IMPACTS OF
"THE OTHER JUSTICE."

ISAAC MAMPUYA SAMBA

authorHOUSE®

AuthorHouse™ UK
1663 Liberty Drive
Bloomington, IN 47403   USA
www.authorhouse.co.uk
Phone: 0800.197.4150

Published by AuthorHouse 09/22/2016

ISBN: 978-1-5246-6406-0 (sc)
ISBN: 978-1-5246-6405-3 (e)

Print information available on the last page.

Any people depicted in stock imagery provided by Thinkstock are models,
and such images are being used for illustrative purposes only.
Certain stock imagery © Thinkstock.

This book is printed on acid-free paper.

Because of the dynamic nature of the Internet, any web addresses or links contained in
this book may have changed since publication and may no longer be valid. The views
expressed in this work are solely those of the author and do not necessarily reflect the views
of the publisher, and the publisher hereby disclaims any responsibility for them.

« IMPACTS OF " THE OTHER JUSTICE. " »

5 - « Impacts of the "Other Justice" »
Preceded by:
3 - « Torment of "JULIO, Descent From Poitevese" »
And:
4 - "An Ultimate Therapy To Save Their Children"

DEDICATION

To those who do not know for example that in this world, apart from human justice [sometimes with errors it has despite it], there is "The Other Justice": "Providential Justice" or "Justice Supernatural"; which unfortunately alas!, is not acting for the most time, that untimely.

PRINCIPLE.

"" The Imaginary " first;
then " [1] the Real " after that. ".

---

[1] "The Real" truth "of the Past" but "transplanted", so to speak.

viii

NOTES

With this Fifth Episode of Isaac MAMPUYA Samba entitled: " **Impacts of " the Other Justice " " **, « the " BaLiSambaSty " or " the Literary Walk in Samba – Style " » (And among – others: its scripts, its dialogues, its texts, its scenarios; brief, and among – others: his cinema [his theater] blondywoodian), thus will mark the Epilogue of this Sub – series of the Negritude. But however "the BaLiSambaSty" does not go away for long. Not for long, it is because it will continue for more, soon enough.

If, however, some people would feel ... / ... more or less ... / ... injured ... / ...; because their stories are not really translated (according to them);

or: because their names; or even: because their bad memories experienced in the past, yet look like considerably; ... / ...

or otherwise: because their names; or because their bad memories once lived resemble more or less (or in order to be able to express more correctly:

they still look like "clearly" or so), and painted with those described in this little book [; or rather, in these small works];

these people in question just please accept our apologies sincerely; since it is not at all, at all due to bad faith on our part.

Again in the small Volume **5**, entitled: " Impacts of the "Other Justice" ", in "On Background MARYVONNE Kinese Progeny" and "JULIO D'Background Spanish Descent" and as always, we hope that "Samba-Style" or "Style-Samba", we will try to do everything in order to get along.

One will see for example among others: Following the question as:

In short: Does mom Cathy PEGGY also to "cement" for example "more" link their "wedding", she also simulated, against her "gas"; that is to say: vis-à-vis the father of Cathy PEGGY precisely "the multiple constant false – true" scenes households?

In short: ... / ...?

In short: Does the mother of Todd TEXLER also to "cement" for example "further" their relationship "marriage", she also simulated, vis-à-vis "the bimanous"; that is to say: against the father of Todd TEXLER precisely "the various scenes of households"; but unfortunately alas!, himself the father of Todd TEXLER in question, not knowing actually nothing at all, at all, "all these theatrics" "fashionable" of "Blondinian" for example, he could only take "these domestic scenes" in the first degree, and consequently, he had saved for him?

In short: Does the father of Milène VELASCO also had been the victim of Miscegenation Common Senses; or rather, Cultures?

In short: Does the father of Jay CAREEN similarly, was the scapegoat of Culture Shock?

In short: ... / ... here, here, here!

One example will see again, among others:

How many crimes being committed, shall in no case go unpunished in the eyes of "Supernatural Justice".

Of course, at the end of this little Volume **5**, our "strange Samba – Style" will go away. But rest assured, it will not be for long;

not for long because "Style – Samba" will almost immediately return, in Volume 6; which will follow.

Messy, the characters mentioned in this fifth small volume:

Main characters:

Julio Fernandez;

Maryvonne KEVILER;

Lucilian KEVILER (son of MARYVONNE and JULIO);

Evelyn MULER, which would become for a given time: Ms. Evelyn MULER, spouse FERNANDEZ;

Christian GENEVRAY (a friend of JULIO).

Sisters of JULIO:

Ghislaine FERNANDEZ;

Chatelaine Johannes FERNANDEZ;

Solange FERNANDEZ.

Parents of MARYVONNE:

Maryssa Fouquet, spouse KEVILER.

Mr. Moses KEVILER (or: Monze KEMVILA);

Other people close to this:

Henrietta Mafuta KEMVILA, spouse Nsenga, a sister of MOSES;

Giraud ZEFRINO; which would succeed the "dirty work" to him, by the father of MARYVONNE, to recover JULIO;

Poulain DERECK, a "compagnero" – accomplice of Giraud;

Thierry Glorian, the oldest and most faithful workers, butchers of Moses KEVILER.

Friends of MARYVONNE:

Madam Lillian Quesnel, wife Roger BOUSSARD;

Mr. Alejandro Of Verdun (a Lecturer in Modern and Contemporary History at the University of Paris – Sorbonne);

Madam Louisetta GRIFFIN, Alejandro Of the VERDUN 's wife.

People who had approached closer to LUCILIAN or his grandparents:

Corinne KIMBERLIN (Mistress of the last class of the Kindergarten where LUCILIAN attended);

Miss Jeanne CABROL, the babysitter that was hired to MARYSSA interest LUCILIAN;

Madam Joubert Menie, the Mistress of the CPB "School JOFFRE."

Mr. Augustan LAMARTINE, a child psychologist; or rather, a child psychotherapist in Benedict MARCONI Center for children, at Rueil-Malmaison;

Ms. Paloma ORNELLA, a child psychologist; or rather, a child psychotherapist at the same Benedict MARCONI Center;

Madam Léonie COLBERT, a child psychologist; or rather, a psychotherapist with children, always in the same Benedict MARCONI Center.

Children who were receiving therapy together with Lucilian KEVILER in the Benedict Center MARCONI:

Magdalena MATT;
Regina BLAIN;
Betty MANNERS;
Laurie Zuker;
Janet SANTINI;
Bennett WEAVER;
Jacob BERGER;
Stephan Lorentz;
Delfino STESCHER;
Jonathan Henks;
Dave RABWIN;
Steve Shiban
Adeline KAPLAIN;
Damien HOWE.

Secondary characters:

Gary ULRICH and Aziz OF ROBIAN: Without accommodations Fixed capita for a time in the Relay Center Social Atlantis [122].

Brats of children ages that followed the therapy in the Marconi Center; which was observed behaviors, through different tapes – videos:

Paula BERC;
Dorothy Amann;
Marilyn HANEY;
Cathy PEGGY;
Austin STEWART;
Todd TEXLER;
Milene Velasko;
Jay CAREEN;
MARION Sebastian;
Anaïs ARMIN;
Jacquelyn DORIS;
Andreas NELLY.

Other secondary characters:

Gilles Carpentier, another worker of MOSES;
Yves MULER, the father of EVELYN;
Simone Durand, wife MULER, the mother of EVELYN;
Laval BRICE and Loïc MORIN: loyal colleagues working of Yves MULER.
Annick Tyssandier "the subversive" used by the father of MARYVONNE, to "make" "a dirty job";
Patrick Fernandez, the little brother of LUCILIAN;
Yolanda FERNANDEZ, little sister of LUCILIAN and PATRICK.

Claude Roland, the Chief of Staff of the Company Guarding "the SECUDARGAUD";
Regis HARISSON, the Chief Executive of "SECUDARGAUD."

"The SECUDARGAUD Guards " serving in a site located at Saint-Quentin – En – Yvelines:

Bertolotti Foppiani;
Lionel REYNALD.

People barely mentioned in this fifth volume:

Roger BOUSSARD's husband of LILLIAN;
Elian BOUSSARD, one of two daughters of LILLIAN and ROGER;
Nicole BOUSSARD, another of two girls LILLIAN and ROGER.

People who had tried in vain to recover [And how! And what for] in ways deplorable JULIO:

Elvira AUBRY;
Vincent GILBERTO;
Henrique LEFEBVRE;
Alfred Peuron;
Marc THIÉBAUT.

Other friends of JULIO:

Nelson RUDNIK;
Roz LORENZO;
Eric BATTLES;
Jeffrey MAXWELL;
Arthur RAVER.

The others barely mentioned in this Fifth Volume:

Johm Christopher WINDSOR;

Giordano COROLIAN;

Norberto MAURY;

Kevin DE SOUSA;

Alexander NAVARRE;

Olivier Gauthier;

Lucia GAUTHIER;

Lucian CHAPERON;

Cleopatra MOULLER, the former worker of MOSES;

Agatha LEROUX;

Mvila KEMVILA, the dad of MOSES;

Adolphina Nseke (or Mama ADOLO), the mother of MOSES;

Patrick Fernandez, the late father of JULIO;

Yolanda ROUSSEL, the mom of JULIO.

PREAMBLE

In short, the parents of Maryvonne KEVILER, they would use methods for managing and transferring the nervous breakdown of their daughter, to another person, by the way. Which no one would recover little of this new situation and she just died. But for the parents of the only child: "There is no getting around as it was then, **the ultimate therapy in order to save our children, and ensure the legacy of our fortune with the utmost tranquility**". Is this would also be accepted by the "**Other Justice**"; or to better express it: This would also be accepted by the "**Providential Justice**"?

In "**An Ultimate Therapy To Save Their Child**", we saw that the conversation between JULIO and MARYVONNE became very, very interesting. There was for example seen as MARYVONNE, change the subject, so it was "make returns to the species". Did JULIO, he had that time yet again [as indeed he always accepted so far, to no longer continue a discussion; which could turn into a fight]; accepted? Or was he angry this time? To do this, go up – so a little further back, as a reminder; and therefore, let us hear him: How was it at the time addressed to the attention of MARYVONNE: "Ah!, it's always that, change the subject for you?". Ask Julio Fernandez, in his "Fatima", the Miss Maryvonne KEVILER.

Miss Maryvonne KEVILER: " So. This is not the first time that we proceed in the way that I know, not! And so today; here's your astonishment you no longer want (alas!, unfortunately), what you had always accepted so far! ".

Julio Fernandez: " You also say [I quote]: "So what? "The dopa" ... / ... ".

MARYVONNE: " Yeah!: So what? I shed tears? ".

JULIO: " "Dopamine" and ... / .... ".

MARYVONNE: " What I whining? ".

JULIO: " And "sero"... / ... ".

MARYVONNE: " What I weeps? ".

JULIO: " "Serotonin" – oblige, I would say aye!, aye, aye! ".

MARYVONNE: " What I sob? ".

JULIO: " Yet weep every time a: Yes; or a No, you do not know what to do it with me you Maryvonne! And because of this, neighbors of the building come watch us! Always wanting and yet always wreck me greatly! ".

MARYVONNE: " But no ohm! It should hardly see things that way! ".

JULIO: " Yeah!, yep, yet! If so ih! We should just start seeing things that way; since, it is high time now! ".

MARYVONNE: " That is to say, eh!, eh, eh! ".

JULIO: " That is to say, eh, eh, eh! Me JULIO, I'll tell you what "that is to say, eh, eh, eh! – that"! That is to say, that it was exactly that way just that you'd done the shame ... / ...! ".

And so for him Julio Fernandez: " "This Descending Parisian and Outback Descending Kinese" loved and yet combine both: **horror *and* beauty**; "Incredible beauty"; "Although incredibly beautiful"; but especially "shaped" to "mixed character"; even on **"a terrifying character"**; "That character" turns out to be just for: Miss Maryvonne KEVILER. ".

And so for him Julio Fernandez: he did not think, just take to their heels. And he actually ended up taking it; leaving behind him MARYVONNE **in a mental state, you could not dismal**. "**There could so more lamentable**"; so much so that a Professor Alejandro Of Verdun try to help as; he could to find his "gentleman".

So let us hear precisely this ALEJANDRO, continues his conversation with the depressed MARYVONNE; a conversation begun in Volume N°. 4, entitled: "**An Ultimate Therapy To Save Their Children**".

We had too much too spoiled since childhood! And worse, we never wanted for example dare contradict his very, very poor whims; when she was growing up! And now the work!

CHAPTER: FIRST

"The Professor Alejandro Of Verdun": And what was the reception, once arrived at the scene where there is the Headquarters of the Guard Company? ".

MARYVONNE: " The I was treated as being "less than nothing"! The I was treated, as "a sausage very, very depressed"! The I was treated, as "a real crazy"! The I was treated, as "a real mental haywire"! The I was treated, as "a real bitch"! The I was treated, as "a real plague"! ".

ALEJANDRO: "Ah!, you saw eh! ".

MARYVONNE: "Yeah!, ih! And like that ah!, you ALEJANDRO, you had suggested to me as anything, that you will recover my Julio Fernandez, "Of Poitevese Progeny and Progeny Background In Spanish"! And like that, you ALEJANDRO, you had suggested to me "blithely" Julio Fernandez will return! Frankly, I think about – me MARYVONNE, he will never return at all! ".

ALEJANDRO: " But if ih! He will return! ".

MARYVONNE: " So despite the fact that the situation regarding the search for "what JULIO" is as it appears! But nevertheless, you confirm me anyway as yours – ALEJANDRO, like what, Julio Fernandez will come back? ".

ALEJANDRO: " I can confirm that anyway; since I'm sure. ".

MARYVONNE: " But then when he returns? ".

ALEJANDRO: " Soon. ".

MARYVONNE: " Soon? ".

ALEJANDRO: " Absolutely! ".

MARYVONNE: " But how can you be so sure and so confident like that ah? ".

ALEJANDRO: " I told you I was going to see [even if he had to, for example], a medium! You remember that right? ".

MARYVONNE: " Yep!, I remember. So you had already consulted? ".

ALEJANDRO that in reality, it was there, that lie about a medium, to try to make go as he could, the morale of MARYVONNE; he wouldn't consequently little, answered in the affirmative: " Absolutely!, I had already consulted. ".

Miss Maryvonne KEVILER: " And what did he answer you this medium in question? ".

Alejandro VERDUN: " It's like I've already said," Soon". ".

MARYVONNE: " This medium had actually said to you: "Soon"? ".

ALENJANDRO: " Of course! "Soon", he told me actually indeed! But he had also suggested to me that it would take this time 'it, treat him well! Treat him properly, like a spouse or rather are treated: a husband at home! That is to say, especially not to leave to him no deal almost alone, of all the household chores! In addition, you should make him, more wilt in the presence of people; when they come to visit you here in Montrouge! ".

MARYVONNE: " My mother had her all and you just told what ah! ".

ALEJANDRO: " Absolutely. She had the opportunity to have me once on the phone. There was a lot done. And therefore, she finished among others, for me also mention, uh – huh!, ih! ".

MARYVONNE: " No, if he comes back! If JULIO back, I would not behave me again as "a hysterical mad at its worst and having in hers veins", "a vampirian blood"; "vampiric blood" "flowingly"; and when it goes down to her nerves and to the throat; it makes her do stupid things; which among others, are the shame [to her "ape"]. "I promise that if JULIO returns; I would not behave me again at all, at all, as "such a **butterfly**" I just describe some characteristic features psychosomatic! ".

ALEJANDRO: " "Such **maidenly**" like the one you just described, it is really you? ".

MARYVONNE: " It's ah!, my mother did not say you had and she stands out! You do not believe much in your ears eh! You do not believe much in your ears; but it's really me "this **girlish** then"! But then, I promise you that if you ever as the medium has spoken; and Julio Fernandez returned! I would not behave me again at all, at all, as "the prostitute" which I have just described "psychosomatic some characteristic features"! I now would behave properly. I would not do more JULIO suffer with my very, very bad characters. ".

" And of Verdun had returned home. " ".

LILLIAN, at MARYVONNE: " Oh!, you really did her disgrace in the apartment huh! ".

MARYVONNE, at LILLIAN: " I admit that I am ashamed to answer your astonishment; because the answer is actually: Aye! ".

LILLIAN: " What kind of obloquy you were doing it for example? ".

MARYVONNE: " Today for example, when there were guests at home; me MARYVONNE, it looks like something made me nervous; and it made me uncomfortable and very, very anxious. And on the other hand, in my mind (and I know this is "the sort of vampire blood", one would say, that in my mind: "this kind of Vampiric Blood", that one, I have definitely me): it seems like something in question always told me like what, that not only that there were only **carnal knowledge that could take away the nervousness and put me at ease**; but also that no matter how, there were more visitors from us; which might hinder us; that they had already returned home. And therefore. ".

Lillian QUESNEL, wife Roger BOUSSARD: " Aye, aye!, ih!, ih, ih! And therefore? ".

Miss Maryvonne KEVILER: " Hmm mm! We really need me to do a drawing! Finally is! And therefore I did to him: "Do you suppose; that is to say: what a couple; or to better express it: it was that two lovers should do that by being hidden; or by being sheltered from prying eyes". And you my dear LILLIAN quite frankly! Have not you ever behaved in this way, vis-à-vis Roger BOUSSARD, the father of your two daughters Nicole and Elian BOUSSARD? ".

LILLIAN: " I quite frankly! I've never behaved this way, vis-à-vis Roger BOUSSARD, the father of my two daughters Nicole and Elian BOUSSARD!

What for? This is because the "legalistic" lessons I received from my father and my mother since my early childhood – force! ".

MARYVONNE: " But as for me – MARYVONNE, I acknowledge that I am "a crazy-hysterical **empress** of the worst kind that can exist". In this regard precisely, I have to admit that it was some GHISLAINE, a sister of JULIO, who frankly made me realize what I really was. I am "this crazy chick – hysterical – there"; which grew up with very, very bad characters. But still is! Besides, this is what had finally led to serious problems between on the one hand, I MARYVONNE who speaks to you now; and on the other hand, him, JULIO "the fugitive"! It's really weird! He is the coward who fled the marital home; and it is I who thinks and continues to also think of him! ".

LILLIAN: " We should think about him anymore! Only wish that your friend Alejandro Of VERDUN finally find him anywhere; and, when so found, he agrees to come back alive with you, in Montrouge. And at that time, you'd all really should be done in order not to hurt him; and you would see yourself my dear friend and colleague MARYVONNE, it would work as if for example, it was on wheels! ".

MARYVONNE: " Many thanks for all the advices my dear friend and colleague. ".

"You'll never understand
how could all be sad,
if someone you really love,
flees, without saying where he goes!".

Like all moral consolations, Alejandro Of VERDUN used to lavish on "The Background Kinese Descending"; the moral comfort; LILLIAN had lavished on this one, had restored precisely this, they hope to live. Hence, she had begun to take hers antidepressants. She began taking pills against depression. She also began again anyway to have the love and taste, her job as Secretary – Trilingual Management This is because before, though still went to work; but only here, in reality, she had in fact at all, at all, desire. She did not at all, at all, envy or "believes" whatever it may be in fact work. Now, with the comfort that her colleague and friend LILLIAN granted her; like all comforts her friend ALEJANDRO (and his wife) offered her; MARYVONNE had taken "a taste" of life. She began to repeat very well housework, Three rooms of her apartment. But only here, Julio Fernandez still be, to long, to return at Montrouge; and it had been several months; to not even say: it was already more than two years that she was still waiting in vain. MARYVONNE that, yet again had very frankly to have the love and the taste of her work; another day at lunch time to the service, she was all sadly sitting on the chair; and she would not eat. She sat for ten minutes in his chair in the canteen at work, with her great friend Lillian QUESNEL, wife BOUSSARD. She did not even have the courage to eat the meal she ordered herself. Her friend Lillian QUESNEL asked: The reason of the fact that she was apparently, and it suddenly became so sad; so discouraged and very, very bad shape? But at first, she even refused to answer.

LILLIAN, at MARYVONNE: " MARYVONNE? But why are you so sad apparently became suddenly like that ah? Why did you become so discouraged like that ah? Why are they become so ill so suddenly? Why do not you answer me when I talk to you? ".

5

After urging of her great friend Lillian QUESNEL, Maryvonne KEVILER 's response was; and that one, a very low voice and very sad: " You'll never understand my love LILLIAN! ".

LILLIAN: " I cannot understand what? ".

MARYVONNE: " You'll never understand how we could be very sad if someone you really love, runs away, without saying where he goes! ".

LILLIAN: " Ah!, I was sure: you think again and again forever, about your "guy" Julio Fernandez, the father of LUCILIAN? ".

MARYVONNE: " Certainly!, ih! ".

LILLIAN: " Since the headquarters of his job security, we will not send you all the information concerning! So, why were you not part of yourself in person, visit for example for several nights in a row in his job? Do you know at least its sites assignment? ".

MARYVONNE: " Of course! Of course I got to know his reporting site! But I was gone! Before my friend ALEJANDRO and myself, we went to his place of work, I had obviously begun and there. It is at N°. 113 Avenue President Sadi Carnot. But only, it is far! This is very far! It's still very, very far! This is the fifth area! It is a site that is to Saint-Quentin – En – Yvelines, and even beyond! It is, so to speak, one of the suburbs of that City what; JULIO though he used to call it "the Site or the Station Saint – Quentin". But only here, the problem is that almost nothing, nothing at all, is marked! The problem is that there is virtually no information! ».

LILLIAN: " I should have suspected! I said that too, as you would have certainly had a chance to get at least one day on himself Julio Fernandez; or otherwise, on one of his colleagues; which would have been very kind to possibly provide you with valuable information about the father of LUCILIAN! ".

MARYVONNE: " You bet! I was gone for three weeks; and that every night. But only here, I encountered only other "heads". This position is located next to the bus station! ».

LILLIAN: " What a pity there only to meet other "heads" and not, him JULIO! ».

MARYVONNE: " In addition, I do not even tell you that in order to get there; order to reach this place; to get this job for the first time (the Central Station Of Security) located at "Level 0", in a large eight – floors building; he had to deal, in a "sacred Chinese puzzle so to speak"! But nevertheless, I was out in anyway somehow. Arriving at the Central Station Of Security (and this: even for several nights), I unfortunately had unfortunately found the one item that I left in search!; that is to say: he Julio Fernandez. ".

LILLIAN: " Who did you find there? ".

MARYVONNE: " Hmm mm, I found several other people. I found it such an Italian national, appointed Bertolotti Foppiani; which also did not speak French very well. But he was very welcoming anyway vis-à-vis me, after all. I also found another "course heads", for example a certain Lionel REYNALD. ".

LILLIAN: " Why did you hardly asked these other "heads" so they can provide you information about the father of LUCILIAN? ".

MARYVONNE: " But that was precisely what I did every time. But unfortunately that's just, unfortunately, I always came across people!; or: who had never known at all, JULIO; or who had known and worked with him for two or three months, for example; then they met again, again. "This is a very sensitive position" that post here in "Saint – Quentin"; this is a position in which guards would remain almost never long enough; even if they want to stay long anyway. "They told me everyone, each in his words, of course; but the content of remaining always the same message". ".

LILLIAN: " Go therefore whether it was true that they told you all! ".

MARYVONNE: " It was unfortunately then, alas!, the whole point! ".

LILLIAN: " And yeah!, ih!, a great question! ".

MARYVONNE: "Over time, I realized that I was there, that simply make me "fool" myself by constantly wanting to extract information about JULIO; and that, wanting sometimes insist several times from the same guards; and asking them and always repeating them, the same issues; when they had already told them that they knew! From where ... / ... ".

LILLIAN: " Where? ".

MARYVONNE: " Where, I just decided to give this track there. ".

LILLIAN: " Holy shit! ".

MARYVONNE: " When I remember that I had never left there where JULIO worked before; when we were together; while he in his case, he came almost every time here in our workplace! ".

LILLIAN: " But you also MARYVONNE! Why you did not go there? ".

MARYVONNE: " And yet he wanted and he was telling me and I repeated the same all the time, he also had to me, I go and see where he was working! But it was me who did not want; or not yet in those moments! And here is what comes next, how it is? ".

LILLIAN: " And like that, much later, you would feel in this ultimate burden of collecting all alone, his place of work! And that's how, that this series presents what! ".

MARYVONNE: " And yep!, ih! Given the current turn of events, I was obliged to go! I was forced to go to "My Computer then this Saint – Quentin" and lose myself! ".

LILLIAN: " Is it far? ".

MARYVONNE: " It is very far! It is in the Fifth area! It is a site that is to Saint-Quentin – En – Yvelines, and even beyond! ".

LILLIAN: " Shame! ".

MARYVONNE: " The problem is not even the distance; because I went there, to the edge of my Mercedes. But only here, the problem is that. ".

LILLIAN: " Aye!, ih!, ih, ih! The problem is that? ".

MARYVONNE: " The problem is that almost nothing, nothing at all, is marked! The problem is that there is virtually no information! ".

LILLIAN: " This is what a new City! ".

MARYVONNE: " Absolutely! This is a new City; and virtually nothing, nothing at all is scored town. ".

LILLIAN: " What a pity! ".

MARYVONNE: " I turned the vacuum several times; when I had gone there for the first time. ".

LILLIAN,:" Oh!, the cow! ".

MARYVONNE: " I was forced to park my car away; and walk again for a long time to finally go and see the place. ".

LILLIAN: " Well, it was at least that is essential. ".

MARYVONNE: " Sounding; or rather, by pressing the button onto the ring; a course electric bell; and then speaking immediately "hygiaphone" (communication device); or rather on the intercom, the night watchman answered me that I was there, in "Level: ¾1"; and that ... / ... ".

LILLIAN: " Hmm mm! "At Level: ¾1"! Will therefore know! Since this level ¾1 gives indeed on the street and the vehicles are parked next the door! ".

MARYVONNE: " Huh! As you say yourself, my dear friend: Go therefore know that it was then "Level: ¾1"! Finally is! That I was there, "Level: ¾1"; and it was absolutely necessary that I get on the ramp next to go "up to Level N°. 0"; "Level 0" where he was; and there he would receive me. ".

LILLIAN: " What a **hassle! What a drag**! ".

MARYVONNE: " I asked the guard to the question: How I was going to get there? ".

LILLIAN: " And what the guard had said to you? ".

"MARYVONNE: "That Night watchman had answered [I quote]: (

The guard, at MARYVONNE: " It's easy Madam, I'll explain: How do you go! OK? ".

MARYVONNE, at the night watchman: " Yeah!, agree. ".

The guard, at MARYVONNE: " First, you will cross the asphalt which is right behind you. ".

MARYVONNE, to the night watchman: " " ... / .... Cross the asphalt which is right behind me". Ih!, yep!, Ih, ih! ".

The guard, at MARYVONNE: " You will then head to the left; "left"; that is to say, in the direction of your walk, to your left! ".

MARYVONNE, to the guard of the night: " " ... / ... Me going left"; "left"; that is to say: in the direction of my work, to my left, "Aye!, ih!, ih, ih!". ".

The guard, at MARYVONNE: " You will find right on this street, a concrete ramp that goes up of course. ".

MARYVONNE, at the guard of the night: " " ... / ... In this street, a concrete ramp that goes up of course. "Ih!, aye, aye!, Ih, ih! ".

The guard, at MARYVONNE: " You will simply up above the. ".

MARYVONNE, at the guard of the night: " " ... / ... I'll just go up. ". Ih uh!, Ih, ih! ".

The guard, at MARYVONNE: " And at the end of the ramp in question, you ... / .... ".

MARYVONNE, at the guard of the night: "" And at the end of the ramp in question, I will ... / ...? ". Ih uh – huh!, Ih, ih! ".

The guard, at MARYVONNE: " You will immediately once turn right again! ".

MARYVONNE, at the guard of the night: "" ... / ... Once again turn to the right! "Ih all right!, Ih, ih! ".

The guard, at MARYVONNE: " And you'll finally arrived Madam! That's okay? ".

MARYVONNE, at the guard of the night: " Ih!, very well, that's okay Mr. The Night Watchman! I arrived and immediately! ".

The guard, at MARYVONNE: "" So I'm waiting. "! ".).".

MARYVONNE, at LILLIAN: ""I did it like that ah! And when I was in front of this nice guard of the night; I obviously was presenting (MARYVONNE, at the night watchman" ": "" Hello Sir! ".

The night watchman, at MARYVONNE: " Good evening madam! ".

MARYVONNE, the night watchman: " By all means!, good evening! It is true that the day is already over now! Good evening Sir. ".

The night watchman, at MARYVONNE: " You saw yourself that this is not rocket science eh! You noticed yourself that it's not difficult to get there at this Central Station Of Security huh? ".

MARYVONNE, at the night watchman: " It's true that it's not difficult. You only need to follow your valuable insights; and there comes into effect, quite easily. ".

The night watchman, at MARYVONNE: " So, what do you want lady? ".

MARYVONNE, at the night watchman: "I am the wife of night watchman Julio Fernandez who works here with you. Does he work today tonight? ".

The night watchman, at MARYVONNE: " I am the guardian Bertolotti Foppiani. As my name is easily noticed, I am an Italian; and as my way of expressing my further notes, I just arrived in France, he is no longer. I sometimes prefer the report in advance to strangers, so we do not make fun of the way I express myself in French, later. ".

MARYVONNE, at the night watchman: " You're not wrong you know! But only with respect to me, I think on the one hand: you express yourself very well in French, for an Italian who just barely, that arrived in France eh! And secondly, that it's not even worth really pay attention to other people; because here in the Paris's region, we will generally not care about other people's problems, exactly! ".

The night watchman, at MARYVONNE: " Certainly, I'm in a new "box", let alone at this very sensitive Station Saint – Quentin – here; where you change guards all the time. But yet, I can only tell you Mrs. Fernandez, that ... / .... ".

MARYVONNE, at the night watchman: "Mrs. Maryvonne KEVILER, wife FERNANDEZ! My surname is KEVILER; and my first name is MARYVONNE. ".

The night watchman, at MARYVONNE: " But still, I cannot tell you that Mrs. Maryvonne KEVILER, wife FERNANDEZ. I'm really sorry! I am very sorry! This is because: Not that your husband JULIO not working tonight; since, if it were not such as this ... / ...! But I'm really sorry; because your husband Julio Fernandez is not at all in that post – here! It's no wonder Madam; because in that post – here just very sensitive, the guards did not stay long. But it is anyway very funny you Madame, as his wife, you are not even kept abreast of the situation! ".

MARYVONNE, at the night watchman: " There had been some minor marital disputes or household; he was angry; he had separated a little bit; the story of first calm those little marital dispute in question; then here now, came what happened; and therefore I am not actually kept informed of this situation! But where is he working now? ".

The night watchman, at MARYVONNE: " So then, I do not know! Besides, for starters, I'm just another in "the box" of the Security; and consequently, I know nothing about other positions of " the Company SECUDARGAUD"; although, it is true that "our box" provides guarding lot of Companies; including among others: SNCF example where we, we are working on outsourcing! But if you want Madam, I'll give you right now, the address of our head office located in Paris; and therefore, you will you learn yourself in person. ».

MARYVONNE, at Foppiani: " Thank you very much; but in any case, frankly speaking, I have it. It is in the Ninth Arrondissement of Paris! Is not it? ".

Foppiani, at MARYVONNE: " Yeah!, that's right! ".

MARYVONNE, at Foppiani: " So, it's not worth me spinning this address; because someone had already done this step for me! But only here, we do not want at all, at all, to provide the slightest information concerning my husband JULIO. Thank you anyway because for thinking give me the address of your head office. ".

Foppiani, at MARYVONNE: " You'll probably tell me that you've already suggested to me, and [I quote]: " There had been some minor marital disputes or household; he was angry; he had separated a little bit, the story of first calm those little marital dispute in question; then here now, came what happened; and therefore I am not actually kept informed of this situation! ". And you will surely add me that: it's not about me; and I give you right of course! But just now, I do not understand at all and I admit, a husband, and for a few small domestic disputes; he can get angry and go well in nature, without, giving news to his wife! ".

MARYVONNE, at Foppiani: " You cannot understand! You really cannot understand; since it is a long and complicated story actually! ".

Foppiani, at MARYVONNE: " I'm sorry Ma'am. ".

MARYVONNE, at Foppiani: " You're welcome! I would also tell you that myself too, I left at the Registered Office of the Company. ".

Foppiani, at MARYVONNE: " You yourself in person? ".

MARYVONNE, at Foppiani: " Aye!, ih! And once there, I had proof that someone I have mentioned earlier, he did not lie to me. Once there at the Headquarters, I was made me realize that aye, aye!, this is someone there who had been there before me; he did not lie to me. Besides, he could not even lie to me about it. That someone is a Lecturer at the University of the Sorbonne. He's not anyone. This really is a very serious Man. ".

Foppiani, at MARYVONNE: " Madam, I once again repeat that I am very sorry. Anyway, if I could actually provide information about your spouse; I would not hesitate one little moment to do so. But only here, where quite frankly, I cannot do anything for you! It is only yourself as his wife, who can truly overcome this one! Once again I'm really sorry! ".

MARYVONNE, at Foppiani: " Never mind. Thank you anyway. Bye for now. ".

Foppiani, at MARYVONNE: " "Goodbye **Ma'am!**". " ".).

MARYVONNE, at her friend LILLIAN: " It was then my dear friend LILLIAN, the results of the first evening. I would rather say: It was then my dear friend LILLIAN, the results of the first night; where I left there, where worked in principle, JULIO. ".

LILLIAN, at MARYVONNE: " Pity! ".

MARYVONNE: " I even imagined that he too Bertolotti Foppiani, he would not at all tell me the truth! Then, as the guards are not always the same! ".

Lillian: " I thought so! ".

MARYVONNE: " As attendances vary greatly and consequently, we do rotations at this site; as indeed in all other sites. Then I thought I needed to come back the next day, try again my luck; it was because he could maybe I'd find another Vigil; which could very possibly find out about JULIO! ".

LILLIAN: " Good idea. ".

MARYVONNE: " But only here, wanting to go home in Montrouge, I was looking for my Mercedes – Benz; I did not rediscover it at all, at all ooh! ".

LILLIAN: " It was stolen? ".

MARYVONNE: " Not even! ".

LILLIAN: " But! ".

MARYVONNE: " You're right and surprise you. Not that my Mercedes – Benz was stolen; but the fact was that: only I did not find it more! I do not even found it; it's simply because I do not even remembered me from where I had parked it! I even remembered me from this place where I had "parked" my car; so I had a long walk [off and it goes without saying], to find the address I was looking now finally; but unfortunately, alas!, I do not even found quickly, the address in question. ".

LILLIAN: " Oh!, the cow! And what you had done? ".

MARYVONNE: " As it was already too late at night; therefore I preferred to first let this car where it was; and take a taxi; which had brought me home in Montrouge. And since it was a Saturday night; ... / .... ".

LILLIAN: " Fortunately for you; otherwise: "Hello the Trials Verbal's [T V].". ".

MARYVONNE: " And since it was a Saturday night; I thought, "well, the next morning I'll take care of this Mercedes – Benz". And the next day, too, I took another taxi to take me there. I do not even speak to you of the amount that the two taxis had cost me: it was a true rip – off, what! And very fortunately!, that I had enough "liquid winkles" on me; otherwise, hard, hard! It was really a rip – off! But just now, I could not do anything else, than pay; because before this awkward situation ... / .... ".

LILLIAN: " I doubt it! ".

MARYVONNE: " Besides, I do not even talk to you that: the fact that prompted me to throw myself on board the first taxi that showed up coincidentally very happily, close to me was the fact that a band of [hooligans] was going to rape me! ".

LILLIAN: " In addition! Bummer! ".

MARYVONNE: " All that night, I was not able to get sleep. ".

LILLIAN: " You were just thinking about this sad evening then what! ".

MARYVONNE: " Absolutely. I especially prayed that Heaven should ensure that this band of thugs then, does not come by chance, on my Mercedes – Benz; if not, no need to even describe to you later! ".

LILLIAN: " Otherwise, no need to draw me a picture what! My poor! What a sad story! ".

MARYVONNE: " When I was back there in Saint – Quentin – En – Yvelines; that is to say: where JULIO the next day worked; that is to say: on Sunday morning, I had searched for two and a half hours to finally find my big car! ".

LILLIAN: " Finally! ".

MARYVONNE: " It was very close to a place where I went and ironed for at least a dozen times; or more! ".

LILLIAN: " What a pity! It was perhaps that way you were done you noticed by this band of disaffected; which idle wanted to rape you; before you can throw you in the taxi passing by chance very happily, to your near what! ".

MARYVONNE: " For sure myself and besides, I had thought. ".

LILLIAN: " Finally, the key is that it went well! That is what is important; and the remaining one is ultimately fun. ".

MARYVONNE: " But as in my program I had finally provided the day before, like what, I should return the same evening to workstation's JULIO ... / .... ".

LILLIAN: " You were back too? Or rather: You were also distributed? ".

MARYVONNE: " Absolutely. I also picked the same particular Sunday evening. But guess LILLIAN: Who I unfortunately had unfortunately met the other night, there!? ".

LILLIAN: " Bertolotti Foppiani! ".

MARYVONNE: " That's right. Yeah!, it was him Bertolotti Foppiani I found there for the second time consecutively. ".

LILLIAN: " Not very funny! Anyway I can ask you a question MARYVONNE? ".

MARYVONNE: " Yep!, I know I should not have again, introduce me to him, as soon as I found me, to him again! But only here, it was stronger than me; and consequently, I was me again presented to him anyway! ".

LILLIAN: " Again! It is true that it was indeed this one I was going to ask you this question as a fact! So what? ".

MARYVONNE: " Aye!, again! And I rested him again the same questions as in the last day; that is to say: "the early Saturday night!". ".

LILLIAN: " It was really ridiculous and it must be admitted anyway! ".

MARYVONNE: " I totally agree with you LILLIAN, righto!, ih, ih! ".

LILLIAN: " But it was such Bertolotti Foppiani believe he was there, case maybe, to an "Iphigenia" dingo! ".

MARYVONNE: " It's ah!, that's for sure! ".

LILLIAN: " So what? ".

MARYVONNE: " And then what BERTOLOTTI still had obviously passed on to me the same answers; and therefore it was of course for me, the same results, as the day before early Saturday night! ".

LILLIAN: " This is a true story that crazy ah! ".

MARYVONNE: " Righty – ho!, absolutely! ".

LILLIAN: " But at least you had no more lost your Mercedes – Benz, at this time? ".

MARYVONNE: " No, I was more cautious at this time precisely. I was more cautious; because I had [with each increase I was doing, meter by meter in this new City] taken very seriously benchmarks. ".

LILLIAN: " In any case, it really is a true story of **madness** it ah! ".

MARYVONNE: " Hmm mm! "True Story" of "**foolishness**"! As you repeat it! Then I would say: "Yes" and "No". ".

LILLIAN: " It's to say? ".

MARYVONNE: " That is to say, I would answer, "Yes!, this is indeed a true story of **craziness**!"; since, on two occasions, I was indeed find that the same person; and consequently, I was of course, to repeat myself, the same things. And I would say: "No!, this is hardly a history of crazy!". What for? This is simply because I learned a lot of others new things. I tell you in short, they [quote about them, those that let me also hear, the Night watchman Bertolotti Foppiani]: " " """

(The night watchman Foppiani Bertolotti, to Maryvonne KEVILER: " ... / ... This is as I have already said to you Madam, yesterday: " I am the guardian Bertolotti Foppiani "Certainly that, I'm a new" in "the Company SECUDARGAUD."; and even more so in that post so sensitive of Saint – Quentin – here, which often turns the Security Guards; but nevertheless, I can tell you that Mrs. FERNANDEZ, I'm really sorry I am really sorry, since your husband is not at all in this post – here, where he had been transferred [like so many other Security Guards before him, and of course, like many others, among others myself Bertolotti Foppiani talking to you right now in this room, and I know full well, I will be after him sadly alas!] ".

Maryvonne KEVILER, at the night watchman Bertolotti Foppiani: " He is no longer in this post here? Or: He's not at all, at all squarely in the "SECUDARGAUD Company"? ".

The night watchman Bertolotti Foppiani, at Maryvonne KEVILER "Yeah!, ih! Aye!, so ih! Aye, aye!, it makes you feel, he is still part of "the SECUDARGAUD Company"; but only – here, in another post of assignment;

even in several other positions at once eh; as it turns out to be common in this profession guard, that we, we do. In short, JULIO currently found in another post; or even: in several other positions at once; where he is definitely his night shifts. ».

Maryvonne KEVILER, at the night watchman Bertolotti Foppiani: " What is the name of this post; or: what are the names of those positions where he was affected now then? ".

The night watchman Bertolotti Foppiani, to Maryvonne KEVILER: " So then, I do not know. I've only heard whispers by some colleagues as anything: Julio Fernandez currently end up [he would seem] to a large tower in a business cited in western Paris, especially in the City of Defense. But anyway, I do not know any more. ".

Maryvonne KEVILER, at the night watchman Foppiani Bertolotti: " Why did he go from here exactly; while he is still remained there several years without he was fired; and [of] this staying long, long time here in this post; he knows, therefore, very, very good ones that are to be executed in the latter, exactly! And not even counting the fact that finally, by dint of being kept here very long, you are made to feel very, very comfortable! ".

The night watchman Bertolotti Foppiani, at Maryvonne KEVILER: " The fact is that he had not asked to go by himself alone, Madam! He was forced to do so! He was perhaps for a long time escaped being kicked out of here! But the wheel turns and therefore turn that delayed hitherto arrived, had finally arrived anyway! Hmm mm! Although your husband for him in his case, he had been lucky to still be assigned elsewhere; this is because after all, he has always been until then a very, very good conscientious night watchman! ".

Maryvonne KEVILER, at the night watchman Bertolotti Foppiani: " " ... / ... Even your husband for him in his case, he was lucky to still be assigned elsewhere; this is because after all, he has always been until then a very, very good conscientious night watchman! "? ".

The night watchman Bertolotti Foppiani, at Maryvonne KEVILER: " Absolutely! But unfortunately alas!, ... / .... ".

Maryvonne KEVILER, at the night watchman Bertolotti Foppiani: " Yep!, ih!, ih, ih! "But unfortunately, alas!, ... / ..."? ".

The night watchman Bertolotti Foppiani, Maryvonne KEVILER: " Uh – huh!, but unfortunately alas!, he is a very, very good conscientious guardian, who was in fact, very, very disturbed by the fact that most never stop to think about his mother! ".

Maryvonne KEVILER, at the night watchman Bertolotti Foppiani: " ... / ... Never again, thinking of his mother! ".

The night watchman Bertolotti Foppiani, to Maryvonne KEVILER: " Absolutely! In the words of many people who trusted your husband Julio Fernandez in this site – here in Saint – Quentin; the latter told them; and even, he stopped almost little, to cause them [I quote]: " ... / ... This is my mother! I have many affections for her. But only here, she finds herself in a shit now; an almost indescribable shit! This is not the time of the dump now! In any case, certainly not! "[Unquote]. ". In short, your husband was in fact very, very upset thinking of his mother. Or precisely, given the fact that he likes a lot her; then he cannot: not to think about her. ".

Maryvonne KEVILER, to the night watchman Foppiani Bertolotti: " Okay, my husband Julio Fernandez was in fact very, very upset! But realistically, ... / .... ".

The night watchman Bertolotti Foppiani, at Maryvonne KEVILER: " All right!, ih!, ih, ih! "But realistically, ... / .... ". ".

Maryvonne KEVILER, to the night watchman Bertolotti Foppiani: " But realistically, what he actually does just wrong, so that finally turns him also, the site where he stayed for quite yet very long time? ".../.... "). ".

"Anyway, I was definitely" idiot "but
when you love someone like I love JULIO,
and that someone is saved, without saying where he went huh!".

What Julio Fernandez had really done? MARYVONNE had "star" fall coincidentally, another night, during hers repeated investigations on another night watchman by the name of Lionel REYNALD. However, she would benefit the most, to know a little more, about "her bimanous Julio Fernandez" precisely. After the usual introductions, she would raise the night watchman Lionel REYNALD several questions; among – others:

(Maryvonne KEVILER, at the night watchman Lionel REYNALD: " ... / ... But what my husband Julio Fernandez had done exactly, so that the turns like that here?".

The night watchman Lionel REYNALD, at Maryvonne KEVILER: " ... / ... Mrs. FERNANDEZ! I do not know: What he had in him, finally, these last days; but he spent here in this station so sensitive of Saint – Quentin; but his mind was always somewhere else! He was always distracted; he was always thoughtful; he was always worried! ".

Maryvonne KEVILER, at the night watchman Lionel REYNALD: " He was always distracted; he was always thoughtful; he was always concerned! ".

The night watchman Lionel REYNALD, to Maryvonne KEVILER: " Absolutely. It is said that he became so before me Lionel REYNALD, I come to this position; before I met him. I've been here; and he worked for about two months together with me too. When I asked him, for example: Why was he so distracted; so thoughtful and so anxious? He replied to me: "My mother!". Agreed!, his mother, he had a lot of conditions to her. . ". " " ".).

MARYVONNE, at LILLIAN: " And indeed! So they were also among – others, those whose, the guardian Foppiani Bertolotti, had suggested to me. """

"« (That said [and I quote the night watchman Lionel REYNALD]: " It's my mother I have many affections towards her but only, she is in a shit now, an almost indescribable shit, so! Say! This is not the time to drop her, now! Anyway certainly not! ". Answered me your husband Julio Fernandez, **Ma'am**. On those, he deliberately refuse, to tell me more. » « ».).

LILLIAN, to MARYVONNE: " His mother? ".

MARYVONNE, at LILLIAN: " Indeed his mother has a lot of problems! ".

LILLIAN, to MARYVONNE: " That's why he was so distracted; so thoughtful and so concerned, all these last days he spent there, in that post so sensitive of Saint – Quentin! That's because he simply thought of her; that is to say: his mother! ".

MARYVONNE, at LILLIAN: "[I continue to quote the night watchman Lionel REYNALD: """

"« (" ... / ... So back to your question Madam, your husband Julio FERNANDEZ not stopped at all, to earn malpractice more or less serious, it's because his head was obviously elsewhere.". » « ".).

LILLIAN, to MARYVONNE: " Of course! Obviously when the head is actually elsewhere eh! ".

MARYVONNE, at LILLIAN: "[I continue to quote the night watchman Lionel REYNALD: """

"« ("... / ... And despite several warnings, that he had received from our branch in this regard precisely, he unfortunately changed alas!, to nothing at all! Until one day ... / .... ".

Maryvonne KEVILER, at the night watchman Lionel REYNALD: " Yeah! Until one day? ".

The night watchman LIONEL, to MARYVONNE: " Until one day, in the same night he had committed three serious professional misconducts, following! The warnings that he was being repeatedly therefore used to anything. ".

MARYVONNE, at the night watchman LIONEL: " And that was what and what and what, like three serious professional misconducts? ".

The night watchman Lionel REYNALD, to Maryvonne KEVILER: " First: Every level of the third floor was flooded due to a major water leak. There was for it, the synopsis, multiple alarms, as bright as sound; but Julio

Fernandez, who headed elsewhere; he had not noticed anything. However, he had not done enough that a guard should absolutely do in such cases. ".

Maryvonne KEVILER, at the night watchman Lionel REYNALD: " But why did he not make the need for a guardian should absolutely do it, in front of such situations, too? ".

The night watchman Lionel REYNALD, to Maryvonne KEVILER: " As I said to you **Ma'am**, he had not done enough for the simple reason that he did not realize anyone actually spent in this table; this great synopsis you see their behind you, Madam! ".

MARYVONNE, at the night watchman Lionel REYNALD: " He had not realized; it was because he had his head elsewhere! ".

The night watchman LIONEL, to MARYVONNE: " Absolutely! ".

Maryvonne KEVILER, to the night watchman Lionel REYNALD: " And he had his head elsewhere; that is to say: it's because he always thought simply to his mother! ".

The night watchman LIONEL, to MARYVONNE: " Exactly. ".

MARYVONNE, at the night watchman Lionel REYNALD " Numerical and physical difficulties that his mother must have surely! ".

The night watchman LIONEL, to MARYVONNE: " It is possible. ".

MARYVONNE, at the night watchman Lionel REYNALD: " Cleopatra MOULLER had he not right? ".

The night watchman LIONEL, to MARYVONNE: " Sorry **Ma'am**? ".

MARYVONNE, to the night watchman Lionel REYNALD: " No! Nothing! I was just going to ask about the result of the flooding of the entire level of the third floor! ".

The night watchman LIONEL, to MARYVONNE: " OK: All offices were upstairs ... / .... ".

MARYVONNE, to the night watchman Lionel REYNALD: " The third floor? ".

The night watchman LIONEL, to MARYVONNE " Affirmative! All offices upstairs were like pools; and he missed very, very little, that there was a great, great risk, for a short circuit; which would eventually cause a large fire in the building. ".

Maryvonne KEVILER, to the night watchman Lionel REYNALD: " And all these, it was my husband did not even notice? ".

The night watchman Lionel REYNALD, to Maryvonne KEVILER: " And all these, it was not your husband noticed anything Madam, actually. ".

Maryvonne KEVILER, to the night watchman Lionel REYNALD " This is anyway a thing eh! ".

The night watchman Lionel REYNALD, to Maryvonne KEVILER: " I would say instead: Your husband should definitely have some **bad lucks** with him! ".

Maryvonne KEVILER, to the night watchman Lionel REYNALD: " "... / ... Must definitely have some **curtains** with him!". Finally is! And the second? ".

The night watchman LIONEL, to MARYVONNE: " Certainly! And secondly: All fire dampers and all the sprinklers had fallen in curtain; and your husband Julio Fernandez had hardly called "The Permanence Technique"; in order to turn the necessary; that is to say: to immediately contact a Team of Technical Experts in the field; and send it as soon as possible on the site which one was touched! ".

MARYVONNE, to the night watchman Lionel REYNALD: " "And all those; this is for the simple reason that because him, my husband Julio Fernandez, had not noticed anything! Humm!". ".

The night watchman Lionel REYNALD, to Maryvonne KEVILER: " This is exactly right, **Ma'am**. ".

Maryvonne KEVILER, at the night watchman Lionel REYNALD: " What "**casualty**" indeed! ".

The night watchman LIONEL, to MARYVONNE: " And yeah!, ih! ".

Maryvonne KEVILER, at the night watchman Lionel REYNALD: " And finally, the third [and therefore: the last severe fault], that my husband JULIO had committed consecutively in the same night? What fault? ".

The night watchman Lionel REYNALD, at Maryvonne KEVILER: " Aye! The third fault was: The air conditioning of all three computer rooms; located in the Third Level Basement; namely that the largest administrative building in Saint – Quentin has everything: Eight Floors and Four Levels Basement; all [; especially the four levels of basement] aired by a network or a circuit, sophisticated air – conditioning; to distribute; [Or rather, to determine; and therefore, in principle, to correct, automatically; when everything is going very, very well], atmospheric moisture, offices and other premises, according to a given degree of temperature well paid in advance, for many operate machinery. In short, this sophisticated air conditioning system maintains constant: the humidity of the air, in all offices and other premises of all four levels of basement above. Again **Madam**: Third: air conditioning in all three computer rooms; these computers and then, they are not any computers huh office! Rather: sacred machines; it is rather: the very giant machines worth millions of dollars, to put this in this currency. Air conditioners of all three large rooms of computers so finding, the Third Basement reached the second threshold in the temperature scale, in our Field of Security [; and for your information **Ma'am**, once the third threshold is reached, all these sacred machinery worth millions; all these sacred computers would simply curl; and that, without exception!]. In fact, with all that we have to watch in the Eight Floors + The Level 0 or the Ground Floor and + finally Four Levels Basement; we should inevitably work several guards at once by night. And several, problems like those who arrived to your husband **Madam**, would be avoided! But only this: Saving money on wages to be paid to ensuring the Security of personnel – obliging; then in this Site of St. Quentin, the night watchman works alone by night! ".

Maryvonne KEVILER, at the night watchman Lionel REYNALD: " "... / ... Until one day, in the same night, he had committed three serious professional misconducts, following! ... / ....". And despite all the warning lights so that sound, my husband Julio Fernandez still had noticed anything? ".

The night watchman LIONEL, to MARYVONNE: " Nothing at all, at all, **Ma'am**! ".

Maryvonne KEVILER, to the night watchman Lionel REYNALD: " In any case, Cleopatra MOULLER had he not right? ".

The night watchman Lionel REYNALD, at Maryvonne KEVILER: " Sorry **Ma'am**? ".

MARYVONNE, at the night watchman LIONEL: " No! No, no! Nothing! I would only say that despite all these, him my husband had always do little notice? ".

The night watchman Lionel REYNALD, to Maryvonne KEVILER: " No, no! In any case, one thing was certain: he had his head buried in his family problems; ... / .... ".

MARYVONNE, to the night watchman LIONEL: " Including: marital problems! And why hesitate to say very explicitly! ".

The night watchman Lionel REYNALD, at Maryvonne KEVILER: " It ah!, I do not know! He had his head elsewhere; because even if he slept for example; as is repeated everywhere as often happened eventually; whereas before he had no problems of this nature one! Hence, because even if he was asleep; but at least he was going to wake up anyway; wake up as a result of repetitions not light alarm signals; because he fell asleep; and he could not see; or collect them; rather, he would wake up anyway as a result of repetitions of sound signals; and if he was going to wake up as a result of crackling printers, repeated; the printer that you see here has, **Ma'am**! ".

Maryvonne KEVILER, to the night watchman Lionel REYNALD: " It was because of all these, he had been fired by what? ".

The night watchman Lionel REYNALD, at Maryvonne KEVILER: " It ih, by all means! Although ... / .... ".

MARYVONNE, to the night watchman LIONEL: " Yet that? ".

The night watchman Lionel REYNALD, at Maryvonne KEVILER: " Although he had many chances, so he still continues to work in "SECUDARGAUD Company", after committing such mistakes eh! Otherwise ... / .... ".

MARYVONNE, at the night watchman LIONEL: " Aye!, ih! Otherwise? ".

The night watchman Lionel REYNALD, to Maryvonne KEVILER: " Otherwise, he would be returned mercilessly as a result of multiple serious misconducts of this nature, recognized by "The Collective Agreement Companies Watchman!". ".

MARYVONNE, to the night watchman LIONEL: " ... / .... ".

The night watchman LIONEL, to MARYVONNE: "... / .... " " " ").

Maryvonne KEVILER, to her colleague and friend Lillian QUESNEL, wife BOUSSARD: " Furthermore, after these days of interviews with the two guards; that is to say: with Bertolotti Foppiani and Lionel REYNALD, I left again; I am stubborn and I admit that I recognize myself; I left on the road to Saint – Quentin – En – Yvelines, to do all in all, a good three and a half weeks! ".

LILLIAN, at MARYVONNE: " But why do so eventually insist on that point? ".

MARYVONNE, at LILLIAN: " It was just in the case probably not impossible, where: Bertolotti Foppiani and Lionel REYNALD would me much at all, spit the truth about him "my hominid JULIO"! Although apparently they seemed to me to be undoubtedly very, very nice; very, very welcoming and very, very honest; like that ah!, I was going to have possibly the vein! Instead, I was going to say like that ah!, I would have possibly the opportunity to be able myself, by chance, meet me finally with himself JULIO in person! And so I would persuade him to return home; I would rather say him to return home [; with him as our son and Julio Fernandez Lucilian KEVILER] in Montrouge; although the latter is still temporarily until this moment here with my parents in Rueil–Malmaison ! ".

LILLIAN at MARYVONNE: " But what you said, these days, to Bertolotti Foppiani; to Lionel REYNALD and to possibly others of their Security Guards colleagues? Or to ask this question quite poetically: "Were you" "every again", "back"? Or: Were you "every again", "back"? ".

MARYVONNE: " I do not understand! ".

LILLIAN: " Let me explain: Were you "every again", "back" in the Central Station Of Security, to talk with these other agents Watchman? Or: You were resolved you to "return" only empty – handed, with you in Montrouge? ".

MARYVONNE: " That's it! I understand now! Of course, "that every again," I was determined me to "return" home empty – handed only to Montrouge! Otherwise expressed: "But what I said, all those days at Bertolotti Foppiani; Lionel REYNALD and possibly others of their Security Guards colleagues? "! "Well, eh!, eh, eh! Nothing eh! Nothing!". ".

LILLIAN, at MARYVONNE: " Nothing? ".

MARYVONNE, at LILLIAN: " Nothing; this is because they do not even see me! ".

LILLIAN, at MARYVONNE: " It's to say? ".

MARYVONNE, at LILLIAN: " Oh!, they do not even see me! They do not even see me for the simple reason that I hided off; and I "kept under surveillance"; I "watched" and their own well camouflaged at various street corners, for several hours and several days: crepuscular night! ".

LILLIAN, at MARYVONNE: " With all the potential risks of snowshoes; with all the risks of potential hazards; and with all the potential risks still rape; incur – you, to want to stay [certainly well stashed at various street corners] for several hours and several days: twilight evening, all alone like that! ".

MARYVONNE, at LILLIAN: " In any case, thinking well, I was definitely "idiot"! But that's only when you love someone like me MARYVONNE I like him JULIO; and that someone in question is saved, without first saying: Where he went huh! You know what I say? ".

LILLIAN: " With all the risks of rackets, assaults and rapes you were running there, wanting to be alone like that for several twilights then nights for example? But why did you do all those? But why you took all these risks then my dear friend MARYVONNE? ".

MARYVONNE: " In any case, you could never understand, my dear LILLIAN! But that said, I would only say by way of illustration only; which you also saw that with a "Sir"; you are not unknowingly; that's "the culmination" [when I sleep; or rather, when we slept; since it was obviously with him "my crunchy JULIO"]; that's "the culmination to a relaxation"; or rather to "sleep, said repairer"; which is in my opinion, a sleep worthy of the name. You're hardly unknowingly my dear friend LILLIAN, that the improvement of [his] sleep; or rather, "said the culmination sleep repairman"; what is a trigger! Thou art not, without knowing my dear friend LILLIAN that "venereal reports" alleviate concerns or anxieties in the way, so to speak, "a natural tranquilizer"! Or indeed, it turns out that me MARYVONNE, I'm kind: for nothing just a tiny example, be it at work or elsewhere, I'm left with worries and anxieties; for hardly say for example: "anxieties' to express myself in this way"; and in such a case: I lose all my energy; sadness came over me; and what's more, I lose the joy of life! But precisely these concerns and anxieties [; for therefore hardly say these "these anxieties"] "I am the repair just" with "my gas" " JULIO The Descent From Poitevese and Background Progeny Spanish!". [And how! Namely: every night –––]! And there: all my energy back! And there: all my sadness disappears! And last one: my joy of life back! Intense joy of life itself! But now he has taken his legs, around his neck! And what do I do? You are not unknowingly my dear friend LILLIAN, as a result, "these pairings" balance the nervous system. Thou art not unknowingly my dear LILLIAN, that's it, that it is generally found that after orgasm, it apparently feels in itself, be a good absolute and incomparable. So "the culmination to a relaxation"; or rather, "to sleep, said repairer". You're hardly unknowingly my dear friend LILLIAN, that in "the daughter of Eva", "relaxation"; or rather, the "sleep" turns out to be much more gradual. And finally, you're not unknowingly my dear friend LILLIAN, that however, in "the guy", its voltage drop is as it were brutal, "restful sleep" proves consequently, be much faster. ».

Lillian QUESNEL, wife Roger BOUSSARD: " And yeah!, ih! It ah! It shows that, indeed, if only for that reason, "said restful sleep", you really love this "JULIO From Poitevese Progeny and Progeny Background On Spanish" – that hein!, eh! And then, this JULIO in question, took to their heels! ».

MARYVONNE: "Yep!, ih! And this JULIO "Descent From Poitevese and D'Spanish Background Progeny" – that hein!, eh in question, fled without first tell me where he's gone! What I liked in "this archetype here", this ... / ...! ".

LILLIAN: " Aye!, ih! I'm listening! ".

MARYVONNE: "What I liked in "this here", that before making me get that "will eventually be" "my sleep repairman said", what, "eyes closed so to speak" he let himself be guided by blinding me. Ah!, when I thought for example our four combined oral lips together [mixed if you like]! And "this gun" took flight! Certainly there in my memory, other lips; other lips, such as: –Johm Christopher WINDSOR; and –Giordano COROLIAN! But anyway, it was not the same! The four lips here were found to be far below! They "drooled" too often saliva "in my valve". And besides, their languages knew undertake no movement! But, it was only then that poor memories for me MARYVONNE! But then, it is, in my "hymen" JULIO life with him; there were always in moments of great feelings of inner joy and great satisfaction; moments such as those I have always known and yet still with it, even from the moment I began to cohabit with him matrilineal, poor memories crossing [certainly periodically] my mind, as for example, neuralgia and against whom exactly, I did everything to forget; but unfortunately, alas!, I do not hardly could manage! But, it is then not, as souvenirs! And now I am very far from London and most importantly, I am very, very far from Mexico. That's right, this does not prevent that Johm CHRISTOPHER and Giordano COROLIAN also knew [as for himself JULIO] "kick theirs kidneys". Short [and do not have disgust quote this verb LILLIAN] they knew as "overlap". But what made the difference with JULIO; that it in this matter (you know what I mean LILLIAN?), he knew what to do! When I think, for example, in "my valve", his tongue knew perfectly secure synchronization of movements back and just; and those of other movements of the tongue, for example, those of articulation with my tongue in my MARYVONNE. In short, the language of JULIO knew perfectly synchronized movements back and forth and all other movements with my tongue in my MARYVONNE without such "drool me with saliva inside my mouth"; while supporting the synchronized action, using various tongue strokes precisely on my tongue at me MARYVONNE! Hmm mm! In addition, it also knew JULIO "down in the basement"! Otherwise expressed: Also, this JULIO knew as "giving up the sponge" (You can still see what I want to tell you what LILLIAN? The cunnilingus, what?). "He knew me, **give a phone call**", always with various tongue strokes, but of course at the basic of the meatus; just something that Johm CHRISTOPHER and Giordano COROLIAN, they hardly knew make it to me; or perhaps: "they were reluctant" make it to me! Or for him JULIO, there was no reluctance in this; for him, it would be okay; it was going too well, too very well; too very, very well!

I admit that finally my **Nymphae** or my **Rosebud** and **its contours**; Briefly: **my anatomy**, him Julio, in order "**to make the commissioner's hat**", he sucks me Maryvonne, **even better and better and better at superlative; as if it was for example, a bee sucking a flower or sugar. And that ah!, it's magnificence – even.**

And JULIO just decided to slip away without even so far, being asked! And tell me that I MARYVONNE, I had taken considerably risks, going to try to find him, in what I thought was still his job! Anyway, I was definitely "idiot"! But eh! When you love someone like me MARYVONNE, I like JULIO; and that someone in question is saved, without being asked! When one loves her and so do the farce without even tell you where he went huh! So there! ".

LILLIAN: " Surely!, ih! I understand you very well! ".

MARYVONNE: " You know me very well, only apparently it's safe to just enjoy myself! That said ... / .... ".

LILLIAN: " Not at all! It is not: only apparently so just to please you! But it's really true! I understand you very well in all my sincerity! ".

MARYVONNE: " Okay I understand you well in all your sincerity! But that said, I was anyway "bitch" to take such risks, especially a good one evening, I had actually escaped from very, very close to the clutches of a band of scoundrels; which rogues chasing me and they were going to rape me. I was also "dumb"; since in reality Bertolotti Foppiani and Lionel REYNALD did me not much at all, at all lied. They had told me that truth. They had told me that the frank truth. They had told me the truth very frank; the very, very frank truth itself: like what, JULIO that no longer worked in that post. But as to know where he was transferred now? So then, it's a conundrum! ".

LILLIAN: " And yeah! A gang of scoundrels would "delight as it", "a ravishing **mixed – blood,** On Background Progeny Kinese" what! ".

MARYVONNE: " LILLIAN! It's not funny eh!, the rape! Hmm mm! This band of thugs thought maybe it's different for people of color! She imagined that I'm different below the belt, maybe! But, as I've already said many times my dear LILLIAN; and I will once again repeat to you: "In any case, thinking well, I was definitely idiot"! But that's only when you love someone like me MARYVONNE, I like JULIO! And that someone in question is saved, without first saying: Where he left eh! You know what I say? ".

LILLIAN: " Aye!, I understand you very well. ".

MARYVONNE: " You know me very well, for me only perhaps to make me pleasure; but having said that ... / .... ".

LILLIAN: " Not at all! This is not only to make you happy! But it's really true!"

MARYVONNE: " But that said, I was anyway "bitch" to want to take such risks; especially that one day I escaped very closely, being raped by a gang of young rascals. I was also "dumb"; because in reality, Bertolotti Foppiani and Lionel REYNALD had not lied to me at all. They had told me the truth; they told me that the frank truth; the frank truth as anything, JULIO was no longer in that post so sensitive indeed. But as to know: Where was – he decidedly affected? So then, it's all a mystery, then! ".

LILLIAN: " And uh – huh! A gang of jailbirds wanted to "revel as it" "a beautiful mixed race"! ".

MARYVONNE: " Hmm mm! It can be imagined that I am different "under the belt" in comparison of "other **baronesses**"! But in reality, there is less for example some abnormal problems; otherwise "all **countesses**" look alike "below the belt" exactly! ".

LILLIAN: " All that ah!, it was because of the risks you would incur out at night alone! Hence, it was hardly worth it at all, of running such risks outside at night by me, as a "split"! And also, very, very far from home! ".

MARYVONNE: " No, it was actually hardly at all worth it! ".

LILLIAN: " Is Finally! Let this side "risks" in the dungeon; and so back to him "your coconut Julio Fernandez". The preview back at least, not for work, for example, certainly, but at least you had to: this or that any reason given in the position of Saint – Quentin – En – Yvelines, during one of those many nights you did it discreetly watch? ".

MARYVONNE: " No! Otherwise, I would have told you for a long time already! But unfortunately not alas!, I had seen other guards; which turned into this position: Guards guys "African blacks"; Maghrebi kinds; Asian type; Indian kind; and of course metropolitan or European types! And aside from the two guards with whom I had to talk to them; I deliberately refused myself to talk to all the others, that they may not even tell me no more, than the previous two! I wanted to meet me as he possibly with JULIO! But against, I'd never seen him! I had never seen one I was looking obstinately; that is to say: the father of LUCILIAN. ".

LILLIAN: " It took only believe directly, those you said Bertolotti Foppiani and Lionel REYNALD? ".

MARYVONNE: " Of course! So when I think of all the ones I just told you about the position of Saint – Quentin; I confess my dear LILLIAN, I regret greatly from having to follow the track – there. ".

LILLIAN: " Of course! But at least you would have tried as well; because if you had not followed! You would always regret it in the bottom of yourself; and that, for a long time [and nothing else], not having to try to follow among – others, this track too. ".

MARYVONNE: " It's true. In addition, at least I still know a thing, that me and my mother, we did not know. Or to put it better myself: at least I learned one thing; one thing that my mother had hitherto believed just believe; and she had me turn misled. ".

LILLIAN: " What is it? ".

MARYVONNE: "What LIONEL through, I know that" SECUDARGAUD Company is not actually bad, vis-à-vis "my devil JULIO". It did not want it at all. It did not want it; because if that were really the case, a great opportunity presented itself one; to finally put an end once and for all, with him. A great opportunity presented itself then to the final turn of their "Enterprise"! But however, the leaders of the "SECUDARGAUD" had not been developed. They had not been developed; this is because: think a little dear LILLIAN, a guard on his own, and can commit three serious misconducts, clearly recognized in " The art Of The Collective Agreement Guarding"; and not even for all that, be sacked? ".

LILLIAN: " Maybe that attitude ... / .... ".

MARYVONNE: " One thing is very, very safe and very, very certain, as I was saying with the night watchman Lionel REYNALD: "The head of JULIO was elsewhere". ".

LILLIAN: " It ah! ".

MARYVONNE: " Besides, I did not tell you! ".

LILLIAN: " Yep!, ih!, ih, ih! What? ".

MARYVONNE: " What this night watchman ... / .... ".

LILLIAN: " Lionel REYNALD? ".

MARYVONNE: " Yeah! This guard had deliberately; when he was not at all obliged to do so! He had made a deliberate attempt to trigger an intrusion alarm! He did it on purpose just for me. He had done just so I can listen to myself: How does this sound? And: How to repeated crackling printer would prevent someone to continue to snooze, in case it really would snooze in the post, as we finally told everywhere. ".

LILLIAN: " That's a lot of noises? ".

MARYVONNE: " And how! It ah! It ah!, even the deaf hear, so to speak! Even the deaf hear; as he seems, which had voluntarily increased the volume of the ringing tone from a certain given night, a guard had an alarm – conditioning of large computer rooms problem until the third threshold. But since the increase in this volume, there has never been such problems, until ... / .... ".

LILLIAN: " Until it was still arrived with "your funny Julio Fernandez"! ".

MARYVONNE: " Absolutely. ".

LILLIAN: " You know MARYVONNE eh! When you have your head in the well eh shine! ".

MARYVONNE: " According to the guard Lionel REYNALD himself and many other guards, they believed it had done JULIO guess exactly; but they paid little attention at all, at all, to tell it to other people, so as not to add fuel to the fire, as they say. To these guardians then "my paragon JULIO" was just very, very exhausted by its many problems and even fatigue; so much so that he went to lie squarely in one of the offices, by dropping momentarily, the Central Station Of Security; which turns out to be the focal point of this office building! He had to do this, believing lie just a little; then he had forgotten to wake up in time expected. Namely, according to the statements of his guardian LIONEL (except at the last floor of the building, that is to say: except to the Eighth Floor [; where almost majority of offices and other premises are always closed keys out of opening hours], but in any case, in all remnants of Floors, in all remaining levels [, that is to say: Eighth Floor, until Level Basement – fourth]); namely: a near majority of the offices and other premises of all levels are still open. Besides, according to him LIONEL: And even if all the offices and all the various other premises of any such administrative building would be closed anyway in its entirety; guards have always passes (matting); they always have two types of passes (two types of mat): the first type is a pass through Level; and the second type is a single master key that opens almost: all offices and all other local variety of all building levels. I say almost; this is because: for many technical areas, there are sophisticated and specific keys apart. But the guards still have their doubles in wall boxes with keys located in the Central Station

Of Security. And it's better for them and the guards; since then, they only have to carry around during their rounds, with only a few keys; which open everywhere. This is in case of need; because you never know! And so the guards are able to access everywhere, with a view to conduct audits. Going back to "my fellow JULIO" he woke up late. And when he had left the Central Station Of Security; he could only be a fait accompli; and consequently, he could only expect very, very heavy disciplinary practices. But only here, his Company had chosen to moderate the penalty to be imposed. LIONEL for these and other guards as JULIO had deserted his post a good time, going to sleep in one of the offices. As the result of the race, he could hardly at all, at all, to hear such and such other alarms. I must point out to you my dear friend LILLIAN that according to those that think Lionel REYNALD and the other guards: Leave knowingly his job and go to sleep in one of the offices; while one is in operation; "this is much more than a very, very serious". That's why they prefer to keep quiet absolutely deliberately to subject. ".

LILLIAN: " Aye! Aye, aye!, it is a reason that holds up! That must be what the real reason had made sure that him, JULIO had nothing, heard nothing of all those alarms that! ".

MARYVONNE: " That's why I said earlier that commit such serious misconducts; and yet still remain in "SECUDARGAUD"; that it is not at all bad, contrary to what my mother told me! ".

LILLIAN: " And your mother how could she give you that information – there; instead it is you who live; or rather: instead it was you who was living together with him JULIO who can provide it to her mother? ".

MARYVONNE: " Hmm mm! It's simple! That himself "my horse JULIO" just had to provide this information then, to my mother, not me! ".

LILLIAN: " But yeah!, ih! It must be definitely that! ".

MARYVONNE: " That's why, when I was made aware by Night watchman Lionel REYNALD of these faults could have committed that JULIO consecutively for one night; and that no one had even fired! We had just changed her job! So then, what do not want it at all! ".

LILLIAN: " What I was going to say ... / .... ".

MARYVONNE: " You know my dear LILLIAN, my mother was simply wrong about this? ".

LILLIAN: " Indeed! What I was going to tell you exactly about it; and you, you do not stop interrupting me; what ... / .... ".

MARYVONNE: " Go now! I will cut you more speech. ".

LILLIAN: "What: Or maybe your mother was not mistaken about this, as you just said! But it is indeed the attitude of "SECUDARGAUD" who had simply evolved towards "old and experienced", in the "box"! ".

MARYVONNE: " It's possible! You know LILLIAN, anything is possible! ".

LILLIAN: "To return to the attitude; but this time 'it, the attitude of JULIO; irresponsible; "irresponsible" because he fled you! He fled his "split" and his son! So, to return to that attitude of JULIO! ... / .... "! ".

MARYVONNE: " Yep!, ih!, ih, ih! ".

LILLIAN: " My dear MARYVONNE myself LILLIAN I think actually that: Someone who had acted as the father of LUCILIAN had done! ... / .... ".

MARYVONNE: " Righto!, ih!, ih, ih! ".

LILLIAN: " What he did at all, at all, of love for you! This is ... / .... ".

MARYVONNE: " You believe that? ".

LILLIAN: " Righty – ho!, ih! I honestly think the same! It is anyway perhaps incongruous ... / .... ".

MARYVONNE: " No ohm! Myself the question that was leaking; I think not! I think not; since he always had love for me! ".

LILLIAN: " ... / ... Maybe incongruous to me, I would say (to you to know this truth that will follow)! But when you love someone – her or someone – there, very well; it does not hesitate one small moment to say some truthful things in the face! ".

MARYVONNE: " What is there yet? ".

LILLIAN: " But finally MARYVONNE, your story is so very long, not that I get tired of listening to it, quite the contrary! But only the time we allotted for the lunch break, being so small; it is coming to an end! So ... / .... ".

MARYVONNE: " Okay !, ih!, ih, ih! So what? ".

LILLIAN: " Then quickly finish our meal we ordered. They are even any cold already in force long enough chat; and not eat them fast enough. Finish our meal; and tomorrow at the same time; we will continue our conversation! And there, me LILLIAN, I'll talk to you about "some true these things"! ".

'You could never understand how
this "someone" – here, is and will remain
always for me, "irreplaceable" and
"**the Irreversiblestar**" ... / ... "the unforgettable" and
The "**unrecoverablestar**" ... / ... and still remain ... / ... a
"Incontestable and undisputed real man!" ... / ... ".

And next day at the hour of lunch break, MARYVONNE no longer had all the courage (as well as for all those periods) and LILLIAN, her best friend from work were still (as in the usual), parts eat together. Her best friend (LILLIAN) would continue the conversation over there; where they left off the day before. She said in this regard: " My dear friend; MARYVONNE my dear best friend! I said yesterday; when you love someone – here or someone – there very well; we should not be shy, ever so slightly, to tell her or him about some true things. ".

MARYVONNE: " If you did not like to turn around the pot! If you simply and immediately said to myself, as you would just let me hear and there, instead of doing so by procrastination; and therefore by unnecessary postponements! ".

LILLIAN: " In my case I personally LILLIAN; if Roger BOUSSARD, the father of my two daughters Nicole and Elian BOUSSARD was like him Julio Fernandez acted; he would cause me a lot of penalties. In this case, you should only leave him! It is expected to leave him, by the declaring in sharp voice; and therefore the divorce should be declared. And of course ... / .... ".

MARYVONNE: " If we could stop to keep turning around the pot? ".

LILLIAN: " I'm coming! And of course, "a guy" like that; "A sparrow" leaking us; "A sparrow" leaking me and my children; "the pistol" like that, I would replace him by another that I possibly miss much at all to find. ".

MARYVONNE: " But my dear **cicada** LILLIAN! ".

LILLIAN: " OK!, ih!, ih, ih! ".

MARYVONNE: " What would you suggest by these remarks? ".

LILLIAN: " Julio Fernandez cause you a lot of grief's! For this and for me of course, I think "a wretch" like that; you should definitely replace him with another that you will certainly miss much at all, to find; especially when you're very, very beautiful and very, very elegant **mixed – blood** after all! ".

MARYVONNE: " Thank you. But only here, ... / .... ".

LILLIAN: " Roger!, ih!, ih, ih! But only here? ".

MARYVONNE: " But only here, my dear LILLIAN! You could never understand! ".

LILLIAN: " I could never understand what? ".

MARYVONNE " You could never understand: How "that someone out" exactly, is and always will remain still and always for me MARYVONNE "irreplaceable" and "**Irreversiblestar**"! ".

LILLIAN: " If you do not want to replace him with someone else. So, in order that you cannot continue to do so to you and concerns; which are not good for your mental health and your inner peace; you should therefore ... / .... ".

MARYVONNE: " Uh – huh !, ih!, ih, ih! I should therefore? ".

LILLIAN: " You should therefore forget anyway altogether, in spite of you! ".

MARYVONNE " But that's only my dear colleague, you could never understand. ".

LILLIAN: " I could never understand what? ".

MARYVONNE: " You could never understand: How " that someone out" exactly, is and always will remain still and always for me MARYVONNE, "the unforgettable" and "**Irremediablestar**"! ".

LILLIAN: " You surprise me very greatly, honestly! ".

MARYVONNE: " Why? ".

LILLIAN: " " "... / ..." How "that someone – there" precisely, is and always remain for me and yet still MARYVONNE "**unforgettable**" and "**Uncorrectablestar**"! ". You say to me? ".

MARYVONNE: "And why not? ".

LILLIAN: " That "someone – there", who had disappeared as if it was an example of the snow had melted in the nature? ".

MARYVONNE: " So what? ".

LILLIAN: " No, it's not a "real man", that one! And consequently, ... / .... ".

MARYVONNE: " Agreed!, ih!, ih, ih! And consequently? ".

LILLIAN: " And consequently, me your dear friend LILLIAN; I sincerely think you should rather the challenge; rather, you should challenge "that someone – there just". ".

MARYVONNE: " In any case my dearest friend LILLIAN, you could never understand! ".

LILLIAN: " Indeed!, I see ah! I could never understand: How "that someone – there just" I could never understand: How "that someone – there precisely", is and always will remain always and still MARYVONNE for you, "a real man **indisputable**" and "**uncontested**"! Is not that's what you wanted to tell me? Huh? ".

MARYVONNE: " Absolutely! But how did you guess? You become a "medium tow"? That's it? ".

LILLIAN: " Do not turn the conversation MARYVONNE! Have you, for example, signed a pact with this Machiavellian JULIO or what? ".

MARYVONNE: " Who? ".

LILLIAN: " With him Julio Fernandez! ".

MARYVONNE: " Since you insist; so I'll just tell you! ".

LILLIAN: " So, tell me everything! ".

MARYVONNE: " Actually, I will somehow repeat that you, the ones you yourself have guessed! ".

LILLIAN: " Well, in that case, it's not worth it! ".

MARYVONNE: " Affirmative!, ih! Absolutely!, so ih!, Yet! Anyway my dear colleague LILLIAN, you could never understand: How "that someone – there precisely"; "does anyone – here called Julio Fernandez just"; was and would always let me always; in any case, you could never understand: How he remains and always will remain even forever "for me MARYVONNE his **duchess**", "a real man **indisputable**" and "**uncontested**"; though, in front of himself; though in front of himself; I played hypocrisy by refusing me deliberately, to tell him this sacred truth! Did you understand it? ".

LILLIAN: " Hmm mm! So for you, "the male – there" is Julio Fernandez, the father of LUCILIAN; which unfortunately alas!; was saved as a true coward for example? ".

MARYVONNE: " "Descent From Poitevese ... / ...."! Yeah!, ih! For me, "then this anthropoid" is actually Julio Fernandez "The Descent From Poitevese And Background On Spanish Descent" yep!, ih! For me, "then this bimanous" is actually Julio Fernandez, the father of LUCILIAN; which unfortunately alas!; was saved as a true coward e.g. ih aye! "The male then, this is the daddy of LUCILIAN; which disappeared as if it was an example of the snow had melted in the nature, as you already had me very explicitly suggested, aye, aye!, ih!". ".

LILLIAN: " Ah!, I understand now: How you do not stop; and How do not you always would stop from fast to him, as for example, the "Napalm"; that is to say: even after his departure; I would rather say, even after his flight! ".

MARYVONNE: " Exactely!, I think this time 'it, you got it well once and for all, my dear friend LILLIAN: How I do not always would stop, tie me to it, as for example "the NAPALM"; that is to say: even after his departure; or rather [to explain it a lot better: And why not!] Even after his flight! ".

LILLIAN: " All these being said, I will immediately go back; and therefore ask you a question or rather few; some key issues. ".

MARYVONNE: " Go out there and I'm listening! ".

LILLIAN: " All these being said, while I still can more understand: How could you, for example, do so flee, "then this hominid in question"? ".

MARYVONNE: " Actually, I MARYVONNE, I admit that I was really "junk" for it to scare him away and, as you have just explained my dearest friend LILLIAN! I really was "mud" for doing so stupidly run away! I really was "manure"; because, the way I among others, "turned almost slyly"; or rather, "more or less indirectly" from us Montrouge for example, his best friend; for not saying: "his former best friend" Christian GENEVRAY; and that he would never want, never feel ever so slightly; that is to say: he would even want to hear about JULIO; then he just never forgiven me. In addition, I have also caused many, many other sentences to the latter question. ".

LILLIAN: " It was really Christian GENEVRAY his best friend? I ask this question; this is because, if that were the case; he could anyway no matter how understanding and forgiving huh! ".

MARYVONNE: " I might even say it was for JULIO, as more than a friend; as more than a best friend! ".

LILLIAN: " It's to say? ".

MARYVONNE: " Here some borrowed from the mouth of himself and especially JULIO for example, as a passage from a very, very fine example in this regard, so you summarize everything; and consequently, you would understand better this delicate situation. I quote JULIO during our first moments of meeting; [Quote] " " " " "... / ...". "... / ...". "... / ... A Mr. Aziz OF ROBIAN (who had quietly sixties already that time) held the "a" in "Foyer Relay Social Atlantis"; "Atlantis [122]"; Aziz OF ROBIAN occupied the "a"; that is to say: the top of our bed (that is to say, the bed N° 349 [a & b] ["a" is always part ending up on top, or the part top] & "b", [and it goes without saying]: the game is still recovering at the bottom, or the bed at the bottom]) ... / ...! And given the fact that the promiscuity was often poor; then, as one of the consequences of these living conditions precisely me Julio Fernandez, "The Descent From Poitevese And Background On Spanish Descent" I'd catch: Nearly on all over my body, small uprisings inflammatory skin; which became purulent. Fort fortunately these were hardly malignant pustules; otherwise, hard, hard for me JULIO!

As another consequence, I would catch even the "corny" ([mean by that] [mean by it], as I already stated there is not a very long time: lice and crabs).

As a further consequence, I also would catch maggots' toes.

As if all these consequences – here are already not enough for me; I also have the disease of scabies; when I would sleep on a bunk bed in one of the four Centers Of Relay Social; which reads that Mr. Aziz OF ROBIAN; that is to say: the gentleman who occupied the top, was not only full of lice and lice; not only that stopped almost not pissing in bed; and thereby his piss sometimes dripping, straight to my JULIO; but also, and above all that Mr. Aziz OF ROBIAN had very swollen [especially his toes] feet; which began already to deform little by little; and which, at times, they were even trickle "of water and blood". Also, "this bum" often vomited, so he stopped almost little booze "the bottle" [The alcohol, what!].

Although, we ["we"; that is to say: me Julio Fernandez and many others homeless as I do eh]! Where: though, we had also failed, for example nab, scarlet fever; since it was often in direct and close contact with some people suffering among others also, then this contagious febrile disease, characterized by the existence of scarlet patches on the skin and the mucous membrane.

Although, we had also failed, for example nab, tuberculosis; since it was often [and without prior knowledge at the right time], in direct and close contact with some people suffering among others also, this infectious, contagious, caused by Mycobacterium tuberculosis, and characterized by the formation of tubercles in various organs; such as the lungs; vertebrae (Pott's disease); the kidneys; the skin (lupus vulgaris); brains (tuberculosis meningitis); and intestines. "... / ... There was frequently and without prior knowledge at the right time ... / ..."; that is to say, what to do? That is to say: in fact, that "It is not always clear point in time"; "the right time"; that is to say: we still had no information on a timely basis; that is to say: Before for example, be able to make direct and close contact with those individuals who have been infected and were met themselves, by Mycobacterium tuberculosis. If and only if you could know in advance, then the individuals in question; it would, for example, in front of such situations, breathing masks; these objects are respiratory would advance before such cases; we put them, before they can even get in direct and close contact with those individuals then precisely. But the problem was that we knew them little in advance, and those individuals affected.

There was beautiful to have vaccinations up to date;
> but unfortunately alas!,
> those ones did not cover; or rather,
> did not protect people Hundred per Hundred;
> and therefore, regularly and continuously,
> is reported; and we still continue and still
> report, cases of new infections.

But the problem was that we knew them little in advance, and those individuals affected.

Anyhow elsewhere and apart "diseases appearances or visible forms" or apart then "those diseases that had arrived at more or less advanced stages", one could hardly at all, at all, knowing for example: "Who and who actually suffered from what and for what?".

Anyhow besides, we hosted the other, we had no way of knowing really. But the problem was that when it was done, for example, up to speed as anything: "Such and such other persons, for example, were all emergencies is channeled through the Nursing Home, in specialized hospitals, to seek treatment of Mycobacterium tuberculosis; they had had contact; they had to become contaminated; and had consequently, could actually fall ill with tuberculosis. "; and it was actually only at this time exactly ... / ....".

[These were some of the borrowed very, very long narrative stories experienced by him JULIO sentences; which story him, himself among others had told me MARYVONNE.]. In short, it was just for that one: horror. And when he had spoken among others, all of them; that is to say: of all those he had experienced for quite a little while here in the Paris's region, this Christian GENEVRAY even before he and I, we meet at the Sorbonne; the latter had immediately taken; and this not only without asking prior notice; but also, without having the slightest hesitation, to his home in Nanterre; while he occupied only a small room. And for him JULIO was [I quote]: » « »"

"« » " ... / ... It's this that I Julio Fernandez "The Descent From Poitevese And Background On Progeny Spanish", I call a real help. It is this real help; aid without calculation. Help someone who was only sickly and sickly appearance; a someone who could possibly do transmit any contagious disease to another healthy person! And bring him, at home and host him for a long time! Do care! Him find work yourself! But quite frankly, we should really do it eh! ... / .... ".

And so it goes without saying and, as a CHRISTIAN would be: much more than a great friend of JULIO. You see my dear LILLIAN that make him flee definitely such a great friend; it is a real sacrilege huh! Really! Scare him such a great friend like that! And it, deliberately! And I MARYVONNE, I did, anyway! It ah! " « » " ".

LILLIAN: " Indeed, I understand that scare such a great friend like that, someone; and especially that it was not him Julio Fernandez who had actually done it! Rather, it was you who had done; and it deliberately; and unfortunately alas!, for this great friend – there!; he could not know! He could only think that you MARYVONNE and him JULIO, you – you are arranged in order to be able to do that and to be able to make them leave to you; and that, finally! ".

MARYVONNE: " I honestly admit that looking at me through the mirror! I frankly admit that looking at myself in the mirror! I want a lot! And I would always and still always significantly, all the rest of my life, thinking about what I had done! ".

LILLIAN: " Well, forget all these and eat; or rather: finish our meal; which once again have already cooled! ".

MARYVONNE: " Yea!,, forget all those and finish our meal. ".

LILLIAN: " So eat. Finish our meal that one, we ordered; even if they have already been cooled. ".

MARYVONNE: " Ih!, Yep!, that's all cool. ".

LILLIAN: " It does not matter. Take courage my dear MARYVONNE; because I am now convinced that the way you want him to Julio Fernandez; it ... / .... ".

MARYVONNE: " I will not say it! ".

LILLIAN: " It's ah!, I'm finally understood. The way you hold him Julio Fernandez; thereof; even with the assistance of others; people like your dad, for example; to mention only thereof; Julio Fernandez precisely what would end one way or another, by back in your arms. ".

At work, Lillian QUESNEL, wife BOUSSARD consoled now as she really had, Miss Maryvonne KEVILER; and at home in her apartment in Montrouge, her friend by the name of Alenjandro Of Verdun and his wife Louisetta GRIFFON went console from time to others. In the state MARYVONNE finally found, and living alone in her big apartment; hers parents felt in this ultimate obligation to leave also, as often as possible in her home in Montrouge; to visit her; and to monitor more closely the evolution of health. One Sunday evening, Mr. Moses KEVILER and Mr. Thierry Glorian, the oldest and the most faithful of his workers, butchers and at the same time, one of his closest friends; went to see Mr. Gilles Carpentier, another worker – butchers of MOSES, who was hospitalized. They had decided to do, the way back, a short stop – surprise, at Damsel Maryvonne KEVILER, in her apartment in Montrouge. Once there, she would not cause with them well.

Mr. Moses KEVILER, to his daughter Maryvonne KEVILER: " But MARYVONNE? Why your apartment is so messy like that? ".

Miss Maryvonne KEVILER, to her dad Moses KEVILER: " It is not messy as I know me ah! ".

MOSES, at MARYVONNE: " Yeah! ".

MARYVONNE responding with contempt enough and with enough disdain to MOSES: " No! ".

MOSES: " Yep! ".

MARYVONNE continuing to meet with enough disdain: " No! ".

MOSES: " But aye!, ih! ".

MARYVONNE meet with a lot of aggression: " But not ohm! ".

MOSES: " Do you want me to send you a housekeeper, for example, two to three times; that is to say: two to three days I was going to say, a week, for two or three hours per day; and it's me who pays course! Are you agree with this proposal? ".

MARYVONNE did in fact not really want to talk to her dad: " No, I do not agree. ".

MOSES: " But why? This is for your well – being and it is very good heart eh! ".

MARYVONNE always having indeed not eager to meet her father; but nevertheless, she would reply anyway, anyway; and in this condition, she often meet him at half and maliciously: " Myself, I have hands to do that; and therefore, I hardly need a maid. ".

MOSES: " I want to help you! ".

MARYVONNE: " It's not worth it. ".

MOSES: " Besides, you're too weak apparently! Consequently, it would be much use to you this maid! ".

MARYVONNE: " I am not weak as I know me! Things are going well. ".

MOSES: " Why are you so aggressive like that MARYVONNE? Why do not you do not mind cause we? We talk to you; and thou hast not seemed eager to answer. Or if you answer us; you do not answer that half of it! If our presence bothers you; you just tell us! And we're going to save for us! ".

MARYVONNE: " Excuse me you two, my attitude! I keep asking myself: Where can I pick Julio Fernandez? ".

MOSES: " My daughter! There is a saying that [I quote]: "There are only mountains that never meet. But men as to them; they always meet, not even for a single day!". I think you know not ohm!, This proverb? ".

MARYVONNE: " Absolutely!, I know. ".

MOSES: " Especially for "your parishioner JULIO", you might inquire you to his family! It will inform you, about him! ".

MARYVONNE: " It is not worth talking to me, about his family. ".

MOSES: " Why? ".

MARYVONNE: " This is because, if it was only her; JULIO if people listened to the advice of the family in question; he would have saved for him, a long time. But he would not listen to this family fairly. And that was why he always remained with me. ".

MOSES: " But the fact is that it is indeed gone anyway! And leaving you in this psychological and physiological state then! ".

MARYVONNE: " Aye!, but ah!, it's not because of his family! It's because of me! It is because of my unworthy behavior towards him and his friends, like a certain Christian GENEVRAY! ".

MOSES: " Do not be so hard on yourself, my girl! ".

MARYVONNE: " It's because of my malice towards him; this is ... / .... ".

MOSES: " Do not be too harsh vis-à-vis yourself! ".

MARYVONNE: " It's because of my selfishness dictated by my very, very strong attacks and recurrent incurable anguish; because I ... / .... ".

MOSES: " Do not be too hard against yourself MARYVONNE! ".

MARYVONNE: "... / ... Because I did not care for others; and I only saw him Julio Fernandez! I did not care of his family and his friends! Finally, it's ... / .... ".

MOSES: " Do not be too hard on yourself! ".

MARYVONNE: " Well, it's because of "**my madness**"; this is because of "**my hysteria of the worst kind that can exist**"; **hysteria dictated precisely by my very, very strong attacks and recurrent incurable anguish; which hysteria when she said; "she turned me"; and even "it continues to transform me", as for example: "a real sex obsessed**"! ".

MOSES: " Know this that everyone here on earth, has his qualities and his faults of course also. So eh! Do not be too hard on little yourself! O. K.? ".

MARYVONNE: " It is because of these multiple faults that I have all to myself. It is because of all these, Julio Fernandez had decided to go for him. He had even informed mom a few days ago; that is to say, a few days before he flees. And I'm even sure and certain that Mom had to tell you Dad, in turn! But anyhow, she'll say to you as the dad or not, it does not matter. What is important, what mom had in turn also reported that the decision on the horizon, to the person concerned; that is to say, to myself, MARYVONNE. Mom told me that if I was improving my habits developed; JULIO that was going to save all. But only here, as to me, and as usual, I had that at my head! And it's time for me to admit very solemnly, in your presence! ".

MOSES: " Me too; I would rather say that we also; as it is about me and your mother, of course! This is mostly because of myself and your mother, that you MARYVONNE you are currently suffering "sentimental"; or rather "psychically" if I could say so; and of course "physiologically" too! ".

MARYVONNE: " How are you ah? ".

MOSES: " Think very well and you would understand that as you are to us, "an only child"! In doing so, for us your parents "wealthy" to hardly say for example "wealthy"; ... / .... ".

MARYVONNE: " So? ".

MOSES: " It is because we have not touched thee gave to you a very good basic education. That is why, we are trying to catch us now; if and only if this adage: "It is never too late". Hold in our context; otherwise ... / .... ".

MARYVONNE: " Otherwise? ".

MOSES: " If not, we will catch up anyway nevertheless for example, LUCILIAN! And again: If and only if you agree! In short, we try to catch up with us now; this is because, once you were as they say: "spoiled child". ".

MARYVONNE: " Hmm mm! Say you knew that! And to further myself the question, I did not even complain! And on the contrary, I was very, very happy and very, very proud of being "spoiled child"! I do not even have any idea as what, thus, my character became ill; very bad; very, very bad! Hmm mm! Say you knew that! ".

MOSES: " We certainly knew; but we should understand us! This is because we only had you! And we could do to correct your very, very poor habits nothing! We just afraid to cause you pain; and thereafter, the penalty turns for example, and this, in one way or another, against ourselves! ".

MARYVONNE: " Is Finally! ".

MOSES: " All remains; that is to say: all your folly; all your hysteria; short, all your very, very bad habits against "JULIO your lover"; as to so many others, were not there, that the consequences of the way we educate you; this is to say: that there are only consequences of our own mistakes. ".

MARYVONNE: " Is Finally! Finally, mom and dad yourself, you loved me and you continue to love me a lot. For this, you have committed unintentionally so to speak, these faults; these mistakes including myself MARYVONNE, I pay the consequences today. The bottom line is this love that you have vis-à-vis me. That's the most important. ".

MOSES: " That's why I told you; and I will once again repeat, to visit his family; to see the family of "your honest Julio Fernandez"; and ask forgiveness; to apologize; at the same time you ask them for information about him. ".

MARYVONNE: " It's not worth it to try to insist on this track then Dad! It's not worth it; since for that family; it really is: "a fallen sky opportunity"; so that Julio Fernandez gets rid once and for all, from me! ".

MOSES: " So INFORMED up at the headquarters of his Company for Security Agents! ".

MARYVONNE: " You speak late dad! I tried; but since we are not married; they; that is to say: those responsible for the Company called "the SECUDARGAUD" had simply refused to give me these kinds of info. In addition, they had treated me, as it were: as a premium; they ridiculed me mercilessly. ".

MOSES: " Damn! Oh!, I forgot! And why do not you go yourself, see JULIO directly into the workstation? ".

MARYVONNE: " Dear Dad? ".

MOSES: " Yeah!, ih!, ih, ih! ".

MARYVONNE: " You do not doubt it for a moment that I was going to wait until you ask me, that I do it, right? ".

MOSES: " No, no! I had really no doubt at all about it! So what was it given? ".

MARYVONNE: " It gave nothing! ".

MOSES: " Nothing? ".

MARYVONNE: " Absolutely! ".

MOSES: " How are you ah? ".

MARYVONNE: " The party had already changed the site of job. ".

MOSES: " Ah!, the manure! He had it all planned! ".

MARYVONNE: " It's not that oh!, daddy! This change was not requested by him. He had been imposed as a result of a certain disciplinary action. ".

MOSES: " Had you asked his colleagues found that you were there, so they provide you with information about him JULIO? ".

MARYVONNE: " Yep!, I saw two of them – them, in particular: Bertolotti Foppiani and Lionel REYNALD. And I had a lot done with them and especially with this one. I had talked at length with both Security Agents! And they also welcomed me and answered me very nicely. ".

MOSES: " And Bertolotti Foppiani for example! He said what? ".

MARYVONNE: " Nothing special about the current housing JULIO; or his new site of job. ".

MOSES: "Ah!, there is no way to forward for example, a private investigator, for now what! ".

MARYVONNE: " In any case no! For the moment no! But it's sure a little later and one way or another, if you persist with this track to follow with example from the simple address of their Headquarters Company of Security Agents at rely on the private detective; certainly there is no doubt that we would eventually find him! ".

MOSES: " I have taken note of those you just said; and therefore, I will consider those I could do! ".

MARYVONNE: " Thanks in advance dad, for all you're going to take at the right time! ".

MOSES: " I want to know anyway if the other guard with whom you had yet done; if ... / ...? ".

MARYVONNE: " Aye! This is Lionel REYNALD. ".

MOSES: " Aye, aye!, ih!, this Lionel REYNALD!. If you had provided anyway less track about him JULIO; a lesser track to help us to begin again without wasting time; a lower index for example about the place where you could quite easily nab this Julio Fernandez; because after all, he runs anyway no! It runs, were it only to go [to ¾] and return [the] work! ".

! MARYVONNE: " Alas!, unfortunately: no one, and no one, and no one wanted to tell me about the new home of JULIO; or his new duty station. I had only heard very superficially and with no conviction for that matter, like what, he is currently in a tower (High Rise Building [HRB]) in the City of Defense. But you know dad, put it this way: the City of Defense is vague! So I'd rather give up this other track there! ".

MOSES: " It is anyway better than nothing, as ohm!, Not! I see how I could use! ".

MARYVONNE: " Thanks in advance. ".

MOSES: " Good MARYVONNE! We will save for us now; it is because we were out early; and we are very, slashed. We left to visit one of my workers butchers who is ill and hospitalized. ".

MARYVONNE: " Okay Dad. ".

MOSES: " But first, I'd ask you just give me the address of this old site of JULIO and obviously the name of one (, or even outright and why not, [the names of these two colleagues]); which had caused with you. Then I will promise you anything very sure now! But anyhow, I see people I could possibly do on my side to try and find him "your horn JULIO" in question! ".

MARYVONNE: " Thanks Dad. ".

MOSES: " Do not thank me; because, as I told you there is not long: Myself and your mother, we are the real cause of your emotional pain. We're sort of in this ultimate moral obligation to try to make everyone we could do, so that "your sparrow Julio Fernandez"; even if, for example, he is already present with "another companion", so that they leave, in one way or another; and come back as a result, with you, our heiress! ".

MARYVONNE: " Thanks in advance. ".

MOSES: " Give me the address that I asked you. ".

MARYVONNE: " Here one[1] this address in question: What is the N° 113 Avenue President Sadi Carnot in Saint – Quentin – En – Yvelines. These are the names of the two guards who had caused with me; and which were also very welcoming me and very kind to me: Mr. Bertolotti Foppiani and Mr. Lionel REYNALD. ".

Then Moses KEVILER and Thierry Glorian said: "Goodbye!", to MARYVONNE. They went back in the car. And finally they went on their way, towards where his first THIERRY worker lived.

---

[1] " Which has a point of reference essential "Bus Station". If you do not notice this here; I am writing to you both; if you do not notice this here; you would find a little of everything, at all, that sacred address; it's simply because we have one, case to a new City! ". MARYVONNE clarify his two visitors.

"... / ... I'm not going to take my pills; because I have
really tired to continue living in
uncertainty. I am really fed up to continue
to live while having the hope that someone
I really like return; whereas
actually, I realize that I do
illusions do nothing.".

The week that followed, Mr. Moses KEVILER asked Glorian if he could help in caring for him, this little investigation, of course, in return for a good adequate remuneration. For this, he had given her "fifteen thousand new francs"; a sum that could be used for such activities. Mr. Moses KEVILER had granted several days of "compensated absences" to his worker Glorian; so he takes very good care of this little survey. The result of this track, made possible by a good sum that had been given to one of the guards, by the name of Foppiani Bertolotti, was eloquent. That said, Glorian would tell his boss: " ... / ... Boss! ... / ... It was not easy to find yourself actually eh! Moreover, there is good news. ".

Mr. Moses KEVILER: " Go! Give birth! I burn with desire to listen to it! ".

Thierry Glorian: " Subject to the sum of ten thousand new francs, which I had bribed one of the guards to; ... / .... ".

MOSES: " That is to say ... / ...? ".

THIERRY: " That is to say, Mr. Bertolotti Foppiani, not only that I got to know how great tower defense works our "wanted" ["our desired"]; ... / .... ".

MOSES: " That is to say our Mr. Julio Fernandez, what! ".

THIERRY: " That is to say: our Mr. Julio Fernandez; but also, and especially, ... / .... ".

MOSES: " But also, and above? ".

THIERRY: " But also, and above all, I had gone there; I had seen; and even ... / .... ".

MOSES: " Yeah!, ih!, ih, ih! And even? ".

THIERRY: " Nay, I had a little talk with him. ".

MOSES: " Very well done. ".

THIERRY: " Thank you boss. Moreover it is quite normal for me to issue such a service to my boss; which trust me; otherwise he would entrust me not this delicate mission! ".

MOSES: " Very good. I only ask you not to say anything about it, to MARYVONNE or to someone else. ".

THIERRY: " Not even MARYVONNE? It's best to reassure her, give him this information! ".

MOSES: " Certainly not; or rather, not yet! When she goes ask me, the news about it; I will answer her for example: this approach has not led to anything good! ".

THIERRY: " Okay boss. ".

MOSES: " This is great. ".

THIERRY: " Moreover, at this point, consider boss, like it was already done! ".

MOSES: " Very good! So you had a little talk with him? With him JULIO? ".

THIERRY: " Boss! I probed! But that's only what I can say in all honesty and in short: he has enormous practical difficulties; and for that, you, you could without difficulty; and that, by one way or another, buy or handle! ".

MOSES: " Okay! That's great that ah! As I already told you, we should talk about this to anyone; the life of our only daughter depends on it! ".

THIERRY: " Boss! Consider if it was already done; that is to say: as if the secret was already very well kept! ".

MOSES: " Alright my very faithful worker. ".

THIERRY: " Thank you. ".

MOSES: " As to me, I would study what I could possibly do it later; to recover this JULIO on behalf of MARYVONNE. ".

THIERRY: " This will greatly arrange her, boss. ".

MOSES: " Finally, as you very well conducted these investigations; then five thousand new francs that remained; this is your pay for this little survey you agreed to carry for me. Remuneration so to speak, net of tax what! ".

Another day, a Saturday afternoon, was MARYVONNE part in "the Establishment-Butchery's Moses KEVILER". That said, she had asked her father: " ... / ... Dad! ... / ... You were gone to see the address I gave you? ".

Moses KEVILER: " Yeah! Yep!, but it was actually much easier to find eh!, this place in the car! ".

Miss Maryvonne KEVILER : " Ih!, Certainly!, I know! Even for me, when I left there for the first time; I do not even tell you the hassle I'd have known! ".

MOSES: " Finally, either! ".

MARYVONNE: " And what was the result of the race? ".

MOSES: " I saw the night watchman Berpiani FORTOLOTTI. ".

MARYVONNE: " Okay!, the night watchman Foppiani Bertolotti, OK!, ih! ".

MOSES: " Excuse me: the night watchman Bertolotti Foppiani. ".

MARYVONNE: " Agreed!, ih!, ih, ih!? ".

MOSES: "I had talked with him! But ... / .... ".

MARYVONNE: " But? ".

MOSES: " But he told me that he knew neither about the new home of JULIO; nor his new assignment post! He had no info's about them!".

With such a response, MARYVONNE who entered in the daddy 's Butchery, so full of optimism; she emerged there was therefore very, very fast and above all full of pessimism; and she left her dad and went back in her home. She had decided in her little noggin: " **As soon as I'll get home at Montrouge; I will not take my pills; because I am really fed up to continue to live in uncertainty! I am really fed up to continue living while having the hope that someone I really love return; when in reality, I realize that I am under no illusions that eh!** ".

Fortunately, that Saturday – there in the end of the evening, Mr. and Mrs. VERDUN were going to visit her, for as usual, they made for her one time, occasionally, to cheer her up. After the usual greetings, MARYVONNE told at ALEJANDRO: " Today I was part in the Establishment of my father. I wanted him to tell me if he could get info's about JULIO! ".

Professor Alejandro Of Verdun: " Had he obtained them, these info's? ".

Miss Maryvonne KEVILER: " No, unfortunately! ".

Alejandro Of VERDUN: " We need to understand; it is because myself as well, I was not able to get them, despite me ah! ".

Maryvonne KEVILER: " But it was he himself who had asked me the address of the site of JULIO and the names of the two guards who had welcomed me very nicely for two days; or rather, three days away! ".

ALEJANDRO: " Did he also went to check that address? ".

MARYVONNE " Of course!, or at least that he had suggested to me! ".

ALEJANDRO: " If he had said, that it's true! That it is true; since there's really no reason for him, he does not tell you the truth; especially not now! ".

MARYVONNE: " Maybe! But one thing is sure and certain: he had returned empty – handed! He came back with hands empty – handed! As soon as he had given me this information today; I immediately exited from his Establishment; and I returned home here. That said, ... / .... ".

ALEJANDRO: " Uh – huh!, ih!, ih, ih! That said? ".

MARYVONNE: " That said, I decided in my little noggin that as of today, I no longer take my antidepressant drugs! That way I would let myself simply damage slowly and surely; as I had predicted by a certain Mr. Cleopatra MOULLER there is this, a very long time! ".

ALEJANDRO: " But no MARYVONNE! Do not do it especially! ".

Of VERDUN provided MARYVONNE to the moral support, that she really needed in such situations; and therefore she was agreed to reconsider her decision. Alejandro Of VERDUN always give her whenever he would visit her in Montrouge, to see her again; he would always give her hope to wait a little more, JULIO; and she still would take therefore hers therapeutic seals. During another weekend and during another visit to the same kind, Alejandro Of Verdun and his lady Louisetta GRIFFIN, wife Of Verdun had even given to Miss Maryvonne KEVILER, some idea, not too bad at all; but which unfortunately alas!; she had been systematically denied.

ALEJANDRO: " But at least you know where live some of the family members of JULIO by example? For example, his sisters; the truth being that is the current between sisters sometimes goes better! Then go see them very kindly; and try to tell them to go to Julio Fernandez, where he now lives; since they, as members of his family; it must obviously know! ".

MARYVONNE: " But damn! So why this initiative? ".

ALEJANDRO: " Try to tell them, for example, to bring their brother to reason; to fly back with you "his regular", with whom he already had a son: LUCILIAN! ".

MARYVONNE: " Hmm mm! A son who does not even bears his name; or at least not as we know, you want to say! And that's it, did you really say! Is that right? ".

ALEJANDRO: " But MARYVONNE? Reasoned why you like this? I'm just asking you to try this other track one; because it could possibly lead to a great result! You do not approve this initiative? Is not that what's great is not it? ".

MARYVONNE: " Sorry! I MARYVONNE fetching members JULIO ' s family? Me? Hmm mm! ".

ALEJANDRO: " One looks like it will catch this proposal? Is not it? ".

MARYVONNE: " But you two: " "Adam" and "Eva" "! Have you fallen in the head or what! And you also push such a proposal! Have you fallen from heaven, by the head or what? Did you come by your heads? Have you gone mad's or what? Do you not know that they were the ones we had rotten existence for me? Especially his sisters! "These **gamestersns** – there!". ".

ALEJANDRO: " Do not say that MARYVONNE! Do not say that, especially where there are a lot of people! ".

MARYVONNE: " "These stools that"! Which husbands rob them! "These **bitches** – then" you're referring to! And I MARYVONNE, pick them up; and therefore, chatting with them? No, they do not like at all, at all, feel! And given such an atmosphere of understanding that exists between me and them, I could not in any case go find "these **strumpets** – ones"! At home or elsewhere for that matter! I could frankly speaking, in any case, go find "those stews that"! Including "their areas of choice" for "their love parades" are none other "areas" that "the spouses of their own sisters"! Yeah!, ih! "These sisters – there"! Do not appreciate that their own brother! Furthermore, I do not even tell you ALEJANDRO: How, their irreducible ways to win (the ways of "the creatures that!"), Emit virtually "real dirty poems, worthy of the name"! Ah!, "these **hustlersns** – there"! Eh! This is something! It's really something, "these **adultery stars** – then!". ".

ALEJANDRO: " But always try and see MARYVONNE well: What it could possibly give for example, as a result of the race! As said – on: "You never know!". ".

MARYVONNE: " No, I will even be several years at home; and I hope that eventually JULIO understand the wrong; and consequently, he would eventually decide to come back home just as the two of you yourself have already had occasion to tell me and let me repeat again and again; rather than seek his sisters: "These **fornication stars** – ones"! Shamelessly! "Shameless" and "light"! Yep!, ih!, "These **whoringstars** – there" are more "light"; they give themselves the immense joy of conquering "the husbands of others" (and not just any "husbands of others" eh! "These professional one"! give themselves the immense joy of conquering "**husbands of their own herrings**". "These **mistressesns** – there" give themselves the immense joy of conquering "theirs brothers – in Law". "There's brothers – in Law" of course they are, where they find, that is to say: at home)!. And they are already with them immediately "immediately"; that is to say: the same day of the conquest, which will still return tomorrow; and after tomorrow; and later, after tomorrow; and so on; that is to say: "the **horizontal boogies**". Hmm mm, for "**these junks – ones**"! "**Do – cuckold**" **theirs own sisters** [and under the impulse of that? That ah!,] is we say, "a determining factor" "in the family" ["the family of FERNANDEZ"]. Hmm mm, for "the **lobsters – ones**"! "**Do – cuckold**" **theirs own sisters,** it looks like it's "a way of them" "can enter into osmosis" "with the world-sublime"! Ah!, "**the prawns – ones**"! Eh! ".

ALEJANDRO: " You do not stop to dress up for "these synonyms of **lobsters – ones**"! Pejoratives as well as each 's other's eh? ".

MARYVONNE: " I walked by "marriage covenant" in their family! And because of this, I am very, very well informed about those I say about "these **trollopsns** – there!". I am still very, very knowledgeable about "their very, very Long Journals Coded.". "Very, very Long Journals Coded. "Of" these **hustling 's – stars** ones! "! "Coded", certainly, but perhaps not so coded it eh! Because no matter how: " **The insidious and ruthless fight** "**sisters – Fernandez – idyllic**" "**buttocks**". ", For example; it could only mean: what it could mean that eh! "These **hooking 's – stars** ones"! Launch towards their brothers – in Law "cries of the heart"; "Cries" for "them reach their hearts" ("the hearts of the latter") to "to pamper"; or rather to "to tame"! For people who do not know "the sisters FERNANDEZ" themselves from the moment that the approach that we cause with them: "What are" "nice – wives"; these are "great – mothers"! But as to me MARYVONNE example I am "the **harlotrystar**" "a FERNANDEZ": " Sisters FERNANDEZ precisely, "it is apparently" the nice – mothers "certainly; however", "beyond" "accents": "the nice – wives", it is only " the authors of the insidious and relentless fighting "sisters – Fernandez – idyllic" "buttocks" ". "; otherwise: "the revanchists targeting their evil targets!". That's what they really are "the genuine **whoringstars**"! ".

B ut that's only after waiting a little longer; and JULIO did not return; that said, a good day, Miss Maryvonne KEVILER had clearly told at Alejandro Of VERDUN and Louisetta GRIFFIN, wife Of Verdun; that is to say: to "the legitimate of ALEJANDRO"; which as usual again; they had gone to visit her: " I'm sick to hope in vain. I'm totally stop everything. Today I'll just quit hoping. I will stop taking the tablets. I will stop to clean and fix my apartment; and cetera and cetera ... / .... ".

And yeah!, ih! As might be seen: it was a desperation to MARYVONNE. It was: a hopeless cause for her. It was: a desperation. But only here, "impregnated" so "certain habits" "Blondinians", Maryvonne KEVILER, did not succeed [we say] little, understand herself really: What had she done exactly, in desperation.

ALEJANDRO: " But no ohm! Do not do that ah! Above all, we must not abandon absolutely taking the drugs; otherwise it would prove to be very dangerous for you! ".

MARYVONNE: " Yep!, agree! I will not give up taking my pills; as this would prove to be very dangerous for me; is heard. I will not give up taking my tablets; this is because no matter how my father MOSES would hardly happy! Speaking of my dad exactly! ALEJANDRO you know that my dad is, so to say, "From Kinese Descent"? ".

ALEJANDRO: " So what? ".

MARYVONNE: " And you also know that my mother MARYSSA is almost "Descent From Alsatian?". ".

ALEJANDRO: " So what? ".

MARYVONNE: " Ih!, aye!, I too say: So, where is the problem? Besides about it breeds; even though my father is "black"! ... / ... ".

ALEJANDRO: « Aye, aye !, ih!, ih, ih! ".

MARYVONNE: " Even though my mother is white! ... / ...! ".

ALEJANDRO: " Uh – huh!, ih!, ih, ih! ".

MARYVONNE: " Even though my father is Congolese, a native of Kinshasa! ... / ...! ".

ALEJANDRO: " Okay !, ih!, ih, ih! ".

MARYVONNE: " Even though my mom is French, a native of Strasbourg! ... / ...! ".

ALEJANDRO: " OK !, ih!, ih, ih! ".

MARYVONNE: " But if I think for example that my dad had been "adopted to express myself in this way", by a Mr. Adrian Of SAINT-HILAIRE! ... / ...! ".

ALEJANDRO: " Indeed!, ih, ih, ih! ".

MARYVONNE: " "An adoption" which certainly does not even say his name! So ... / ...! ".

ALEJANDRO: " Agreed!, ih!, ih, ih! ".

MARYVONNE: " So given the fact that Adrian Of SAINT-HILAIRE happens to be the uncle of my mother! Hence thus: my dad MOSES and my mom MARYSSA, are somehow that the "cousin" and the "cousin"! That said, in order not to hurt them, I no longer would stop taking my pills! ".

" ... / ... You can never understand: How
Julio Fernandez this "Descent From Poitevese
On and Rear-Spanish Descent" ultimately remains for me ... / .... ".

In reality, MARYVONNE was said in the background of herself: " Take home first; take home real Of Verdun; and so, right after, I would stop everything! ".

ALEJANDRO, at MARYVONNE: " MARYVONNE, I will still ask you something; or to better express it: I'll make you another suggestion. Will you listen to me this time 'it; or just shut me up? ".

MARYVONNE, at ALEJANDRO: " Go! I'm listening! ".

ALEJANDRO: " I was going to say, like JULIO and you, you were not; or to put it more correctly: like JULIO and you, you're not married ... / .... ".

MARYVONNE: " Not married yet, so ih!, ih, ih!? ".

ALEJANDRO: " That's it! You only live "conjugal" ... / .... ".

MARYVONNE: " As married, yeah!, I'm listening! ".

ALEJANDRO: " So, if you found you another ... / ...? ".

MARYVONNE: " Go! Another one? ".

ALEJANDRO: " Another "noble man"? ".

MARYVONNE: " What surprising question! Not to say: What a surprise and all at once stupid question! Damn it! But what my faithful colleague and you both husband and wife, you like that make me a stupid suggestion! ".

ALEJANDRO: " We will ourselves (my wife LOUISETTA present – here and myself) to help you, for example, to find someone else; someone else good, I'd rather tell you! He turns out that anyone else concerned that we know very well by the way, is also a University; since he is an Assistant – Professor at the University of Poitiers, in the Faculty of Arts; Option: Modern and Contemporary History ... / .... ".

MARYVONNE: " Hmm mm! Coincidentally, it speaks to me of the same University where JULIO started its academic programs; and as for that other random coincidence, the same Faculty of Arts also! Just one question: "Progeny Poitevese And Background On Spanish Descent" too? ".

ALEJANDRO: " Excuse me? ".

MARYVONNE: " It someone else okay with that, you two would make an arrangement for me! Is he also "Descent From Poitevese And Background On Spanish Descent"? ".

ALEJANDRO: " No ohm! But why this question? No, do not answer; it's because you've already actually provided all the elements of the answer! Ah!, I see! This is because, I told you about from the University of Poitiers, is it not? ".

MARYVONNE: " Aye!, because you talked about this wizard; This Lecturer at the University of Poitiers; and as if by chance!; and it ah!, I just realize now that I did you had not shared so far: Julio Fernandez is also a native of this City; and especially that at any moment he almost never stopped to say (much like myself MARYVONNE also, coincidentally, except for me, adjectives, or rather change places, and he does almost never stopped to say [I quote]): "Me Julio Fernandez Of Progeny Poitevese And Background On Progeny Spanish". So that's why, I wonder if this is not by chance also become such **a slogan of the natives of Poitiers**? ".

ALEJANDRO: " But no ohm! I do not know you spoke of that friend like what; he is a native of Poitiers as I know me ah! ".

MARYVONNE: " No? ".

ALEJANDRO: "And well no! This friend; Lecturer this, I would rather say that someone else good, is originally from Brittany; but he did all his graduate work at the University of Paris – Sorbonne; and he was stationed now, in Poitiers, just in the course of his work. ".

MARYVONNE: " But say so! ".

ALEJANDRO: " Excuse me? ".

MARYVONNE: " Definitely! Even the University of Paris – Sorbonne! Me MARYVONNE: Paris – Sorbonne; one of my friends and especially MARLY: Paris – Sorbonne; anyone else good, from whom you both husband and wife you want to connect to me: Paris – Sorbonne; JULIO: later, Paris – Sorbonne; ALEJANDRO yourself: Paris – Sorbonne! Definitely actually! ".

ALEJANDRO: " Excuse me? ".

MARYVONNE: " No! No, no ohm! I said nothing! ".

ALEJANDRO: " There had sympathized with the Lecturer of course, in an International Conference of Historians in the United States. That someone else is well widower; and he trusted us: proof that he is all the time in correspondence with us, since we had met and befriended him. One phone is further from time to time. ".

MARYVONNE: " I'm sorry! ".

ALEJANDRO: " You do not even wish to know his name? ".

MARYVONNE: " No! No, it's not worth it and I'm really sorry eh! ".

ALEJANDRO: " You do not want? ".

MARYVONNE: " Negative! ".

ALEJANDRO: " Not at all! ".

MARYVONNE " It's negative! ".

ALEJANDRO: " Not at all, at all? ".

MARYVONNE: " It's negative! It's not worth the stress! It's really not worth it to try to stress; because no matter how, I will not change my opinion on it! ".

ALEJANDRO: " But just try and see: What this could possibly give! ".

MARYVONNE: " No, no way! It does not really matter and I'm adamant about it! For me MARYVONNE is Julio Fernandez or anyone else! ".

ALEJANDRO: " Definitely! ".

MARYVONNE: " It is not even bother to tell me:" Definitely! "; because I have weighed my words answering you, ALEJANDRO, how I answered you! Otherwise, I could have answered you very systematically, "Nyet!". I could send you two ("Adam" and "Eva") walk! And therefore you, you would not even have had such courage to still continue to talk to me about this stupid suggestion! I wore gloves to meet you again nicely, if not hard, hard! ".

ALEJANDRO: " Okay! I clearly got it now! We understood very well now! ".

MARYVONNE: " Besides just about that, it's like I already suggested to one of my work colleagues Lillian QUESNEL wife Roger BOUSSARD, you two; that is to say: you ALEJANDRO and your lady LOUISETTA: You could never understand: How "this gentleman – there" Julio Fernandez called "Descent From Poitevese And Background On Spanish Descent" precisely, is and always will remain and yet still for me MARYVONNE: "**Irreplaceable**" and " **Irremediable** "! ".

ALEJANDRO: " Is it by any chance, it's not the fact that my friend Lecturer, you refuse to even know no, is not Poitevese origin, which makes you automatically reject, any marital cohabitation with him, right? ".

MARYVONNE: "Not at all! MARYVONNE myself talking to both of you now, I am not a native of this Region – there! My parents either! My father was born in Leopoldville (the Belgian Congo [now today: Kinshasa, Republic of Zaire; The Democratic Republic of Congo or DRC]); and my mother, she is Alsatian; she was born in Strasbourg. And I MARYVONNE I am: "A Mixed Descent From Paris (my birthplace) and On Background Kinese Progeny (the birthplace of my father)". If I say: "Julio Of Descent ... / ....". ".

ALEJANDRO: " ... / ... From Progeny Poitevese. ".

MARYVONNE: " Exactly! This is simply because the latter himself, liked to call; or rather: likes to call many, many times so; it is because I am sure and certain that where there is currently found, he does the same! Hence the fact that: him, himself likes to call many, many times as well. ".

ALEJANDRO: " It's fun there? ".

MARYVONNE: " Absolutely. This amuses him greatly. That was why, when you told me this Lecturer, citing in Poitiers! So right away, I thought of him Julio Fernandez "Descent From Poitevese"! ".

ALEJANDRO: " No, he has nothing to do at all with "Descent From Poitevese" as place of birth! ".

MARYVONNE: " And that, I emphasize that it was not at all; or to put it more correctly: and this without me, a slightest intention of Regionalism eh! ".

And those, Of Verdun could not even dare to propose another possible suggestion. He could not do anything else. He and his lady LOUISETTA they could therefore say that everything nicely: "Goodbye!", to MARYVONNE; and go for them.

ALEJANDRO, to "his Venus LOUISETTA": " You know what LOUISETTA with this depression to her MARYVONNE? ".

LOUISETTA, to "her everyman ALEJANDRO": " No! I know nothing! ".

ALEJANDRO: " When she let me hear for example [I quote]: " It is not even bother to tell me: "Definitely!"; because I have weighed my words answering you ALEJANDRO, how I answered you! Otherwise, I could have answered you very systematically, "Nyet!". I could send you two ("Adam" and "Eva") walk! And therefore you, you would not even have had such courage to still continue to talk to me about this stupid suggestion! I wore gloves to meet you again nicely, if not hard, hard! ". ! ".

LOUISETTA: " Yeah!, ih? ".

ALEJANDRO: " It was very serious this depressive eh! ".

LOUISETTA: " It ah! Very serious! ".

ALEJANDRO: " I would say eh! ".

LOUISETTA: " Too serious! ".

ALEJANDRO: " That's right, yep!, ih! I would say she was too serious! ".

LOUISETTA: " I totally agree with you ALEJANDRO! This was stamped in fact his words carefully in responding to you the way she answered you! ".

ALEJANDRO: " This was clearly schizophrenic, too serious! Otherwise, she could have answered me very systematically, "Nyet!". ".

LOUISETTA: " This psychopath was undoubtedly too serious! Otherwise, she could have sent us we walk, we two ("Adam" and "Eva")! ".

ALEJANDRO: " This was really skewed too serious! Otherwise, she could have acted in ways we express it: " And therefore you ALEJANDRO, you would not even have such courage to still continue to talk to me, about "the stupid suggestion", in his words! ". ".

LOUISETTA: " This was obviously unbalanced, too serious! And she therefore wore gloves to meet you again nicely! Otherwise: hard, hard! ".

ALEJANDRO: " Between us LOUISETTA though we find ourselves in this hallucinatory one, she should in any case, that one of us can, for example, spit ears: "This **imbecility** was undoubtedly too serious! Otherwise, she could have ... / ...!". ".

LOUISETTA: " We should in any case, that one of us can, for example, to spit in the ears; or even just talk in her presence, for example: "This was certainly goofy, too serious! Otherwise, she could have ... / ...! ".

ALEJANDRO: " Or for example: "This was undoubtedly alienated too serious! Otherwise, she could have ... / ...!". ".

LOUISETTA: " Or for example: "This crank was indeed too serious! Otherwise, she could have ... / ...!". ".

ALEJANDRO: " Or for example: "And cetera and cetera .../...!". ".

LOUISETTA: " No ohm! It should under no circumstances tell her that, I know that, uh – huh!, ih! ".

ALEJANDRO: " That's ah! Otherwise, she'll think! ".

LOUISETTA: " That we made fun of her! ".

ALEJANDRO: " Yep! Above all, that I did not even want to go to a psychic for her! But I do not even have the courage to say to her face! How cowardly of me! ".

LOUISETTA: " It's ah!, you did well expressed! ".

Maryssa Fouquet, wife KEVILER, the mum of MARYVONNE, had passed some good days where Alejandro Of Verdun lived and his **"noblewoman**, Louisetta GRIFFIN, wife Of Verdun", to talk to them about her only daughter MARYVONNE. That said, they all talked together. Maryssa Fouquet who entered in Of VERDUN's house, every pessimistic, thinking about the evolution of the health of her downward; she came out all optimistic. MARYSSA same pass again several times, in Alejandro Of Verdun's house, to talk of course about her maiden MARYVONNE. As also it also happen frequently in Of VERDUN; then, a good day when she came to find by chance, her mother in those; she was right after, retraced the way, without even so far to say beforehand: " Hello!"; even less: "Goodbye!" ", to anyone whatsoever. However, Alejandro Of VERDUN says to Maryssa Fouquet: " Do not worry about that lady! I'll arrange that! ". And he had also arranged that.

EVELYN greatly loved Julio
FERNANDEZ. For her, too, he is
very frankly: " "**Irreplaceable**" and
"the **Uncorrectable** "; "**Indisputable**" and "**Uncontested**";
and finally "**Unforgettable**" and "**Irretrievablestar**"; do for
hardly say, for example:
"The **Inevitable**" and "**Unavoidable**". ".

But that's only as Miss Maryvonne KEVILER actually had pretty much stopped; and it fell by chance in August; when Mr. and Mrs. VERDUN are on vacation for two months in Reunion Island; and they could not even be aware of psychic evolution and even outright physical of MARYVONNE; they telephoned her; and the phone did not answer; and they sent to her postcards; which unfortunately remained alas!, "dead letters!"; this one was not taking hers pills for almost two months; and nobody knew, in order to force them to take. One day, the dad MARYVONNE, Mr. Moses KEVILER and Thierry Glorian, his oldest worker butcher, had gone home to see MARYVONNE in Montrouge, on the request of the Company, where she was working to learn: Why was already three days, she [left] more at work? Arriving there, they knocked on the door; or rather, they rang the doorbell. Once MARYVONNE had heard the doorbell ring just. She imagined it was JULIO who had returned. She was very happy. She was [part] open; and she stated that it was only her father and one of his faithful workers. MOSES and THIERRY on their side, they had obviously found a near pandemonium that reigned in the apartment of MARYVONNE; and they had also found: How she had became quite weak; because in reality, not only that she was not taking hers medications for almost two months already; but she had stopped eating altogether for three days ago. MARYVONNE seriously believed at first that it was undoubtedly her "gentleman Julio Fernandez" who had turned in hers arms, "as predicted [in the words of

Mr. Of VERDUN], the medium; realizing that in fact, her dad and one of the workers of the latter, it was"; …/…!

MOSES: " Hello MARYVONNE! ".

MARYVONNE with weakened her way: " Hi Dad! ".

MOSES: " You will provide me MARYVONNE, JULIO's news today? ".

MARYVONNE: " Who? Me? ".

MOSES: " Yeah!, you! ".

MARYVONNE: " No ohm! ".

MOSES: " Yep!, ih! ".

MARYVONNE: " No! This is because: I do not have! By against dad, you'll provide me with you, JULIO news today! ".

Hence MARYVONNE took advantage, to ask them (with its very weak and barely audible way): " Have you heard from him? ".

MOSES: " Who? ".

MARYVONNE: " But let ohm! JULIO of oh! Julio Fernandez! ".

MOSES: " No, we actually came to you MARYVONNE; this is because "your Direction"; Management of your work phoned us to know: What happens exactly; since, it's been three days exactly, that you are not part of your work; and that you do not even have anything reported about it to anyone! Your Management had obviously tried to reach you during the three days in question; but unfortunately alas!, your phone does not respond! We, too, we first tried to reach you by telephone; but alas!, it still does not answer! ".

MARYVONNE: " Yep! Most of time, I would say, almost at any time and for quite some time now, I always unplug my phone; and yet I'm still at home. But I act this way; this is because I want peace to ponder my very frequent errors; I would even say on my frequent mistakes squarely; which had pushed "my man of honor Julio Fernandez" to save, and this: not to tell me where he's gone. ".

MOSES: " Ah!, he certainly should not have this habit then, unplug the phone! This is not good! ".

MARYVONNE: " And why would not it although I know me? ".

MOSES: " This is not good; since this could for example … / …. ".

MARYVONNE: « Aye !, ih!, ih, ih! This could for example? ".

MOSES: " ... / ... For example, simply be ... / .... ".

MARYVONNE: « Aye, aye !, ih!, ih, ih! For example simply be? ".

MOSES: " Simply the unexpected blow over "your man deserves Julio Fernandez"! That's what I wanted to say for example! ".

MARYVONNE: " Oh!, ohm! If that's why, I think: Dad, you're not wrong about that! Are you sure you're right! ".

MOSES: " And ben! You see! ".

MARYVONNE: " But I do in fact, for about almost two months I think, and especially during the night! I do it the more the couple Of Verdun who often came to comfort me morally, went away on holiday, for the same period almost already! Do you think for all those days, JULIO might have tried to reach me? ".

MOSES: " I do not know. I said just like that eh! ".

MARYVONNE: " I solemnly admit that I was wrong to finally unplug my phone; JULIO since had certainly tried to reach me and in vain, as you said yourself Dad! ".

MOSES: " Maybe not! ".

MARYVONNE: " And maybe: Yeah? ".

MOSES: " Absolutely! ".

MARYVONNE: " And well you know! Ah!, it annoys me that I was doing! Now I understand: JULIO had certainly tried in vain to join me! ".

MOSES: " Maybe not! ".

MARYVONNE: " Yep! Aye!, so ih! Oh!, I still had again been stupid! ".

MOSES: " JULIO might have tried to reach you indeed! But maybe not, and it is not excluded either! In addition, I would lean more balance, the fact that: Maybe not! ".

MARYVONNE: " And how can you know Dad? ".

MOSES: " It's simple! ".

MARYVONNE: " How that's simple? ".

MOSES: " It's simple, for the simple reason that if he really had unsuccessfully tried to call you on the phone ... / .... ".

MARYVONNE: « Aye, aye !, ih!, ih, ih! ".

MOSES: " If this had been the case, after insistence, and as he knows the apartment [And for good reason!] he would simply moved himself, as other – we just do it! This is because, obviously, as I said, we have also tried in vain to reach you by phone after receiving the call from your Department. And saw that indeed at home, it does not answer the point; and given the fact that we know very well your apartment quite logically! So we – we moved ourselves, to see first – hand, what happens exactly. That said, "your noble man Julio Fernandez", so really, he had tried to reach you several times; after insistence he would obviously proceed in the same way as us move squarely to come and see himself on the spot: What's going on here. ".

MARYVONNE: " Yeah. ".

MOSES: " Yep!, what? ".

MARYVONNE: " Aye!, I think your reasoning is logical. It makes sense.".

MOSES: " Of course! So do not you Add other concerns, about this phone disconnected almost two months, and especially the night; because you already have too many problems in your head like that, about "your noble JULIO"; which still returns yet! I admit that it is even worse, for example, ... / .... ".

MARYVONNE: " You confess that it is even worse example than what?".

MOSES: " No nothing! ".

MARYVONNE: " Aye!, aye, aye! If you have to tell me dad! ".

MOSES: " Finally, I would only say that someone who runs away like that, without giving news; it is even worse, for example, than someone who died outright; since then, everyone knows! Since then, everyone has worries! Then these concerns eventually disappear; and it almost completely. ".

MARYVONNE: " Oh!, oh! What idea did you dad behind your head? ".

MOSES: " But nothing eh!, eh, eh! ".

MARYVONNE: " I say daddy in the presence of your faithful worker Thierry Glorian that ... / .... ".

MOSES: " What? ".

MARYVONNE: " What if you're trying to do ... / .... ".

MOSES: " What would you do? Besides, if I try to do what again myself huh? Can you be more explicit than that? ".

MARYVONNE: " I would say that if you try to remove Julio Fernandez, for some people, who, you would pay much of your fortune! Know – dad, that ... / .... ".

MOSES: " Who ih!, ih, ih! What? ".

MARYVONNE: " ... / ... What I would end up knowing too! I would eventually know that Julio Fernandez died for example, as a result of a particular accident! And from there, I simply conclude that it was sponsored by you, dad! ".

MOSES: " And if that be the case? ".

MARYVONNE: " And if that were the case, I would delete downright, me MARYVONNE, too! ".

MOSES: " But have you thought about the implications of such a situation one on one's mental state[1] LUCILIAN your son? ".

MARYVONNE: " Of course I thought! It is very sensitive to him one too! He died[1] therefore: slowly and surely, simply an indirect impact of the case

---

[1] "He would die ... / ....". Looks MARYVONNE, his father MOSES. This was certainly true; all the more so when one remembers that "Benedict MARCONI Centre" had already indicated to the attention of the maternal grandparents' child LUCILIAN "as anything that" mental state "remained very fragile and consequently, it was essential to humor from worry! So when you consider the implications of such a situation" like a child" exactly? Or whatever Miss Maryvonne KEVILER knew "mental state" of her kid; that: "... / ... Lucilian KEVILER [is] he also very sensitive.". But she did not even know he was already, because of his fragile mental state; like what, he already was, for a period of two years [as it were, to the day], followed by psychologists of "Benedict MARCONI Center", located on the Avenue Georges CLÉMENCEAU [at the junction with Street Of The Source; that is to say, to the right, heading towards Paris]; which he administered two types of therapies: the group and the individual.

MARYVONNE hardly knew this episode in the life of her son; it's because hers parents, knowing that she herself had not at all an excellent mental health: she was suffering from a nervous breakdown; then they had an absolute obligation of not to keep her informed: this episode in the life of her son; afraid to do then, matters worse; which already proved to be very, very complicated way.

as "the flight of our family home", of his father Julio Fernandez. But that's only ... / .... ".

MOSES: " Aye!, ih!, ih, ih! But only here? ".

MARYVONNE: " But only here, me MARYVONNE, I would not be here in this world, to see with my eyes, this catastrophe! I would not be here to see with my eyes, this situation! In addition, ... / .... ".

MOSES: " Aye, aye!, ih!, ih, ih! In addition? ".

MARYVONNE: " Also me as such, I hardly have a fortune to bequeath, to be afraid that the state simply takes up, by the default of an heir or heiress e.g. ! ".

MOSES: " MARYVONNE Enough blackmail one! ".

MARYVONNE: " No it's not blackmail! ".

MOSES: " If it is not; but anyway, it looks like it considerably. ".

MARYVONNE: " Maybe so! Or maybe not! ".

M OSES: " It was not worth thinking that I could have Machiavellian ideas to this point; since it's really gruesome! I just wanted to say that someone who is lost as in the nature; it's worse than someone who died outright for example! And you're gone very far in your thoughts! ".

MARYVONNE: " Not at all! Because, no matter how: JULIO is lost as the true nature, but against me! But I do not think that it is also vis-à-vis his family, too! ".

MOSES: " I wanted you to understand that: If JULIO really tried to reach you by phone repeatedly; and it did not answer; because it was ... / .... ".

MARYVONNE: " Yeah!, I of course: because it was unplugged! It would just be moved to come see for himself there. But as there was hardly come; where he had not even tried to contact me; I know! ".

MOSES: " Yep! Absolutely. It's even there, a logical reasoning. ".

MARYVONNE: " Why do not outright say for example that it's even there, a more than logical reasoning? ".

MOSES: " Here for example! Your mother and myself, when we call you for trying to know the statement of your health; and when it does not respond; one insists, but it still does not respond! So in this case, it simply moves until your house of Montrouge – here! ".

MARYVONNE: " It's true. Ohm!, good! We forget that little moment of madness. ".

MOSES: " Okay!, we forget all that ah! ".

MARYVONNE: " Going back to what was the beginning of our conversation! Frankly especially joking aside, you, you two, got news of him JULIO? ".

MOSES: " No! No, well, we did not come here for that. We are, as I said, you see; it's because you realize you most in your work; and it was already three days. We phoned to tell you about just the phone; but only here, it does not even answer! For this, we absolutely, we decided to move ourselves till here! ".

MARYVONNE: " Oh! ".

MOSES: " Ih!, Yeah!, this is hardly to bring you news of him "your gentleman Julio Fernandez"! ".

And when dad MARYVONNE had only finished saying: " ... / ... This is not to bring you news of him "your gentleman Julio Fernandez"! ". This one just had slowly [and as it were also "slowly and surely"], began to sink. She was beginning to fall slightly in a first time, in a state of semi-consciousness. And then his dad MOSES and THIERRY (worker and faithful friend – one); which found themselves seated right next to her; they both, had been standing; they stood with their four arms; and that's before for example, they have had the slightest moment: really dip: Those were happening exactly, suddenly? Then, there, in a second stage suddenly MARYVONNE instantly had slipped into unconsciousness. And yep!, ih!, she had fallen into a swoon!; or to better express it: she had already fainted. There had phoned any speed "The Emergency Medical Service [acronym: EMS]". Then a few minutes later, one of the cars of "the Service" was already there on the spot; and it was already too, to proceed with resuscitation on site; so as not to waste time; or to better say, to save time already. Then we had brought MARYVONNE in[1] hospital. She remained in a coma for two days. After two days, she "had found knowledge"; she was conscious again; and wondered quite naturally: Where was it located? [Oh!, that destiny is frail! Oh!, that last sleep, is never "the devilish!"]. The doctors had suggested to the parents of this one, that: "It happened not only because she is fed for three more days; but above all, because he had systematically stopped taking hers pills, there was this, about two months.".

---

[1] In " Our Lady Of Good Help 's Hospital", located on the Street Giordano BRUNO, in the Fourteenth Arrondissement of Paris; that is to say: Montrouge near where she lived.

MARYVONNE remained in hospital in all, a good whole month; which for two weeks, with sensors in their body; which artificially fed in key nutrients that the human body is absolutely necessary in order to continue living. When she was out of this Healing Center, his parents; that is to say, Moses KEVILER had suggested that she [comes] just live with them in Rueil–Malmaison, if only for a short definite period, for just the time she can regain her strength of old. That way they could at the same time, although the monitor and protect the well during this short period. But only here, unfortunately, the response was interested: "A categorical Nyet!". It's nice parents; or rather his kind parents had yet offered to come live with her squarely in Montrouge with her; or, if the three of them (that is to say: Moses KEVILER, his lady Maryssa Fouquet and of course, the child of their daughter who was sick, that is to say: LUCILIAN); or, if the three of them, at least one of two adults and in turn, by sharing days or weeks; to better monitor her health. But again and unfortunately, the answer to MARYVONNE was again: "Another systematic Nyet!". Finally, Moses KEVILER still had proposed to their only daughter, they pay her a stranger to the family; a caregiver for example; which would totally live with her, to not only monitor her mental and physical development; and take steps quickly in case of extreme urgency; but also to take care of the various works: cleaning her apartment by example. But that was stubborn; the response of the interested MARYVONNE in question had been: "Another absolute Nyet!".

That said, her dad MOSES not found more than before the only alternative, to left to her, reiterating that the promise he had made to her and even remade in hospital; which is to help to find and push him back to her home in Montrouge, "his pistol Julio Fernandez". In doing so, he was still assigned; or to better express it: he still sent his faithful worker Thierry Glorian; which finally knew: You can find one, so he was gone again, have a second interview with him; maintenance significantly more advanced one. But only here, there was unfortunately alas!, a big problem. What exactly was the problem? The man in question; that is to say: Julio Fernandez had already for some time, put together with "another **mama**"; and this time, it was totally a wedding at City Hall. He had already been married for only a short time with another **princess**[1]; with Evelyn MULER; which had become quite logically: Ms. Evelyn MULER, wife FERNANDEZ. And it was also coincidentally, an only child she also; but after only child of poor parents, as in the case of Julio Fernandez himself. EVELYN this was not "a Trilingual **Gentlewoman**, Secretary of Direction", as in the case of MARYVONNE; but was rather: "a cashier part – time" in a big – box in Eleventh Arrondissement of Paris; and particularly on the Street Saint – Maur; that is to say: close to home actually. His parents; that is to say: Mr. Yves MULER and Simone Durand, wife MULER, living in their apartment on credit, in Corbeil – Essonne, were poor people [since this one was a worker – Specializes in highway maintenance] work. The contrast with MARYVONNE and her family was quite evident.

---

[1] And the new couple should live on Street Oberkampf in the Eleventh Arrondissement of Paris; where it would rent a "three – pieces" in an old building.

Given the new state health of MARYVONNE; which could not stop worsen, Moses KEVILER decided to do what was suggested to his faithful employee Thierry Glorian; whereas previously, in the bottom of himself; though he had accepted the concept; but nevertheless, he hesitated so far yet. That was why he was delaying to act in that path. But now that the health of MARYVONNE not stop hardly get worse; he was determined to do what we had suggested him to do.

EVELYN greatly loved Julio Fernandez. For her, too, he was quite frankly: "**Irreplaceable**" and "**Irremedial**"; "**Indisputable**" and "**Uncontested**"; and finally "**Unforgettable**" and "**Irremediablestar**"; for hardly say for example: "the **Inevitable**" and the "**Irremedialstar**".

Furthermore, there was a very big concern in their recent home; and which could quite frankly, to simply shatter their new household. What was this very big worry? This very big concern was the fact that Evelyn is, as was already the case for "MARYVONNE, **the old rave**" of Julio Fernandez, an only child; as she held to her, to have lots of kids. EVELYN for her, it was a choice she had drawn in her head; and she was keen to meet. She had to respect him and that, regardless e.g. weaknesses of income. Why was it set such a choice? It was not to be like hers parents, for example; which is saying that the economic universe only stopping little darken; hence, "one **toddler**" they had had; that is to say: her EVELYN, enough for them very widely. For the latter: " ... / ... This is so that a later date; I do not find myself in such an eventual loneliness ... / .... ".

Or just for Julio Fernandez: " ... / ... I have in my little head, several wonderful macro – economic projects, according to my calculations! It is in order to succeed once and for all in our lives! ". And for that, he would say simply to "his **empress**, EVELYN" the only daughter of Yves MULER and Simone DURAND: " ... / ... Anyway my dear beauty, I'll tell you one thing! ".

Mrs. Evelyn MULER, wife FERNANDEZ: " Say it! ".

Julio Fernandez: " For this I am going to express myself without any complacency! ".

Evelyn MULER: " Go! ".

Julio Fernandez: " I know very well that you dream to want to have a real family! You dream of desire to have a real family life; and I know it very well! ".

EVELYN: " If you were a little more explicit than that ah? ".

JULIO: " This is to say that you dream of having many children, to do the opposite of your parents. ".

EVELYN: " It ah! I will no longer do tell! ".

JULIO: " Know this right now, as I do also, I love many children. ".

EVELYN: " But? ".

JULIO: " But just now, I have in my little noggin, a great economic project; and I would even say very good economic projects; in order to succeed once and for all, in life. ".

EVELYN: " So? ".

JULIO: " Therefore, it will be necessary that we first wait quite a few years to finally begin to have offspring. ".

EVELYN: " It will be necessary that we first wait quite a few years? ".

JULIO: " Indeed! ".

EVELYN: " Otherwise? ".

JULIO: " Otherwise, we will do all fuck up; and stay forever, with only very low incomes; which might one day, to ensure that it is even more able, for example, to pay our costs of rents; to see this offspring, thrown out; or rather to see it, to eject out, as was the case with my mother, there is this, a few years, with consequences, rather melodramatics. ".

EVELYN :" But no ohm! ".

JULIO: " But yeah!, ih! ".

EVELYN: " But no ohm! ".

JULIO: " But yep!, ih! ".

EVELYN: " But no ohm! ".

JULIO: " But aye!, ih! ".

EVELYN: " But no ohm! ".

JULIO: " But aye, aye!, ih! ".

EVELYN: " Do not be too pessimistic at this point, my husband Julio Fernandez "Descent From Poitevese And Background On Progeny Spanish!". ".

JULIO: " The economic universe is dark enough for now! So I do not see: How could I do to hardly be too pessimistic, as you say! ".

EVELYN: " You know eh! ".

JULIO: " No, I do not know if you yourself do not tell me: What is it? ".

EVELYN: " My parents have almost paid off the debts Twenty years of funding their apartment in Corbeil – Essonne. ".

JULIO: " So what? ".

EVELYN: " Now they have only one child: me! ".

JULIO: " So what? ".

EVELYN: " I am their sole heir! ".

JULIO: " So what? ".

EVELYN: " Certainly they are not rich because they are the only workers! ".

JULIO: " But? ".

EVELYN: " But never if they were to die; it's you and me, whom shall live in their apartment in question! ".

JULIO: " So what? ".

EVELYN: " So, I implore you: we will have our offspring! ".

JULIO: " I say no! We'll have to wait absolutely! ".

EVELYN: " According to you, he will have to wait approximately how many years, for example? ".

JULIO: " Maybe the chance of success would come my economic projects such little immediately; it may well be that in ten years, would come quietly; and that in such a case, we should also expect for example ten years quietly; and it is not rocket science! ".

EVELYN: " How much? ".

JULIO: " Perhaps even more eh! ".

EVELYN: " But! Do you speak seriously? Or you're just joking? ".

JULIO: " It will not head, not ohm! Me: joking with the future? ".

EVELYN: " But anyway! ".

JULIO: " Maybe we just expect that less than ten years! But I'll never know exactly how long it would take; for two simple reasons: I am not a magician to know the future; and further, it is because the projects I have in my head are ambitious; and that for the moment they seem to be utopian, for the simple reason that the funds are still missing! In short, for the moment, I do not even see: How to start making these projects! I have nothing but great ideas in my head! But in reality, what we could buy for example, just by having very good ideas in the head, in this present world "Britannia metal" dominates? ».

EVELYN: " You know JULIO! ".

JULIO: " Uh – huh!, I'm listening! ".

EVELYN: "I could have such good offspring "behind your back" as they say, and you can only see the fire eh? ».

JULIO: " It's to say? ".

EVELYN: " This is to say that thou shalt trust me as if I was taking regular contraceptive measures, ... / .... ".

JULIO: " Yes ih!, ih, ih! ".

EVELYN: " When in reality! ".

JULIO: " Okay!, ih!, ih, ih! When in reality? ".

EVELYN: " When in reality, I simply would stop; and quite naturally, I would have my pregnancy; which I would keep jealously! ".

JULIO: " In any case my dear EVELYN, not that! ".

EVELYN: "What if just by to please you, I told you verbally or theoretically, for example: " Okay, I would not do that!". When in reality or in practice, on the contrary, I did it anyway, anyway? ».

JULIO: " If you dare do it! ".

EVELYN: " OK!, ih!, ih, ih! If I dare do it? ".

JULIO: "If you dare do it! I assure you most sincerely, that you never see me again; and God knows, that I have experience in this area of "flight of a matrimonial home"! For I know very well that I will not have it yet caused, until just now; but in any case, I have already done that, with some lady! I had fled a certain lady called MARYVONNE; Maryvonne KEVILER; which also very, very suspiciously like myself JULIO, she likes to display her Progeny and Progeny Background (mean here: the place of birth of the person concerned, and of course, places of birth of parents, or else the birthplace of one of the two parents); as she liked to appoint herself the occasional "Me MARYVONNE, A Mixed Descent From Paris And In Background Kinese Descent". Anyway, I've dropped a "marquee", before I met you EVELYN; but, I never wanted to tell you about it, until just a while ago; to spare you the trouble which you could possibly experience, listening to the news. Currently, I am certain that "this Countess" is on and still looking to hear from me. So eh!, "drop the chicks", I know perfectly well I do JULIO! So I repeat: Do not make me repeat the same thing with you, please! This is because ... / .... ".

EVELYN: " By all means!, ih!, ih, ih! This is because? ".

JULIO: " This is because of course, that I love you a lot! But ... / .... ".

EVELYN: " But? ".

JULIO: " But if you dare to me what you just described me! You never see me again! ".

EVELYN: " That's it? ".

JULIO: " Excuse me? ".

EVELYN: " I said: Just that as punishment to inflict on me? ".

JULIO: " But EVELYN! You provoke me or what? ".

EVELYN: " Okay! OK!, I'll stop! I Quit! This is because I clearly cottoned your message! ".

In fact, EVELYN had anyway deliberately omitted to take her birth control pills. She had stopped taking them altogether. Yet now Julio Fernandez himself in person reminded "her **Queen**, EVELYN" to take every day, "the contraceptive precautions". That said, it vis-à-vis "the parishioner", pretended to drink hers pills. But in truth, she drank only water; and that, usually, in the presence of her "gentleman's JULIO"; then she hid the pills; and she swung cleverly into the sink. Julio Fernandez who apparently saw that his "**shepherdess**" indeed took hers pills regularly; and that, as often as possible in his presence; he could not one little moment think any deception on the part of "his **queen bee** EVELYN". Race result of this trick: "the latter split" would be pregnant. But expect a little more than three months to announce it to her "devil JULIO". Pregnancy was actually the one she wanted, in her secret calculations. EVELYN was said in the background of herself: " ... / ... Oh!, well, even if at first, Julio Fernandez goes away! But I know he would only anger; which would make him do that! But after very long and hard, like anything; he would have had little reason, if only vis-à-vis his own conscience! He would quite naturally, in his home, find me, "his **ticket** EVELYN"; and that, as soon as possible. ".

˝You will understand immediately, because I'm going to have [to not accept that one and put a spoke in the wheels], not, for example, hesitate a little while, to screw you, and disguising the fact, rather than "bury like that, all my plans for the future". ˝.

When a good Sunday morning when they were first naturally take their breakfast; then get ready to go visit relatives of his "**mistress**" Yves MULER at home in Corbeil – Essonne; Julio Fernandez and EVELYN were going to have a heated discussion. While we ate breakfast at the table, quietly EVELYN said: " "My dear gentleman"! I do not know how it happened! But I think I'm pregnant with a little more than three months ah!, ah! ˝.

JULIO: " You said what? Are you sick or something like this? You became "**flakiness**" or what? And your pills? You always took or what? Pregnant with a little more than three months, you tell me too? But it will not head, not ohm! ˝.

EVELYN: " Aye!, aye, aye! I take them at night regularly; and indeed very often, you're even my witness, when I take them! ".

JULIO: " Yeah!, it is true that very often, I'm even your witness; when you woods. That's why EVELYN, I have to tell you not to formalize about it for you! This is because I am certain that this is not "puffiness". It could being, any shift your cycle of menstruation. ˝.

EVELYN: " You cannot! ".

JULIO: " How could you confirm this? ".

EVELYN: " This is simply because ... / .... ".

JULIO: " Yep!, ih!, ih, ih! ".

EVELYN: " I was part consult my gynecologist; and she confirmed to me herself, after of course, some appropriate tests. ".

JULIO: " What is this story? ".

EVELYN: " In addition, we spent an ultrasound! My gynecologist suggested to me that I had: not a single zygote; but two; two scalable zygotes thirteen weeks. Clearly, it was found that I had in me, twins. ".

JULIO: "But what is this story? In addition, not one mouth to feed, for example, but twice! Two mandibles to feed! But you kidding me or what? These are children that we do not want; it's ah!, of course! It's a bit like "the Foyer Relay Social Atlantis [122]"; where there was for example the case of a certain Monsieur; a rich farmer; this rich farmer there, was from one of these countries beset by various rebellions in Africa in those years already; years which had followed their independence. This old wealthy farmer named Mr. Gary ULRICH. This had a huge area of land, with several houses; many of which they were built of durable materials; and in which among others: himself Gary ULRICH; his family; its many workers [; these workers were among Thirteen]; and families of his many workers lived there. That Mr. Gary ULRICH had three large trucks to ensure the transport of its various products. It told me, this some Gary ULRICH example, in one of these countries at war then, there were among others, as "processions of misery": "children" ("fruit of rape" which of course is rejected! ... / ...)! ".

EVELYN: " Stop this poetic mockery; Humo ... / ...! ".

JULIO: "But there is no question of a mockery! Him, sure Gary ULRICH even said to me that there was only ever for example, the number of girls raped and shot ourselves! Him, sure Gary ULRICH even said to me that there was only ever for example, the number of girls raped; and then, in "their baskets", we did not hesitate at all, at all, for a moment, to introduce outright, ears of corn! ".

EVELYN: " But stop this poetic mockery; even humorous! ... / ...! ".

JULIO: " But there is no question of a mockery! ".

EVELYN: " Affirmative! One had spent an ultrasound; and it was found that I had in me, twins. ".

JULIO: " Twins and more! ".

EVELYN: " Yeah! Do not you think it's wonderful? ".

JULIO: " "Two noses" to feed more at one go! And you think that's wonderful! ".

EVELYN: " But JULIO! It's wonderful for the simple reason that having twins is a providential grace; since it is not a lot of couples who have this good fortune to have eh! ".

JULIO: " But this is not possible, it ah! ".

EVELYN: " But aye!, ih! It's possible! ".

JULIO: " I dream or what ah! ".

EVELYN: " No, you're not dreaming! ".

JULIO: " And like that ah!, you took as your regular birth control pills? ".

EVELYN: " Absolutely! ".

JULIO: " And that, most often in my presence; when I was at ease night; or even when I was leaving my vacations ensure many nights before I go! ".

EVELYN: " Affirmative. ".

JULIO: " But it is not possible that ah! ".

EVELYN: " "This gynecologist tow" suggested to me that unfortunately happens, unfortunately, very rarely, "a **female**" who regularly takes hers pills, can anyway despite her fall "bell"! ".

JULIO: " Never mind; since I know a very, very good gynecologist me also; and which might; or to say explicitly: which should definitely make you a Voluntary Termination of Pregnancy [an abortion, what!]. ".

EVELYN: " JULIO But oh! I never told anyone that I wanted to practice of abortion as I know me, not! ".

JULIO: " But look! Let's see! Should we be soon decided to make the practice; since more weeks passed; plus it would be too late; and therefore it would be more dangerous for the mother, in this case for you EVELYN! ".

EVELYN: " Think well JULIO! There is on the one hand, a deadline for the "age" bubble "that we would stop"; and it is for me EVELYN precisely this period is already over! Since abortion as permitted by French law passed by Parliament in 1975 should absolutely be done before the twelfth week of "**pregnancy**", and demand generally "the partner concerned". And on the other hand, the abortion is too expensive; and as far as I know, it's not too reimbursed by Social Security right now. ".

JULIO: " Never mind! We will pay anyway, anyway! ".

EVELYN: " You always suggested to me that you had very good economic projects in your little noggin; where you wanted to achieve; and that "white metal" was still missing! ".

JULIO: " Absolutely. ".

EVELYN: " And now, you want to spend "Britannia metal" for nothing eh! ".

JULIO: " It is not for nothing eh? ".

EVELYN: " Yep! ".

JULIO: " No! ".

EVELYN: " If it is spending "of German silver" for nothing; because eventually, it could, for example, may be repeated again involuntarily; and therefore, we still think of another Voluntary Interruption of Pregnancy? ".

JULIO: " No, it is not spending "of **Ackers**" for nothing! Thereafter, it will never repeat; and therefore we would not need to think again to another abortion! ".

EVELYN: " How could you be so sure and so certain as anything, that it will never repeat? ".

JULIO: " And you, how can you be so sure and certain as anything, it would be repeated again absolutely? Huh? ".

EVELYN: " I did not say that: "I was so sure and certain as anything, it would be repeated again absolutely!". I'd rather say: "... / ... Because eventually, it could, for example, may be repeated again involuntarily; ... / ..." ".

JULIO: " There would be no "... / ... OF possibly ... / ...?". It's ah!, you could trust me! ".

EVELYN: " How could you be so sure and so confident like that ah? Huh? Anyway, I do not want at all I hear about. Make a Voluntary Interruption of Pregnancy (VIP)? And as it is indeed my own body! So no one but myself, could not make a decision for me; and above all a decision of this magnitude, with its moral, if not physiological, pretty **dire**! Oh!, no! Nobody will decide about it for me, except of course **docs** and for purely medical reasons! And I hope you understand JULIO? ".

JULIO: " If you do not want to hear of an abortion; what you had wanted to have "the blister – there"; and therefore you had done deliberately! ".

EVELYN " But you unlock or what? Not at all! ".

JULIO: " No, I do not release! I do not get mad! This is the logic of reasoning huh! ".

EVELYN: " But how I could do it deliberately; while I was taking my birth control pills every night? ".

JULIO: " I could not tell you myself; for myself, I'm asking myself the same question: How, indeed! ".

EVELYN: " Calm down JULIO! ".

JULIO: " It's to say? ".

EVELYN: " This is to say that we keep "this bloat"; as: "Wine is already shot! So it must be drunk!". The guard is "this swelling" and therefore, it is allowed to go to term! Then ... / .... ".

JULIO: " Then? ".

EVELYN: " Then we would change birth control! The other would adopt much safer means of contraception; finally, be sure and certain that it will never repeat. ".

JULIO: " No, no, no, no! There is no question that the guards "phlebitis then this!" And besides, "gestation" that will lead to one, two mouths to feed! ".

EVELYN: " Why such firmness of you? Why such a demand? ".

JULIO: " There is not even three to four months, you spoke to me: "To have offspring behind my back!". And now as for "just a fluke", "a blister of a little more than three months" has arrived! Hmm mm! It's both actually happened! ".

EVELYN: " It's just a coincidence! ".

JULIO: " You bet! "It's just a coincidence!" And I have to swallow it ah? ".

EVELYN: " Of course it's just a coincidence! ".

JULIO: " And I'll swallow that, you sincerely believe? ".

EVELYN: " But what happened to you? You think the wait two babies at once, is it a tragic situation? ".

JULIO: " "Two throats" to feed more, in one fell swoop? ".

EVELYN: "So what? ".

JULIO: " You obstinate to continue to deny a Voluntary Interruption of Pregnancy (VIP)? ".

EVELYN: " In any case, none of that on my body! I do not even want to continue to hear about it! ".

JULIO: " If you continue to refuse as well, this could be very serious, you know? ".

EVELYN: " Oh! What would you do? ".

JULIO: " I think in this case, I am even forced to become ill; very bad; or very, very bad, even forgetting in my belief in God! ".

EVELYN: " I still do not understand: What would you mean by that? ".

JULIO: " Besides, I still had hitherto respected moral or religious ethics! And what does this respect has he really brought me? ".

EVELYN: " Where is ... / ...? ".

JULIO: " Nothing eh!, ... / ...! ".

EVELYN: " Where is the report ... / ...? ".

JULIO: " Nothing hey, if these are just concerns and bud lucks! ".

EVELYN: " Where is the report in regard to us now? ".

JULIO: " I've always been honest with the society and its people; and I always ... / .... ".

EVELYN: " Where is ... / ...? ".

JULIO: " I have always respected other people and especially "beautiful sex" or "weak sex"! ".

EVELYN: " Where is the ... / ...? ".

JULIO: " But what does that me he brought about? ".

EVELYN: " Where is the report in which ... / ...? ".

JULIO: " Nothing! Nothing, if it is not, that worries and miseries. ".

EVELYN: " Where is the report in regard to us now? ".

JULIO: " Now I ... / .... ".

EVELYN: " Yeah!, ih!, ih, ih! Now? ".

JULIO: " Now I go back to "Providence"; and I will ... / .... ".

EVELYN: " No! Never say that! ".

JULIO: " And I will do harm to others if it suits my example projects. ".

EVELYN: " Never say that ah! ".

JULIO: " That way, if truly "this Providence" exists; it punishes only me and never mind eh! ".

EVELYN: " Attention eh! Do not say that; because in this case, even unintentionally, "that Providence just" going very, very severely punish you!".

JULIO: " So it would be too bad for me; since, with all the trouble that I had to endure so far! And "This Providence" sees me! And apparently it does nothing to my favor! ".

EVELYN: "I understand very well your reaction against "the Providence"! Because, actually, with all the trouble you had to endure until the day here! You think that, "the Providence" does not see you! Or even, "It" has forgotten you! But no ohm! "It" has not forgotten you! This is indeed a simple look! And tomorrow you will see: How "this Providence" will reward all the efforts [for you] made so far, to really succeed; and this, once and for all, in life! It is for this that "I EVELYN your **Gentlewoman**", I ask "the Providence", sorry for thee this is because with all those you just made a very, very poor against "It"! If "It" ever decides to punish you! For you, it would then be: other additional penalties to endure! Or have you already widely, suffered like that! It really would not be good to have to suffer more! But alas!, no ... / .... ".

JULIO: "Never mind! I would rather say: "Thank you anyway! "; though, I know ... / .... ".

EVELYN: "But alas!, it never repeats. Do never put in your head, such ideas; because "Providence" could actually punish you very, very severely, both immediately; that, untimely; and that, by one way or another! ".

JULIO: "Although I know very well indeed, "This Providence" does not exist in fact; as asked me the question with "some Trilingual **Female** Management", responding to the first name of MARYVONNE; that is to say: that one I had just dropped [I quote]: ... / ...? ".

EVELYN: "Hmm mm! "Your old mouse" that you had dropped! ".

JULIO: "She asked me the question [I quote]: "Do you know where "It" lives "this Providence?". ". "Do you know where God lives? ". ".

EVELYN: " What a question! ".

JULIO: "Yep! What question indeed! Otherwise, "It" would help me for a very long time! He would help me, as to many others who's [that is to say, her God] always pray elsewhere and unfortunately alas!, are still suffering and still always! ".

EVELYN: " But yeah!, ih! God does exist! But only ... / .... ".

JULIO: " But only? ".

EVELYN: " But only, it is sometimes not right away; not to say: It works for most of time, not right away, unlike many other various supernatural forces that exist and I do not even cite an example! ".

JULIO: " No, I know that He does not exist! Otherwise, ... / .... ".

EVELYN: " Yep!, ih!, ih, ih! Otherwise? ".

JULIO: " Otherwise, He would not ignore the millions; even billions of people, in the world today are being affected; but in ... / ...! ".

EVELYN: " Aye!, ih!, ih, ih! Who in? ".

JULIO: " Who in all their sufferings, they have the divine prayers in their valves! ".

EVELYN: " But there! He sees everything and therefore He knows exactly whom He will do and at times He would make! And men's to them ... / .... ".

JULIO: " Yeah!, ih!, ih, ih! And men's to them? ".

EVELYN: " And men respect to them, they are blind; and they do not see! Besides, it is not even easy to see eh! ".

JULIO: " Tell me! You've become a spiritual person or what? One would think that we have such case, a female pope! Hmm mm! You've become a "Pope Joan", you eh! ".

EVELYN: " Can you believe those you want! But what I'm telling you, is an absolute reality; and is known to many people. ".

JULIO: " Anyway, I do not believe in "Providence"! Or to better express it once: I always believed in "this question of Providence"! But now ... / ...! ".

EVELYN: " But now? ".

JULIO: "But now I do not care of It! ".

EVELYN: " Do not say that ah! ".

JULIO: " Now, even if "It" is I work for "the many various other supernatural forces that exist and which you do not even will be mentioned example"! As you said; ... / .... ".

EVELYN: " I had mentioned: "... / ... In contrast to these various other multiple supernatural forces that exist and I do not even cite an example!". ".

JULIO: " So, even if "It" is I work for "these various other multiple supernatural forces that exist", as you said; and which act right away, I would not hesitate more. And it would be so ... / ...! ".

EVELYN: " So then JULIO! This is ... / ...! ".

JULIO: " And that would be too bad for ethics! ".

EVELYN: " So then JULIO! It is you yourself who causes divine wrath! ".

JULIO: " Oh!, you bet! ".

EVELYN: " Anyway, I do not understand at all, all you talking about me then! ".

JULIO: " You will understand immediately! Because, I'll be obliged; to not accept that one and put a spoke in the wheels, not for example, hesitate a little while, you totally screw up and make-up does! And so the killing would be neither seen nor known, as they say; rather than bury it as stupidly, all my future plans! ".

EVELYN: ""... / ... Here today and gone tomorrow ... / ...!". What demon!".

JULIO: " You just have to accept the abortion; and it is more in talking all over again. ".

EVELYN: " And you're not ashamed to say? ".

JULIO: " You just have to accept the abortion; and it is more in talking all over again. ".

EVELYN: " It is no longer a run out powder you'd take! Rather, you would systematically eliminate me ... / ...? ".

JULIO: " You just have to accept the abortion; and it is more in talking all over again. ".

EVELYN: " ... / ... But instead, you would totally eliminate me physically?".

JULIO: " Wait ahn! Only if you do not accept the abortion; and that's it! ".

EVELYN: " Why this hardening of thy heart? ".

CHAPTER: II

And there, "one would say" as Julio Fernandez had received "legacy"; "Untimely inheritance" from "that thereby he had dropped": "delusions"! Yeah!, ih! "Delusions"!

Induction:

JULIO: " It's simply because I would not want to run away at all! I would not want to save me at all! I would not want anything at all to flee, as before, I had already fled "another **baroness**"; in case some MARYVONNE! Some Maryvonne KEVILER "A Mixed Descent From Paris [by her place of birth] and D'Background Kinese Descendants (by the birthplace of her father Moses KEVILER [formerly called, Monze KEMVILA]).". """

" " "This very lovely Shepherdess"; "such a charming **Countess**," I had, alas!, unfortunately, leaked anyway! This all natural female beauty, I had fled anyway! I had dropped despite the fact that she was: "A beautiful **mixed – race**" (and surprising in this: that the **Mestizos** are still generally very nices!). """

" " "Such dazzling **matron**"; "such an elegant otter", I unfortunately had alas!, fled anyway! I had dropped anyway despite the fact that she was: "A beautiful **mulatto**"! """

" " "This **Eurydice**"; "such an **Iphigenia**", I unfortunately had alas!, dropped anyway! I had dropped anyway, despite the fact that she was "a very attractive **hybrid**"! """

" " "Such **Joan of Arc**"; "such a **Judith**", I had, alas!, unfortunately, leaked anyway! I had fled anyway despite the fact that she was "**a very lovely latte!**" " "

" " "This **Rebecca**"; "such a **Juno**", I had, alas!, unfortunately, dropped anyway! I had dropped anyway, despite the fact that she was "**a very charming feminine person**"! "**A very charming feminine person**" which has ... / ...! ". " " "

And just thinking to operation of Evelyn MULER, JULIO would become as he were "crazy, crazy ally", "like hell". He would blow at astonish. He would tell at the attention for example: himself; and she, this Evelyn MULER precisely: words without heads or tails; lyrics such as:

" " **A**h!, women"! " "

"" Ah!, women! They imagine themselves to be the Center of the world!""

"" Ah!, women! But they are evil creatures! ""

"" Seek to offspring behind the backs of their husbands! " " " " " ".

Evelyn: " Oh!, oh, oh! You delusions! You're currently wandering one! Hmm mm! Say you pedal and in sauerkraut; because I tell you that I'm having babies! "... / ...". "A very charming feminine person" which has all the qualities of a dream creature! "Such **Salome**" which has all the qualities; all of the natural qualities of course! But "such **missus**"; "such a **Venus**" like that, you were anyway eventually flee! And especially for me EVELYN which I do not even have all these qualities, all natural; such as any that has "The **Mixed – Descent** Kinese On Back", which you mention here! So eh! Run away from me, could I believe that it will really put you in trouble? In any case, not at all, at all! And that's what you'll tell me just now as a result of your delusion! "... / ... A very charming person female ... / ....". It is observed that, me EVELYN, next to her, I am nothing, nothing, nothing, nothing at all! And it shows, too, that you regret now having dropped such a creature dream to finally stumbled onto "a disgusting chicken" as me, EVELYN! Huh? ".

JULIO: "Actually it is very, very exactly that ah!, I'm going to let you hear just now as a result of "my **delirium tremens**"! ""

"« ... / ... "A very charming feminine person"! "A very charming feminine person" which has all the qualities of a dream creature indeed! Such a young lady that has all the qualities; all of the natural qualities of course; turn to me until I die, my head; like me saying my sisters! But "as a daughter of Eva"; "such a shepherdess", anyway I ended up running away! And especially for you EVELYN that indeed you do not even possess all these qualities, all natural; such as any that has "The Mixed – Descent Kinese On Back" which I mentioned here! So eh! You run, do you think it will really put me in trouble? In any case, not at all, at all! ""

"« But, as I had told you earlier EVELYN: " It is no longer I would take a run out powder! ". And if you ask me: The reason for this is that I do not want to save me? Me JULIO, I would answer simply: "It's because if I allowed myself to escape! And given the fact that we are married after all that I know! Given the fact that we live in a couple legally! I always have and that, in one way or another, to suffer from such or such other potential impacts on the heels I would have just taken! And because of this, I could never be alone! That is why, to be quiet, I did not flee; but only, **I will bump off**! And that is all the answer you want to know why and I'll provided without the slightest complacency!". » « » ".

EVELYN: " And you say so explicitly like this? ".

JULIO: " And why not? ".

EVELYN: "But damn! Why curing heart? Why this stubbornness? Why this obsessive decision? Why this wickedness? Why such evil to me? Huh?

To me, "me EVELYN, your **Arian**"? "Me EVELYN, your **Contessa**" who loves you greatly? ".

JULIO: " The answer is simple! This is for me the ultimate way to dissuade you, you can change your opinion; and consequently, to make you accept to perform this abortion! ".

EVELYN: " But if I never, ever and never accept? But if I continue to refuse? ".

JULIO: " That is to say, you still refuse despite the ultimatum? ".

EVELYN: " Affirmative! I still refuse despite the ultimatum! I reject this threat which is more like a bluff rather than anything else! ".

JULIO: " It's not a bluff EVELYN. This is the straightforward truth! ".

EVELYN: " I say that I refuse, a point and a line! ".

JULIO: " Okay! I understand that I could not really at all, at all, to make you change your mind what! ".

EVELYN: " No, no! As you say yourself: could you really not at all, at all, to change my opinion about it! ".

JULIO: " So forget all that I said. ".

EVELYN: " Forget them! It is understood! ".

JULIO: " It was just to fuck you cold feet! ".

EVELYN: " Hmm mm! Say it was just to scare me! To be afraid, I was really scared huh! But fact remains that no matter how I was not going to yield much! That was why, I told you this was a bluff, this threat there! ".

JULIO: " And as you would hardly give in! So ... / .... ".

EVELYN: " Hmm mm! I concede that point? But frankly JULIO! It would be very, very badly about myself eh! ".

JULIO: " So forget all my excitement there! ".

EVELYN: " It is understood! That's all forgotten! ".

JULIO: " And finish our breakfast. ".

EVELYN: " Okay. ".

JULIO: " And we will prepare ourselves to go visit as scheduled today, Sunday, to your parents. ".

EVELYN: " Okay. ".

And actually, Julio Fernandez was only stifled discord; he was only muffled the din; for he had plotted immediate improvisation so to speak, and that without the slightest hesitation, a macabre plan in his head; which plane he would definitely run on the same day in order to "respect" his "new principle"; that: "From trashing same example, one who would prevent it; or rather, that interferes with one way or another, be able to meet the realization of economic and other projects, of the future; whom he had plotted for the short term; for the medium and long terms". We will now know this macabre plan outlined by immediate improvisation, in the head of Julio Fernandez.

... / ... JULIO came out virtually unscathed; because the seat belt helped him a lot. But that's only for "his filly" that the seat belt "prove to be defective [And rightly so!]"; the shock was a bit more violent.

B efore you go to the parents of his "stretcher EVELYN" JULIO had gone to prepare the car; "Renault 4". In reality, he was gone altogether a traffic safety belts. He had gone deliberately fiddling one end that attach the seat belt and especially the right side of the front; that is to say, the side that usually put "his crate EVELYN" when they were dating by car. Then, when they had gone to her in – laws, they were very well arrived and there was no problem on that side. They had been well received. They ate well and even so to speak, of drinking. On the way back, Julio Fernandez had voluntarily left his path and he had gone to the front stamping knowingly and specifically the right side of his car against a street lamp poles. It was pretty serious as accident, fire – rescue workers had come fast enough. ... / ... JULIO came out virtually unscathed; because the seat belt helped him a lot. But that's only for "his **filly**" that the seat belt "prove to be defective [And rightly so!]"; she had seen "type" more or less violently her head against the windscreen. And yeah!, ih!, The shock was a bit more violent. This one started already lost a lot of blood. She would be in a coma. Before her transfer to hospital[1], we could not even know, for example, if: She was going to make her or not? And if so, with what kind of effects? In truth, JULIO had wanted and systematically knock EVELYN. And thus, there is not even so he wished. He was keen in the bottom of herself, that she died. There was thus led her precisely in the hospital. JULIO was released only a day later, after multiple observations; which would prove, very happily be, for him, good. But for "his **pile** EVELYN" remained in all three good weeks in intensive care at the hospital. And as a further result, she had an

---

[1] At the Intercommunity Hospital, Street Emile Zola on at Villeneuve – Saint – Georges.

accidental abortion; and she no longer had "turgor" to which she held yet considerably. The twins were now no longer with her. Naturally, Julio Fernandez was going to visit his "**Delilah**", almost every day during his short stay in which she found herself in the hospital.

JULIO which, in truth, did not even hesitate to try expressly outright trashing "his **Eurydice** EVELYN"; since according to him; and he would say, without interfering with any degree; and this, in the bottom of himself: " ... / ... She wanted to put a spoke in the wheels! ". He was always by himself: " ... / ... I finally and very fortunately for me, if I could still in the depths of myself, allow me to express myself in this way; I finally and very fortunately for me, got what I wanted in the beginning; that is to say: "**the imperative abortion**" from "my **butterfly**, EVELYN"; even if it did not happen in the best conditions; such as those I wanted her to practice initially. On balance, ultimately it's good for us! So much the better; since "the two cavities to feed mouth" are no longer one; although so far, their mom was able to escape after all, to this tragic end that I had, as it were, programmed! But it ah!, no other man than myself, no one will know! It's top secret! ".

However, one day, JULIO would suggest to his "**Artemis** EVELYN" while the latter was not yet out of the Intercommunity Hospital where she was being treated: " You've seen the rubbish eh! ".

EVELYN: " Please, let's forget all these! I almost died; and now I'm out of business; that's ah!, the most important! ".

JULIO: " You wanted to do something very serious indeed; but ... / ...! ".

EVELYN: " Please JULIO! ".

JULIO: " You wanted to do something very serious indeed; but unfortunately alas!, "behind the back of someone else!; and in case of me ah!". ".

EVELYN: " Please JULIO! Not again! ".

JULIO: " Did you see the "**denouement**" eh! ".

EVELYN: " Okay! Aye!, I saw the "**unhappy**"! Aye, aye!, I saw it! But forget that! ".

JULIO: " As a "**calamity**", an accident happened to us, we do not even know How? And it is this pregnancy that you cared so much that goes! That eh! Did you see it a little ah? Although, very fortunately we are still alive! ".

EVELYN: " Yep!, I saw. ".

JULIO: " Although, very fortunately you're still alive you "my **dame** EVELYN", which have more particularly suffered from this accident! ".

EVELYN: " Uh – huh!, ih! And I say thank you in Heaven who protected me. ".

JULIO: " But we must at all, at all, such a thing again, unbeknownst to the husband; which mostly has his good plans for the future; which would not accept any item of clutter for example! Okay got it? ".

EVELYN: " Of course!, I got it very well! ".

JULIO: " We should never, ever, never, ever and never again dare such a move; since it provides only "the worst **adversities**" which may exist, as it! ".

EVELYN: " Okay. Besides, I have seen very clearly "this **Cataclysm**"; or rather: "these **calamities** worst in question". So, I swear that I not do it again never, ever, never, ever, and never, dare to put such an act indeed. I swear I will never start again, ever and ever, without your consent first obtained. ".

EVELYN was discharged from hospital; but only here, not knowing in fact, the "scheming" made by her husband JULIO; she thought about the latter. She no longer wanted at all, at all, dare again yet again, to ask such an act, "behind the back" of one. Day flowing; then the weeks; then months and years as well; and realizing that her husband absolutely did not want to kids; while for her to her side, she was very fond; she thought only one idea: to separate quite naturally of JULIO; then possibly go redo a home elsewhere; and optionally, having therefore the progeny. EVELYN finally took to the idea. She would want to do this, to have also the vein can meet someone else; that he would facilitate this task. But only here, again, it would not at all easy; sincerely loved since Julio Fernandez "Descent From Poitevese And Background On Spanish Descent" (as he liked very, very often say, and he also loved very, very often repeat.).

EVELYN still continued and even still, to love greatly Julio Fernandez. For her: conclusively, she continued to remain quite frankly: "**Irreplaceable**" and " **Incorrigiblestar**"; "**Indisputable**" and "**Uncontested**"; and finally "**Unforgettable**" and "**Irretrievablestar**"; for hardly say for example: "the **Inevitable**" and "**Unrecoverablestar**".

"... / ... Or to ask me this last question differently: Do I risk, over time, to regret it when everything just be too late for example? ... / .... ".

But when MARYVONNE was leaving the hospital, her father had promised her that he would help to find his "Julio Fernandez"; and therefore, the cook in one way or another, with it; that is to say, in his **old woman, MARYVONNE**". For this, he had committed "subversive people"; whom he had sent in pursuit. Or indeed, it was only when he was found; one was coincidentally, already married for a few years only, with some Evelyn MULER [wife FERNANDEZ]. Moses KEVILER and Thierry Glorian not forgetting the faithful worker butcher from Moses KEVILER had found it necessary to keep secret, these news; and do not release them to MARYVONNE (and for good reason). Therefore, they decided to do something fresh, to save "their heir youngster" of their property. What are they going to do? They had decided at first to systematically assemble a great Machiavellian shot against Mrs. Evelyn MULER, " " self " ", " " legitimate " " Julio Fernandez.

The **donor** or **sponsor** of this **Machiavellian mission was certainly Moses KEVILER; but nevertheless, the mentor or rather, the director of "task" would prove to be unquestionably his right-Thierry Glorian.** The idea of MOSES blown by it, because Julio Fernandez and Evelyn MULER could not even, for example, give yourself the luxury of having an apartment, as owners at that time[1] precisely. Hence, Moses KEVILER had decided to launch several million of centimes [new francs] to save indirectly **"the unique hussy"**. Initially, he had paid people to whom he had given many "**accounts**" so that we deceive EVELYN; and thus the scare from her husband; so as to pave the way for a possible return of common life of Julio

---

[1] At that time, JULIO and his wife EVELYN were tenants on Street Oberkampf in the Eleventh Arrondissement of Paris, in an apartment Three rooms, located in an old building.

Fernandez, with his "**gal** MARYVONNE". In this connection, five attempts were ordered by[1]

Mr. Moses KEVILER, to close; and consequently, seduce Mrs. Evelyn MULER, mainly using arguments; or rather, the sales pitch of numerical and material orders; they all literally failed. And the sixth attempt, that of a gallant, elegant and seductive Mr. **Giraud ZEFRINO**[2] that he too had been commissioned; or rather sent by Mr. Moses KEVILER and Thierry Glorian in order to approach and therefore to seduce Mrs. Evelyn MULER, wife Julio Fernandez had just managed accordingly. In fact, through Mr. Moses KEVILER precisely, Thierry Glorian had paid: and Mr. Giraud ZEFRINO; and other intermediary Sir, by the name of Poulain DERECK.

The mentor or rather, the director of the mission that we are busily perform on behalf of the couple [MOSES – MARYSSA], would prove to be unquestionably THIERRY.

---

[1] The very first one, from Mr. Elvira AUBRY; the second, that from Mr. Vincent GILBERTO; the third, from Mr. Henrique LEFEBVRE; the fourth, from Mr. Alfred Peuron; the fifth and also the last attempt, that from Marc THIÉBAUT.

[2] Giraud ZEFRINO, nicknamed Casanova Giovanni GIACOMO, said Jean – Jacques Casanova Of Seingalt; that is to say: considered Adventurer and writer Italian, born and died in Venice [1725-1798]; including its non CASANOVA passed into everyday language to describe a **seducer**. We shall see a little further: Who was it exactly that gallant, elegant and seductive Mr. Giraud ZEFRINO; which would document not bad at all, at all, before, in some important notions of medicine, even before going to discuss with Evelyn MULER, to scare her; to make her very afraid; to make her very, very scared even. And then we would: Who this Casanova, Giraud ZEFRINO, would have happened when Mrs. Evelyn MULER, wife Julio Fernandez would address. This seductive Giraud ZEFRINO, to maximize its chances, to break up the household of the former; he would have time accomplice, a Mr. Poulain DERECK; which apparently would solo; but in reality he would duet with him Giraud ZEFRINO in question [surprising in this, since both "bandidos" **follow to the letter, the script, although tweaked by THIERRY**].

And for that, THIERRY **write the draft and "finish" the script; and distribute consequently, the roles**. The main role should whichever mentor, be awarded "to the hoodlum" "would consume"; and that "for the past: some time", "narcotic". But precisely, this would correspond as closely as possible, Giraud ZEFRINO. Hence the fact that THIERRY would grant the principal role in question, to the latter. It would just be ultra – left – thoroughly respect: very, very strict prohibition, to focus thereafter; and this: so little, "emotionally speaking" with **"this naive bitch"** who was that EVELYN. It was to make the transition very, very bad, "a naïve **duchess**" whatever. This is because **the real issue was that of leaving the field open for** MARYVONNE. And with such a goal: What he could do, that ZEFRINO attaches thereafter "sentimentally speaking" with just **"this naive frog** named EVELYN"?

That said, THIERRY attribute the supporting role in Poulain DERECK. And then all three here [; that is to say: THIERRY; Giraud and POULAIN] **bring their keys in the scenarios. In short, we had somehow written the script "is getting ready to play", three: namely: first: Glorian; and on the other hand, "the bandidos" Giraud and POULAIN**. Furthermore, **THIERRY had even "one would say", writes, "The role of the bitch" [EVELYN], to whom they were going to hurt, simply anticipating, on many details as possible, about the possible reaction; or rather the possible reactions they might have.** Hence, the fact that "one could even pretend somehow" that **"THIERRY had granted the third role in EVELYN"** [the course knowledge of that fact]. **The latter would prove consequently, to be "the third man", "a theatrical piece", "played four"; "That is to say + JULIO also the husband of her"; "Which simply would grant, the latest role" ["the fourth part, and of course also unwittingly"]; "The fourth part", which THIERRY, "the specialist detail on the matter", also planned reactions in anticipation [also]. One had set as he really had this script in question. And it was again and again, especially with the setting provided, the roles of the two main characters; which were Giraud and Poulain; and that with all possible details. Each of these "desperadoes" should absolutely learn and relearn again and again, his text to perfection.**

"His text", which for Giraud: "And here I Giraud, ... / ...!".

"His text", which for POULAIN: "And here I Poulain, ... / ...!".

"His text" and "His text", which we will see "The Machine!"; or rather, "The Demonstration!". "In LARP!" (or: In Life – Size!); or to be able to express more correctly: "The text" and "His text", which will be seen "theory!"; which happen to "The Practice!". A little further.

Worse, THIERRY had obtained "fairly strong painkillers", which he susceptible to the main actor; that is to say: to **Giraud**, that he consumes, so he gives no signs of fatigue in his role he would be eager to play: harm to the household of Madame Evelyn MULER, wife FERNANDEZ, defiling precisely enough copiously, the latter, for JULIO repudiates her. **And even worse, THIERRY would advise Giraud, "to eat" also "these powerful amphetamines"; and it insidiously to that. What a story! So it was a history precisely to release this one in question, the home of Julio Fernandez, in order to recover Maryvonne KEVILER in the hands of him.**

Through Thierry Glorian, Mr. Moses KEVILER was therefore paid [first, a well endowed first part, as a "down payment"; and "any account balance", also well endowed, would be paid after] and Mr. Giraud ZEFRINO; and other intermediary Sir, by the name of Poulain DERECK; which had the task to approach and learn by all means, Julio Fernandez. Mr. Giraud ZEFRINO as to him, he had the task to approach and learn very well, with Mrs. Evelyn MULER, wife Julio Fernandez.

That said, Giraud ZEFRINO also succeeds; but only just, the task that was set before him. How? Giraud ZEFRINO had just managed; it was because he had made them aware of "some valuable informant" that Julio Fernandez's husband of EVELYN did not want at all to have children; or at least not very quickly, since he wanted to first perform better life, economically and materially speaking. But as against, it's very strongly wanted to have them. Therefore, Giraud ZEFRINO had used the important argument, using some knowledge of medicine; the argument like that "... / ... Evelyn MULER, you never know: How long you are going to wait, with your husband Julio Fernandez, to start having offspring; however, if and only if he desires, really have offspring just! What I'm not even sure! You do not know at all how long it will last! If it's a year; or two years; or even three to four years, in addition, with respect to all time lost so far, as Madam! There, it'll still eh!, eh! Though!".

Evelyn MULER, wife FERNANDEZ: " It is true that reasoning more! ".

Giraud ZEFRINO: " But if it is ten; or fifteen years; or more, compared to all time lost by example, so wait! ".

Evelyn ZEFRINO: " It is true that most reasoning that! ".

Giraud ZEFRINO: " **It would be heavy impact**. ".

EVELYN: " For example? ".

Giraud: "For example, "is growing" fibroids "in her womb"! Yeah!, ih!, I say: "fibroids"! That is to say: "These benign tumors" composed of "muscle fibers"! Namely, there are two types: "leiomyomas" which consist of smooth muscle fibers! And "rhabdomyomas", which as to them, they are made up of striated muscle fibers. And that "these myomas in question" could possibly turn beget "fibroids"! Yep!, ih!, I say: "fibroids"! That is to say: formed "these tumors" "fibrous tissues". Joking aside EVELYN more you and leave empty for long enough, your uterus! More also, "these myomas" can generate "uterine fibroids precisely", which are formed at a time, "fibrous tissues" and "muscles". And I do not even talk to you, "the fibrochondromes" or "fibrolipomes" or "fibromyxomes" and cetera and cetera ... "these myomas in question" could therefore result in your womb! This is simply because it could not bear "zygotes", for several years. In short, my dear EVELYN, thus to wait longer before they can finally decide to have babies at your age now, could even possibly make, that you be not at all, at all, of childbearing potential; or even. ".

EVELYN: " Do you really know in medicine eh!, Mr. Giraud, you know! And you frighten me one! You make me very afraid! You make me very, very afraid that! Aye!, ih! Go for it! Or even? ".

Giraud: " Do not vouvoyer (the "vous" form of "you") me! Or even conceive, but give birth to offspring with ... / .... ".

EVELYN: " Go! Finish your sentence! Do not be shy! Offspring with? ".

Giraud: " Okay, I'll finish my sentence. ".

EVELYN: " Finish it there and I listen! Anyway, for someone who is not even a gynecologist, you really sacred knowledge Gynecology eh! ".

Giraud: " I was going to say: The more time passes! Over the years do pass! The higher your chance to procreate decreases! Or even, for example, you run a risk of an ectopic pregnancy; gestation where eggs are normally not implanted into the uterine cavity. However, it will crash rather, in one of both tubes; or in the ovary; or even in the peritoneal cavity; thus creating clear contingency serious bleeding! Or even, you can design a pregnancy; but giving birth for example, an offspring with a genetic disorder characterized by a supernumerary chromosome in a pair; this anomaly causes malformations of varying severity. So it is really not desirable to have such a pregnancy! ".

EVELYN: " What you are strong in medicine uh! That's right everyone you say? ".

Giraud: " Oh!, it's even more than true! If you want to take your time; and check with several gynecologists or "gynaecologists" of your choice; and you would find by yourself; that almost all ... / .... ".

EVELYN: " Nearly all, in order not to tell everyone! ".

Giraud: " Absolutely! ".

EVELYN: " That's good. This means that you take precautions to be careful! ".

Giraud: " Absolutely. Should you find yourself, as almost all gynecologists you are accessing, you would answer the same. ".

EVELYN: " That is to say: they will corroborate what you said ah! ".

Giraud: " Absolutely. At that time, you could come to see me, if you like well; for me. ".

EVELYN: " You hesitate to pronounce what? Go for it! Do not stop dry and free as the point! Do not stop like that without much finish your sentence! For you? ".

Giraud: " For me, I like you a lot, that's what I was going to say; and I hesitated to pronounce the word; love that word! ".

EVELYN: " "... / ... That you were going to tell me; and you had hesitated to pronounce the word; love that word!". At that word; love that word! ".

Giraud: " Affirmative. To me, **you are a cherub came from Paradise! Yeah!, ih!, I repeat, an angel from heaven!** And therefore ... / ... ".

EVELYN: " And then? ".

Giraud: " And therefore, I wish to marry you and have kids with you; many kids; and this, without losing more time. In addition, ... / .... ".

EVELYN: " Apart? ".

Giraud: " In addition, I have a very good trade: a trade that still has his whole future ahead of him; **Because I'm a Computer Programmer and**

Programmer in a large architectural firm, called "syllogism". It is in any case not you all, all that I am a braggart; but is it in the eyes of everyone in my job, we definitely consider myself: **"An Ace[1] Aces of Computing"**. And so, we will have a better material life and our own house; us is to say: me; you; and not forgot to mention our children's future. ".

EVELYN: " Me also I have a very good trade: a trade that still has his whole future ahead of it! ".

Giraud: " What do you do for a living? ".

EVELYN: " My job as yet his whole future in front of it; since I am a cashier in a supermarket; although only half time! But I was promised like what, they were going to make me do a full time basis. I say me too; I have a very good job indeed! But I'm not talking in terms of wages; because I would be lying if I said I was very, very well paid! But I'm talking in terms of job security; because we have always and still always need cashiers! ".

Giraud: "Oh!, okay! But **I'm a Computer Programmer and Programmer in a large firm that markets into many foreign countries. And because of this, I travel widely**. ".

M rs. Evelyn MULER had separated from Giraud ZEFRINO – deceiver. She started seriously thinking about the latter's proposal. But first, she had herself asked questions:

"What Giraud ZEFRINO really looks serious! But he told me the truth?

---

[1] Giraud ZEFRINO lied to Mrs. Evelyn MULER, wife FERNANDEZ, like what he was: *a Computer Programmer and Programmer in a large architectural firm*, **called "syllogism".** He lied like whatever it was seen as: " **"An Ace of Aces Computer"**; when in reality him just Giraud and his partner with him in this sad story; his accomplice named Poulain DERECK they were indeed as **"desperados"**; it was not actually as **"desperate"**. In short, they were not really, as **"bandidos"**; or rather **"bandits" "**; it was not actually that, **these bandits**; they were, in truth, that, the **hooligans**; which to live, they were the scum of the people.

Or does he just want to ruin my marriage with Julio Fernandez?

Although my marriage with him right now, floundering?

Would he only **spoil** my marriage with Julio Fernandez?

Which I EVELYN I continue again and again and yet still, to love greatly?

What for?

This is simply because for me EVELYN quite frankly, "JULIO Descent From Poitevese And Background On Spanish Descent" still remain conclusively "**Irreplaceable**" and "**Irretrievable**"; "**Indisputable**" and "**Uncontested**"; and finally "**Unforgettable**" and "**Irrecoverable**"; for hardly say for example: "the **Inevitable**" and "**Unrecoverable**"?

This famous ZEFRINO does not he risk in the long run to dump me?

"Over time"; that is to say when exactly for me EVELYN, everything would be too late, for example?

Or to ask me this last question differently: " Do I risk in the long run, to regret it when everything just be too late for example?

But for him Julio Fernandez too! It's his fault!

This is because: How long would he wait for me again so exactly?

A year?

Two years?

Five years?

Ten years?

Fifteen years?

Twenty years?

Huh?

How long would he wait for me again so exactly?

Twenty years?

Fifteen years?

Ten years?

Five years?

Two years?

A year?

Huh?

No one knows! No person really knows! This is the most complete uncertainty! Anyway, I'll see several gynecologists, as I had been told

Mr. Giraud ZEFRINO; Then I would see: What would they say to me! And depending on their answers precisely, I would take a decision obviously! ".

When Mrs. Evelyn MULER had inquired, as she had been advised by Giraud, almost all gynecologists she had been consulted, had actually corroborated the statements of the latter. Consequently, EVELYN who has always wished she had a lot of kids, to do the opposite of hers parents; she had been tempted; and therefore, she had just accepted the proposal of the **Lothario** Giraud ZEFRINO.

"... / ... Because what matters to us, it is not moral; but the dough! Consequently, he never would have people on this earth to be naive, and listen to "manure" as we – others; if not, too bad for them! ".

T hat was, why Evelyn had agreed, after much considerations, the proposed Giraud. That said, one part of the program established by Mr. Moses KEVILER was already done. In doing so, the program continued quietly and reliably. However, it would be that Mr. Poulain DERECK; which would operate in fact a duet with Giraud ZEFRINO, he was tasked, to approach and learn by all means, Julio Fernandez; and above all as a consequence, to tell to him the story of "binding" "his **old bag** EVELYN" "with this certain Giraud ZEFRINO". And it would also be what him DERECK in question precisely, there would bustle about, to very, very accurately. And execute this task beautifully. It is truly one had: affair, **to "detail – there" "very, very carefully developed"**; "**Details very, very meticulously planned for the script**",

written together between – others: on the one hand Poulain DERECK and him, himself ZEFRINO Giraud; and on the other hand: their direct sponsor Thierry Glorian; which himself was controlled by Mr. Moses KEVILER, to whom he reported, gradually and step by step, progressively and as we progressed in ["subversive this sacred mission."].

A s one might imagine, POULAIN and his "compagnero" Giraud had this obligation to know; and therefore, to work together virtually, And to each his own well-defined "directors" role; or rather by the sponsors, of course. However, one day, JULIO himself had almost "busted" his wife EVELYN, "in the act of infidelity, so to speak" with the famous Giraud precisely. How it had happened? On the eve of the incident; that is to say: a Friday night EVELYN who had already informed her husband JULIO from "three days"; that is to say: since "Tuesday morning past", like what, she would go to visit one of hers cousins who lived in the town of Chartres, which was supposedly "very, very ill at this time"; she recalled that one, the eminence of this visit. EVELYN would tell her husband JULIO, she would spend the night there. Or just, "before Thursday", Poulain DERECK had a dual mission to do. The first: he would go take some conversation with Julio Fernandez [And what a conversation!]. And the second: he would go to meet with his accomplice Giraud ZEFRINO to remember; and this: **to perfection stage script, scheduled for when we reach for EVELYN "the stage of no return"**; otherwise expressed, "the stage where EVELYN with the most used business [would find] going to join his "Executioner Giraud ZEFRINO" in the Metro Parmentier; or else: in the Metro Oberkampf".

"The Thursday before just arriving"; therefore, Poulain DERECK was already party also find his new friend, Julio Fernandez. And he had suggested to him: "... / ..."Your **split** EVELYN" you she said when she would visit on Saturday morning?".

Julio Fernandez, at Poulain DERECK; "Yeah!," my **crate** EVELYN" said she would visit one of hers cousins who lives in Chartres; which is very, very ill. ".

Poulain DERECK, at Julio Fernandez: " Is not it intends to sleep there, right? ".

JULIO, at POULAIN: " Yep! But what would you like to suggest by that?".

Poulain, to JULIO: " What I want to tell you over there! ".

JULIO, at POULAIN: " Aye!, ih!, ih, ih! ".

Poulain, to JULIO: " What if you want to catch "your **girl** EVELYN" almost in the act of infidelity, so to speak! ... / .... ".

JULIO at POULAIN: " Ay, ayes ih!, ih, ih! ".

Poulain, to JULIO: " Then hurry to go tomorrow to the Station Of Lyon! ".

JULIO at POULAIN: "At the Station Of Lyon? ".

Poulain, to JULIO: " Tomorrow at 09 Hours 30 Minutes accurate, she would take a train. ".

JULIO, at POULAIN: " In 09 Hours 30 Minutes accurate? ".

Poulain, to JULIO: " Affirmative! But you would not go to 09 Hours 30 Minutes accurate! Course before you go! ".

JULIO, at POULAIN: " Of course before? ".

Poulain, to JULIO: " Absolutely!, if you really want to catch almost! And so, you would see with that, "your **binge** EVELYN" flirts for some time! You would see with whom she will leave, on holiday; to not say for example, flirt; or, on a picnic, not to Chartres, as she'll let it herself heard; but rather, in Lyon! ".

JULIO, at POULAIN: " But rather to Lyon? ".

Poulain, to JULIO: " That's right! Now ... / .... ".

JULIO, at POULAIN: " Now for? ".

Poulain, to JULIO: " Now to go to Chartres is at Station of Montparnasse we will look for trains. But in the case of "your **Agnes** EVELYN" ... / .... ".

JULIO, at POULAIN: " But for the case of "my **Agnes** EVELYN"? ".

Poulain, to JULIO: " But for the case of "your **pile** EVELYN" is at the Station of Lyon; she will take the train. ".

JULIO, at POULAIN: " It's Station of Lyon; she will take the train! ".

Poulain, to JULIO: " Absolutely. In 09 Hours 30 Minutes accurate, the train would leave for Paris. ".

JULIO, at POULAIN: " In 09 Hours 30 Minutes accurate, the train would leave for Paris! ".

Poulain, to JULIO: " Absolutely. she would be with someone. That someone is called Giraud; Giraud ZEFRINO; and he is his Lover "your ticket EVELYN". This Giraud is bad! This Giraud, so to speak: "This is the real Italian adventurer and writer born in Venice in 1725 and died in that city in 1798": "reincarnated" in "this Casanova Giraud ZEFRINO"; or rather in "the womanizer Giraud ZEFRINO"! You understand a little, "archetype" of **"yeoman"** which I would like to refer here to illustrate "this"? Huh? ".

JULIO, at POULAIN: " No ohm! I do not see ah! ".

Poulain, to JULIO: " Otherwise explained that Giraud was not born in Venice, and more importantly, the Eighteenth Century; or even that he is not dead! I just want to let you know that by this comparison, this "Sir" is really comparable to the Venetian adventurer and writer Giacomo Casanova Giovanni; says Jean – Jacques Casanova Of Seingalt; which his name is commonly CASANOVA passed into the language as a **Prince Charming**. This Giraud fact that accumulating amorous adventures and deceptions. We should admit that he can afford to behave this way; since by his craft, which in their box, he turns out to be the "**Ace of Aces**"; and he is pretty darn paid! "It's just **a man in fortunes**"! And consequently, he could afford to behave this way. He is "a **Womanizer**" of **Petticoats**. ! "He's just a **heartbreaker**"! This "Sir" Giraud gives promises of marriage to "the **baronesses**"; to "naive **countesses**" course; then he drops! And he will immediately seek others and so on. He is vicious; since he finds his sentimental pleasure to that way. "This is just a **ladies' man!**".

He is particularly interested "to **bitches**" of others; as it were; he is simply to dissolve their unions. And once he spotted his prey; "Prey"; that is to say: "a naïve **Contessa**"; he did break again! He shrinks as it were, at nothing! "This is just **a charmer of hearts**". And in order to achieve his objective, he is always ready to engage "**both pesetas**" in its business of seduction and conquest "of **empresses**" and especially those of others. And so he is really safe and certain to eliminate all chances of failure. It's that way, he broke several households. "He is **a tomb of hearts**"! That said, with "your **broad**, EVELYN" it would hardly ZEFRINO then, in his first attempt. In short, if you want to save your household with her EVELYN precisely; there is still so much to do something now that it's not too late! If not, then it would be too late! It is not necessary that your wife is "**a naive lettuce!**" Since I do not know: How he proceeds? But anyway: Is it that this "**lady – killer**" knows precisely locate fairly easily "naive **bitches**". He focuses exclusively as "naive **females** " such as you; that is to say, EVELYN; to be well! This is because, if they are not naive; it may be difficult enough for him! He looks "as naive bitches!" Then once he has duped; once he got what he wanted in them; that is to say: once he has finished fornicate with them; he dropped them just, mercilessly! And so he feels the desire of the flesh. And for that, he did not even hesitate to put into play, lots of numerical means. And **money market** means precisely, he have so much; since he is after all, "**An Ace of Aces of Informatics**". And as such, he is pretty darn paid. Thus, he could well afford to indulge in his hobby after work! In short, "he is only a **Romeo**"; "he is only a **woman chaser**" " **that Giraud ZEFRINO!** ".

JULIO, at POULAIN: " How do you know all of them my friend Poulain DERECK? ".

Poulain, to JULIO: " But JULIO? Is it not that you have become my good friend? ".

JULIO, at POULAIN: " Affirmative. ".

Poulain, to JULIO: " Now it gives me great sadness, my great friend, and you my dear occurrence Julio Fernandez, **be cuckolded** and, for some time without knowing it yourself! ".

JULIO, at POULAIN: " If it's true what you say then me! It is indeed sad! ".

Poulain, to JULIO: " But it's true! This is why, given the degree of friendship that ultimately connects us; I decided to tell you, that my conscience is quiet. After, you are perfectly free, to those you want huh! ".

JULIO, at POULAIN: " Thank you my dear friend Poulain DERECK. Tomorrow I'll do the audit. I'll see with my own eyes, what you breath me ears' infidelity as it turned out, "my frog EVELYN"! That said, again: thank you for this tip! ".

Poulain, to JULIO: " At the Station of Lyon; and it should be there by 09 Hours 30 Minutes in the morning! ".

JULIO at POULAIN: " It is understood! ".

That said, Julio Fernandez and his friend Poulain DERECK had taken leave.

And immediately after he left his new friend Julio Fernandez, Poulain DERECK would begin his second mission planned for "the same particular Thursday just before". He would leave actually meet with his accomplice Giraud ZEFRINO **to remember**; **and** this: to perfection stage script, scheduled for when we reach for EVELYN "the stage of no return"; otherwise expressed, "the stage where EVELYN with the most used business [would find] going to join" his **smooth operator** Giraud ZEFRINO "in the Metro Parmentier; or else: in the Metro Oberkampf".

Poulain DERECK leave consequently hearing, his accomplice Giraud ZEFRINO: ""

"« » " "Before coming immediately after Giraud home here, today, I went to see" this "**gentleman**" from "**yeoman**" from "JULIO" " " ""

"" I told him (**as was planned in the script**): ""

"« "Let him go the next Sunday in the morning to surprise you all with" "this silly EVELYN" of, "almost in flag adultery" at the Station of Lyon. ""

"« Well now, "the two of us" me and you Giraud POULAIN! ""

"« "**B**etween us", go together "to the latest settings of our script"; ""

"« "Our unstoppable script!". ""

"« ("Unstoppable" at least "in theory"; ""

"" But I hope with all my heart, that: ""

"« "Practically also" it's the same! ""

"« [The we'll see: What comes of it "Virtually" "Day" "D"; and "Time" "T"; to "Time" "T"; that is to say: in the late afternoon. ""

"« That is to say: "on Sunday, just"; when "the Machine" "actually starts";""

"« Or rather when "Execution" "three characters": "I Poulain"; " you Giraud" and "this silly of EVELYN in question"; ""

"" Where – about of it as such, it is not in the game; ""

"« And it is hardly in the game; because: it is "our pigeon" that will make us acquire fortunes from MOSES; ""

"" It is hardly in the game; because: she is the victim]; ""

"« [So we'll see: What it will "virtually" the Day "D"; and "Time" "T"; that is to say, "on Sunday, just"; when "this script in question" will be well and truly in place, in fact]); ""

"" Script that we actually designed and developed at three: me Poulain; you Giraud and her, the naïve EVELYN. ""

"« Between us go together, "the latest settings for this script"; because there are only two days before "Practice"; »"

"« Before "Practice": "Life – Size" [obviously]: »"

"« "Friday" and "Saturday"; »"

"« Then "Sunday" by the end of the afternoon, it will already effectively the "Day – D" and the "Time" "T"! »"

"" What time goes really fast eh! ""

"« It will be already "fateful day"; »"

"" And by extension, you and me, we have absolutely no right to error; ""

"" And especially no, no and no fault at all, at all! ""

"« It will be "the day we will reach with this fun to EVELYN": "the point of no return"; »"

"« "The point of no return" in " "his" **"Sir"** of "coco" of "JULIO" ". »"

"« Listen to me very, very well Giraud! As provided in the script that we developed all three together: When EVELYN would indeed repudiated by "her **Military**"; and she would come and join you in the mouth of Metro, as you are forced to tell her and telling her several times even when you will end up in Lyon, to do so in "this inexorable case elsewhere" where this "puppet" would be repudiate; ZEFRINO you, you will speak to me until I Giraud, I will finish those I'll briefly remind you! »"

"" No, you ZEFRINO, do will chat me anyway: not there in the Metro; it would be too difficult! ""

"" And of course I POULAIN also, I will chat you anyway: not at all, at all, there in the Metro; it would indeed be too much too delicate! ""

"" No imprudence! ""

"" Not there in the Metro! ""

"" That's because she EVELYN, who would join you, she would hardly be far from you! ""

"" She would even be all the time, walking almost as it were together with you over there in the subway station and in the corridors! ""

"" And indeed, she could hear us even if we are talking about more or less silently, as elaborated in the scenario! ""

"" And consequently, she could understand the plot! ""

"" However, if you have stuff to say absolutely, in some small, short days only; we will meet with Mr. Thierry Glorian, our direct sponsor (and himself being controlled by Mr. Moses KEVILER), to make him, report on the success of this first stage of the mission. ""

"" And therefore, there could be cause as we please; that is to say: freely and without following any text! ""

"" But for that moment, as expected, it would be essential that you Giraud, you're immediate attention with "this naive **lobster**" of EVELYN until substantially the final phase of the mission! ""

"" And now Giraud, I'll remind you again very, very distinctly; very, very cleverly and sooner or later: our texts; our facts and our actions to be implemented in that fateful moment then very, very precisely! ""

"" There you Giraud, you will continue to cause me nothing at all, at all! ""

"" There, I Poulain, I'll pretend to strangle you. So I will really like it's true! I will do like I wanted to, for example, to avenge the honor of my new friend JULIO! ""

"" I will really pretend to strangle you. ""

"" Here I Poulain, I go with my two hands, grab your shot at you. ""

"" Here I Poulain, I'll pretend to shake you; shake you so much; and even very, very strong. ""

"" And then, for you to Giraud, you're going to try to pretend to defend yourself in me suggesting very, very strong, "but let me go! But you'll let me, yeah!". ""

"" And in doing so, there me POULAIN, I will also let you go. But that's only when I'm going to let you go! ""

"" There you Giraud, you will save so to speak, "at 100 Kilometers per Hour"; and this, without requiring any degree thy rest; and that, without looking so slightly back. ""

"" And then you Giraud, you're downright run; and this without looking back; me POULAIN where I am stood still, accompanying you to my nasty look! ""

"" And then you Giraud especially, you're going to run by speaking very loudly (; so that above all, "the naïve **sultana**, EVELYN" you listen very, very explicitly): "Oh!, ah! This guy is really just crazy! It is really sick! He wanted to strangle me!". ""

"" And then I Poulain, my answer will be as provided in the text we have stored: In a first time and still quite quietly; that is to say: more or less silently, so that "the naive calf" "Evelyn MULER" cannot listen, your answer will be: "Okay! ... / ...!". ""

"" In summary: ""

"" When I POULAIN I will rebuke apparently; and there you Giraud, you will also try to defend you too apparently: while also shouting very, very strong: "But let me go! But you'll let me, aye!". ""

"" And then I Poulain, I will also let you go. ""

"" **A**nd then you "assaulted the Giraud", you will be released. And therefore you will save current "in Cent Time"; while saying very, very hard for me POULAIN abuser: "Oh!, ah! This guy is actually a siphon! It really is "crazy, crazy!" He wanted to strangle me! ". ""

"" And all the time that we would spend together, trying to solve our roles under the scenery, "the naive prostitute EVELYN" you waiting a little further away: that you Giraud you go fast join her; but that, as precisely you will not go quickly join her! ""

"" She would have suspected! But that too was expected! Hence, our semblance of fight is mainly intended to remove her immediately from her mind, these suspicions! ""

"" Here Giraud yourself, you're going to pretend to go get on the subway and go away immediately after me POULAIN, I would have released you! ""

"" And there for me Poulain, for that day here, my task will be completed; and therefore I will take the subway; and let me go! ""

"" But moreover, as to you Giraud, your day is not yet over! It is not yet completely finished. This is because right after that I Poulain, I left! ""

"" There you Giraud, you will leave to EVELYN; to continue talking to her. ""

"" It is in fact, to start with her immediately: the next stage of this subversive mission we're executing on behalf of Mr. Moses KEVILER, against a whopping remuneration! ""

"« » " But, "prevents much for all that", "this mouse EVELYN just" "you certainly will ask": Do you know what, this "Sir"? ". » " »"

"« And you Giraud you tell lies: "No ohm!". »"

"« This whore of EVELYN you even ask for example: "Why did he want you bump off by strangulation; and that, in the presence of all "walkers" nearby? But why you are saved you like that, saying [I quote your words]: "Oh!, ah! This guy is really a jerk! He's really come! He wanted to strangle me!". As if it were for example two antagonists; two enemies who once knew; they had lost sight of; and which, when they meet again; they wanted to fight with fists; or rather, with a duel to the death of one of the two? »"

"" And you Giraud you will lie her again: ""

"" Not at all! I do not know him at all! ""

"« I had only preview today, trying to talk to "**your Mark Antony**"; when I escorted you home! »"

"« And coincidentally, I saw almost all come with you so far in the station, so really, to take his Metro. I really thought he was coming to get me and that in any case he would find me; he would pass me by example, mercilessly beaten, because of this act of adultery that I made with you EVELYN; and this: at the expense of his friend JULIO; that is to say: at the expense of "**your bird**"! »"

"" So, I got cold feet ever! I seriously believed he had to impose me, a sacred correcting; it is because I have so break the household of his friend JULIO with you EVELYN! ""

"" Hence, I started to greet him, lest he be angry, for example, much against me. ""

"" And then I tried to continue the conversation by saying anything that came into my head. But ever in fear, I said more or less silently! ""

"" I stammered anything; and this more or less silently; such that: ""

" " Not only that he "this clown", the friend of "your zebra JULIO", he hears nothing, really; so that not only he does not understand anything, really; because having heard nothing; and more importantly, for having nothing got it; ""

"" But also and even primarily for: he says at the bottom of himself, for example: ""

" " " " "But! But she is not a patsy this Dredger of "**Delilah**" for others!". » « »"

" " And as a result, rather than him the friend of "your coconut JULIO", he finally fear me Giraud! I Giraud, the goofy, which might have eventually to assault him! ""

" " And, moreover, he can save himself; especially not me; and that, "at Cent Time"! ""

" " And alas!, it was more, this friend of "your horse", the cuckold JULIO put me through! ""

" " And yep!, ih! Rather, it was him that made me flee "to Hundred Kilometers per Hour"! ""

" " And aye, aye ih! Myself Giraud, who believed scare "in Hundred Kilometers per Hour"! ""

" " It was more to myself that we did flee "to Hundred Kilometers per Hour"! ""

"" And it was as a result, I let him hear that Giraud precisely: ""

" " "Oh!, ah! This guy is actually a come!"! ""

"" That's all! It's fear! It scared me, I thought, yet scare him! ""

"" Me Giraud who finally, I actually thought him more afraid; that I would have done! ""

"" Remember Giraud very, very well what this script especially for word!""

"" What for? ""

"" That's because our fortunes to us, depend on it! ""

"" And it would be only then that you have good recall: ""

"" All that and stuff and stuff ah! ""

"" And thou have gone all to practice it yourself, but you will in the remembering, as a solo repeat that: ""

"" "The Machine" "size", "so to speak", "could start"! ""

"" Or rather, that ""

"" "The Execution" "size", "so to speak", "could start"! " " " " " ".

And as to him Julio Fernandez, when he returned home, he was just thinking about all that his new friend POULAIN had spoken to him about his "bug Evelyn MULER". All that night, he did not even get to sleep; since he was just thinking about all those we had to tell him. And the next morning, as expected, Julio Fernandez lied "his trollop" like what, he was going to work the day that Saturday; that is to say, 07 hours to 19 hours. In doing so he was already found in 08 Hours 15 Minutes before the Station of Lyon. He asked, with a tobacconists, an Office of Information this station schedules for Lyon and their numbers docks. And therefore it is planted; or rather, he just covered well behind a kiosk of sandwiches from the Station, around the dock that was shown him. In 08 Hours 25 Minutes accurate, he saw "his **missus**, EVELYN" alone; which looked everywhere, as you might say she had lost someone female or someone male that she absolutely wanted to find. Then, 08 Hours Thirty Minutes; that is to say, only five minutes later, a "Mister" tall or giant; elegant; and not very fat; came to her.

So it was [undoubtedly] " the **Fair sex's "Faller ¾ Down"** " Giraud ZRFRINO "in person. Which will bustle about" "who better, better", "to be better able to succeed" "the subversive Mission"; which he had already given way to "deposit", "a very, very large sum"; and to be sure and certain, yet touching "very important, after he had left very touching", as a "balance on balance"; especially:

For Greater Success "battles" that would announce to him, "The Lady Killer Giraud ZEFRINO" and the naive Evelyn MULER, for "all afternoon, almost: nonstop", "Saturday, the day of their arrival in this city of Lyon";

to be more successful "low – dances" that announce "copiously" for them, "almost overnight: nonstop" ["the night from Saturday to Sunday, the day of return to Paris"] ;

to do better "the shallow steps" that would announce, for "all morning" "almost: nonstop", Sunday; ["All the morning on Sunday"; that is to say, "to the surroundings, a little before Twelve Hours"; since, anyhow, "the Heartbreaker Giraud ZEFRINO" had paid the hotel room; a luxury hotel, just to "Twelve Piles up precisely". Hence the fact that later, "12 Hours 30' ", "torque – fornicator" should imperatively be clear out of that hotel room in question].

In short, then: Thirty Minutes to 08 hours; that is to say, only five minutes later, "the **Rebecca's Killer** Giraud ZRFRINO" came to join the naive Evelyn MULER. They were heading to a fast food restaurants, train station, to take a quick breakfast too, pending the arrival of the train they were going up. One thing was sure and certain: they had fixed an appointment at Thirty Eight hours in the morning; and Evelyn, for example does not to be late, she had even pointed it ahead of Five Minutes over Thirty Eight Hours, the time of appointment. Julio Fernandez, who had more hidden behind the kiosk; when its "tow" was still only herself to get a better look; he chose precisely that moment; "at precisely that moment"; that is to say, when "the devil" had come to join in order to get out of his hideout. However, he continued without the slightest complacency [since after all, she was his wife], even in the restaurant where they met; and he said consequently the latter: "EVELYN!".

EVELYN (surprised then, "her Adam JULIO" and she would meet her): " But! But since when are you following me like that? ".

JULIO, to EVELYN: " EVELYN? ".

EVELYN, at JULIO: " Yeah!, ih? ".

JULIO, to EVELYN: " Would you like you get to Chartres? ".

EVELYN, at JULIO: " So what? You are not the owner of my body as I know not! ".

JULIO, to EVELYN: " Would you like you get to Chartres! But Chartres is at the Station of Montparnasse that we will not find the train! ".

EVELYN, at JULIO: " So what? ".

JULIO, to EVELYN: " But! ".

EVELYN, at JULIO: " There is no" But! '".

JULIO, to EVELYN: " But! ".

EVELYN, at JULIO: " Ah!, JULIO! How long have you been doing this job as a private detective, to allow you to follow me like that? ".

JULIO, to EVELYN: " Also, Who is this "Sir" – here – present; which allows to take quietly coffee and croissants with you? ".

EVELYN, at JULIO: " Why are you to know? ".

JULIO, to EVELYN: " I do have a right to know; This is because: do not forget one little moment, we're married eh! ".

EVELYN, at JULIO: " Since this is so, then I am no longer ashamed to tell you. ".

JULIO, to EVELYN: " Then say it! ".

EVELYN, at JULIO: " This" Sir" – here – present, that ... / .... ".

JULIO, to EVELYN: " Aye!, ih!, ih, ih! ".

EVELYN, at JULIO: " This "Sir" – here – present, that has coffee and croissants with me ... / .... ".

JULIO, to EVELYN: " Aye, aye!, ih!, ih, ih! ".

EVELYN, at JULIO: " This "Sir" that is watching you trying to ask me questions and ... / .... ".

JULIO, to EVELYN: " Yep!, ih!, ih, ih! ".

EVELYN, at JULIO: " This "Sir" is listening to all your questions ... / .... ".

JULIO, to EVELYN: " Uh – huh!, ih!, ih, ih! ".

EVELYN, at JULIO: " It's "Mister" Giraud ZEFRINO. And he promised me a lot of joy and happiness! ".

JULIO, to EVELYN: " You bet! Hmm mm! "A lot of joy and happiness"! But you want to laugh or what? But "this" is " **Shrew's "Faller ¾ Down"** "! ".

EVELYN, at JULIO: " Not at all! ".

JULIO, to EVELYN: " So let me laugh alone! ".

EVELYN, at JULIO: " So laugh all alone! ".

JULIO, to EVELYN: " A lot of joy and happiness! But you talk EVELYN! But "this" is "a brain – heart"! ".

EVELYN, at JULIO: " Righto!, and simply! "A lot of joy and happiness!". ".

JULIO, to EVELYN: " Righty – ho!, and simply! ".

EVELYN, at JULIO: "Absolutely! ".

JULIO, to EVELYN: " "Okay!, and simply!". ".

EVELYN, at JULIO: " Absolutely. And it hardly needs to first make very large economic projects for this! ".

JULIO, to EVELYN: " But EVELYN! Open your eyes; since it is being conned you all! "This is just a charmer", "this gentleman"! It should hardly succumb to his good words; these are just **the wind**! This elegant **Delilah's Killer** is fooling you! He would only break your marriage with me and that's it! ".

EVELYN, at JULIO: " He would rather that my happiness. ".

JULIO, to EVELYN: " I am aware of how to behave in this " **Agnes 's "Faller ¾ Down"** "! ".

EVELYN, at JULIO: " This is not true. That said, I do not want at all, all you hear. ".

JULIO, to EVELYN: " It **"Eva's Killer"** is wrong! ".

EVELYN, at JULIO: " This "Sir" is not bad. ".

JULIO, to EVELYN: " This **Antigone 's "Faller ¾ Down"** is bad; and you must listen to me, so there's still time! ".

EVELYN, at JULIO: " This guy is good. ".

JULIO, to EVELYN: " This **Daughter of Eva's Killer**, this is not good; and you must listen to me, as long as it's not too late to listen to me if you want! . ".

EVELYN, at JULIO: " But then, it turns out there: Me EVELYN, I do not want at all, at all, to listen to you! In addition, this individual is a good one. ".

JULIO, to EVELYN: " It's only a **Giovanni** ... / ...! ".

EVELYN, at JULIO: " I do not understand anything at all, from what you tell me then! ".

JULIO, to EVELYN: " This is only Homo sapiens **Giovanni GIACOMO** says ... / ...! ".

EVELYN, at JULIO: " But? ".

JULIO, to EVELYN: " ... / ... Said: **Seingalt of CASANOVA**! ".

EVELYN, at JULIO: " But JULIO! You've become "crazy, crazy", or what? But you drunk me, ah! ".

JULIO, to EVELYN: "But listen to me ah! This is to warn you before it is too late, as I do! "It's only a **Don Juan**" this human! ".

EVELYN, to JULIO: "You pump me, ah! ".

JULIO, to EVELYN: "It's for your own good! ".

EVELYN, at JULIO: "This "Sir" Giraud is a good one. ".

JULIO, to EVELYN: "This hominid named Giraud ZEFRINO is an adventurer by accumulating its credit: the amorous adventures and deceptions! "This is just a flirty"! ".

EVELYN, at JULIO: "This "Sir" Giraud is a good one. ".

JULIO, to EVELYN: "But this human race is just a **Arian 's "Faller ¾ Down"**! "It's a winning"! ".

EVELYN, at JULIO: "It's a good one! ".

JULIO, to EVELYN: "This is a deceiver! "This is a sorcerer!" "This is a cruel and wicked sorcerer"! Short, this is a **Juliet's Killer**! ".

EVELYN, at JULIO: "Are you going to stop getting drunk me, a little? ".

JULIO to EVELYN: "Only " **Artemis 's "Faller ¾ Down"** "! "This is just a **Penelope's Killer**" ambidextrous this creature! ".

EVELYN, at JULIO: "Are you going to stop just to pump me with your talk of honest appearance; but actually untrue and harmful to me? ".

JULIO, to EVELYN: "Only "a Seducer of Petticoats"! "This is just one suitor" this talented creature supposedly reason; and please believe me EVELYN! ".

EVELYN, at JULIO: "But quite frankly ah! I'm really tired with you JULIO you know eh? ".

JULIO, to EVELYN: "But this creature endowed with intelligence is saying, "this is just a thief of honor"; where does that accumulating on his own, multiple-night stands! And for you too, he will inevitably treat you like this, EVELYN! ".

EVELYN, at JULIO: "Enough JULIO huh! This Giraud is a good "Sir" a point and a line! ".

JULIO, to EVELYN: "He pretends to be: a good "Sir"! But it is a well – known ways in which **Celimene 's "Faller ¾ Down"** use! That said: This **"Cleopatra's Killer** " is "a **Eurydice 's "Faller ¾ Down"** "! ".

EVELYN, at JULIO: " It is not a " **Eurydice 's "Faller ¾ Down"** ", "this biped". It's like a serious, honest and sincere! This is a "Sir" bitterly hates one-night. ".

JULIO, to EVELYN: "This man, this is not a good one. About this human being just this week here just someone; a certain "Sir" Poulain DERECK has put a flea in my ears. He told me among others, [I quote]:

"... / ... This Giraud is wrong! He gives promises of marriage to "the **grandmas**"; "to naive dolls" of course. Then he dropped. And he will immediately seek others; seek "other naive hens"; and so on. He is vicious; it's because he finds his sentimental pleasure of that way. He is particularly interested "in stretchers" of others; as it were; it is simply to: to dissolve their unions. And once he spotted his prey; "prey"; that is to say: "a **naive mouse**". He did break again. It shrinks as he were, with nothing. In order to achieve its objectives, he is always ready to engage both "**species**" in its business of seduction and conquest "of **baronesses**" and especially those of others. And so it is really safe and certain to eliminate all chances of failure. It's that way, he broke several households. That said, with "your **sweet thing**, EVELYN" he would hardly ZEFRINO then, in his first attempt. "In short, if you really want to save your household with her EVELYN precisely; it is still high time to do something now that it's not too late! If not, then it would be too late!". "... / ....". "This Seductress" is interested exclusively as "naive **tootsies** " such as you; that is to say, EVELYN; to be well; this is because, if they are not naive! It can be difficult enough for him! It looks "as **ladies** naive"! ... / .... ". [End of quote]. ".

"" So EVELYN! I will repeat to you too, the end of the present summons; since he shows very, very well and at the same time, he also summarizes very, very well, our situation: ""

"« "... / ... However, with [you] EVELYN, it would hardly ZEFRINO then at his first attempt. In short, if you still wish to save your household with [me JULIO] exactly! It is still high time to do something now that it's not too late! If not, then it would be: indeed too late!". ""

EVELYN, at JULIO: " Ah!, ah, ah! You JULIO! You drunk me! ".

JULIO, to EVELYN: " It **Judith's Killer**" only gives promises of marriage to "the **females**"; to "naive **lassies** " such as ... / .... ".

EVELYN, at JULIO: " Ah!, ah, ah, you JULIO! You fatigue me!!! ".

JULIO, to EVELYN: ""... / ...". "At **womanishes** naive", as you EVELYN: "... / ... In order to have the ... / ...! Then once he has **screwed** them! Once he got what he wanted in them; that is to say, once he has finished fornicate with them! He dropped them mercilessly! And so he feels the desire of the flesh. And for that, he did not even hesitate to put into play heavily on numerical media! And "numerical just means" he is so much; since he is after all, "**An Ace of Aces for Computing**"; and as such, he is pretty darn paid. Thus, he could well afford to indulge in his hobby after work. ". [End quote.]. Like my friend always said this Poulain DERECK. ".

The so we understand that, for all the arguments made in vain alas!, by JULIO, to discourage "his **ticket** EVELYN", not to fall into the trap of the **Iphigenia 's "Faller ¾ Down"**, he still loved her very, very significantly, that. But then, this one just made his decision: JULIO leave, she certainly loved him, also very, very considerably; leave with nostalgia, of course, and then remarry the newcomer; that is to say: the **Fatima's Killer** Poulain DERECK. EVELYN, at JULIO: " You do not get tired JULIO? ".

JULIO, to EVELYN: " But it's for your own good, I'm hoarse! It's for your interest I do not get tired! ".

EVELYN, at JULIO: " You do not want me I know a lot of joy and happiness? ".

JULIO, to EVELYN: " You ... / ...! ".

EVELYN, at JULIO: " This is why you me pumps ears with your great speech that you'd sincere? ".

JULIO, to EVELYN: " You're wrong ... / ...! ".

EVELYN, at JULIO: " This is why you do not hesitate one little moment, to lie, to dissuade me from that way quite Machiavellian, not to accept this good "Sir" Giraud ZEFRINO? ".

JULIO, to EVELYN: " You are mistaken EVELYN! ".

EVELYN, at JULIO: " No, I do not deceive me at all! ".

JULIO, to EVELYN: " You are mistaken. This " **Juno 's "Faller ¾ Down"** " does just that! He cheats "naive **queens**" to get what he wants; and then he dropped mercilessly and simply. ".

EVELYN, at JULIO: " It's not true! And besides, stop repeating the same thing for quite a while eternity! ".

JULIO, to EVELYN " If it's true. It will ruin your life and this one, forever!".

EVELYN, at JULIO: " This is my life for that matter as you said! So if you want to do me a big favor, let me now direct all alone this one! ".

JULIO, to EVELYN: " Even if it is beginning to spoil? ".

EVELYN, at JULIO: " Even if it is beginning to spoil, absolutely! ".

JULIO, to EVELYN: "EVELYN! Do not accept this " **Joan of Arc's Killer** "; this is because when you will break your marriage with me; ... / .... ".

EVELYN, at JULIO: " Yeah!, ih!, ih, ih;! I'm listening! ".

JULIO, to EVELYN: " He that " **Salome 's "Faller ¾ Down"** " ZEFIRIN, you ... / .... ".

EVELYN, at JULIO: " He that "Sir" yep!, ZEFRINO ih!, ih, ih! ".

JULIO, to EVELYN: " He that " **Countess 's Killer** " ZEFRINO, you will drop also. ".

EVELYN, at JULIO: " How do you know? ".

JULIO, to EVELYN: " I know this is because a friend of mine which I not stopped talking with you here; which friend you got to know, there is not very long; and which is called Poulain DERECK, knows very well that " **Sulamite 's "Faller ¾ Down"** " ZEFRINO! And he let me hear about it too among others that: ""... / ...". That gallant **Duchess 's Killer** "eventually dropping" your "**petticoat**"; then go get some elsewhere; and they also act in the same way as "your **squaw**"; as did so many others before her and so on. And it's precisely that way; he has already broken a considerable number of households. It's a vicious this **Venus 's "Faller ¾ Down"**,who finds his sentimental fun that way; that is to say, being very, very bad to other people. That said, it ZEFRINO is hardly there at his first attempt. ". In short, your question: "How do you know?"! I know through Mr. Poulain DERECK; which became for me, as a sincere friend; while in the meantime, "your gallant Giraud ZEFRINO", is indeed a vulgar **Princess 's Killer!** ".

EVELYN, at JULIO: " Stop me you tired and JULIO and it is the same, that stops you tire yourself and also for the simple reason that I do not believe at all, at all, in a word, all those you have started to tell me, since if what time, until now. ".

JULIO, to EVELYN: " And yet it would have to believe me; because after that he would be disgusted with you! And therefore, he is simply save for him. And at that point, you would have missed him: and too, you would have missed I JULIO your husband speaks to you and very, very long; to discourage you not to make the mistake of falling into the net of this subversive ZEFRINO; and the latter himself precisely. ".

EVELYN, at JULIO: " If you want my opinion JULIO about him! Frankly, ... / .... ".

JULIO, to EVELYN: " Ih Yeah!, I admit yep!, ih! ".

EVELYN, at JULIO: " Quite frankly, he will not run away. ".

JULIO, to EVELYN: " What do you know? ".

EVELYN, at JULIO: " I know something, since I'm so sure and certain that this is a good guy "this crisp ZEFRINO". ».

JULIO, to EVELYN: " How can you be so sure and certain? Huh? ".

EVELYN, at JULIO: " Just by the way he talked to me. There is no doubt he is sincere; even very sincere and see: very, very sincere, "this gas ZEFRINO". ».

JULIO, to EVELYN: " It is not true; inevitably he will save a good someday fairly close. And at that time, it will ... / ...! ".

EVELYN, at JULIO: " "This guy ZEFRINO" will not run away. ».

JULIO, to EVELYN: " This will save; and this time, it will be too late; far too late; this is because, me JULIO, I could never, ever, never and ever take you with me! At that time, I could never, ever, never and ever accept you again! That's why my dear wife, I tell you that I love you enormously; and because of this: go home in our apartment while he is not yet too late! ".

EVELYN, at JULIO: " No, "this zebra ZEFRINO" will not run away. ».

EVELYN, at ZEFRINO: " Is it not that you will not save you? Huh? ".

ZEFRINO, at EVELYN: " Me? I save myself? I once together with you, to save me and I Hate About You? In any case I ah!, never, never, never! ".

EVELYN, at JULIO: " Did you hear yourself JULIO? ".

JULIO, to EVELYN: " But these are just words in the air! But he's lying! He lies as he breathes! Go home in our apartment, before it's too late! ".

EVELYN, at JULIO: " No, I do not go with you in the apartment. I go with him on a picnic in Lyon! And when I return tomorrow, too bad for any consequences that I would undergo! ".

JULIO, to EVELYN: " " ... / ... For the possible consequences ... / ..."! Possible only? Not "possible"; but rather "real consequences", it should say! In every way, you get back tomorrow, I'd rather tell you right now before you go with "what **blade** of ZEFRINO" to make you change your mind if you persist in wanting ... / ... . ".

EVELYN, at JULIO: " Yeah!, ih!, ih, ih! I'm listening! ".

JULIO, to EVELYN: " What if you persist in wanting to go with this **Baroness 's "Faller ¾ Down"**! On your return, it would be ruthlessly legal separation in a first time, waiting for the divorce itself a second time; which undoubtedly would be pronounced as soon as possible by a matrimonial judges considering assault, so to speak! ".

EVELYN, at JULIO: " I told you I did not go into the apartment with you today; as I leave earlier with "this guy of ZEFRINO", that one you hate so much, then you ... / .... ".

JULIO, to EVELYN: " I'll say it a little more clearly to you: You're not going further back into the marital home; if ever that you persist in following this **Archduchess 's Killer** in your flirt at Lyon! It is imperative that this decision is this; and will remain: constant; immutable and irreversible. ".

EVELYN, at JULIO: " I told you I did not go into the apartment with you today; as I leave earlier with "this type ZEFRINO", which one you hate so much, when you come to meet him, only just though! In doing so, for me also, that this decision is; and will remain: constant; immutable and irreversible. Besides about from earlier; he will make a few small moments only: New Hours Thirty Minutes and therefore our train will leave the dock! In short, I will not go into the apartment with you today! Because I'll take that train a little while to another, will ring the hour of departure dock! I go with "this archetype ZEFRINO" in Lyon and nobody can stop me; except himself "Sir" Giraud ZEFRINO, of course! Or just him, he would issue. He would not do that, for the simple reason that the idea of leaving, me EVELYN and him Giraud, "we take good weather unforgettable", "set in a luxury hotel", of Lyon; this idea comes from himself! And it comes from him Giraud! What for? This is simply because he loves me and would make me happy. Also with this "Sir", I have little need for example, to take contraceptive measures. On the contrary than for you, it is important not at all, at all, to take them. I am going with him. And then when I get back with you in the Eleventh Arrondissement of Paris: too bad for the real consequences thereof as a result of this I'm going to flirt with this "Sir" Giraud, as you yourself have so very, very well expressed! Or to better express it: So much for the real consequences that result as a consequence of this very act, adultery I am about and most highly deliberately commit with "the crunchy"; "with this elegant"; "with this gallant" Giraud. ".

Finally, Giraud ZEFRINO, at Julio Fernandez: "Sir"? "Mr." FERNANDEZ? "Mr." Julio Fernandez? Have you heard those your wife just left you hear herself without him they are forced? So eh! If I were in your place; I understand there: it would be nothing at all, at all, it can still save between me and this "Joan of Arc" who spit in my ears, of such truths! ".

Julio Fernandez who listened such a response; which was just to show him the reality; he remained a few seconds at first speechless; before finally actually accept him despite this reality just in front; and therefore, to finally meet this Giraud: " Okay " **Shepherdess 's "Faller ¾ Down"** " lover "my prostitute"! Okay I quite understand! I'll let you continue your journey; and I go home in the Eleventh district of Paris! ".

So Evelyn MULER and "the **Madam 's Killer** Giraud ZEFRINO" go get on the train HST [High Speed Train]; and they would go quietly to Lyon, where he had booked by phone, a room in a luxury hotel. And that ah!, he could really afford it. "The **Countess 's "Faller ¾ Down"** Giraud ZEFRINO" could really afford, because: many baboons already received as an advance for, that mission work (and what work and what mission that is more a subversive mission of course!) a mission funded by Mr. Moses KEVILER "The Butcher" [And rightly so!]: [Many so – Barbary forced].

And always, just thinking to operation of Evelyn MULER, JULIO would still become "crazy, crazy ally", "like hell". And once back home in the Eleventh Arrondissement, he would again to rave. He would tell the attention for example: himself; and that all who wanted to listen him, so slightly: lyrics, without heads or tails; lyrics such as: """

"" "Ah!, those who are fornicators and Giraud EVELYN!". """

"""" They are just animals! """

"""" And they also act as real animals! """

"""" The real animals, with males, irresistibly, they excite or who would overexcite by pheromones released by the females in heat! """

"""" Ah!, women! """

"""" Ah!, **Bimbo 's Killer**! """

"""" Oh!, the animals! """

"""" Ah!, those animals that are: Giraud and EVELYN! """

"" The whole thing with them, takes place as for example that looks like: Five Million Cells Olfactory nostrils of EVELYN were irresistibly excited and even excited by "pheromones" "generated by Giraud"; and no, the opposite!"""

"""" It's quite mysterious! """

"""" Go therefore understand this mystery! """

"""" Go therefore understand something in it ah! """

"" The sham of **Chick 's "Faller ¾ Down"** Giraud had just fought the simplicity of JULIO. The elegance of "his devil", her Iphigenia EVELYN "is a flat street, a look postcard; which is simply to prepare everything under the heat of the moment". This could be a stage apart. And the problems do not they dying eyes? The start = violence and more! The end = indolence less! But it was not, is not? " " """

"""" Is it to put me under pressure? """

"" Is what it is to bring down the sky on my head without there being the slightest warning? ""

" Is "the **Damsel 's Killer** Giraud him, my rival" has other arguments to be seduced "EVELYN my companion", and first, his job as Computer Programmer? ""

" Is that Evelyn is "Rebecca," which in any case could not say "No!". To "the new guy, the **Girl 's "Faller ¾ Down"** Giraud"; and, in any case, could not say: "Yep!" To "her former, the horse JULIO" either? ""

" To "me, the coco JULIO", "my little housewife EVELYN as such" is essential! And "her funny, the **Rebecca's Killer** Giraud", it is not great; it is a science fiction film anything! It is "an adrenaline" to "pure"! ""

" Does "his horn Giraud" embodies both: the vital energy of masculinity rather young; the robustness of a wrestling champion and the beauty of a "Sir" Universe? ""

" Cuckolded and "me, her **wight** JULIO" with "her new boyfriend, the **Fair sex's "Faller ¾ Down"** Giraud", to explain the unexplainable! ""

" They become poets; they become dreamers; and they were gone in Five Hundred kilometers from Paris; that is to say: in the City of "romantic poetry"; where they are damned given their heart, "to absolute romanticism"! They reserve me other surprises, they have not yet finished, to show myself? "This bourgeois EVELYN" not interested "as dormant dreams of offspring"? "That" has the air only to be this appearance? In less than "the look" ¾! "
« » « »
.

And here in a room of hotel accommodation in Lyon, they (that is to say: she Evelyn MULER and him, "the **Delilah's Killer** Giraud ZEFRINO concerned") would "delight in" to express ourselves in this way "mutually multiple repeats" [even for one night, to be sure, "a white ¾ night"], as ever, never, ever and never, "they would have previously, one as the other or as a the other (of course)" taken "of such lively pleasures". In one night (admittedly "all the night", or "the white ¾ night", or "a night without sleep so little"), Evelyn MULER would with "the **Shrew's "Faller ¾ Down"** Giraud ZEFRINO": "a loving couple's life rather intense and quite sultry". It would do "this adulterous then", as if it were for example "a real foot"; which would exchange his body against "several hundred billion kopecks"; when it was not even at all, at all the case. It was "a formal verbal guarantee of promise of marriage" after divorce with Julio, "this thief of honor Giraud ZEFRINO" pushed her to apply to her husband Julio Fernandez (; "a formal guarantee of promise marriage" and yet "tacit" and "unwritten" "certainly not"; "which formal guarantee of promise of marriage" could actually happen overnight, "being a mere buzzword, no future just", since there was not even a "written proof" for that).

And Julio Fernandez was actually returned home without his "Agnes EVELYN".

Just thinking to operation of the latter, JULIO would become as it were "crazy, crazy ally", "like hell". At home he would start to talk nonsense. He would tell to the attention e.g. himself; and that all who wanted to listen to him so little, lyrics, without heads or tails; lyrics such as: " " "

" " "But yea!, ih!". In less than "appearance" exactly! That's good "nomenclature" that could indeed dress up in "his new fellow, the **Eva's Killer** Giraud", and in addition: use it in every way! ""

" " "In every sense of actually"; As the promises of a better life that gives him appear "apparently" true! ""

" " "In every sense of actually"; As the promises of a better life that gives him, the look "unquestionably" chimerical! ""

" " Is for "this half EVELYN", "it is a challenge" always "hardly listen to me" "I her sparrow JULIO"? ""

" " Is for "this regular EVELYN", "it's a challenge" to "always listen" " her new horse, the **Agnes 's "Faller ¾ Down"** Giraud "? ""

"" Is for "her, this minister EVELYN", "it's a challenge" to "always start with" "his new number, the **Daughter of Eva's Killer** Giraud" in the agglomeration of Lyon? """

"" Frankly, "me his bird JULIO", I cannot be that to really dip: what is real in this real story here? """

"" And what is not? """

"" Do "this **Archduchess** EVELYN", she would flee me because the clouds clouded over my aura? """

"" Do "this beautiful sex EVELYN" does not, she flee little "her new zebra Giraud", since "the sun shines on his aura?" """

"" Did she would upset, since most would desire to continue to wear his same look on a "Sir" full of **Cataclysms**? """

"" Is she not desire to continue wearing her same look on a "Sir" from the "Descent Poitevese and background Spanish Descent"? """

"" Speaking of the "Descent Poitevese" exactly! But this is my home Agglomeration and I cannot help me ah! In addition, this is where a near majority of the members of my family together (this near – majority)! Moreover, this is where I recharge better! """

"" This is the City of Poitiers, where I know the best, every nook and corner of streets. The streets in which I often do, "walks, health", "to burn my calories too"; then, I'm also "walks, health", "to relax"! Or just, "this moment of relaxation" "perks up" "my brain cells"! """

"" These nooks and crannies of Poitou streets turn out to be for me "the **Fellow** JULIO", ingenuity "structure" """

"" and "ingenuity", all at once! """

"" These nooks and crannies of Poitou streets turn out to be for me, "the man JULIO", "the structure", "good – natured" and "authority" at once! " " " " ".

It was that way, Julio Fernandez was therefore actually returned home without his "Artemis EVELYN"; that, where she would end up with him, the

Antigone 's "Faller ¾ Down" Giraud ZEFRINO in a hotel room in Lyon, there would not even picture; because:

as was for example the case for Ghislaine FERNANDEZ and Olivier GAUTHIER in "**A True Untimely Awareness**";

or as was also the case for Chatelaine Johannes FERNANDEZ and Lucian CHAPERON in "**Nervous Depression or Grief of Love**";

or as it was still also the case for Chatelaine Johannes FERNANDEZ and Lucian CHAPERON in: " **Torment of "JULIO, Descent From Poitevese**" ";

or as was also the case "delusional memories", "raised" by Maryvonne KEVILER, about "their somersaults" with Julio Fernandez, in "**A Therapy For Ultimate Save Their Children**";

or like this would therefore also, as became the case for her: Evelyn MULER; and him the **Juliet's Killer** Giraud ZEFRINO in this monograph present here, entitled "**Impacts of the**" Other Justice " ";

and the couple "in one nighters' – here" would be yet immensely apparently; and he also expresses intensely with "sulfurous physical practices".

She, Evelyn MULER and he, the **Penelope's Killer** Giraud ZEFRINO, ensured by example for "the love life of the couple"; and that, by "multiple positions and variants", "an extraordinary intimacy" and a "coring" "rear" very deep. "And about precisely" "the rear infiltration", he loved Evelyn MULER squats for example; and he, the **Arian 's "Faller ¾ Down"** Giraud ZEFRINO, liked to sit with his "**forks well hung's**" ("And that ah!", she Evelyn MULER and him, the **Cleopatra's Killer** Giraud ZEFRINO, certainly, these were "parts of hams" for "all the afternoon, almost: nonstop", "on Saturday, the day of their arrival in this City of Lyon", "and there they were the same immensely"!). And always, for "their pileups" and as was the case for Chatelaine Johannes FERNANDEZ and Lucian CHAPERON; hence, to Evelyn MULER and Giraud ZEFRINO, and coincidentally also love to Evelyn MULER "coring" "rear". And as a just "variations" "the infiltration" "back", she Evelyn MULER loved to sit with hers "drumsticks" "very, very torn"; and entering "knuckles" "well flexed her **Artemis 's "Faller ¾ Down"** Giraud ZEFRINO, Evelyn MULER and the latter Giraud ZEFRINO" ("And that ah!"!; course, these were "parts of hams" for "all afternoon, almost: nonstop", "on Saturday, the day of their arrival in this City of Lyon", "and there they were the same immensely"!). And tenaciously for "their **boom – boom**" and as always was about "the transformation" of "the infiltration" "back", she Evelyn MULER sitting for example; and "hams"; "the suburbs"; "hers **bridges player**" and hers feet resting on him, the **Judith's Killer** "Giraud ZEFRINO". (And that ah!, "she Evelyn MULER and him, the **Celimene 's "Faller ¾ Down"** Giraud ZEFRINO, of course, these were" parts of hams "for" all afternoon, "almost": "nonstop", "on Saturday, the day of their arrival in this City of Lyon", "and there they were the same immensely"!). And "ineradicably", "tucked in their" we do not even telling not: How "you had for example, inflate the Nymphs". ("And that ah!," she Evelyn MULER and he, the **Fatima's Killer** Giraud ZEFRINO!, of course, these were "butter" to "almost all night: no stop", ["the night from Saturday, to Sunday, the day of return to Paris"], "and there they were the same **gigantically**"!).

It is not even telling item: How to "**multiple intensive inter – gender frictions**", "we did for example, inflate the **glans**" ("And that ah!", she, Evelyn MULER and he, the **Iphigenia 's "Faller ¾ Down"** Giraud ZEFRINO!, of course, these were "**belly dancing, bingo**" to "almost all night: no stop", ["the night from Saturday, to Sunday, the day of return to Paris"], "and there they were the same **immeasurably**"!).

It is not even telling not: How, for "**multiple intensive inter – gender frictions**", "we did for example, make red – hot labia". ("And that ah!", she, Evelyn MULER and him, the **Joan of Arc's Killer** Giraud ZEFRINO, certainly, these were "property" to "almost all night: no stop", ["the night from Saturday, to Sunday, the day of return to Paris"], "and there they were the same **inexhaustibly**"!).

It cannot tell the point: How to "**multiple intensive inter – gender frictions**", "it was for example, make red – hot nymphs". ("And that ah!", she, Evelyn MULER and he, the **Juno 's "Faller ¾ Down"** Giraud ZEFRINO!; certainly, these were "parts of **bones dancing**" for "all the morning on Sunday" [, that is to say, "to the surroundings, a little before Twelve Hours"] "and there: They were the same **prodigiously**"!).

It is not even telling item: How to "**multiple intensive inter – gender frictions**", "we did for example, to flush acorn". ("And that ah!", she, Evelyn

MULER and he, the **Countess 's Killer** Giraud ZEFRINO!; of course, these were "parts bolsters" for "all the morning on Sunday" [, that is to say, "to the surroundings, a little before Twelve Hours"]; "and there they were the same **monumentally**"!).

It is not even telling the point: How "**you had for example, burning, big lips**" with "**multiple intensive inter – gender frictions**". ("And that ah!", she, Evelyn MULER and he, the **Salome 's "Faller ¾ Down"** Giraud! ZEFRINO, certainly, these were "bolsters parts" for "all the morning on Sunday" [; that is to say: "to the surroundings, a little before Twelve Hours"], "and there they were the same **immensely**"!).[1].

And so it was for them (and this is to say to him, "the **Duchess 's Killer**" Giraud ZEFRINO" and for her, the naive Evelyn MULER) "compelling events"; "**Compelling** events"; or rather "**concretization indisputable**"; "**Incontestable embodiments**", "**charming sins**", "**impetuously made**".

---

[1] Cf. Isaac Mampuya Samba:

1 - "A True untimely Awareness".

2 - "Nervous Depression or Grief Love".

3 - "Torment of" JULIO, Descent From Poitevese.".

4 - "An Ultimate Therapy To Save Their Children".

In short, to be better able to succeed beyond measure: all this and all that and all that, "**the Seduce of the hearts**, Giraud ZEFRINO" had agreed to consume bluntly: "the Methamphetamines" to better "perk" or "rejuvenate" "masculinity" or "manhood". He also slip; and that, "smart", in "cutting" "champagne" of the naive EVELYN ["intelligently" and above all without her knowledge, of course]; when in fact, before we can begin, "**their low justices**", "**they would sip**" "**golden champagne**". And in this way, without really too much, too much, do it by example, attention [How?], The Naive EVELYN in question would notice that in "this adulterous then", she would do and yet for the first in her life, "femininity" or rather "libido" is tenfold; and moreover, she would not feel "apparently" "not at all", fatigue in action.

And so, it would be for them (and that is to say: to him, "the **Sulamite 's "Faller ¾ Down"** Giraud ZEFRINO" and for her naive Evelyn MULER) "**compelling events**"; or rather "**compelling realizations**" "**charming sins**", "**impetuously made**".

And so it would be combos of "**lovely soft**" on "**charming nicer**" on "**cute charming**" on "**charming pleasures**" on "**charming sins**"; except of course, when multiple short breaks, "**both sinners-adulterers**" would, when, occasionally, they would have "little hollow bellies"; and "they would devour", "sandwiches they acquired in the same City of Lyon", and also, they would order meals in the restaurant of their luxury hotel; which meal they had been served in their room, of course. They "would swallow" while continuing to "sip" "pink champagne".

And so, "**with of course the help of these substances that stimulate their central nervous systems**", "the two fornicators" not feel "extrinsically" not [; or otherwise: at least not yet] fatigue; which, indeed, "the invading" already, but only "inherently". And they would feel in virtually effects, once, indeed returned to Paris on Sunday, in the afternoon. And even in the HST back, "these two fornicators in question" would stop only little doze.

Speaking of "almost" exactly, it should be added that, "virtually":

Plus, "the two sinners", "charming sins" "were their sweet charming";

Moreover, they still had the urge to want to immediately follow up with "other pretty charming";

and they had finished chain immediately with: "other pretty charming";

Moreover, they still had the urge to want to immediately follow up with "other" "cute charming";

and they had finished chain immediately with: "other cute charming";

Moreover, they still had the urge to want to immediately follow up with "other" "charming pleasures";

and they had finished chain immediately with: "other charming pleasures";

Moreover, they still had the urge to want to immediately follow up with "other" "charming sins";

and they had finished chain immediately with: "other" "charming sins";

Moreover, they still had the urge to want to immediately follow up with "other" "lovely sweet"; and so on; for not even say for example and so endless, what!

Ah!, "Amphetamines" or rather: "Methamphetamines": it is something huh! This really is: a thing eh! They will "destroying" intrinsically; but you do not even realize, yourself! "You do not even realize you yourself"; this is because: extrinsically, you are very, very "refreshed as" or "refreshed".

And so, it would be for them (and that is to say: for him, the "Flirty Giraud ZEFRINO" and for her, the naive Evelyn MULER) "impulsive and enthusiastic ardor"; if not, and so, **it would be for them, "an undeniable vicious circle"; which would prove to be "very, very difficult to stop to be caught up in the system".**

In short, **with "these powerful enhancing drugs"; with "these powerful painkillers"** and it would therefore be **"formidable cravings** increasingly frantic", "dive" and "actively continue", "falling back" "in the sins of the flesh".

In one night, certainly a "white – night" Evelyn MULER really had with "the **Princess 's Killer** Giraud ZEFRINO", "**a love life enough sulfurous couple**". Him, "**the ladies man**; that is to say: "he, the **Venus 's "Faller ¾ Down"** Giraud ZEFRINO" that, yet he found himself far in the City of Lyon, on mission of work [And what a job! A subversive work of course.]. Rejoicing for "**this charmer of hearts**; that is to say, for him, the **Archduchess 's Killer** Giraud ZEFRINO" was ultimately to him, "**a bonus in kind**". [**And what a bonus! "A pretty herd prime" and "fairly fiendish", of course.**]. This "Seduce petticoats"; that is to say: "he, the **Baroness 's "Faller ¾ Down"** Giraud ZEFRINO" can certainly be delighted [And how! With "**a sulfurous joy**"]; **but above all, it hardly forgotten at all, at all, he found himself then to Lyon, on mission of work, very, very highly paid; which he would still feel, very, very large sum, as a "balance any account of the mission"; "when it would end to repudiate Evelyn MULER well actually, from her marital home"; and that, therefore, Julio Fernandez remain with "free rein", "to be able to get back together with Maryvonne KEVILER".**

And stuff and stuff and all that, unfortunately! Her "poor" Evelyn MULER precisely, she knew nothing at all, at all. She did not see that far, that "**the fire**". And when she knew the reality of this adventure, it would actually alas!, indeed too late; and consequently, she would only have eyes for whining.

In short, in one night, certainly a "white – night" Evelyn MULER really had with "the **heartthrob** Giraud ZEFRINO", "**a love life enough sulfurous couple**". She had really had ("**the love life**") as if it were for example "a real **brutalizesv**"; which would have exchanged her body against "hundreds of billions dollars and cents"; when it was not even at all, at all the case. It was in fact, as "just a formal verbal guarantee of promise of marriage" after the divorce, that "**Madam 's Killer** Giraud ZEFRINO" pushed her to apply to her husband Julio Fernandez.

And yeah!, ih! With "nothing but a mere formal guarantee of promise of marriage" after the divorce that he uttered request to her husband Julio Fernandez, her Evelyn MULER and he, the **Shepherdess 's "Faller ¾**

Down" Giraud ZEFRINO (; "a formal guarantee of promise of marriage and yet" "tacit" and "unwritten": "certainly not" and in "one nighters' so to speak"), **they would live "moments of intense fullness".** They amuse **"acrobatics" "high – flying"** to express ourselves in this way; while with him Julio Fernandez precisely, it was not the same; or it does not even accept that it, "makes him" "play" (as opposed to [her predecessor] or better express it: "her predecessor" Maryvonne KEVILER). For her, Evelyn MULER be honest it was actually just lived for her: as **"a true synonym of venereal fullness".**

And after finishing "deliver" "of such very, very intensive battles"; and this: without sleep, they [; that is to say: he, "the **Bimbo 's Killer"** "Giraud ZEFRINO" and her naïve, Evelyn MULER] **would return to Paris, completely punctured; completely exhausted.** They would say to each other, consequently: "As soon as we arrive", one and one "or" "one and one" ["home"], "the first thing to do" and that is to "shoot up quite a nap".

Illustration:
And already in the HST train back to Paris, if not already would stop, to snooze [and for good reason].
In short, with **"these doping products",** it would be so, so **"formidable cravings increasingly frantic", "dive"** and **"actively continue", "falling back" "in the sins of the flesh".**

Just by trying to imagine how his wife was **"plowing"** with **"another prankster"** in Lyon, JULIO would not stop to derail; and he would say, for example: » " »"

" « "These nooks and crannies of Poitou streets turn out to be for me", "the model JULIO": "the structure" of "innocence" and "intelligence", all at once! »"

" "This paradigm Giraud" is simply "a sacred predator"! "Quite a predator"; which "prints triumphantly his grip" on the miserable JULIO! It "throne and his power" to me, whatever! This is surely a way "Computer Programmers", "tamp pawns" to "poor" "fellows" "Security Guards" who got married with "charming **queens bee** " what! Honestly, it Giraud who grows perhaps be "a funny hero"; which had managed to "getaway" with "my muse EVELYN"; but that he just forget what it is unquestionably "the first" and also "the latest" "Getaway" it has taken with "like a bird" or even "any other bird also" eh!, in his life! ""

" It is now for me, "the cuckolded JULIO" high time to begin to regret MARYVONNE! "A MARYVONNE" a priori, to be honest: at a time, "so like with this EVELYN" who decides decidedly want any cost annoy me, but for all that, "so different too", aye!, ih! The proof is: MARYVONNE was hardly challenged me in such a way here; which is beyond belief! ""

" And aye, aye!, ih! The extravagance of "**sultana**" is to: ¾ and yet always, will thwart any cost "her **yeoman**"! It's very, very certainly, to understand: What is possible with "her **gentleman** in question"? And what can be done with him? And ben eh!, eh, eh! And well no! I do not! For, "the stories of manners – here", nothing is in any case possible to do with "the **foal**, JULIO", exactly! ""

" "This Saturday morning", "the **blade** JULIO" was actually returned empty-handed; that is to say, without his "trollop EVELYN"! And so, it was believed that returning "the next Sunday night", I was going to accept her! And so, it would just once for example, that I accept "well, well soiled" with "**another prankster**"; and that would be elsewhere, like every night in the same conditions of filth: and I would still accept her! Hum mm! Always go with "another **Sir** " and always come home with "her **Swain**" and be as still, still, still, accepted by this one! Not me JULIO anyway! Anyway I no longer touch, ever so slightly, to "**such a carnal pollution**"! I would not even feel her next to me! " " " " ".

And on the eve of "this unfortunate adventure – here so", he, Julio Fernandez, he was actually returned home without his "prostitute Evelyn MULER". He was a great dive tantrum. JULIO had become as it were: "Crazy, crazy ally", "like hell". And Sunday that followed the next day, his new friend Poulain DERECK had gone home, to "make him a courtesy call" and asking the same time: If those he had spoken to him about "his **little woman** EVELYN" were also true. In reality, him, POULAIN being paid for power also play a duet but slyly [; that is to say, neither seen nor known] a role no less subversive. He was paid to support a reality quite so tactile, the **Damsel 's Killer** Giraud; POULAIN this one, was indeed, come check: If the Machiavellian task they undertook, followed well and truly underway. And if she was going to do well; and that he and his accomplice POULAIN and the **Countess 's "Faller ¾ Down"** Giraud, would indeed be substantially paid; as he had promised; because they relied heavily on "these washers" they would touch, in carrying out this mission. Now the challenge is based on the fact that Evelyn accepts challenge "his **Master** JULIO" and therefore go with the **Chick 's "Faller ¾ Down"** Giraud; and so "this sordid task" would have freed thus: "**a process of no return**". And in doing so, every step of the mission that remained, they would be "as the nougat"; or rather, "that train wheels, rolling course on track".

Arriving at home of JULIO, POULAIN rang the doorbell. And that one would ask: " Who is it? ". And Poulain replies: " I am Poulain; Poulain DERECK, your new friend. ".

JULIO, at POULAIN: " Okay. And I get a moment you open the door. ".

And JULIO had left open the door. He had brought with him; and he told him, to sit down.

JULIO, at POULAIN: " Hello my dear friend POULAIN! What you bring me? What news? ".

Poulain, to JULIO: " Hello my dear friend JULIO! ".

JULIO, at POULAIN: " Take up my dear friend! ".

JULIO himself also take place to sit; but first he would ask his new friend, though: " You want a drink? ". ("And if yep!". "What he wanted to drink?". It would be a sweet drink. ".). And it would be so, it would look as a sweet beverage; and they would use that little by little, the drink in question; to do too much, too fill their bellies and their bladders. Once seated Poulain DERECK would ask Julio Fernandez: " Have you been able to verify for yourself, which I blew the ears you last Thursday? ".

JULIO, at POULAIN: " Indeed! What you bring her? What new POULAIN? ".

Poulain, to JULIO: " You're all alone in your room, right now here? ".

JULIO, at POULAIN: " Of course!, I am alone in fact aye! It's like you had me ... / .... ".

Poulain, to JULIO: " It's good and well, we can talk quietly without fear of being disturbed, so slightly! ".

JULIO, at POULAIN: " Affirmative! That's what I wanted to immediately tell you just now. It's like you had said my dear friend POULAIN! I could check myself, what you had blown my ear! ".

Poulain, to JULIO: " So what? ".

JULIO, at POULAIN: " You really were right indeed. ".

Poulain, to JULIO: " You were able to prevent her anyway, to follow **this manure**, of Giraud ZEFRINO, right? ".

JULIO, at POULAIN: " No! Despite all the many efforts that I had to deploy about it! Unfortunately alas!, I am not able to do exactly! I am not able to prevent her anyway, to follow **this manure**! ".

Poulain, to JULIO: " But! And why you did not succeed? ".

JULIO, at POULAIN: " This is to say that I had tried everything; but "my ugliness" was limited; and she did not want at all, at all listen me. ".

Poulain, to JULIO: " She thought you wanted to inhibit what happiness!".

JULIO, at POULAIN: " Excuse me? ".

Poulain, to JULIO: " She thought you were doing everything to prevent her happiness to have anything! ".

JULIO, at POULAIN: " Absolutely. ".

Poulain, to JULIO: " It took him and talk it in the presence of "this **Girl 's "Faller ¾ Down"** ZEFRINO in question", all those I had known you, about him precisely. ".

JULIO, at POULAIN: " But it was what I had done. ".

Poulain, to JULIO: " So what? ".

JULIO, at POULAIN: " My dear friend POULAIN! If I kept telling them that "my own bug" was suggested to me! You do not believe much at all, at all, in your ears! ".

Poulain, to JULIO: "What she told you, for example? ".

JULIO, at POULAIN: " She told me, for example, [I quote]: " ... / ... In short, I will not go into the apartment with you today; since I'll take that train a little while to another, will ring the hour of departure, its dock! I'm going with this "Sir" ZEFRINO, at Lyon and nobody can stop me; except himself Giraud ZEFRINO! Or just him, he would issue. He would not for the simple reason that the idea of taking from "good time" "me and him together," so from just himself. And it comes from him; it's because he loves me and wants to make me happy. And also with him, I **hardly need to take contraceptive measures**! On the contrary, above all, not at all, at all, take it! I go with him; and then at my coming with you; too bad for the real consequences thereof as a result of this I'm going to flirt with that Giraud! Or to better express it: So much for the real consequences that would result as a result of this very act, of adultery; which one I am about to commit eminently with this stylish and gallant Giraud. ". [End of quote.]. ".

J ULIO at POULAIN: " Hmm mm! "... / ... As a result of this very act, of adultery; which one I am about to commit eminently with this stylish and gallant Giraud!". Hold such derogatory remarks to her husband! ".

Poulain, to JULIO: " She said that? ".

JULIO,at POULAIN: " Absolutely! ".

Poulain, to JULIO: " Anyway, it's like you had said it yourself: I do not believe at my ears! Really "the **females**" eh! It ah! Incredible! ".

JULIO, at POULAIN: " It is yet true! This is yet frank truth! And please believe me! ".

Poulain, to JULIO: " But I think eh! But only such things anyway: "... / ... As a result of this very act, of adultery; which one I am about to commit eminently with this stylish and gallant Giraud!". Actually hold as you say yourself my dear friend JULIO, of such derogatory remarks in her husband eh! Say so! Frankly eh! In any case such a response was undoubtedly strengthened the position of the **Fair sex's "Faller ¾ Down"** ZEFRINO, absolutely want to go with your wife eh! ".

JULIO, at POULAIN: " How! ".

Poulain, to JULIO: " It ah!, that's for sure! ".

JULIO, at POULAIN: " And how! ".

Poulain, to JULIO: " And what he had said this **Rebecca's Killer**, listening to such a response from the lips of "your lobster"? ".

JULIO, at POULAIN: "Listening to it, it had systematically, the **Shrew's "Faller ¾ Down"** just told me [I quote]: " "Sir"? "Mister" FERNANDEZ? "Mister" Julio Fernandez? Have you heard all those "**your old bag**" just let you hear herself without she, they are forced? So eh! If I were in your place; I understand there, there would be nothing at all, at all, to save between me and a "Rebecca" that spits me in my ears, such truths! ". [End of quote.]. ".

Poulain, to JULIO: " Hmm mm! Like that ah! And without the slightest complacency!".

JULIO, at POULAIN: " Without the slightest complacency ih!, yep!, indeed!".

Poulain, to JULIO: " It ah! G 'has something to let someone speechless!".

JULIO, at POULAIN: " Indeed! ".

Poulain, to JULIO: " It ah! ".

JULIO, at POULAIN: " Indeed I had stayed a few seconds speechless. I was completely stunned, before pull myself together and meet him after all ... / .... ".

Poulain, to JULIO " Aye!, ih!, ih, ih! And meet him after all? And what you had told him? ".

JULIO, at POULAIN: " Before the last EVELYN response and the response of this **Delilah's Killer** about it; I was really freaked! ".

Poulain, to JULIO: " I understand that indeed! ".

JULIO, at POULAIN: "And I could only answer that " **Agnes 's "Faller ¾ Down"** "Giraud ZEFRINO [I quote myself]: " Okay **"Eva's Killer"** lover of **"my lettuce"**! Okay I quite understand! I'll let you continue your journey! And I go home in the Eleventh Arrondissement of Paris! ". And actually I had returned home so far this Street Oberkampf! ".

Poulain, to JULIO: " It's really sad, we get there, overnight eh! And when she goes back home, you'll also accept again **to resume with "such ugliness" that would copiously dirty like** that? ".

JULIO, at POULAIN: "Who? Me? Accept again **to resume with "such a bitch" who would heartily dirty like that**? It ah!, never, ever, never and ever! Never in my life! There is no question! Look! She'll be back today Sunday, according to their program! And since it is already beginning to make tonight! I think she will perhaps more to come soon! Hence, if you want; you might expect here at home a little longer. Thus, you will yourself to witness live, to put it this way on her return. And consequently, you listen everyone I will tell to her! ".

Poulain, to JULIO: "Okay. And besides, I bet this " **Antigone 's "Faller ¾ Down"** ";Iwould rather say: And in addition, as a **Daughter of Eva's Killer** who was comforted in his position as subversive than anything else really, for "your own bitch"; he would not hesitate, to walk her home so far; that is to say, far from what you JULIO! ".

In truth, it was a well – hung scenario; that is to say, according to the well – established first plane, Poulain DERECK would precede this apartment located on the Street Oberkampf, only a few hours before the scheduled time of the return of his accomplice, the **Arian 's "Faller ¾ Down"** Giraud ZEFRINO and "the slut" Julio Fernandez. And like that, he would inevitably attend to what had been planned by them these subversive as **"the point of no turning back**; that is to say": **the point where the cuckolded Julio Fernandez, he could never, ever, never, ever and never forgive "his bitch"**. And within a few short moments only more effectively, we rang the doorbell of the apartment of JULIO. He left open that one and it was also "called his EVELYN" returning; and she was actually escorted as provided by the **Juliet's Killer**; like Poulain DERECK had previously said to Julio Fernandez. Hum mm! and she was actually escorted as provided by the

Artemis 's "Faller ¾ Down" Giraud ZEFRINO, to the front of the door where lived between others – EVELYN. EVELYN and the **Penelope's Killer** Giraud just seemed to be completely crappy [And for good reason!] what's more, **"they felt the bottle"**, **"two – meter radius"**. Poulain DERECK and one which, in reality, they knew very well [And for good reason!] and who knew exactly: those they were doing and they were even so to speak, to perfection; they had done "a blink of eye fast and unnoticed, to express ourselves in this way", before Giraud, the gallant and elegant **Celimene's "Faller ¾ Down"**, not forgot to tell EVELYN: "Goodbye EVELYN; and at the next!". In reality, the **Cleopatra's Killer** Giraud ZEFRINO who knew what was going to be the sequence of events; or rather, that he knew what was going to be the reaction of Julio Fernandez; he had gone to wait at the mouth of the nearest Metro N°1 Previously he had told EVELYN: Where he never expected one if it was actually more accepted among JULIO. And EVELYN also agreed. What neither EVELYN or JULIO knew what all that front, also known Poulain DERECK, for the simple reason that he, too, assisted in its preparation. When Giraud had finished saying only: "Goodbye EVELYN; and the next!"; Julio Fernandez, had replied: " Wait " Sir **Eurydice 's "Faller ¾ Down"** "! Hold on! You'll come away with her pronto! Because not only that you love; but also "an otter" and copiously soiled myself Julio Fernandez "Descent From Poitevese And Background On Spanish Descendants"; I can find most of all, at all of interest! I do not wish at all, at all! In doing so, I could accept her anymore! It is now up to you to promise her so much joy and happiness! ".

But the **Judith's Killer** Giraud ZEFRINO just, would not wait either. He would leave as for example an arrow. He would go back to full speed. In reality, he would not go too far; since only go wait at the mouth of the nearest Metro[1]. And all those details – here just were also meticulously planned in the script, written together between: him, Poulain DERECK and the **Iphigenia 's "Faller ¾ Down"** Giraud ZEFRINO, first; and on the other hand, their direct sponsor Thierry Glorian.

---

[1]   The nearest to where JULIO and EVELYN praised Metro, it was "pie" in the Eleventh Arrondissement of Paris; or otherwise: Metro Oberkampf.

Julio Fernandez told to "his **femininestar**" to take hers most important cases; and walk away with the **Fatima's Killer**; as for hers other businesses, she would return another day during the day, to recover them. And she would also make it so. Poulain DERECK who had witnessed at this sad scene; he said immediately afterwards, to Julio: "Goodbye Julio Fernandez!". And he would go around the same time that Evelyn until the Metro Station [1]

But, POULAIN about him, he did then verily, that cling to the character that was yours; he was then actually activate that, to perform the steps of the proposed roles for him in details that were meticulously orchestrated in the script, written together between: him POULAIN and he, Giraud, first; and on the other hand, their direct sponsor Thierry Glorian.

Once in the latter place, Poulain DERECK seeing the **Juno 's "Faller ¾ Down"** Giraud ZEFRINO waiting there [And for good reason!] he wanted to beat him up; or rather, he wanted to fight with him; he wanted the same bump off; the bump off by strangulation. But only here, "it was not for real!". [Scenarios – forced]. The **Joan of Arc's Killer** who knew this also be a very, very good actor; and also knew memorize the details of his role; he not therefore: How to dispel suspicions that suddenly begin to fester in the mind of EVELYN. [But these suspicions precisely which begin abruptly already hatching in the mind of EVELYN were also meticulously planned in the script, written together between: him POULAIN and he, the **Salome 's "Faller ¾ Down"** Giraud, first; and on the other hand, their direct sponsor Thierry Glorian]. This Poulain DERECK recall anyway, in accomplice (the **Countess 's Killer** Giraud); and that, more or less quietly and speed, without really noticing Evelyn do something, those that were predicted for both of them, rushing to perform at this stage, their mission. And all would unfold in fact, as if it were for example clockwork. It should be added that even the fact that "POULAIN talk to his accomplice, the **Sulamite 's "Faller ¾ Down"** Giraud, more or less quietly and speed, without really noticing Evelyn do something!". Was carefully detailed in the script, that would activate two accomplices to carry the letter.

POULAIN therefore face the **Duchess 's Killer** Giraud executes any theatricality that had been provided for this purpose.

Short, and the reaction of the **Venus 's "Faller ¾ Down"** ZEFRINO was also as expected in the first time and still quite quietly; that is to say, more or less silently, so that "the naive **broad**" "Evelyn MULER" " Cannot hear, "Okay!". The fact is, as was provided for in the script, written together between: me POULAIN and you the **Princess 's Killer** Giraud, first; and on the other hand, our direct sponsor Thierry Glorian; that is to say: we do like you just remind me, what! ".

Then in a second time actually; suddenly; and to the astonishment of all "loafers" who found themselves very, very fast, around him; POULAIN taking with her two muscular hands, shot the **Baroness's "Faller ¾ Down"** Giraud; he would seem very, very strong, while also shaking the apparently very, very strong too. In doing so, he also tried to defend himself apparently shouting also very, very strong: "But let me go! But you'll let me, aye!". And they were also released. And "assaulted the **Archduchess 's Killer** Giraud" was released. And therefore he had escaped by running "at Hundred Kilometers an Hour's Time"; while saying very, very strong, about her attacker: " Oh!, ah! This guy is really just a batty! He really is "crazy, crazy!". He wanted to strangle me! ".

However, EVELYN which had anyway, anyway, preview some signs; some facts and passed quietly enough gestures (although, to be placed a little further than the two gentlemen, who would speak, or rather: which would murmur more or less silently, and that it in turn, and she could therefore not listen to words) between "Sir" Giraud ZEFRINO, "her lover" and the other "honest man" whom she met by chance, chatting with her "coconut JULIO"; and which furthermore be found "friend" of the latter; **she would only see the fire**. However, she started for a few brief moments, to have within him, some feelings of suspicion. Therefore, she would remove immediately from her mind, all these few feelings of suspicion in question precisely.

When the **Shepherdess 's "Faller ¾ Down"** Giraud fled "to Hundred Kilometers an Hour's Time"; immediately after also POULAIN would go get his Metro and he was gone. And immediately after, the **Madam 's Killer** Giraud would return to EVELYN; to speak to her; or rather to continue talking with her, as they were already together since the day before, in the morning. And for that, she had asked the question [whether] to "his lover" Giraud: " Do you know what "Sir"? ".

Giraud, at EVELYN: " No ohm! ".

EVELYN, to Giraud: " But why did he bump off you, by strangulation; and that, in the presence of all "walkers" nearby? But why you are saved you like that, saying [I quote your words]: "Oh!, ah! This guy is really a jerk! He's really come! He wanted to strangle me! ". As if it were for example two antagonists; two enemies who once knew; they had lost sight of; and which, when they meet again; they wanted to fight with fists; or rather, with a duel to the death of one of the two? ".

The Response of the **Countess 's "Faller ¾ Down"** Giraud, to EVELYN was: " Not at all! I do not know him at all! I had only preview today, trying to talk to "your **Samson**"; when I escorted you home! And coincidentally, I saw him almost come together with you so far in the Station, so really, to take his Metro. I really thought he was coming to get me and that in any case he would find me; he would pass me by example, mercilessly beaten, because of this act of adultery that I made with you EVELYN; and this: at the expense of his friend JULIO; that is to say, at the expense of "your bird"! So I got cold feet ever! I seriously believed he had to impose me, a sacred correcting; it is because I have so break the household of his friend JULIO with you EVELYN! Hence, I started to greet him, lest he be angry, for example, much against me. And then I tried to continue the conversation by saying anything that came into my head. But ever in fear, I said more or less silently! I stammered anything; and this more or less silently; so that not only that it "this clown" friend of "your zebra JULIO", he hears nothing, really; so that not only he does not understand anything, really; because having heard nothing; and more importantly, for having nothing got it; but also and even primarily for: he says at the bottom of himself for example: " But! But it is not a patsy this Dredger of "Delilah" for others! ". ".

˝And that therefore he rather the friend "your coconut JULIO" he finally fear me Giraud! I Giraud, the goofy, which might have eventually to assault him! And that, moreover, he can save himself; especially not me; and that, "at Hundred Kilometers per Hour's Time"! And alas!, it was more, this friend of "your horse", the cuckold JULIO put me through! And aye!, ih! Rather, it was him that made me flee "to Hundred Kilometers per Hour"! And aye, aye!, ih! Myself Giraud, who believed scare "in Hundred Kilometers per Hour"! It was more to myself that we did flee "to Hundred Kilometers per Hour"! And it was as a result, I let him hear Giraud who just: "Oh!, ah! This guy is actually a come!". "That's all! He's fear! He scared me, I thought, yet scare him! Me Giraud that finally I actually thought him more afraid; that I would have done!". ˝.

Anyway, when the **Bimbo 's Killer** Giraud had apparently fled "to Hundred Kilometers per Hour". Immediately after also POULAIN would go get his Metro. And he was gone. And right after too, the **Chick 's "Faller ¾ Down"** Giraud returned to EVELYN; to continue talking to her. It was actually, to begin immediately with her; and that, without that herself cannot understand something, **the process of the second phase of their sordid mission**. (But all those details just were also meticulously planned in the script, written together between: him POULAIN and he, the **Damsel's Killer** Giraud, on the one hand, and on the other hand, their direct sponsor Thierry Glorian).

The **Girl's "Faller ¾ Down"** Giraud just him, he would suggest to EVELYN: " Ooh! What I was hot just now! What is he scared me that guy! ".

EVELYN, to Giraud: " I confess before you did hot just now! I confess that before this guy, a friend of "my guy JULIO" do you fear! That for a while, I watched him speak more or less silently indeed! And while almost all the time you spoke to him; he did not meet you too. And I confess that for a while I was watching you; even though I was listening to nothing those you darling Giraud, you were talking to "this issue" "friend JULIO"; it's because I was away! I admit that some signs; some facts and gestures that conversation as I watched from afar; reminded me that you did and the Giraud you express; so it looks like you did not want me to understand those you said to him! And I admit very, very solemnly! ".

Giraud, at EVELYN: " It was no more, no less, the fear that I felt, seeing "this horse ", one would say: head straight to me, so to speak; fear that had driven me to this course of action almost sneaky; consisting in the back that same fear; and this in a much more subtle way; and that, in a much more refined way; and that's it huh! Hence, it would just understand me! ".

EVELYN, to Giraud: " But I've come to understand you very, very well eh!".

Giraud, at EVELYN: " Thank you! ".

EVELYN, to Giraud: " You're welcome! ".

Giraud, at EVELYN: " Thank you! ".

EVELYN, to Giraud: " Okay! And now, what we gonna do; since as expected, and you knew beforehand that JULIO does not want at all, at all from me; because I had challenged? ".

Giraud, at EVELYN: " I think: I'll let you hear now EVELYN, does not go shock you: At the moment, it would be essential, I'll walk myself Giraud, even your parents to Corbeil – Essonne. But I want you to report it immediately; I'm not going to meet them! Or at least, not now! It's a little too early and too brutal! ".

EVELYN, to Giraud: " At my parents to Corbeil – Essonne? ".

Giraud, at EVELYN: " It certainly should not take it bad huh!, EVELYN! Let us displease one or the other; or rather one and the other! The people love so much too! So we will not start now especially to shock us! But only here, is it that for now, there is no other alternative than this! And then there; we would see! That said, it should certainly not be angry! ".

EVELYN, to Giraud: ""And then there; we would see!". In the conditional plus: "And then there; we would see!". ".

Giraud, at EVELYN: " Absolutely! But I repeat: it should certainly hardly put you in all your statements! Stop and offend against me ah! ".

EVELYN, to Giraud: " But I dream or what! ".

Giraud, at EVELYN: " You are not dreaming. That's the reality. But do not be angry for that ah! It would eventually work out eh! Eh! Stop and offend against me ah! Eh! ".

EVELYN, to Giraud: " Always the conditional: "It would end ... / ...!". "But?". ".

Giraud, at EVELYN: " But what? Once you let go yet to anger! Then stop and have you against me! ".

EVELYN, to Giraud: "Last Saturday all afternoon; all night from Saturday to Sunday was spent; and this without sleep so little; this morning today Sunday you so to say, a non – stop manner (: and this, it seems as a result of strong performance – enhancing drugs), abused me! **But me EVELYN, I said nothing; since I was your partner, accomplice of adultery! I was even happy to rejoice with you quite copiously Giraud! And all this vast time I still liked you wonderfully! And now: now suddenly, I do not please you more, it seems! And this, after copiously polluted me! And that, after "my gentleman JULIO" I challenged, following your advice, do not want "a bug" and copiously dirty! Hmm mm! And just today; you would not want me anymore, it seems!**

You do not want me, just at a time when "my good man" fired me (and for good reason and I do not even give it wrong elsewhere! Since I would be in his place, I would do the same !) But "what penury!". ".

Giraud, at EVELYN: " There, you're still violently irritated EVELYN! Wait! It's not that ah! It's not what you think! So, stop and scramble against me! Quick, I do not have enough time; plus I have very, very sleepy! It goes ... / ...! ".

EVELYN, to Giraud: " But I also like you, I did not sleep that night (and for good reason! You know this because besides!) doing so, I also I have very, very sleepy! ".

Giraud, at EVELYN: " What violent discontent! Wait! It's not that ah! It's not what you think! All the more reason I bring you quickly to your parents; you to go to sleep; and that I, too, go back to sleep with me! Hence, we will have, I wanted to tell you, I'll walk you to your parents for now; and later, we would see! So stop your quarrel against me about this! ".

EVELYN, to Giraud: « **"And then we would see!". Anyway, JULIO was right: You just want to get what you wanted; that is to say, "pollute me" "copiously enough"; and then dump me mercilessly; and now it happened; and yeah!, when: it is too late; such as JULIO said! What do I do? Oh!, I do not find an answer! From whom, shall I cry? But what do I do? Ah!, it annoys me that I cannot find an answer! ».**

Giraud at, EVELYN: " What aggressive towards me moving! Wait! It's not that ah! It's not what you think! Come quickly and without wasting time again, I'll take you home to your parents! So do not put yourself at odds against me more about that ".

EVELYN, to Giraud: " If this is really so! ... / ...! ".

Giraud, at EVELYN: " You're suffering from severe irritation there! But wait! It's not that ah! It's not what you think! But is it: it is really so ih! And this is not a joke! So do not fret against me! ".

EVELYN, to Giraud: " If this is really so! So I answer: No! ".

Giraud, at EVELYN: " Anger take you forever! But wait! It's not that ah! It's not what you think! Not take you much against me! You said, "No!". So not what? ".

EVELYN, to Giraud: " No, it is not worth it, to escort me to my parents; it is because I know the way myself! ".

Giraud, at EVELYN: " Again and again always angry! But wait! It's not that ah! It's not what you think! I'll walk you to your parents; because I very thoughtful indeed, in the meantime, while I was waiting for you here in the Metro Station! And I very, very well understood: in order that we do not is wrong both us and especially you in the eyes of the Law; or to put it more precisely: so that we do not have both of us wrong in the eyes of justice; the eyes of the State; you should absolutely first; and that, as soon as possible, get the divorce, from the matrimonial judge, before I can have that freedom as it were Lawful, can coexist; and later, to marry you! In short, do not pretend this crisis of wickedness that you just suddenly feel against me; since I just, I love you immensely; and I swear that in wishing me EVELYN legally marry you! ".

And it was "**that way quite clever and quite particularly Machiavellian**" that the household of EVELYN was ruined; and it was also "**that way quite diplomatic**", that she had agreed to go back to her parents. But only she was a party alone anyway. In short, it was this way that the household of "this naïve **womanish**" had been wasted. It was as a result of false promises from a certain **Rebecca's Killer** Giraud ZEFRINO [and for good reason]. EVELYN had left all alone with hers parents. And another day; and that with a courier vehicle, rented with his driver, it was distributed as planned, recover all hers other businesses, she had left JULIO's home.

Decidedly EVELYN was sad; and therefore, such as depression MARYVONNE known threatened. And some small, short days only, as expected, " the **Fair sex's "Faller ¾ Down"** " Giraud ZEFRINO and "Sir" Poulain DERECK actually had gone to meet with "Sir" Thierry Glorian, the faithful worker butcher from "Mr. and 'Madam" Moses KEVILER and at the same time, the man who was responsible for carrying out this subversive mission; to save this ultimate way there, the only daughter of the latter. THIERRY asked these two people there: " And then guys? First wait for me to go pick you refreshing! A second and then I get and I am yours! ".

And a few minutes later, too, He would meet Thierry Glorian and Poulain DERECK: " We are on track! The first stage was very, very well. We have virtually reached now, "**the point of no turning back**"! All steps to come that would take place as smoothly! ".

Listening this reply from his friend Poulain DERECK, "the Giraud ZEFRINO" add same to the attention of their direct sponsor THIERRY: " The mission is the same, almost completed chef! This is because "**the chick**" in question; that is to say, "the doll" of Julio Fernandez, is finally returned to hers parents! ".

THIERRY, to Giraud: " How can you be so sure and so confident, to express that:" ... / ... That "Baroness" in question; that is to say: "The Countess" of Julio Fernandez, is finally returned to hers parents! ". ".

Giraud, at THIERRY: " This is because the decision had taken her husband Julio Fernandez, had finally sworn that, Evelyn will not to return to the marital home; if ever that "his crate EVELYN just" stubbornly follow me; before we go in to flirting at Lyon; this decision is and will remain, he said: constant; immutable and irreversible. ".

THIERRY, to Giraud and Poulain: " Well guys! I am very pleased with you! You have very well done the first step of this delicate mission. I'm going to share it with "Sir" Moses KEVILER; which will pay you considerably, as expected. Ohm!, good, I let you keep your drink chilled; and I come back soon; since I have small storage space to the kitchen. ".

And when Poulain and Giraud remained in the living room of "Sir" Thierry Glorian; they were consequently, begin their conversation; which, in fact, it was impossible to start quickly on Sunday night in the Metro Station. However, Giraud ZEFRINO told to Poulain DERECK: " POULAIN! That night in the subway, we were brilliant! This naive EVELYN not even made unaware of our plot against her! Hmm mm! But she felt anyway in it, even if that just for a very short time, some feelings of suspicion from us! But that was not surprising, since such a reaction from her, was also included and studied closely in our script. Hence, according to this fact, I ended up doing everything to "dazzle"! Otherwise, hard, hard! ".

Poulain DERECK, to Giraud ZEFRINO: " Is she also believed in this movie that you played to her? ".

Giraud, at POULAIN: " Absolutely! Finally, she had actually understood that but **fire**! And thank goodness it was all planned in the scenario, in an attempt to dazzle! Otherwise, hard, hard! ".

Poulain, to Giraud: " It's wonderful. That's great how our texts had planned to stifle hers feelings of suspicion! ".

Giraud, at POULAIN: " It ah! ".

Poulain, to Giraud: " No matter how the situation had reached "**a level of no return**". **And therefore the household of "this poor lady" with JULIO was already doomed!** ".

Giraud, at POULAIN: " It's true. And that was the most important. ".

Poulain, to Giraud: " Yeah!, that was it, the goal of our mission. And consequently, there is nothing at all, at all, that we can do this for so damn household, in order to possibly fix things. **Because no matter how the decision of her husband JULIO, turned out to be: constant; immutable and irrefutable**! ".

Giraud, at POULAIN: " It's true! Well now, you could cause me all you wanted to cause me to the Subway Station Sunday night, waiting for the return of "Sir" Thierry Glorian making his cupboards in his kitchen; pending his return here in his living room; we, we – we find ourselves to rejoice in the misfortunes we have unfairly cause to "a poor woman"! ".

Poulain, to Giraud: " Okay! I just wanted to say that this is it! It was passed our mission! ".

Giraud, at POULAIN: " For that ah!, there is no doubt! ".

Poulain, to Giraud: " One win many "slices"; and I'm glad! ".

Giraud, at POULAIN: " Me too! ".

Poulain, to Giraud: " When I will receive this large sum "of wheels behind", representing the balance on balance; I believe that. ".

Giraud, at POULAIN: " Yep!, ih! You think? ".

Poulain, to Giraud: " I think that, I'll be able to do such a lot of traveling! This is because, since my childhood, I always dreamed to do a lot of traveling. But. ".

Giraud, at POULAIN: " But? ".

Poulain, to Giraud: " But I've never done; because. ".

Giraud, at POULAIN: " Because? ".

Poulain, to Giraud: " For even from my young youth, I never had enough money to make anything! ".

Giraud, at POULAIN: " For even very young since your youth, you've never had "sufficient **auriferous**" "in order to do anything"! ".

Poulain, to Giraud: " Absolutely! ".

Giraud, at POULAIN: " Me too, I think when I will receive this huge sum; which will be the balance after all; I will also make some trips. ".

Poulain, to Giraud: " It would really enjoy it; since with these huge numerical means that we will eventually at all! If we do not take advantage! So there is no benefit in again until the end of our lives here on this earth! ".

Giraud, at POULAIN: " You are right my friend Poulain. Also for me. ".

Poulain, to Giraud: " In addition to you? ".

Giraud, at POULAIN: " Also for me, I had as a reward in kind, to go with "this silly then", "a whole night of romance"; otherwise expressed: I had the added bonus of this mission of subversion, **to "enjoy copious nectar"**; if I could use the term "enjoy"; rather, these two terms [terms "copious" and "nectar"]! Hence further for me Giraud, I had to have the added bonus of the mission of subversion, to "savor" "copiously" "nectar" **"the delights of carnal pleasures"**, **with "this pretty EVELYN"**! And not forgetting our stay in a luxury hotel in Lyon; without that I spend one small subset of my own pocket. Instead, I'll even touch; touching enough; "touching enough", doing only a mission; a difficult task indeed; yet which on the contrary, it made me enjoy some advantages. ".

Poulain, to Giraud: " They were good" duped "she EVELYN," this naive lady "and him JULIO, **"her stupid bastard of husband"**! ".

Giraud, at POULAIN: " I will not say it! But only. ".

Poulain, to Giraud: " But only? ".

Giraud, at POULAIN: " But only, **"her stupid bastard of husband** just, (as you express it, yourself so well)", the other day; the other Saturday morning ... / .... ".

Poulain, to Giraud: " Before you go on holiday in "subversive purpose" and "well engineered" for "the City of Lyon"?.

Giraud, at POULAIN: " Absolutely. This Saturday morning, when I finally got himself very, very afraid! I had anyway been in fact very, very scared; **although the details of all these scenarios have been carefully and methodically especially prepared by ourselves the conjurers**! I wondered: If the final form was not there, the back of the success of the very, very good editing scenarios? Anyway, I really had very, very afraid! **I even thought we were inevitably fall into our own trap**! ".

Poulain, to Giraud: " Finally, the substance is that we did it! The key is that we have done our job! The key is that we finally win in all, a lot of "front wheels"! And this is the most important! ".

Giraud, at POULAIN: " Aye!, that's the most important! ".

Poulain, to Giraud: " Oh!, I'm really happy; because I can finally find myself with a good amount! ".

Giraud, at POULAIN: " If you knew how the last Saturday morning, JULIO talking about you, Poulain DERECK "as a sincere friend to him"; and me Giraud ZEFRINO, "as a vulgar adventurer"! Hmm mm! Me Giraud ZEFRINO, "as a vulgar **Delilah's Killer**"! ".

Poulain, to Giraud: " Are you kidding! Me Poulain DERECK, "as a sincere friend of him Julio"! Hmm mm! I was only there that fulfill my part of this delicate subversive mission to earn **money matters** eh!; to win many **wherewithal's**! ".

Giraud, at POULAIN: "Really I do not really stop to think how" that idiot of JULIO "not stopped talking for you my dear friend Poulain"; when "his **lettuce** EVELYN" asked him: Who he was acquainted, about me! ".

Poulain, to Giraud: " It ah! ".

Giraud, at POULAIN: " But still, I would have to recognize that for a while; I really ended up being afraid that "his stretcher EVELYN" finally listen to his persuasions! And therefore, everything falls apart before they can even begin! I was honestly afraid that this delicate mission definitely fair! ".

Poulain, to Giraud: « **It was very, very important, to take him too, like our partner; cause, without him knowing himself in the scenario; otherwise it would take place without his knowledge; and it was certainly not, ah!, that the aim sought by us, the subversives!**

It was only that "the flick well mounted and well regulated in detail" by us; to make it look real! When in truth, it was not even true! And that, consequently, it would be OK, likely to derail that delicate mission permanently. ".

Giraud, at POULAIN: " But I admit anyway that I really got scared, for a short time; or rather, for a while; this delicate mission to come to nothing! And therefore, I began to regret already, this amount of **pecunious** that "we would" miss! ".

Poulain, to Giraud: " That 'would be very sad for us eh! ".

Giraud, at POULAIN: " Fortunately, "this silly"; such as the same as saying "his own guy JULIO"; had believed in my promises, they can assure him there: a life with lots of joy and happiness; which promises I will keep obviously never, ever, never, ever and never! [And for good reason!]. ".

Poulain, to Giraud: " As soon as the mission lead; that is to say: as soon as the divorce is well underway; it will actually be: "**The Time of a large and goodbye forever**" to be there, sounded! ".

Giraud, at POULAIN: " Absolutely! It will indeed: "**The Hour of great goodbye and forever**"! To be there, stunned! ".

Poulain, to Giraud: " It ah! ".

Giraud, at POULAIN: " I told her to go to hers parents; then we would see later what we will do, of course! I told her to wait this divorce certainly! But if we reflect very, very well indeed; However, one could say without hesitation that it was already there; and as it was written in our script, "**The Goodbye and forever!**". ".

Poulain, to Giraud: " This is great; because what matters to us; it is not morality; these are not feelings; but rather: "taffeta"! Therefore, it should never, ever, never and ever that people on this Earth to be naive; Manure and listen guys like us more! If not, too bad for them! ".

Giraud, at POULAIN: " Absolutely! If not, too bad for them indeed ih!, yeah! ".

And on that last sentence, "Sir" Thierry Glorian came back into the living room. And gave them to everyone, "a large sum"; which in reality was not one: "the balance after all"; but rather, "a second installment". "The second installment much more off than the first"; so that the mentor; which had to call Moses KEVILER was very, very happy with the pace that took the mission. In short, it was not there, "a second installment". He gave them; because in truth, all the time he said he was doing in his kitchen cupboards; he actually talked with Moses KEVILER over the phone on almost all the details of this first phase of the delicate subversive mission; which was to heal and subsequently indirectly MARYVONNE; or to put it another way: which indirectly concerned, the subsequent healing "unique **butterfly**". And as Moses KEVILER was very happy; and saw that he had given so to speak, a huge sum in cash to his faithful and discreet worker butcher Thierry

Glorian; he had therefore ordered; or rather, the authorization by phone, to share part of the money which had remained until then, into two equal parts; and reward, "as the second installment to each", "two bandidos"; that is to say: to Poulain DERECK and Giraud ZEFRINO. MOSES had authorized THIERRY to use this part of "these remaining **sinews of war**", promising to pass it instead, "another large amount of sorrel" for further operations. The latter two had taken "their second installment"; they were very, very happy; and they were returned home. However, with regard to the pair [JULIO – EVELYN]; it was already: ruthlessly, legal separation, pending divorce; which showed up very, very quickly, on the horizon.

And again: just by remembering back to that dry answer to Evelyn, JULIO would again become once again as "crazy, crazy, ally", "like hell". For this, he would again to unlock. He would tell for example, he and his new friend Poulain DERECK **who listened carefully**, words without heads or tails; lyrics such as: " " ""

" " "Um mm! When I think that I was watching" "Saturday morning", "his new **sample** Giraud", "which swelled so to speak", "his twisted" by bringing in Lyon; "Lyon"; that is to say: out of sight and therefore, out of control of me "her hominid, JULIO"; and that I was powerless over this guy then just! So, I want to have inexorably: eh!, eh, eh! Of "puke myself"! It really is this: I want inexorably "throwing myself", that the term – so right! I admit frankly that this story of infidelity proved "bothers me quite considerably"! **All this ends "by straight away, send my nerves" in "the kettle"! ""**

" " Does "the Initiator" "does not mystify" already "the artist" in this way – here! Will it this latter could really become a good some day, "a director" of consciousness? ""

˝« Is the goal in that story – here exactly, would it not honestly "to feed" EVELYN; but rather, to "gorge her" or: making her, room with excess? ˮ˝

˝« Are some of the most beautiful stories of "blotters" would they not honestly born this way – here, quite provocative? ˮ˝

˝« Do Giraud is one of those who like to "wet" even before owning "sectors of alluvial"? ˮ˝

˝« Does not him Giraud, reduce and little, the "evelynians"'s "hemispheres" in "portioned"? ˮ˝

˝« Do the "festival" of "task" to address "the frogs" of others; grant them enticing promises; making escapades with them; moreover, make them "who better, better", "escalation"! Is it actually that, that would be called a "festival" of "task"? ˮ˝

˝« Is that "intentionally" JULIO, is "the **Adam**" which "most cuckold" of all "the cuckolded"? ˮ˝

˝« Is that "involuntarily" all "the most cuckolds" best would console with "most cuckolded"? ˮ˝

˝« Is that "imperatively" that's how the nature works incredibly "the repairs" in "the stories of hearts"? ˮ « ˮ « ».

"... / ... If you agree to relive MARYVONNE, I would pay for you, a large villa with five rooms in the Paris's region; which would offer you a gift, of course, on the sly; and this, even before you leave find MARYVONNE. Not me ... / .... !".

After breaking the marriage of Julio Fernandez and Evelyn MULER, the gallant elegant Giraud ZEFRINO and his friend Poulain DERECK were able to meet so the first part of their course contract subversive. However, and just for this first stage, they were paid generously, as "their payments already received so far", from the hand of Thierry Glorian, with of course, the order of "Sir" Moses KEVILER himself same. Therefore, and with regard to the argument provided by Giraud vis-à-vis EVELYN, that would of course there, a pure lie, in order to obtain a divorce from her precisely. Divorce which would according to his calculations, indeed obtained in very, very short time only. For Poulain and Giraud (this gallant and elegant **Shrew's "Faller ¾ Down"**, or rather: this **criminal**) and with respect to their promise to win obtained significantly "**numismaticals**"; quite frankly, they had no concept of morality in their heads. **About Giraud, this gallant and elegant Eva's Killer, though he had had time to advise Evelyn MULER to accept the divorce of course asked by Julio Fernandez as quickly as possible. And that thereafter, he Giraud justly, he would marry her; and offer him a better life and children**.

For JULIO not yet want to hear about her, that question of offspring; before he could find a job based on his multiple degrees, for example. This gallant and elegant **Agnes 's "Faller ¾ Down"** him, more or less artfully (; little to say, more or less diplomatically) demonstrates another Sunday night in a Metro Station; he could not bring her straight home to his apartment, before she can legally get her divorce with JULIO. This is because according to his argument; or otherwise: as his excuse: He was going to have, for example, serious problems in the eyes of the Law. And it was so, Evelyn had come to accept; and return (though she herself) with hers parents. The lady was so naive, first accepted the idea of divorce; and then later, the idea of considering marriage with Giraud; or rather, remarriage with Giraud ZEFRINO.

As to Poulain DERECK already even when he was still in a very first time; that is to say: the time of separation between body first, EVELYN; and on the other hand, JULIO; then this other thief who had played the second part; the role of approach; to learn; and finally terminate with the latter, the binding of one, with the gallant and Seduce petticoats Giraud; POULAIN this one was once again asked by the boss Moses KEVILER, and through the course of his faithful worker Thierry Glorian, do even so, Julio Fernandez, "resumes only" Maryvonne KEVILER.

For POULAIN (which eventually he would start to think very carefully apparently on if only a small notion of morality proof: it was really risky!): " It's really risky, as new, it is still me Poulain DERECK who can accept this other phase of the subversive mission! ". That said, it seems to Thierry Glorian (himself controlled by Moses KEVILER) about it precisely: " ... / ... It's true that I have great need "**treasures**"! But anyway, ... / ...! ". THIERRY and interrupted him, asking: " But anyway? ".

Poulain, to THIERRY: " But anyway, given the risk that there's always myself Poulain, continue to want to rub JULIO; and consequently, ... / .... ".

THIERRY, at POULAIN: " And therefore? ".

Poulain, to THIERRY: " And consequently, also want to continue to handle him, I ... / .... ".

THIERRY, at POULAIN: " Aye!, ih!, ih, ih! ".

Poulain, to THIERRY: " I believe that if ever a way or another, he got caught up in all this scheme! So he could react very, very badly; and consequently, I Poulain, I might possibly find myself in trouble. ".

THIERRY, at POULAIN: " In bad posture! But it will not! You are bound to know that Mr. Poulain DERECK: Since from the beginning, you have accepted this task pretty darn subversive paid! Since the outset, you read the script! Since the outset, you read the script; and you even repeated several times until the very, very good store! **As a result, you are forced to bring it to completion, this task pretty darn subversive paid! Then, a point and a line!** Already, in a: How is him JULIO would he know, especially since this mission is top secret! Unless it is for example Giraud ZEFRINO that can go just disclose this secret! Or him, as I understood finally, he would not do that! **And two: You do not believe anyway, after agreeing to conduct the first part of this delicate mission; and therefore, you know, of course, very, very secret; and thereafter, you will refuse to continue in this direction? And therefore, we will still hire other people to continue this subversive mission? And that, with all the risks of disclosure of "top secret precisely this" it has not? You do not believe all the same, that we are going to accept that? Not ohm?** ".

Poulain, to THIERRY: " That is to say eh!, eh, eh! ".

THIERRY, at POULAIN: **« No! No way: "That is to say, eh!, eh, eh!". You agree to go through with the mission; then, a point and a line! If you thought of refuse! He should have done already from the start! Now it's too late! In addition, I will report this to my boss himself Mr. Moses KEVILER, your sense of reluctance; or rather disobedience, consisting of the fact that you refuse to prosecute the said mission. And it's really useless to you the description of what would be his anger and reaction to you! Should he, for example, to learn that! Because, do not forget that it was he the real sponsor of the mission! This is because in fact we are talking about, save for the ultimate way there, certainly quite Machiavellian, "his unique doll"! ».**

Poulain, to THIERRY: " Okay! I agree! I agree to continue this delicate mission! ".

THIERRY, at POULAIN: " Well! But only here, by way of your punishment for having first expressed some feelings of reluctance; or rather disobedience; I am, by my loyalty to my boss, in the obligation to report it to the latter anyway still ooh! ".

Poulain, to THIERRY: " I reiterate the most! Now I accept directly pursue this delicate mission, as subversive and sordid that it can be! ".

And Poulain DERECK was forced against his will, to continue to play his role as sordid and subversive. It was hard, the other part of this mission for him! For Julio Fernandez really believed enjoy an extraordinary opportunity, to have a friend like him Poulain DERECK. Hence, morally speaking, it was not easy enough for him Poulain, to continue to manipulate quietly one, Julio Fernandez. But since this latter justly had never understood the spiel; given the fact that he never understood the role played by his new friend Poulain DERECK. And he does not even suspect anything at all, at all. Hence, he would accept him despite the constraints of Thierry Glorian. When POULAIN would eventually suggest to his new friend JULIO, wanting simply resume with her; or rather, to better myself: just want to relive with "his old Arian Maryvonne KEVILER" in his life; would be surprised to hear that Julio Fernandez just could answer to him, for example; and this quite explicitly: " ... / ... I agree! I agree; since I still had quite a while already observed; and I had always been loyal to "my Delilah: Evelyn MULER"! But what does that me she brought? Nothing! Nothing, if these are just concerns and additional **afflictions**! ". Poulain DERECK would among others, the minutes of this last service to his direct sponsor Thierry Glorian; which in turn would pass it to him, too, to his patron; that is to say, his boss. And meanwhile, the boss himself; that is to say "Sir" Moses KEVILER, the dad of MARYVONNE finally had been made aware; and this fresh, JULIO found; and he was consequently suggested: " ... / ... If you agree to relive with MARYVONNE, I would pay a large villa with five rooms in the Paris's region; which I would offer you like a gift, of course, on the sly; and this, even before you leave find MARYVONNE. And I will find a good job for you, depending on your academic qualifications. Do not answer me immediately to this offer I'll make for you, quite generously! Take your time even for a few days; to better reflect on this proposal; and therefore, to sincerely answer me later! I want to tell you right now, that regardless of your answer, I respect her! Hence, the importance of wanting to first think very, very carefully, before you can answer me! ".

Julio Fernandez who eventually sought only really succeed in life; he was surprised to hear of such flattering remarks, from the mouth itself, of "Sir" Moses KEVILER, and sent for him. In doing so, he even missing words; and it was only to put as a question: " Is it true? ".

The boss Moses KEVILER which himself also did not expect at all, at all, that the concerned Julio Fernandez could for example not react badly to these words as flattering sent for him by himself in the head no one; which were more about the announcement of a huge real close corruption; phenomenal corruption; rather than anything else; he looks for that, it just: " But because I tell you myself in person! ".

JULIO, to MOSES: " Since this is how ah! So my answer despite everything anyway immediately for this job you will do me quite generously! I took my time for just a split second, so to speak, to better consider your proposal. And therefore, to sincerely respond later! I want to tell you straight away, that I agree! I accept this offer you will do me! ".

MOSES, at JULIO: " Moreover, I will let you boost in a large International Organization; where you will be considered, depending on your multiple degrees. ".

JULIO, to MOSES: " I agree. In addition, I can find my son LUCILIAN; and that, as soon as possible; which was already missing me a lot; and which continues even miss me greatly finally; and I have not even ashamed to admit very, very solemnly! ".

MOSES, at JULIO: " Finally, in order to close. ".

JULIO, to MOSES: " Aye!, ih!, ih, ih! ".

MOSES, at JULIO: " I give you another promise like whatever, I'll help further; and it widely, your mom. This is because I am very well aware that you hardly stop at all, thinking about her. ".

JULIO, to MOSES: " Thanks in advance for all that you are going to do for us. ".

MOSES, at JULIO: " I will help you greatly; This is because, without being conceited; but I have extensively and see themselves very much, material or numerical means, to be able to do of course. ".

JULIO, to MOSES: " Many thanks in advance! ".

MOSES, at JULIO: " Tell me more now: "Thank you very much in advance Stepfather!"; because after all, you are actually eh! Since when do you have known her, "my **filly**"; and even when you had a son with her precisely; I did not see you influenced so little, eh? ".

JULIO, to MOSES: " I totally agree with you dear Stepfather! ".

MOSES, at JULIO: " Finally, finally, I want to assure you ever like anything: everything I'm going to do for you and for your mom, I will of course, sweet. ".

JULIO, to MOSES: " Thank you dear Father – in – Law! ".

In short, through the POULAIN and THIERRY, MOSES succeed "phenomenally corrupt, finally," JULIO; because he would give him a villa Five pieces; or rather: a Five pieces pavilion in the Paris's Region. In short, Julio Fernandez, **only a few short months after the dismissal of EVELYN**, he already would arrange in the villa; or rather, the five pieces in the Paris' s region ; where he had become decidedly himself the owner [And how! Or rather: And with that]!.

In short, after the departure of Evelyn MULER of the apartment rented by Julio Fernandez and after finally accepted "phenomenal corruption of MOSES"; and this, even in anticipation of divorce, that one would relive (almost, but hiding anyway so to speak a little, as expected really do before any marriage in the Town Hall, before then, power squarely appear with her, outside their new home) already as married, with "his former MARYVONNE stretcher". Therefore, this divorce [between JULIO and EVELYN] had actually held as soon as possible. It was held as soon as possible especially because there was a "hymen" mistake "serious and proven" committed "willfully by her, this latter". And furthermore, it is because the latter herself precisely, she apparently not wanted most of all, to continue to live with, Julio, to be able to remarry with that one who had given her a lot of good promises.

This divorce was obtained under the wrong course, that latter herself. But by the height of paradox for her, unfortunately, alas!, "this gallant and elegant Maw appointed Giraud ZEFRINO love", he finally would any more to want, at all (then really: any more at all, at all feel her Evelyn) [and for good reason].

Julio Fernandez has finally cottoned well as: " Fighting alone at any time in life, without the slightest nudge; is good; if not that's fine; and if we want to see yourself it's very, very good; this is because, no matter how, in almost majority of cases in life precisely; it could hardly be otherwise. But only here, in the vast majority of situations when it is so. People have unfortunately alas!, no luck, to make working life, those they still want to do. ".

Julio Fernandez had finally cottoned on that well: " In short, it's very, very nice to find work that is to be always, alone. But however, this does not often results in practice what we want to do in real life actually. ".

In doing so, JULIO having very, very well understood this (and because he was still very, very long time, loaded with the big diplomas! But nevertheless, he hardly managed to find work according to them precisely.). Hence the fact that: in doing so, JULIO having very, very well understood that. He consequently immediately agreed to take all the benefits they were promised, to offer him. And above all, he had accepted; this is because: finally, it was not even matter that concerned him; he does for example, something subversive to someone or someone else. But rather, it was no question for him, but to agree to simply relive conjugal speaking with a "**Eurydice**" who had lived together with him before; and with whom he had already had a son named Lucilian KEVILER. That "**Iphigenia**" which definitely waiting for this after all. And so it was; that is to say, **after the perspicacious discrete 's intervention of Moses KEVILER himself**; and not forgetting the new proposal Poulain DERECK, suggested to the attention of Julio Fernandez; the new proposal to take with him, Maryvonne KEVILER; that it just was again left with that one. **And this one in question was not at all, at all finally sick** (And due, she had found one who cared above all, that is to say: "His Julio Fernandez": "From On the Descent Poitevese And Rear-Spanish Descent", "Her **Irredeemable Irreplaceable**", "The **Undeniable** and **Undisputed**" and finally "The **Unforgettable** and **Monumental**").

M ARYVONNE understood very well, reliving that "this time" with "**The Unforgettable** and **Illustrious** " JULIO; she would definitely explain **decidedly**; and this: **very, very explicitly**, "**morals**" and "**customs" of the people from "the Blondinia**". And for that, she would let him hear:

Maryvonne KEVILER, talking to her husband Julio FERNADEZ: " Finish "the past" JULIO! ".

JULIO: " Amazing and that's good like that! ".

MARYVONNE: " Listen to me very, very well JULIO; this is because I want to talk to you long enough; and that, by monopolizing the floor."

Julio Fernandez, meeting his wife Maryvonne KEVILER: " I'm listening! Go! ".

Maryvonne KEVILER, continuing to talk to her husband Julio FERNADEZ: "Apart from my **very, very strong anxiety attacks**; which I could manage little to actually curb; and which, in addition, also made me overcome with really anxiety; **making me "crazy, crazy"**; JULIO indeed, about all our quarrels we were doing before you run away, ¾! JULIO indeed, it would remind you that: my dad; that is to say: Monze KEMVILA [or rather: Moses KEVILER] is from the village "Guigo" ("Guigo" in the Region of Nsoundi, on the right bank of the great river Congo); that is to say: he's from "the Blondinia". JULIO indeed, it would remind you that: My paternal grandmother (and this is to say, the wife of Mvila KEMVILA, that is to say, the father of my father or my grandfather paternal hence: my paternal grandmother that is to say: Adolphina Nseke, commonly known as Mama ADOLO) as to her, she was from the village "Guillodo" ("Guillodo", a neighboring community of "Guigo", needless to say, it is still very much here, in the Region of Nsoundi in the right bank of the great river Congo, which evokes); needless to say also that my dad Moses KEVILER is from in reality these two villages – there; and needless to say, finally, that this is still very much here, localities of "Blondinia".

JULIO indeed, it would remind you that: My father taught me many stories of manners and customs; or rather several anecdotes of everyday life for people living in communities: from "Guigo"; of "Guillodo" and communities and surrounding areas of these two places then in question; and even: several accounts of manners and customs; or rather several anecdotes of everyday life of the people living to beyond the most distant mountains.

JULIO indeed, it would remind you that; or rather, should you to be aware that:

My paternal aunt Henrietta Mafuta KEMVILA (Madame Henrietta Mafuta KEMVILA, wife Nsenga); that is to say, one of my father's sisters; ("" Shepherdess "so to speak: **the vulgar manners**", "**manners certainly vulgar**" but mostly "a" baroness "mature", " " " " a Countess of experience " " " " [she ¾ above]); and that every time I went; and even, every time I continue to go and visit their family there in Africa, [she ¾] told me several stories of manners and customs; or rather several anecdotes of everyday life for people living in communities: from "Guigo"; of "Guillodo" and communities and surrounding areas of these two places then in question; and even: the people living to beyond the most distant mountains. " " " " ".

Aunt Henrietta Mafuta KEMVILA, wife Nsenga tells me most of all (**above all**):

How to consolidate as "our beautiful old tradition" "Blondinian" good marital harmony; and that, by "multiple false scenes of households"; which, onlookers, as to them, they only see the *fire*. JULIO indeed, all of them would say what? JULIO indeed, everyone me MARYVONNE I did you endure before you run away, in fact, it had nothing to do for example with ¾¾:

That (and this is to say: everyone me MARYVONNE I made you endure before you run away, so) had nothing to do for example with resentment!

That (and this is to say: everyone me MARYVONNE I made you endure before you run away, so) did not even have anything to do for example with hate!

That (and this is to say: everyone me MARYVONNE I made you endure before you run away, so) did not even have anything to do for example with the wrong character!

That (and this is to say: everyone me MARYVONNE I made you endure before you run away, so) did not even have anything to do for example with malice!

That (and this is to say: everyone me MARYVONNE I made you endure before you run away, so) did not even have anything to do for example with cruelty!

That (and this is to say: everyone me MARYVONNE I made you endure before you run away, so) did not even have anything to do for example, with real scenes worthy household name!

Here we only make live "to matrimonial homes": "infernal times of course, but that's only: not in the literal sense; but rather, in the

figurative sense"; or to be able to express even better: there, we only do live "to matrimonial homes", "the enchanting moments".

JULIO should know that according beliefs "Blondinians", "**the dames**" **have unilaterally and undoubtedly the power to live** "**nuptial homes**" in "Enchanting Moments" or "hellish times, not, not in the figurative sense, but in the true "meaning. JULIO indeed, it was hardly anyone there!

But I (and that is to say: everyone me MARYVONNE I made you endure) had more to do with the idea **to consolidate good marital harmony**!

JULIO indeed, **it were that: no more; or less, some of the manners and customs of** "Blondinia"!

JULIO indeed, **it was no more and no less, that "the very spice, very strong", to better strengthen the marital bond**.

And it is an art.

And precisely this art taught "to Blondinians" is not always easy to put into practice by everyone. Those "of bitches", the most deserving who manage to actually put into practice. The art in question, it does not acquire, through deception or by magic. Can be learned. Can be learned from "the damsels" very, very experienced in the field; "colleens of" such as my aunt HEN. Also: Learn "this art" with "the honorable" very, very experienced in the field, that's one thing. But knowing how to create other "very very hot peppers". It's a whole other thing, it would hardly be overlooked especially; and it goes without saying. There should absolutely know how to create new charms.

It is absolutely necessary, that "the Judith" was on the lookout for new ideas about "real – grabbing false" or "true – false wrangling" to introduce "true – false scenes of household" or "false – true scenes of households" in order to be able to attract to herself more and more attention from more and more, "flycatchers"; and moreover, to give spice to the strength "of the hymeneal link". (Cf.. Isaac Mampuya Samba in Vol N°2. "Nervous Depression or Grief Love").

And yeah!, ih! "What fills paradox"! How about me! But there is really nothing can sometimes against certain manners and customs, you know! They were that: no more; or less, some of the manners and customs of "Blondinia"; since, you know that my father, myself MARYVONNE too am a descendant of this hole. When you marry with a descendant of this hole precisely, we need to know many things.

We should know that: When a son of a descendant of these peoples "of Blondinian origin" marries a descendant of the same people (she the daughter) or even: a descendant of another of these peoples "Blondinian of origin"; then, like, "Hello!". So then: "Hello the fights!". (And often than not, so it does not say, and for most of the event for that matter), the "man of honor" to him as he is not even a descendant of such a tradition cultural. And it is quite JULIO your case for you. But as long as the wife as to her, she's the tradition. So, it is enough, there is also often these fights in their household; "Man of Distinction in question" will simply learn to live with from now on. And it is "the daughter of Eva", the "train"; and that, absolutely.

And so, then, like: " Hello endless shouting matches; false, indeed; and endless fights, also: false; or fighting; also false; that can actually exist in order to express ourselves that way! ".

"So, like: " "Hello!". "The skirmish" "regular"; "successive" "regular" and "continuous"!, In the household! Of course in this show that we offer; or rather, we provide periodically; successively; regularly; and continuously "to various penguins" gestural and verbal elegance women [among others]; would deploy with retaliation; or rather with fags; tears; female cries; loud calls; very strong; very, very strong [among others]; which would compete ardently (but certainly not all, at all, snapped anyway), with demonstration of boldness and power of the head of household.

Brief: sour and unpleasant female screams (very, very acute, or very, very strong, whatever); scolding's on a sour and unpleasant tone; Brief: discussions; brief: shrieks (among others) would face graceful and smooth, with burning; but not aggressively against: bold; insurance; power and authority.

Induction: Just for example, one such; or that another brawl household; just "Adam" would touch on the skin of "Eva"; suddenly,

that latter would start immediately after, crying; first, crying quietly; then, shouting; while squawking; while squawking strong; very strong; very, very strong; as if such were burned her "chest" with a burning cigarette butt at the fiery red color; or as if for example, tore her skin! When in reality we did there, barely touching her with "soft palm" "the bitch"; and this, clearly bursting eyes.

What staging!

"A staging well articulated", [of course]; "well timed"; "well established"; briefly: "well done"; with the public as to him would understand nothing, nothing, to this kind of didactic tradition. It would; and he would see again and again, but fire. But only here, do little to prevent the same, with "initiation", if not "initialization" of such a custom, me Maryvonne KEVILER, even if you are hitting me yet not all, at all! But prevented much for all that, I really was considering actually be "a Salome" beaten.

In short, the issue in the eyes of this "daughter of Eva": if "his son of Adam" does not offer periodically; if he does not offer regularly; if he does not continuously offer "to the various caves", dainty to satisfy their curiosity by attending such matrimonial performances; short, the challenge in the eyes of her, "parishioner" if "his prayer" does not offer "the various fools", these shows on the fact of the strike apparently publicly; this would mean simply, that he would never love her. For her, these multiple "taken beaks" are that: the spice of the deal! For her, it spiced love in the day! For her, it's something exciting!

For her, it's just fun!

"For her, it absolutely must not at all, at all (not far wrong), that this pleasure is missing in the home!".

Needless to say, it was also her Aunt HEN who had "initiated" me in "the nuptial sensual trap" of "voyeurism" ["voyeurism" in the "first part"]; JULIO which you know well, for the simple reason that you had been "the victim"; when once your five friends; that is to say: Nelson RUDNIK; Roz LORENZO; Eric BATTLES; Jeffrey Maxwell and Arthur RAVER [many to mention], they had come to some unexpected visit with us!

In "introducing me"; in "initializing me" Aunt HEN told me for example: "You too" "companion", you should therefore: do not ignore at all, at all, with the wedding, it's a whole new life begins quite naturally! And with it: the duties that go with and which "half" bride should absolutely run, and these duties among others: the "mouth"; that is to say: the food; that is to say, the kitchen; that is to say: good cook; that is to say: good food.

Or just for every recipe we have to do, we should not forget any visual appearance. Because we may well have to include all the flavors that one would like (flavors ranging e.g. from sweet to bitter and through salty and acid); but if the recipe hardly has a beautiful visual appearance! It could consequently little either capture sensitivities papillae. Since such a recipe, do not even see the path of the oral cavity. For a recipe comes into the mandible, it has a long way to go, in fact:

It will be observed that.:
The "mouth" will think.
It goes to reason.
It will be projected.
It will enjoy.
And finally, it will eat.

And yeah!, ih!, This path is long.
It is certainly long before actually eating. But however it is done in a few seconds.
And aye!, ih!, Recipes, it can be seen!
But just before the flavors, these are the colors and scents inexorably above. In other words, before the mouth can swallow food, it's first "eye" that "eats". First, there are the "eyes" that "eat". These are first "eye" lurking. Hence, if the eye is such that a particular food is not looking good. So it's damn early. It is grated in advance. It missed beforehand, for the sole reason that "the mouth" will find it disgusting. And when "the valve" finds disgusting. So this food will be hard to go well. » « »"

"« And so ("the bourgeois"), when you understand that: nothing but the look of a dish that is presented beautifully! The saliva is already! When you understand that: it is the eye that eats first! So you've got it! So you will do for "your guy to you"; for yourself and for everyone in your home: recipes for poultry (among others: omelets "Blondinians" dried out and chickens); wild game; fish; of animals; household we eat; plants and cetera and cetera ...; you will do: ""

"" Raw foods; food between cooked and raw; of food slightly cooked; moderately cooked food; highly cooked food; very, very good cooked; and vice versa; that is to say: ""

"" Food very, very good cooked; highly cooked food; moderately cooked food; food slightly cooked; food between cooked and raw; raw food; ""

"" Short, you will make recipes that are noted with very, very hot peppers; number of other very spicy, very fragrant and aromatic herbs; which recipes will tickle the lips and even the nostrils; which revenues sing, sing, sing and sing again, "gastronomy" "Blondinian" impressions; vivid colors and materials, before tasting; before and enjoyed before dining in the company of "nsamba" (or palm wine [palm wine]). ""

"" Anyway, when you understood that: it is the eye that eats first! So you will do for "your devil in you"; for yourself and for everyone in your home: recipes so to speak flavors and magic scents; insightful kitchens; ingenious kitchens; kitchens that have the sagacity; kitchens that have finesse; briefly, kitchens as varied and enjoyable fumes; or rather the subtle flavors well and good bright reflections. ""

"" And all of them is that for "your male you just" know consequently, take good care of him. You know what I say? We should know him well cook for example, various kinds of ratatouille; aye!, ratatouille based on: plantains; palm oils; of butter peanuts; sweet cassava boiled; fresh fish and even smoked fish; and cetera and cetera ...; and all observed e.g. paprika; ginger; pepper and cinnamon. " " " " ".

MARYVONNE: " Finish "the shame" JULIO! ".

JULIO: " Beautiful! ".

"My aunt HENRIETTA let me hear again e.g. [I quote]: " I advise you "the regular" it would let you know for example from rice; or from cassava flour (and especially from the bitter cassava flour: This tuber necessary, recipe – multiple [after special preparation, to root out, the poison] this tuber necessary) to survival of most people in our country (; and it was downright want to express just that in our country precisely, cassava is a unique and unsurpassable shrub)! Hence: I need you to know, for example, from rice; or from cassava flour, make among – others: donuts and especially chili peppers, ginger. In short, it would "minister", you know, for example, treating – among others the delights scents of ginger, chilies etc … and cetera. " " ""

"" In short, it would only from a simple recipe, i.e. make meals taste and tasting, knowing both: Invade: ""

"" Not only (so to speak: the eyes); ""

"" Not only (so to speak: the fingers); ""

"" Not only (so to say: the lips); ""

" (Ahem mm; speaking of "little housewife" chops, I would say precisely with that ah!, we have: the palace, or rather: we have: taste, and consequently, we have: a frantic urge to lick your lips); ""

"" Learn to make food taste and tasting, knowing both: Invade: ""

"" Not only (so to speak: the tip of the tongue itself); ""

"" Not only (so to speak: the language itself); ""

"" Not only (so to speak: the palate itself); ""

"" Not only (so to speak: the back of the throat itself); ""

"" But also, and above all: the stomach itself. " " " " ""

My aunt HENRIETTA let me hear again e.g. [I quote]: " I advise you "the legitimate": it should let you know for example cooking among – others: Bloodspot garlic smoked, grilled; especially: with lots of garlic and precisely with cloves; fish steamed with loads of paprika; fish steamed; that is to say, by packing them in the same leaves, such as those used to cook "of chikwangues"; ("Chikwangue" is a derivative of [Maniot; Maniot esculenta, or cassava]; the Maniots esculentas are shrubs from South America; the tuberous roots of cassava are used to make (after proper treatment) of pasta, of… Maniot esculenta starches, and other flours and cassava (manioc or pulps after they have undergone a specific treatment) in "aqua simplex" in short, to cook [mashed cassava, boiled in leaves] and short, then to cook the fish, by burying them in very, very hot ashes; we the"Venus", we need to know for example, use: cumin, pepper, nutmeg, curry, turmeric, coriander, cardamom, and cetera and cetera ...). " » " »"

My aunt HENRIETTA let me still hear about such chikwangues [quote] (yeah!, besides myself MARYVONNE I watched the preparation of these chikwangues, and in addition: I also confectioned me too):

"« The chikwangue, "this compact paste, extensible framework; or rather elastic" is sometimes called "Kwanga". It is "a classic treat" native "of the great Congo River Basin". This dish very much appreciated, is in itself "a feast ambassador (par excellence)" representing the latter geographic location, across the world. Populations of the latter basin consume considerably; and this: for lunch; dinner; see: dinner; or seef: at breakfast; and yet this: for example more often, that of bread; rice; or millet; or any other condiment also under other horizons. »"

"" How do you get chikwangue? ""

"" Or to ask the question differently: What are therefore the main processing steps in order to obtain paste cooked chikwangue? ""

"" They are nine in number. And these nine key steps in question are: ""

"" Retting is a transformation by immersion for four to seven days of bitter cassava tubers in the water. ""

"" Peeling tubers that we do: ""

"" Or before putting them for several days in water. ""

"" Or if not immediately after leaving the water. ""

"« To know that for "peeling obtained before soaking the tubers in" yawn "the disadvantage is that it's very, very difficult to peel" "these Maniots esculentas"; this is because of their skins; which are difficult to entrench themselves in this case. That said, once we managed anyway despite everything, to spend a lot more time to peel them before soaking them in water; the advantage that it removes is that: these tuberous roots just remain in addition, significantly fewer days in the fleet; to acquire their softening necessary to obtain the destruction or eradication of bitterness (; or poison [bitter] contained in "these Maniots esculentas" bitter, eh?). What for? This is simply because the "aqua simplex" penetrates much faster in the tubers. """

"« To know that for: Peeling obtained: After the release of the tubers of water: the advantage is that it's very, very easy to peel them; because: they just are already well softened "the flood"; which certainly entered it, "easy on – easy on" taking or putting extra lot more time in this stage of treatment; as the fleet gets fairly slowly thereof. In short, the downside is that: "Maniots esculentas" remain much longer in "ranula". And it is anyway quite annoying for "rapid progress"; because, says – not one that "Time is money"? """

"« The "unfiberation" (to flush out the fibers and remove them), which is obtained with a steel comb; or otherwise: by filtration; or: sedimentation; the latter method is commonly called "mpompa" in the dialect of the Region; (As an aside here to Julion]: It is just to point out that many consumers and consumers such as: my Aunt HEN herself and I MARYVONNE are included elsewhere] do not appreciate too much, too a chikwangue obtained from a pulp collected in this way called "mpompa"). They (these consumers and consumers such as: us) do not find it at all [; then really: not at all, at all extensible; on the contrary, they are inelastic; and above all, above all: they are rather bland; you might say that. Swallowed is then for example, paste petrified and uncooked) """
"" The rolling of the dough. """
"" A first cooking. """
"" The mixing of the pre – baked dough. """
"" The modeling dough (large or small models, it depends ¾). """
"« The packaging in "shirts", "lined" with sheets useful plants (genus "Marantaceae" ["Megaphrynium" and "Sarcophryrium" or "Sarcophrynium"] "macrostachyum"); species which sheets are used for example, as aluminum foil; and it would take for the packaging of each stick "Kwanga"; or even for

other foods to cook, use at least three leaves well, well washed, by lot or package or stick. ""

"" And finally: the terminal cooking; which lasts a very long time; much longer than the first firing. ""

"" In short, "chikwangue" is derived from cassava; is this still the staple "in Blondinia" and the circumjacent principalities; which food is consumed daily in various forms. Ah!, "the Blondinia" with the "the cassava"! ""

"" They grow, among ¾ others: "cassava"! ""

"" We are harvesting among ¾ others: "cassava"! ""

"" It transforms, among ¾ others: "cassava"! ""

"" It celebrates, among ¾ others: "cassava"! ""

"" The food, among ¾ others: "cassava"! ""

"" We are present in various feasting, among ¾ others: "cassava"! ""

"" And one on of the best! " ""

"My aunt HENRIETTA let me hear again e.g. [I quote]: ""

"" Me HENRIETTA your aunt, I advise you to you, my niece MARYVONNE: it should let you know, for example, to the "table" among ¾ others: the sweet cassava raw; especially accompanied by raw peanuts recently emerged soil; obviously when it's harvest time of these! ""

"" Me HENRIETTA your aunt, I advise you to you, my niece MARYVONNE: I suggest you "Joan of Arc": it should let you know for instance address among ¾ others: some other medicinal plants; ""

"" Should "Rebecca", you know, for example, "make" among ¾ others: some other roots; ""

"" Should "Beauty", so you know for example prepare among ¾ others: some other stem barks; underground stems or not does not matter; stems many other herbaceous plants; and more particularly, monocots and pteridophytes; ""

"« Should "Marquise", you know, for example, treat among ¾ others: all the one and the other, plants whose bark and rhizomes, are proving to be fleshy and aromatic; which bark and roots are used just as condiments stimulating properties; »"

"« Should "Baroness", so you know for example simmered among ¾ others: "As other meat"; »"

"« Should "Shepherdess", so you know for example prepare among ¾ others: "so many other edible vegetables"; »"

"« Should "Countess", so you know for example, have on the "table", among ¾ others: so many other foods, seasoned of coriander; cinnamon; saffron; paprika and cetera and cetera ... » «. » « »"

"« Should "Shrew", so you know for example that the Secret to culinary success in "our Blondinia" stands foremost in choosing to bring on vegetable species; on species of flesh; on species starchy; on species of spices; and cetera and cetera ...; and not forgot to mention the choices on the right "nsamba" ("palm wine" [the famous "wine that comes from palm", ["palm wine"]). »"

"« And aye, aye!, ih!, "the Blondinians" without this famous palm oil!; this is a people without oil; »"

"« Yep!, ih!, "the Blondinians" without this famous palm oil!; this is a people without "moussaka" "this palm oil, mixed with water"; »"

"« Uh – huh!, ih!, "the Blondinians" without this famous palm oil!; this is a people without giant larvae of giant beetles that are eating "the feast of banquet – up meal" ["the feasting"]; »"

"« All right!, ih!, "the Blondinians" without this famous palm oil!; this is a people without a giant beetles themselves, which also eats "the feasting"; »"

"« By all means!, ih!, "the Blondinians" without this famous palm oil!; this is a people without beds; no chairs; without tables; without closets; without paperless; without hangars; without frames; without roots; without roofs; without burning chapels catafalques; without baskets; without brushless; without brushless; and cetera and cetera ...; (: And they still want to express outright simply, that in our country precisely, palm oil is an unique and unsurpassable tree); »"

"« Short, as everyone knows, palm oil is used in multiple use enough. It is used for example in manufacturing: hats; ropes; carpets; chairs; of structures; partitions; and cetera ...; and especially "the Blondinians" without this famous palm oil; this is a people without the proper "nsamba" "famous" palm wine in question. " It's like, "the Blondinians" without cassava; they are a people deprived of all those that just produces this shrub: starch; soup; boiled; tapioca; and cetera and cetera. .... » « » « »"

"« In short, and not forgot to mention the choices on the right "nsamba." »"

"« And of course!, ih "a good Eva 's Blondinian" was; or rather has always managed to keep the tradition of his moms; aunts and grannies. »"

"« ("... / ... You should know a close family meal with drink "n'samba".)! » « »"

"« We need to know "Parishioner", which brought to table; served in plastic cups and presented to her "son of Adam" and everyone else at the table precisely; there is nothing like that "the n'samba" (palm wine [wine palm]), to better close a family feast. »"

"« It would take "Delilah", so you know for example, have on the "table" in order to help all those, precisely: our fetish – drink ("the nsamba"); which drink you should run afloat; you should be flowing in this strong and soft drinks at a time, to the accompaniment of "good drunk". And you would find out for yourself "maiden" that: more the liquor flows freely; more as the traditional social barrier between "you, the Parishioner" and "your Parishioners"; fall; furthermore, "the bridal ambiance", would become much more user – friendly and so on and gradually; and also (and here I jump first another of the main duties, which I will talk to you "Juno", just now, "one below the hips"); »"

"« and in this regard precisely, we should know that when we go to bed at the same time with the spouse, they should in no case, turn your back (after only a deep sleep for example, there could be the go back)! For this act of turning his back (or her back) to the beginning of sleep, could encourage, not at all, you take into consideration! »"

Hence I told you, "Judith", that the more, the liquor flows freely; more in the "anthropoid", "fireworks" will stimulate; more "her brush"; or rather: her "life and soul joy" still go up a notch; more so, between you and him the author of the organ in question, gradually fall traditional social barriers; and also, "the hymen atmosphere", become much more user – friendly and so on and gradually.

And the more: from the same moment that we would begin to sleep, it should especially not at all, at all, turn back "the Sparrow" because it turns out to be a very foul, very serious. It is absolutely necessary to start her sleep, looking in the direction "of the gun"; and of course it goes without saying that him also, he will do the same. And so we spend so to speak (and here "the Female", it will be necessary that I can call a spade a spade; and there "motherly", we will have one tries to speak without taboo, and that we can address the issue head – on; but of course, with humor and joke)! Hence, I told you "Damsel" from the same moment that we would begin to sleep, we pass so to speak: the sublime intimate, intense sleep. ". ".

Aunt HENRIETTA let me hear again for example: " I inform you that you will notice for yourself when you sleep with "your Brave" at night: How in the morning that follows ¾ [¾ How] (the "sperm" perfume so to speak, or rather: the "seminal" perfume) will make you happy! Just be careful, to be ready for everyday tasks the next day, we should ignore the point of waking up at dawn and wash your body first! ".

Aunt HENRIETTA let me hear again e.g.: " "should" "Fatima", "so you know for example treat: all these" edibles – there "and all those other" foods – there, it looks more or less aphrodisiacs. "Should" "Minister", "that you know for example, have" on the "table", among ¾ others: other "kimbiolongo" ("roots undoubtedly deemed exciting") and cetera and cetera ... ".

Aunt HENRIETTA let me hear again for example: " And we are left with more "Legitimate", but imagine those who would follow later! Because when you do reach "our Male" "such lewd dimension"! You will reach as yourself "the Lettuce", thus: "orgasmic dimension" necessary "to the ecological balance". ".

In short, to be able to get the sack, "very, very powerful", our "Puppet"; and besides, it's not just for him huh! ; because: you too "the Chick" of fantasy perspective, you reap in "orgasmic dimension worthy of the name"! Thou reap more. So then "Lady", you may be sure and certain, you're going to stink "The junk" from "crunchy tone" until such two meters away, before you wash your body, of course. Hmm mm, and it would not even be necessary, for example, be able to read in the guts!; this is because it would be enough thereafter to observe the faces "lovers" to understand that "the magic" "Ingredient – provocative" had in fact done its effects. ".

Aunt HENRIETTA let me hear again e.g.: " Providing power to take her time and also, provided they do little especially after the efforts we will be able to provide that, "and believe me" "Mama" that there is not much in the honeymoon life, a better time than this, to be able to like flat, all the problems that we have, in the home; and in order to find appropriate solutions that work there. ".

Aunt HENRIETTA let me hear again for example: " In short, it would "Salome", so you know for example swallow yourself and of course also to swallow to "Male tone to you of course", among – others: all these other "foods – there", one would say "more or less aphrodisiacs". ".

Aunt HENRIETTA let me hear again for example: " In short, it would "Parishioner", you know, for example, to "table" for the sake of yourself and for the sake of "your Beautiful" company other: several ingredients stimulated supposed "natural desires" [note "little Woman" I do not mean "natural needs, commonly expressed"; but rather "natural desires"; "natural desires, justly"; or rather: "biological pleasures"; "to be much more explicit than that!". ".

CHAPTER: III

"Aunt HENRIETTA let me hear again for example: " In short, we should "little Housewife", you know, for example, treat among – others : several products known in our Region, have aphrodisiacs in order "to get up each and irresistibly; and more particularly, to ride him". And with this demonstration by way of a few examples, I go "bourgeois"; and this without transition to another of the duties for "regular" go with the marriage; this is the "bottom of the hip"; or rather: the "bottom of the belly"; that is to say: "the one to go with" her "zebra", obviously. Hence, one should proceed as above the point in some of these countries to distant horizons, it is done; some of these countries to distant horizons where traditions and evolution does not rhyme; or rather, do not rhyme; and where they are still very, very far from wanting to rub shoulders with each other; .../.... ". """

" In some of these countries to distant horizons where manners and customs die hard they are, they are necessary in Queens, in the field "from below the belly"; """

"" In some of these countries to distant horizons where there are old instructions and prohibitions with which, we could not possibly try to think of them evolve, ever so slightly; """

" In some of these countries to distant horizons, where from himself (according to the beliefs of people living there); upon himself the moment that we would have fun to break so slightly, these instructions and prohibitions in question are systematically would offend the spirits; the spirits of dead ancestors and the same: the spirits of nature! And if it's part of his intimate conjugal relationship for example, that "the Muse" had rebelled! If it's on its carnal life, "Joan of Arc" violated so slightly, rules! So then, spirits (according to their beliefs) would take care of them! They might even get excited; frustration strong; very strong; very, very strong; and consequently, inflicting as punishment, "this sacred award infertility"; "Sentence dreaded" with "hags"; "Primary infertility", if she had not hitherto given birth; or alternatively: "the secondary sterility", otherwise. " " ".

MARYVONNE: " Finish "the shame of the joint" JULIO! ".
JULIO: " This is wonderful! ".

" Hence, according to these beliefs in some of these countries to distant horizons – there, "the Ladies" did that, as part of their "hymen" intimate life: to seek the offspring; and that without the passage, looking to experience, if only a small pleasure. And for that, "their Hominids" do not even have to try to watch "their morphologies" or even their smallest little bulges, to contemplate for example. They only have to "close their eyes, so to speak" at "their busting guts". And woe to the "Venus" that overrides by waiving this rule! Because, if she disobeys this rule precisely! We should even more, she starts to look for or seek new, offspring, according to their beliefs! This is because the spirits would be annoyed severely; or to better express it violently. And in this case – here, if you would like to make reparations to those just past; and that, through "traditional healers talented!". There will be willing to sacrifice several goats or sheep, in honor of the spirits in question that had been so offended. And furthermore, we will buy dozens and dozens of so – alcoholic beverages, and sweet. And we take care of everything during a ritual ceremony, plenary should inexorably advertise on the horizon; a particularly complex ceremony; a ceremony, just thinking, "canopies" in relation to them, they refuse to systematically addition to there to appeal. ""

" And consequently, "a Sparrow", could not possibly be expected to experience joy, from "such a Baroness", when "their pileups". And when the "Bird" falls for example, in the arms "of an old Bitch" from "bad life"; which would be the "pampered" "who better"; or rather: which absolutely would love, though; then really: well, well, "pampered" "the Bimanous" "who better"; that "slut" not good "go with him" "crunchy" "who better"; or rather:

which absolutely would love, though; then really: well, well, "go with her" "the Horn", "who better"! And then in such a case, we should especially hardly surprising "that such Adam" just dropped, "Eva 's" in order to marry in her place, "the former streetwalkersn in question". """

"" Hence, another of the duties for "an old Woman" go with the marriage: it is "the one to go in the crib", with her "Gas", of course. "Go duvet", usually at night; this is because, the day there are numerous enough to perform daily activities. And then, if one already has offspring, then she should not surprise you that anyway. And in doing so, to have the desire (and therefore the desire to better meet each other), you should "old Bag" know that this subject "to go with" his "Honest Man" I wish to notify ("old Lady") that: """

"" there I still talk such as for "food", "this is first, the eye eats; and then the mouth". Hence, it is exactly the same really. What for? This is because: Before "the tail"; or rather, "the heat – seeking moisture missile " from "your Bird" as it can "steal"; or rather: "to go up"; it is primarily "his eye" (even if not expressed verbally, but he expresses feelings) which "fits"; and that it is primarily "his eyes" who "go to check the Melissa's Mop Buckett" before. These are first "eye" lurking. """

"" It is first, the eye that would require "the Bitch" showing off. She shows off all hers curves as much as possible; as well as possible in order to better capture just the "eye of the Sparrow"; to better capture precisely the "eyes of the gentleman"; and to better attract the attention of it on herself; This is because, for a "gentleman", the view "rather large female" embodies the beauty and ... [that is to say: you "the Venus"]; this view embodies its author [; that is to say always: you "the Rebecca"], this view embodies the beauty and delight, the most troubling. And then, the biggest attraction "of the Bimanous"; and indeed, that of the "Arian" eh!, eventually find themselves as a result, concomitant!; or to put it more correctly: synchronized. And then all those who are related to greater mutual appetite find themselves "at the end of four – eyes"! """

"" And there, "guts mutual" will "be jerky" to "mutual exhaustion"! """

"" And there, with considerable opportunities undoubtedly "restful sleep mutual" will grab you; or rather "go with you"! """

"" And absolutely!, ih!, Is "biology"! """

" " This is "biology apart"! ""

" " And "this biology apart – here" inexorably "global"; and in addition, "the same impact that it has" also appear to be "global"! ""

" " And certainly!, ih!, without "this biology aside – here precisely", "there would not even speak such as": "we are no longer"; because no matter how, "we would not even have" "to have so little, ceased to live"; because "it would have been virtually living so slightly, just!! " " " " ".

"**A**unt HENRIETTA let me hear again for example: " That there should be in this matter, "the duty to below the hips", absolutely known "to grant each other the blandishments". And for that, to have the desire (and therefore the desire to get to meet each other), you should know what about it "to go with your Son of Adam just" I want you to report ["Womanishstar"] that, the smell "the everyman" sweaty (and in this case, that "your Gentleman"), turns out to be "the most powerful" "of red – hot"; (female aphrodisiacs; or rather: the smell "of her Man of Honor" sweaty turns out to be "one of the most powerful juicy" that boost the energy of the feminine sensual impulse). The smell "her Man of Merit" sweaty turns out to be one of the most powerful female libidinous racy that: other gingers; raw peanuts; not boiled sweet cassava; and cetera and so on ... I have quoted you high above example. ""

" " These two duties: the "mouth"; and the "bottom hip"; are one: the two best cements fill gaps that would begin to open for example between you, "the Female" and him, "your Male"! And it's very, very important to know! Should be: not much at all, at all, forget these tips for free. I provide you these free just advice; this is because according to our traditions "Blondinians" is indeed me, your Aunt Henrietta Mafuta KEMVILA [she still let me hear for example]: That I am obliged to provide you the specific advice in question – here. " " " " ".

" Aunt HENRIETTA let me hear again: " " " If the "Noble Man" refuses by example; and that, ever so slightly, "to have ridings the pony" with "his Split which one, you are my niece"; when you, the latter asked him often enough; and that, "under the nuptial duty"; forcing by all means, to agree to do it anyway, no matter how; oblige, even if there is, for example, home of the world: not be shy; and so, it will indeed be her "Noble", which, by disturbing the other people watching the scene, it will pronto, accept, to slip away from curiosity; and whether or not he still refuses (as sometimes happens to him to do for that matter), in this case, "the downright hurt"! But beware! Not physically hurt! But rather: with words! By "very upsetting very words"! ""

" " In this case, "hurt" "solemnly"; "methodically" and especially "ruthlessly" his honor; his dignity; and his personality; by insulting him "with all the big words and shocking possible"; uttering his "true, real insult"; "insults with terms very, very rude 's"; or to better express: "with very, very immodest words"; which would hurt him very, very strongly; and for the modesty people; letting him hear for example: it is indeed "a corpse standing"! It is in fact "an impotent"! And moreover, "a banana" for example; or "quite another thing" that looks like this, the case would still be better than him! .../...! ""

" " And then even the "Gallant" most seasoned manners and customs of "Blondinia" he forgets that it is then in truth "as a theatrical" in order to further consolidate the conjugal love. And especially for a "Sparrow" is hardly coming from this tradition "Blondinian" then one! ""

" " So then, is simply the bouquet! ""

" " It is simply unimaginable eh! ""

" " And what else to say! ""

" " And agreed!, ih!, It's simply the tradition! ""

" " The old tradition! ""

" " It is absolutely necessary to know that "the Blondinians" worthy of the name, swear by their tradition! It's like that; and it's stronger than them!

Hence, she or he should not even try to understand: The Why? It's like that and that's it! ""

" In short I said: And here, even the "Archetype" the most seasoned to the manners and customs of "Blondinia", he even forget, that it is then in truth, "as a theatrical" in order to further consolidate love "hymeneal". And especially for "the Type" which is not derived from this tradition "Blondinian" so then, it is the bouquet! ". And it is quite JULIO your case: you're hardly coming from this "Blondinian" 's tradition! Hence: it was really the bouquet! It was sort of, as a result of race: their heels. ""

" In short, in a "matrimonial home" "works perfectly" ("perfectly", as for example in "home to you JULIO and me the "Fatima" MARYVONNE precisely"), and ... / ... (I come back a little further, for now, I would already put the current numbers of other things, that "Blondinians" must not forget you :). ""

" In short, according to the "Blondinian" 's tradition, we never: not knowing that people share the environments in which they live, with not only benevolent spirits; but also with malevolent spirits [; and even this should be: to say]. ""

" In short, according to the "Blondinian" 's tradition, people must consequently often be reconciled and come to terms with the good spirits, in order to cope with spells evil spirits. ""

" In short, according to the "Blondinian" 's tradition; or rather: the fear "of Blondinians" is the question [¾] [question due to fear following [¾] that: the eternal world in which we live is changing too much too soon; and moreover, people are actually just "eternal ephemeral populations"; hence the fear would prove to be the question: ""

" "New Generations" of "Blondinians" (certainly able to adapt "multiple changes" due "to rapid technological intelligence", which ruthlessly challenge their manners and customs) would know they really perfectly continue to properly maintain their tradition? ""

" ¾ Do they ("the new generation" of "Blondinians") would hardly become an example of uprooted within their own territory? ""

"" Otherwise expressed: ¾ Do they developed would become for example, foreigners in their own territory? ""

"« ¾ Do they not be satisfied, for example, live only to "ease" due "to rapid technological intelligence"? »"

"""¾ They that in principle, from their earliest childhood, they have always and still always been used to fight hard in order to be able to earn a pittance? ""

"« Another question asked to the "Blondinians" is: ¾ Do, "ancestral spirits" of "Blondinians" and even all around good spirits of "these Blondinians in question precisely," would they continue to remain on good terms with these new generations who are willing to respect them, to "swing" for example, "their own manners and customs"? » «.

"" I come now to what I wanted to say to you JULIO earlier. " " ". " «» « ».

JULIO, to Maryvonne: " Go! And I'm listening! ".

Maryvonne, at JULIO: " In short, in a "marital home" "works perfectly" ["perfectly", as for example in "home to you JULIO and me MARYVONNE precisely"]; brief: "Parishioner" "and" "Parishioner" should absolutely usually ["**theatrically**" speaking, of course; and what's more: according to course "concept" well – oiled "Blondinian"]: »"

"« "Daughter of Eva" and "son of Adam" are usually absolutely "**will grab**" time to time. **But above all, above all they must remain inseparables**." ". ".

JULIO: " Great! ".

Maryvonne, at JULIO: " For "the Blondinians": "There is here, as in all other minority cultures, a big problem: a balance of majority cultures coming soon in our country; and which we are undeniably format. Just be careful: Even before this cultural threat is actually installed in our area; and thus it begins to undermine our way of ancestral life, it is therefore incumbent on ourselves "Blondinians" to find parades, in order to carry our manners and customs". »"

"" But what are these parades in question? ""

"« We know almost nothing ourselves! But all we can confirm, however: there was real progress in these areas! ". These are all that and stuff and all that, "cultural values" "the Blondinia"; that is to say: the values of Western societies would not hesitate much to qualify for example: "That they still flourish in a" time "," out of time "." Or rather: "That they would find themselves" again in years ",", light years "of difference from" teaching to Western values. " ". But only this: "Tastes and colors are not the same! "They say.". » " » " » " ».

JULIO: "Great! ".

MARYVONNE: " Finish "the joint of .../..."JULIO! ".

JULIO: " Great!

I understand now: The reason of the fact that the other times, there are already several years back now, Judge Alain Mermoz we do not even bring a solution!

He had been for a very, very long time; and that, in colonial times, in Brazzaville.

And as such, it must consequently among others, well be aware, too, of "tradition" "Blondinian"!

"... / ... This is because there is" **"zero problems to solve in your household"**!

And there is only "small kitchen room", "to adjust".

Otherwise expressed: **"There has only a small domestic kitchen set"**! ".

Hum mm!

"There is" "zero problems to solve!".

Anyway MARYVONNE!

Now I need to show you my apologies!

Hence, I do it automatically:

Apologies, MARYVONNE! ".

MARYVONNE: " You're excused! ".

JULIO: " Thank you! ".

MARYVONNE: " Quite frankly, "conscientiously" I made a big mistake with you JULIO! I made a big mistake with you by failing to explain to you in advance; that is to say, **before I practice "theatricality" of "Blondinian" with you,** "all this beautiful tradition" in question – here. If I had not done this omission, you would not even for example, had to take to their heels. ".

JULIO, to MARYVONNE: " This is: **An Awareness** eh! ".

MARYVONNE, at JULIO: " Aye, aye! **A True Awareness**. ".

JULIO, to MARYVONNE: " **Untimely**, anyway! ".

MARYVONNE, at JULIO: " Excuse me? ".

JULIO, to Maryvonne: " **A True untimely Awareness**. ".

MARYVONNE, at JULIO: " Absolutely: **A True untimely Awareness**. ".

JULIO, to Maryvonne: "Ah!, forget about it; because: **What's done is done**, as they say!. ".

MARYVONNE, at JULIO: " Okay!, forget about that. Now that you know the manners and customs of "Blondinia", you know: what will stick with me. And that is, essentially. People like your friend Christian GENEVRAY or even your other friends; or even my friends with me; or even people of my mother's family; and which we are familiar; they had little understanding of this fact; which actually does stop not trot them brains. ". """

" : (And what was that fact that it was JULIO and MARYVONNE loved greatly. But only here, they hardly stopped extend to each periodic tussles. Regular and continuous, and these, even the fishbowl many "silly", which watched the performance and periodically, so regularly and so constantly repeated, that were offered MARYVONNE and JULIO [, even if it was hardly accomplice], but only to an involuntary way, he stopped not of playing the game). """

" "But the truth is that" the curious "ignored (and even what you JULIO, yourself, you did not know)" ; that was then, in fact, a mislead – eye ("trompe – l'oeil"); it was not there, than a theater; a ritual theater; a ritual theater "wedding" that came from a few people of the African 's continent; and some from Africa as myself Maryvonne KEVILER precisely had done; and continue to persist with them so far in Europe, with the mixing of races, of course. " " """

"" (By the way on this, a Maryvonne KEVILER; and Henrietta KEMVILA, wife Nsenga, her paternal aunt, among – others, which had never forgotten, much less denied, their origins, continue to perpetuate these habits and customs.). """

" Do not keep as long, as I Maryvonne KEVILER I was hardly beaten by you, Julio Fernandez! You did indeed, never, ever, never, ever and never raised your hand on me! You did indeed, never, ever, never, ever and never hit me so slightly! You love me too, too, too; and for that, you have me in fact, never, ever, never, ever and never hurt me! JULIO you that in fact you're not even of "Blondinia"! You who are one hundred percent European. Our quarrels were only verbal and no more. But prevented much for all that, I was there then "my ample account" "a trollop" "originating Blondinia". """

"« (And when "the son of Adam" and "the daughter of Eva" come from "the Blondinia"! And they do carry this custom fights, then, then, then, then, "the Honey" would be beaten, and curiously: "»

"« Plus, Sir and Madam would fight; she would find Mrs. behalf. In fact, "the Doxy" would be beaten certainly, but in truth beaten theatrically speaking; but "non – indifference" as to them, they would see that fire! From where: "»

"« Plus apparently "Eva" would battle strongly by her "Adam"! "»

"" Moreover, they would. "»

"" And the more they would like; "»

"" They would fight a lot more. "»

"" And the more they would fight a lot; "»

"" Moreover, they would also like a lot. "»

"" And, they also would love; "»

"" Plus they still would beat a lot. "»

"" And the more they would fight a lot yet; "»

"" Moreover, they would also like a lot again and again. "»

"" And, they also would like to again and again much; "»

"" Moreover, they also would fighting again and again very much. "»

"« And paradoxically, the more "Horse" would not hardly beat "the Mare";"»

"" More also, it would find more than is. "»

"" And the more she grieve. "»

"" Illustration: "»

"" Or rather Initiations! "»

"« When "the Foal" and "the Filly" come from "the Blondinia"; and respect their tradition: The new "Chicken"; or rather, "the young Doll" should absolutely fit; or rather, the young "Chick" should fit perfectly: "»

"" In the initiations; "»

"" Female initiations; ""

"" Initiations female, not to say: ""

"« "The boots"; ""

"« "The boots" feminine's, so to speak; ""

"« "The boots" female variety; ""

"" To the recommendations; ""

"" The various boards; ""

"" The various boards on these customs and practices relating to these periodic tussles; successive; regulars and constants in question in the household; ""

"« Women's initiations for these manners and customs, initiated; or rather initiated by example, by the paternal aunts of "Bride"; ""

"" (And in this case with regard of MARYVONNE by Henrietta KEMVILA, wife Nsenga [the paternal aunt of the bride]): ""

"" And all of them should already be inculcated in the young lady for a long time already true; but above all, it would definitely have in principle be repeated to him only a few days ago, before the date; ""

"" Before the deadline; ""

"" Before the fateful date of marriage. ""

"« As the ancestors of [Maryvonne KEVILER]; and coincidentally also for the ancestors of Madame Henrietta KEMVILA, wife Nsenga; which were "the Blondinians"; they were consequently not forgotten their origin and above their manners and customs. ""

"« It was in fact, no more; no less, in order to maintain and yet still on, the magic of the flame of "marital atmosphere". ""

"" It was actually in the same way as for example, among other nations, we provide periodically; regularly and continuously by non – violent means; by gentle methods and happy (as illustrations: bouquets improvised; persons per capita; surprise visits from loved ones belonging to the family of the wife or husband that you would receive at home example to thousands of kilometers, where people are no longer met that very, very rarely by decade outputs surprises to eat in restaurants, to go to cinemas, to go to theaters, to go to the fairs ... / ...; unannounced trips and cetera etc ...) in order to again and again always keep alight the flame of spousal love. ""

˝« It's also the same way then that, among people such as those of "Blondinia" we offer periodically; regularly and continuously by "apparently non – sweet" and "apparently not happy" methods; by methods in truth non – violent; to achieve the same goal: "keep alive"; "The flame of hymeneal love". » « » « »"

˝« » « » « Henrietta KEMVILA, wife Nsenga said Maryvonne KEVILER e.g.: » " "No living being eternal in this world", adults and experienced "this kind of tradition Baroness will obviously die someday. Hence, it is essential if they want their tradition does not die with them, to carry through the initiations; or recommendations; or advice on this subject just for the benefit of the younger generation of women. Boys, as to them, they obviously receive their initiations, with men. And because of this, they will of course, with these: What to do in order to perpetuate this educational tradition. » « » « »"

˝« Where on the ladies: it is essential, if "Countesses and experienced adults" want their educational tradition does not die with them! They should absolutely have it carry through initiations; which ladies would have no choice but to follow; and to also in turn continue this lovely old educational tradition of silly humor; whims and "fights hymeneals". Or just "fighting double" sometimes rhyme; not to say often rhyme, with some misfortune. »"

˝« The two fighters did not warfare especially with their muscles [; especially not at all, at all]. But they would commitment rather, with their heads. But they rather would Skirmish with their ingenuity and creativity. In short: They are rather would encounter with their minds, so do not get too hurt one or the other [or any]. Thus, they would be entitled to such courses also, their finer spirits; their dreams; to demonstrate to the public as if their quarrels were very, very serious (Finally: it's exactly the same as the Hollywood 's films [in California]; or as the "Bollywood" 's films, [in Bombay]; or as the "Nollywood" 's films, [in Nigeria] or, as the Films also [elsewhere]: where fights and spectators are watching, they appear as a consequence, apparently true, when in truth they are only the results of staged methodically and carefully the orchestrated so we just deal in all these theaters then, to the calculating 's brawlers.).. »"

" " In "Blondinia" also: The so we just deal in all these theaters one: the calculating 's brawlers. ""

" " It even deserves to be called simply "Blondywood"; because: When do the same huh! ""

" " " A "Blondywoodian" 's cinema " concerning so exclusively that, scenes of households, in order to make homes, rowdy and especially crispy, in the eyes of onlookers or spectators more and more numerous, for adulation. ""

"" And so, it would periodically; it would regularly; it would continually, while a calculation to do. ""

"" It would periodically; it would regularly; it would continually, while a series of ideas to surprise; ""

"" It would periodically; it would regularly; it would continually, while an investment of surprises ideas to prepare at any time to find new introductions; new tricks; new pretenses; [New arguments] to constantly renew marital jousting; and of course, having found a range of introductions; ""

" " Short, it would be an investment ideas; of thought and creation; to "tickle so to speak, the pride of the one we would like above all"! "Tickle so to speak, self – love of the one we would like above all"; it would apparently confused feelings; but it would work fine, the couple. ""

" " In short, it's "the thrill of self – love of the one you would like on top"; and it would come back several times; not to say always the same scenarios. And so each would best be initiated for the benefit of the home; and she even rival creations; and originality of imaginations compared to other initiated. And so, each initiated a door to her own touch on "initiation", she would have received. And thereby forge additionally originality. And at the finish, thereby forge her character. " " " " ""

" " **A**nd all the images of the other ladies initiated in "morals" " The Conjugal 's "Movies" "Blondywoodians" " at the same time as me MARYVONNE; and see: all the advice and memories " The Conjugal 's "Movies" "Blondywoodians" " still parade so far, in my mind; they still marching, as if they were "burned" that yesterday. " ".

"" Thus, these calculating' s are brawlers, say for example; and this, in the bottom of themselves: ""

" And if we broke some glasses for example; to do well pleased "to various loafers" who always watching us during our fights? ""

"" After all, a few drinks are cheap? ""

"" After all, a few drinks are easy to replace? ""

"" After all, a few drinks to replace, would not make us poorer than we are already, for example? ""

"" After all, saving the destruction of a few drinks, do not make us rich; or if not more rich? ""

"" Thus, these calculating' s are brawlers – say for example; and this, in the bottom of themselves: ""

" And if we broke for example a few breakable plates; to do well pleased "to various window shoppers" who are always watching us during our fights? "

"" After all, few breakable plates aren't expensive? ""

"" After all, few breakable plates are easy to replace? ""

"" After all, some to replace breakable plates, would not make us poorer than we are already, for example? ""

"" After all, saving the destruction of some breakable plates, do not make us rich; or if not more rich? ""

"" Thus, these calculating' s are brawlers – say for example; and this, in the bottom of themselves: ""

"" And if we swung by example on the floor, a few books? ""

"" And if we swung by example on the floor, a few cans that we have in reserves? ""

"" Thus, these calculating' s are brawlers – say for example; and this, in the bottom of themselves: ""

"" And if by anger, we undid e.g. nuptial bed that is well arranged daily; and we swung all the sheets on the floor? ""

"" Thus, these calculating' s are brawlers – say for example; and this, in the bottom of themselves: ""

"" And if we had a few other minor disorder in the house? ""

"" It does not cost item as it expensive either? ""

"" And so actually the two sides would ignites; ""

"" And so, the two sides would actually few breaks; ""

"" And so, a few breakages and some minor disorders "would multiply" little; ""

"" And so, various "penguins" would love to see all these domestic scenes; and therefore they would ask again for to express ourselves in this way. " " " " """

"" These "bridal" tussles which apparently would: very, very serious; they are limited to operate only a few breaks and a few small disturbances by brawl. And it is perhaps little in the eyes of the "flannels". But only this, these fights would return regularly. And therefore: + little bit regularly = a lot. And besides, even above: this + little bit, it would already be very, very ample, in order to generate those belligerents expect of them: commiseration; compassion; pity and sadness; the pathetic sadness; the pathos of a marital unhappiness. ""

"" And it ah!, it would change the "looks" of fighters, with regard to "the window shopping". ""

"" And that ah!, that would indeed what is also sought in order to further consolidate the "hymeneal" love. ""

"" What a custom! ""

"" The "wedding" ritual theater! ""

"" What theater "marital" ritual! ""

"" It ah! ""

"" The scenes of households would have nothing to do for example with jealousy! ""

"" (It would not even have anything to do for example, adultery or fornication or infidelity!). " " " " """

"« In short, my aunt HEN told me and often told me: "In the vastness of this country" "Blondinia", both populated; but also wild, " The Conjugal 's "Movies" "Blondywoodians" " which, admittedly, their life is hardly ever, an easy one to find day after day, their pittance in fishing; in the hunt; in the collection; but also in culture, certainly; only here, the people have hitherto never provided, betrayed the teachings of their ancestors. And precisely in the context of these teachings, "the dames very, very experienced" have their place far, far apart; a very, very important; and doctrines; or rather, in the convictions of " The Conjugal 's "Movies" "Blondywoodians" " "the females " have unilaterally and undoubtedly the power to live "matrimonial home" in "Enchanting Moments" or "hellish times, not in the figurative sense, but in the true "meaning". """

"« And these teachings (which were sent to my aunt HEN by an aunt, and the latter of whom gets the obligation to pass on to hers nieces, and so on, these teachings) have created in me MARYVONNE: a passion; or rather: a way to love and strengthen love "wedding", of " The Conjugal 's "Movies" "Blondywoodians" ". """

"" One way which is not extinguished. A way that would look commiseration; compassion; pity and sadness; the pathetic sadness; the pathos of a marital unhappiness; a false domestic scene; a true – false domestic scene; a false – true domestic scene. " " » « » « » « » « ».

MARYVONNE: " Finish "the joint of shame" JULIO! ".

JULIO: " Wonderful! ".

"« "In short, my behavior me MARYVONNE, it's not bad character". """

"" This is not selfishness. ""

"" It's not that I only think about **my own sexual desire first**. ""

"" It is not hysteria. ""

"« But it's just a way for me MARYVONNE ["Rear - Kinese Descending"]:""

"" To be able to meet the flavors! ""

"« To be able to spice up the love "hymeneal"! »"

"" To be able to mix the flavors in the couple! ""

"« It is "spice" at " The Conjugal 's "Movies" "Blondywoodians" " ! »"

"« It is "chili very, very strong", forever and yet still stimulate the merger between "**female**" and "**male**". »"

"" And the snot about there? And not just any slime eh! It is therefore an abundant and endless nasal secretion, so to speak! Let's just say briefly about there, as you are at table: you wipe this mucus then; it comes back; you wipe it again; it comes back again; you wipe it again and again; it also comes back again and again; and so on. ""

"« Maryvonne : " " No comment! " " »"

"« Julio : " " Of course! " " »"

"« Maryvonne : " " No comment! " " »"

"« Julio, " " Without forget to mention the immediacy and simultaneity or coincidence of repetitive of dry cough, just for the time of these or other meals by example and the endless sneezing, at least when we find ourselves at the table, what! " " »"

"« Maryvonne " " So there! It's really no comment, you know Julio! " " »"

"« Julio: " " Yeah!, of course Maryvonne, I know it! " " »"

"« And, "this chili very strong", we do not acquire, through deception or by magic. »"

"« It is learned from "very experienced in this field lassies very"; "tootsies of" as my aunt HEN. »"

"« Learn "this chili very, very strong" to "colleens of" very, very experienced in the field, that's one thing. »"

"« But knowing how to create other "very very hot peppers", to include and add a personal touch (; which is also highly recommended by experienced originators in sessions initiations): it is one other thing, she should certainly hardly overlook. »"

"" And needless to say, it should definitely know how to create new charms; new spines; briefly, new flavors. ""

"" And yeah!, ih!, we should absolutely know how to create new scents; new tastes; new pleasant scents; which emerge from certain substances; of certain substances of love of course. ""

" " In short, it would be essential self "the Sweet thing" know how to create new flavors; new flavors certainly carnal; but, always a little provocative taste behind; always with a great – great aphrodisiac taste, in the end; taste which comes into immediate contact with all the reproductive organs; and moreover, that taste and noted, justly puts these pronto reproductive organs in question, in alert. """

" " They were here all the explanations he had previously taken, as I MARYVONNE? I'll explain; and that: explicitly! That said, if I think very, very well. If you JULIO, "you got yourself the trunk", it was hardly your fault! It was my own fault to me MARYVONNE! At the time when you told me about "the manners and customs of " The Conjugal 's "Movies" "Blondywoodians" " [I quote]: "And you would not really tell me more about" the manners and customs too, just too complicated "? ". I should have told you more effectively in that time already! And what do thou be little going on the run! But, remember this great mistake on my part then! It was: a big mistake on my part then! What for? This is because I absolutely refused! I refused absolutely! I refused absolutely to make you understand "the manners and customs of " The Conjugal 's "Movies" "Blondywoodians" "!" " " " " " " ".

JULIO: " Deny absolutely make me know! Absolutely refuse! Absolutely refuse! But it would hardly have had too much, too much, too much, either! It would hardly have had too much "absolutely refuse", either! Otherwise ¾! Otherwise, you're including yourself so that "these too absolutely refuse" had brought us! But hey! **It is the past! It is already behind us**! **Think no more**! ".

MARYVONNE: " These were" the manners and customs of " The Conjugal 's "Movies" "Blondywoodians" " "! And indeed, with "the manners and customs of " The Conjugal 's "Movies" "Blondywoodians" " spiciness; false provocation; boldness; the quaint behavior of "**Sweet thing**"; the humor; exaggeration; eccentricity; specificity; strangeness; extravagance; the absurdity; the oddity; true false domestic scene; nonconformity. Brief as it were, almost: everything and everything and everything and everything and yet all are loyal to the appointment! And so does "**honor**" (or "**dishonor**" huh! Because it depends: if the "everyman" is also derived from its own manners and customs or not! Hence: it will be "**of honor**" or "**of dishonor**") of "**gentlewoman**" way out "of the manners and customs of " The Conjugal 's "Movies" "Blondywoodians" ". In short, if you JULIO you "you were cut", it was my own fault! It would have taken quite frankly, I will clearly explains all these tussles then that I made you [fortunately verbally] **that were then in truth, as scenes of theaters, to further consolidate our love**. Including JULIO? ".

Julio Fernandez, meeting his wife Maryvonne KEVILER: " Absolutely! And back to the same question: Why you did not actually explained to me all those explicitly beforehand? And so, I should not have had to save me! **I even went on the contrary, stay and play the game with you**! Finally, what's done is done! And consequently, it could no longer be changed! ".

MARYVONNE, at JULIO: " And yep!, ih!, finally! ".

MARYVONNE understood very well, by living with "**The Unforgettable and Ineradicable**" JULIO: " That there should be absolutely it can among – others, also absolutely agree; and that, unconditionally, the mother of the latter, for example. For this, she even did better; because not only that she had reconciled with the mother and sister of Julio Fernandez; but even more importantly, she had sworn to estimate; to respect them; and also, everyone of their surroundings, to the end of her life here on earth. ".

MARYVONNE: " Now, it's "this" JULIO! ".

JULIO: " This is perfect! ".

And very, very curious, with this reunion, "unbridled" had slowed; and "sudden"; or rather, the "exploitable" could breathe.

Clearly?

Clearly means that: incessant and recurrent very, very strong incurable crises, anxiety; which MARYVONNE suffer severely from his childhood, had to the astonishment of everyone, volatilized, vanished into thin air, as if by magic; or rather, as by disenchantment.

Very, very oddly with the reunion of Julio Fernandez and Maryvonne KEVILER, with respect "the frantic search forever and ever again, pleasures" of the latter, it was just above and completely vanished into thin air, volatilized; and that consequently, "her noble man JULIO" as to him, well, so he could henceforth lead with this one: "a sensual life" "quite normal"; that is to say: "a private life, not at all, at all; exaggerated", as like the one they once led.

And so, Julio Fernandez was always and still always time to "get back on their feet".

And so, Julio Fernandez did not feel at all, at all, fear of authority "wreck mechanically speaking", for example.

"... / ... I would anyway in your arms; but at this point, I would hope that you'll only just understand me, forgive me, and therefore I avoid this kind of moral judgment, to shame, if not my for personality; but at least for my dignity.".

One day, "Sir" Moses KEVILER and senior workers "Sir" Thierry Glorian had gone to visit MARYVONNE in their new pavilion[1]. Once THIERRY had seen and appreciated; he suggested quite quietly to his boss: "What does she come a long way! Anyway dear master! Your "one Chick" is done well in this real nervous breakdown eh! ". And Moses KEVILER also respond quite discreetly, at Thierry Glorian: " Say instead: " "... / ..." "Your Delilah" "is done well this true eh!, heartache!". Because quite frankly, it is "a real heartache"; rather than anything else! ". ".

MARYVONNE: " Now our vision is trained on "this" JULIO! ".

JULIO: " It's great! ".

Maryvonne KEVILER which in reality, was not at all aware of all the machinations and shenanigans made fresh, under the patronage and supervision of her father;

---

[1] On the Rue des Rosiers in Suresnes, West of Paris.

Maryvonne KEVILER which in reality could therefore not at all, at all, namely the colossal money matters that her dad had spent precisely for these machinations and shenanigans liquidity; she believe with conviction, she was right; when she once said Julio Fernandez, even if it saved; that even if he took "another Chicken"; he would end anyway one way or another, by returning to hers arms;

And Maryvonne KEVILER, consequently; she was just about to make a serious reflection to "her Samson Julio Fernandez"; reflection which would certainly make this reunion switch to some possible deadlock. Hence, she remembered misses, a sentence of JULIO; which was clearly marked well before he flees; which said: " ... / ... If you're right ... / .... I would anyway by returning in your arms; but at this point, I would hope that you'll only just understand me, forgive me, and therefore I avoid this kind of moral judgment, to shame, if not: for my personality; but at least for my dignity. ".

Hence, she had failed to make him this serious thought. She preferred to a clean sweep of the past. She preferred to forget the past. And consequently, she preferred: to see only the present and the future; avoiding decidedly "to make the damned"; or rather to " to make the stupid bastard". Speaking just for the present and the future, some influential friends of Moses KEVILER were able to get to the benefit of Julio Fernandez: and this even before her marriage already with Maryvonne KEVILER: a good job; a good job among the Members of Personnel Services of the United Nations, in the megalopolis of New York. The Poitevese only waiting definitely, that his marriage with the latter, in order to be able to get there. There had also helped the mother of the former; which proved for a long time, being one of the major concerns of the former precisely; especially since she had not contributed much to the Old Age Fund, to for example, claim to enjoy a happy retirement. There had helped this mom to be able to get hired anyway, despite her age more or less fairly advanced at a job that was any more precarious.

In short, after the departure of Evelyn MULER, from the apartment rented by Julio Fernandez; already, while still getting a divorce with the former; which rightly recognized that one course be at fault (Violation of conjugal faith, so to speak, with proof [And for good reason!] ¾ required): not only (and this, only a few short months after the dismissal of EVELYN) that (and this is to say: he Julio Fernandez) would arrange in the villa; or rather, in the pavilion of the Paris 's region; where he had become (and how!) now himself the owner; but, pending divorce, he already live again as married, with "his old claimed MARYVONNE".

When the divorce between JULIO and EVELYN would judge pronounced by the marital (and that, as soon as possible, moreover, the judge by the name of Casmir GARCIA) one, this time 'it, systematically marry MARYVONNE, the Mayor of their town, making their union: legitimate this time. And shortly after only JULIO would work in his new position in New York; and MARYVONNE and her son would follow a few months later. That one would chuck her work "Trilingual Executive Secretary"; and she would follow (herself and their son LUCILIAN, which had about ten years, this time), six months after the departure of her husband JULIO, at New York, in the Megacity, to join him. Mrs. Maryvonne KEVILER, wife Julio Fernandez have again two children (a boy named Patrick FERNANDEZ [, that is to say: as the deceased father of her dad, which was called exactly the same, that is to say : it is for the first name, and it is for the name] and a girl named Yolanda FERNANDEZ [, that is to say: YOLANDA, the name, like the name of the mother of Julio FERNANDEZ, and as the name]). The full name of their eldest son, would remain as such. In short, these two children would from MARYVONNE with JULIO, of course. Hence the fact that their first and last names were related to the family of that fact. The couple [JULIO – MARYVONNE] would in any two son (counting both obviously Lucilian KEVILER, which would keep intact his first and last name) and a girl.

MARYVONNE: " Now our vision is trained on "the future" JULIO! ".
JULIO: " Awesome! ".

" And so with this couple together again, "the hymn to love" could be sung: ""

" Singing for me for a bit, it is like "being thrown" ("singing for you" [and even "singing for others" I would rather say; ""

" It is like "being thrown") in "a world of science fiction"; ""

" Or, rather, in a "universe" of "Anthem"; ""

" Of "the anthem so to speak: that virility" [that is to say: "the hymn actually say what the male"]; that is to say: "the hymn to love, the male"; ""

" That is to say: as in the old "songs or poems in honor of the gods and heroes"; or simply, as a "national song"; ""

" Or even as "the anthem so to speak: that feminizing" [that is to say: "the hymn actually say what the female"]; that is to say: "the hymn to love in the women" indeed; ""

" That is to say: as "religious poetic composition, used in Christian liturgy and often set to music"! ""

" But that's just "the world of the hymn that issue here", "he" turns out to be "locked"; or "very coded"; and see: "very, very locked"! And especially with multiple upper and media phrases! ""

" And here now, "the hymn to love just" ""

" "The sensational fire"; stripped Þ "The blood vampirian" now! ""

" "Sensual requirements"; evacuated Þ "The worst kind" definitely! ""

" "Doping neurotransmitters" resigned now! Þ "Diving as" "In her thoughts"! ""

" "And the vitality", "this kind released already now! Þ of workhorse"! ""

" "Oh!, wretched and miserable", ultimately renounced! Þ not ""

" "The Bouncing bellies" quality!, abjured it clearly! Þ Ah! ""

Þ " " "The top level of embrace" decamped for sure! ""

Þ " " "The terms rather coded" decoded really! ""

"« But that's just, it happens sometimes, that to "rat – in – legs" out; or rather: "the penetrating of lap rocket" who shows much less energy; since, for example, for many a long time already, been under the influence of some of these troublesome Þ libidinal side effects due to daily doses of drugs against hypertension trousers down, of course! »"

"« But that's just, it happens sometimes, that to bring out "the butterfly of Senegal"; or rather "the stick" from his lethargy; it would consequently much more decamped obviously! Þ than female physical beauty »"

"« Is "naturopathy" was actually deflated! Þa plane »"

"« Abandoned Þ "A foolproof plan definitely"! »"

"« Where eh! "Man" with "a" certainly not disinterested! Þ capital "M" is a handyman of solutions »"

"« And so "speed arm drunk"; or rather "the rod of pleasure and be infallibly won! Þ completely drunk" "Broad Faced Chicken" »"

"« And so we finally would realize that "the oblong object"; or rather "the steel rod" would adamantly forgotten! Þ hardly lost its tone »"

That said, this poor Evelyn MULER, how could she get out of this predicament? Stage a blow against the thicket of new household JULIO; driving away for the second time, in one of his Mixed – race lovely, perhaps; so you can recover him exactly; and therefore bring thereafter cleverly enough in the arms of Evelyn MULER; to save this last question?

When the divorce between Julio Fernandez and Evelyn MULER would be so pronounced by the judge marital Casmir GARCIA, the "subversive accomplices Poulain DERECK and Giraud ZEFRINO" have over there and graced the second and final leg of their delicate and subversive mission. They have so briskly: led to the end of the contract of their dirty work;

which they had passed on the sly with Moses KEVILER, through Thierry Glorian, one of his faithful workers 's butchers. However, Poulain and his "compagnero" Giraud actually would affect "their balances all accounts". MOSES would have spent a large fortune. (But alas! Saving the lives of "her" "heir" ["the Brunette"] unique and heiress [too], "only by that way according to his point of view ¾ forced").

However, if the side of Maryvonne KEVILER, things had finally rearrangements [And how!]. But nonetheless with Evelyn MULER by against, things had deteriorated precipitously. And even they were downright destroyed [and for good reason]. This is because after having honored the second phase of their Machiavellian contract; and even before actually moreover, the gallant and elegant Daughter of Eva's Killer Giraud ZEFRINO not looking at all, at all feel Evelyn MULER. And therefore his promise to first get her divorce with JULIO, so that he could quietly marry her; or rather, that she, she can remarry and start a new life with him; this promise remained thereafter simply regarded as a dead letter. It was simply "rubbish" as promise. It was just "the wind" as promise.

As a result of race?

Aye, aye!, ih! As a result of the race, he would just unfortunately alas!, a "direct transfer" of "nervous breakdown" (that had suffered for a long time, Maryvonne KEVILER (; Which no therapeutic drug had been unable to cure [except the return of Julio Fernandez in hers arms]) "to Evelyn MULER", since it will now also think that Julio Fernandez and therefore, nothing on "this planet Earth," that. Only remarriage with him Julio, could be for her: an ultimate therapeutic care short, not any antidepressant medication or something else like this, that only the return of JULIO to hers arms, could not cure "the Poor Evelyn MULER" who hardly knew any… conspiracy mounted against her (and for good reason), she would suffer very, very exactly the same way as in the past, suffered Maryvonne KEVILER. And indeed, she would suffer even "a superlative scale"; since, repeatedly she showed "conspicuous expressions and melodramatic", speaking of her household that was ruined. Now for her and also conclusively, Julio Fernandez "Descent From Poitevese And Background On Spanish Descent", continued to remain quite frankly: "The Irreplaceable" and "The Irreversible"; "The Indisputable" and "The Uncontested"; and finally "The Unforgettable" and "The Impossiblestar "; for hardly say for example: "The Inevitable" and "The Unrecoverablestar".

That said, "this poor Evelyn MULER" how could she get out of this predicament?

Stage a blow against the thicket of new JULIO 's household; driving away for the second times, in one of his half – breed lovely, perhaps; so you can recover him exactly; and therefore bring thereafter cleverly enough in the arms of Evelyn MULER; to save this last in question? But how much would cost such a delicate and subversive mission?

And who would be able to pay him one?
And even if the dad of EVELYN example could afford to finance such a delicate and subversive work precisely for the sake of his "Agnes, Evelyn MULER"; but was it also that dad in question was himself Machiavellian nature to get there?

But alas!, unfortunately, as Evelyn MULER had no relatives Machiavellian in order "to do, make the transfer from her awkward nervous breakdown", to "another Old Bag" and in this case: to Maryvonne KEVILER!"; for it was she who had [as it were] definitely lost JULIO. Although magically too, they did not even have "a lot of money matters" to do so. Therefore, she; that is to say: Evelyn MULER; not be satisfied that taking antidepressants, against her nervous depression; she now suffers greatly. Evelyn MULER stop taking hers pills for nearly two months without hers parents' knowledge; nor hers friends for example. In addition, she also stop eating and drinking for three days towards the end of the two months in question. It was exactly like that, it had proceeded with Maryvonne KEVILER.

EVELYN just had slowly (and as it were also "slowly and surely"), began to sink. She was beginning to fall slightly in a first time, in a state of semi – consciousness. And then her dad Yves MULER and his friends (; which coincidentally, they were presents in –––); which found themselves sitting right beside her, EVELYN in question; they all were put up; they stood with their multiple arms; and that's before for example, they have had the slightest moment: really dip: Those were happening exactly, suddenly? Then, there, in a second stage suddenly EVELYN instantly had slipped into unconsciousness. And yeah!, ih!, she had fallen into a swoon!; or to better express it: she had already fainted. There had phoned any speed "The Urgent Medical Assistance Service".

In short, EVELYN would turn the eye. And they bring in urgently to hospital[1] . Then, she would fall squarely into a deep coma. It was also exactly like that, as it happened with MARYVONNE. EVELYN come into emergency, hospital[1]; where she would remain in all a good two months. The first three days, she would be fed, with probes; that is to say: as MARYVONNE once, at "Our Lady Of Good Helps 's Hospital", in Paris – Fourteenth. When Evelyn MULER was discharged from hospital after her coma; which she had come out of course, not bad at all (oh!, that fate is hail, oh!, that eternal sleep, in no case, so far!) her dad Yves MULER and his followers work colleagues (two in number, which were called Laval BRICE and Loïc MORIN; of labors highway maintenance, which, incidentally already often went to visit her, during her hospitalization and were both gone together with Yves MULER, on a break from Loïc MORIN, to recover Evelyn MULER of the hospital and back her, into the apartment of hers parents, arriving YVES 's home. Arriving YVES 's home justly, Loïc MORIN, the colleague in question of Yves MULER, observing very, very well EVELYN, he would tell one: quite quietly: "What she has come a long Anyway dear colleague". Your one "little Bee" "did very, very well out of her True Depression, huh!".And Yves MULER also respond quite discreetly at Loïc MORIN: " "Say instead": "... / ...". "Your One Religious Mentee" "is

---

[1] In the "Gilles Hospital" located on the Boulevard Henry Dunant at Corbeil – Essonne.

done well this True Sorrow Of Love eh!". Because quite frankly, it is "a real heartache!". "Rather than anything else. "[1]". ".

So they were very, very exactly the same words which were spoken before, about Maryvonne KEVILER; while all these people then precisely did not even have to talk together before. Besides, how could they do it? They do not know each other.

LOÏC, at YVES: " And yep!, ih! A real heartache! It ah! ".

YVES, at LOÏC: " Because, that's what had led her, this depression; and it's also this, which might even win one day, in the world of stiffs; if and only if it does not stop at all, at all, to think about "her ex – Adam, Julio Fernandez"! ".

LOÏC, at YVES: " It's true! But how will she do to forget? ".

YVES, at LOÏC: " Forget it! She keeps repeating to her mother for her, Julio Fernandez "Descent From Poitevese And Background On Spanish Descent" remains; and still remain elsewhere: "the **Unforgettable** and the **Inerasable**"! ".

Laval BRICE, at Yves MULER: " I know it is not easy. ".

Loïc MORIN: " And aye!, ih! It's not easy eh! ".

Yves MULER: " All this, it was also her fault herself. ".

---

[1] In fact, it was actually; and this: very, very curious, very, very exactly the same expressions as already Thierry Glorian suggested to the attention of his kind patron; or rather his beloved boss Moses KEVILER; and vice versa; when we left to visit MARYVONNE; which had just been released from hospital; and that it was causing quite quietly about her.

Listening to this, Mr. Laval BRICE, another friend of Yves MULER, took the opportunity to ask the why?

Laval BRICE, at Yves MULER: " How it was also her fault herself? ".

Yves MULER, at Laval BRICE: " You know very well; because I had told you already! I already told you two; LAVAL yours and LOÏC; as my loyal friends and colleagues, this shameful and sad story! ".

Loïc MORIN, at Yves MULER: " No, it was all by myself that you had told. LAVAL was not there; and you also tell him the counting after yourself. Then you'd probably have forgotten to do so. ".

YVES, at LOÏC: " Since LOÏC to you, I have told this shameful and sad story. Then you could repeat it; and that, in short, at our friend BRICE too, huh! ".

LOÏC, at BRICE: " Okay. It's very charming "goose" was fucking "her hymen" in the air. She had shattered "her hymen" with Julio Fernandez "Descent From eh!, eh, eh ... / .... ".

Yves MULER: " Poitevese ... / .... ".

Loïc MORIN: " Aye, aye!, "Poitevese ... / ....". She had shattered her "conjugal 's hymen" not hesitating at all, "to get plastered the mouth" with a **Antigone 's "Faller ¾ Down"** named Giraud ZEFRINO; and what is more, hesitantly, if at all any, fornicate with him. This precisely who promised her a better life. "Her noble man JULIO"; or rather, "her ex – Adam JULIO" had prevented by all means, go sleep out with the **Juliet's Killer** Giraud ZEFRINO in Lyon (since the adultery happened in Greater Lyon). But alas!, unfortunately, "his **lassie**, EVELYN" (had systematically defying "her hominid JULIO", which he is yet, "the **Unforgettable**" and "the **Unforgettable**)"; she did not want to listen a him, a little bit. And here now, race results of this ridiculous nonsense! He had promised her ... / .... ".

Yves MULER: " That's it, have "one **Filly!**". If we could, while it was not yet too late, have many kids! Finally is! Honestly, I even prefer to be done with her forever! ".

Laval BRICE: " My God! ".

Loïc MORIN: " He had promised her a house on their own and children; especially that "JULIO his ape" who have not yet found a job he wanted so badly; and he also very ambitious to do absolutely economic projects.

He would not, therefore, not at all, at all, to hear in these times, to have children. ».

Yves MULER: " LOÏC, please do not forget to specify him, that Evelyn, she was upset, because she could not even identify, if only more or less about: How long those moments of waiting precisely would last! She could not know: How long Julio would make her wait! Is he going to make her wait until, that 'would be too late for her to have more offspring? And it was there, a big question mark! ".

Loïc MORIN: " Oh!, aye, aye!, ih! It was then, a big question indeed! In doing so, "his **girl**, EVELYN", not knowing: How long do need if only roughly approximate, wait? Not to say: "his **womanly**, EVELYN" not knowing: How much time she took just wait; not forgot to mention the fact, that for her, as the years passed; and also, she might well not any more, at all be able to have the children's. And it is sure that when she thought of it; and that a ... / ...! ".

Yves MULER: " And when a gallant and elegant **Arian 's "Faller ¾ Down"** named Giraud ZEFRINO; a Giraud ZEFRINO who was **"An Ace of Aces Computer"**! And "when a gentleman" as it showed up in the horizon eh! ".

Loïc MORIN: " Now, coincidentally also "the **Spider** EVELYN" our faithful friend and colleague Yves MULER turns out to be "the **only Girl**" who have no one else very safe, except of course her father YVES himself and her mother Simone; thinking and find ... / ...! ".

Yves MULER: " And thinking regain a future family guarantee, only a well – stocked offspring also huh! ".

Loïc MORIN: " Here! Thinking and find a future family guarantee, only a well – stocked as offspring. Then "his **Dignified**, EVELYN" of course, she had naively as she accepted the lies ... / ...! ".

Yves MULER: " She finally agreed the Machiavellian lies of a gallant and elegant "**Ace of Aces Computer**"; which in reality was only thinking satisfy about his "**bestial**" **insatiable instinct**. ".

Laval BRICE: " It's really pathetic for it eh! ".

Loïc MORIN: " And after getting what he wanted; that is to say, after having spent a hectic night together with her at Lyon; where he had taken her on holiday. This Computer 's genius had simply dropped EVELYN, or drum or trumpet, if it could speak like that! ".

Laval BRICE: " It is very sad indeed. But at least for me; for me LAVAL, I would not give too much, too much, hurt EVELYN! ".

Yves MULER: " Why? ".

Laval BRICE: " For the simple reason that it was not she, who had chosen to be: **the only kid** eh! ".

Yves MULER: " Of course not! But ... / ...! ".

Laval BRICE: " But? ".

Yves MULER: " But there are many "other unique **effeminates**" in her case! But they do not act so far ... / ...! ".

Loïc MORIN: " Not as long as it? ".

Yves MULER: " Indeed! ".

Laval BRICE: " However, for she EVELYN, uh − huh!, ih! From where ... / .... ".

Yves MULER: " Where? ".

Laval BRICE: " Where, in order to provide [for] the future; when you YVES and her mother; that is to say "your **Countess** SIMONE", you will no longer be of this world; do not risk ... / .... ".

Yves MULER: " By all means!, ih!, ih, ih! Not to risk? ".

Laval BRICE: " To know possibly loneliness. In doing so, she kept foremost in his life together, to have a family guarantee, only offspring just, well stocked. That's what I wanted to say that about me − LAVAL, I would not give too much, too much, hurt EVELYN! ".

Yves MULER: " Is Finally! ".

Laval BRICE: " A better material life and own their own home, hardly counted it great for her EVELYN; this is because in the long run, she could, of course with her husband and **their possible future** "brats"; it could become the heir to your room; or rather, they could have become heirs of your apartment; which you soon already paid off the debts. ".

Yves MULER: " You really do not wrong LAVAL! But me and "my **Baroness** Simone" when it was still time for children; we deliberately chose to have one; which, coincidentally, turned out to be "a **Ladylike**: EVELYN"; it was because the universe ... / ...! ".

BRICE Laval: " "The **emergency** tail"! ".

Loïc MORIN: " And sure!, ih! ".

Yves MULER: " It was because the socio – economic 's world did not stop darkening. Moreover, even so far for all of us here as small workers (; although it has the qualification of **SW [Specialized Workers]** to do more respectable and respectful. But only here, we do 're only small workers. Hence the fact that I said. besides even so far for all of us here as small workers); I could even say that it (**the socio – economic 's universe** in question) not cleared yet! ".

Loïc MORIN: " We should think about it anymore. It would only advise your cute this time, not to stop taking the pills; and this, three times daily; that is to say: **morning**; **noon** and **evening**; **as was prescribed by the doctor**; and ... / .... ".

Yves MULER: " And? ".

Loïc MORIN: " And to ensure that she no longer makes a hunger strike. ".

Yves MULER: " I'll watch anyway; in order to achieve it, even if it means lying her, for example, by promising simply to bring back very, very soon, the Julio Fernandez "Descent From Poitevese ... / ...". ".

Yves MULER had so effectively given this false promise to "his **Blonde**", for relief. And consequently, it is also believed that he would bring her Julio Fernandez "Of Descent From Poitevese ... / ..." very, very soon.

And given the fact that we do not yet brought him, his JULIO; and as time went on; curiously again: as was already up to four times in total with Julio Fernandez, Evelyn MULER would also become "crazy, crazy ally", "like hell". For this, she would start "pedaling in sauerkraut". She would tell at the attention e.g. herself; at her father Yves MULER and at his work 's colleagues of him (all of them who listened carefully), words without heads or tails; lyrics such as: """

"« » « » " EVELYN becomes downright mad, mad – ally; and she never, ever, never, ever, never, and ever, would stop "to talk nonsense". """

"« B efore " to talk nonsense " EVELYN "talking nonsense ". """

"« After "to talking nonsense", """

"« EVELYN "talked again nonsense". """

"« Between "talking nonsense's states", EVELYN "talked again and again nonsense". """

"« "Tramontana" in the house or "actual disruption"? Will is an evil, "blizzard" in the house? Will is "a flurry" in the house? It's a real problem this: take me "him my new Archetype Giraud". He no longer wants to do it! It would take me more! Yet me "EVELYN," I'm his future self (although he is not yet officially married)! """

"« Me take over "him my Type JULIO " of course; he would want to do more! He did not want under any circumstances, take me back! And yet, "I EVELYN" I'm still so far as I know: his wife (and even if it is almost officially divorced already)! "Him my Man JULIO", he did not want at all, at all feel! He said: "That I am polluted" with "another Romeo"! This is a real problem that actually, indeed!, ih! They are seen methodically first, "these hominids then" before one of them can make a decision in my favor? "Clumsy" observes first "Heavy" "methodically"? "Ulysses" occurs first methodically with "Motherly"? One and the other occurs first methodically? Be observed first methodically "tone" for example? """

"« "The tone" for example, " him my new Partner Giraud ", which is sweeping the tone of "him, my Bimanous JULIO"! "Observer" greenness of "him my new Archetype Giraud " that is sweeping the force "him, my Type JULIO"! ["Observed"] dynamic "him my new Gun Giraud" that is sweeping "the old economic ideas to try first successful projects" that "her my Original, JULIO" was mapped out in his mind ! But Giraud will change everything! """

"" Since JULIO would not change much; Giraud putting a blackout in my past with JULIO, he solemnly told me that he was for my future! The eye of Justice with a capital "J", does he want to take the point already right now, with the apparent kindness of this Giraud, to me; with its promises; with smiles; with his pipe dream to take me first with my parents; with its concept to first realize my divorce; with his idea to marry me immediately; and prospects to grant me a better life, with quite numerous offspring! All these, they were just the can! With "all Lyon Coquettishness' pictures" that are engraved and even now tirelessly and yet in my head; and he has already forgotten the whole story here! """

"" Giraud actually decided to take me out "red card" after "the pipeline" "yellow", followed immediately by "red", for JULIO! Yet "me EVELYN", I am "his future Lady" (and even if he is not yet officially married)! Is celebrated as "ruthless yellow cards" on "ruthless red cards" on "pathetic" "person Sex EVELYN " to be famous! Now "a good nervous breakdown" "already watching me on the horizon", I EVELYN! And now, it is with "the nervous breakdown" "watching me just on the horizon", I'll find a way to bear; "If and only if ¾ " "I could do it too of course": "all the weight of my naivety"; of "my blind trust a Giraud" and "Muse" "stupidly become lonely"! You really had in my life, I met "this Sahib named: Giraud", for I come, where I am now! It ah! """

"" And that's not all! "And that's not all"! That's because he also had to agree to all these empty promises! And that's not all! "And that's not all"! That's because he also had too, that I agreed to go "make me climb" by him! I accept to go for me "plow" through him! It was anyhow, "carnival" of "getaway"; of "naive"; of "blind faith"; "empty promises; "copious climbing"; "hearty plowing" with even "more sagacity" and especially "audacity"! Anyway: "The Getaway" and "Escalation" in question here, beyond of course the understanding! """

"" Um mm! "... / ... Which he is here", "exceed, of course", the understanding! And so, since me EVELYN alternating weak and insignificant dreams; and so, since me EVELYN alternates the most poor and the most pitiful nightmares! Giraud who told me EVELYN "a bitch naturally enjoying hauntingly beautiful"! And he forgot all of a sudden! ""

"" And so, once things are very bad between me EVELYN and him JULIO; and as for the height of paradox, it also goes very wrong between me EVELYN and him Giraud, what! ""

"" And yet, "from one day to the other" (including "some good Saturday morning", to "Station of Lyon"), JULIO do it made me not already hold, as anything "our love disappear"; me EVELYN if I persisted to follow the adventurer Giraud in Lyon?

But that, as to me EVELYN stubborn as I am; I absolutely wanted hardly at all (, so really, " " I really wanted to do much at all, at all, to hear so little)? ""

"" Then here, "that good someday also" (especially "good certain Sunday in the afternoon", and that, in his apartment in the Eleventh Arrondissement of Paris), that our love was actually really gone! Whose fault is it now if I "got silted up" and in "the quicksand"; and even in those "quicksand"; and on and on forever, in "the same quicksand"! Is it the fault of him JULIO? But no! ""

"" And I did it for fun "of bitches"? ""

"" And he earns me what? "Some kids" "into the hands", perhaps? ""

"" Where are they "these kids in question"? ""

"" Him JULIO and yet wanted to hear about "the kids", "because of the money that they ignite"! ""

"" Certainly, by one way or another, there he was not a "continuum" "between on the one hand, him JULIO and secondly, him Giraud"; which is also "a way or another course": "continuo" between "these two Fellows"? ""

"" And yeah! That'll teach me "to me EVELYN", not at all, at all: be naive in life! " " " " ".

"" " " " " EVELYN becomes downright mad, mad – ally; and she never, ever, never, ever, never, and ever, would stop "to talk nonsense". ""

⁽" **B**efore " to talk nonsense " EVELYN "talking nonsense ". ""

⁽" After "to talking nonsense", ""

⁽" EVELYN "talked again nonsense". ""

⁽" Between "talking nonsense's states", EVELYN "talked again and again nonsense". ""

"" Otherwise explained: ""

⁽" Before "to become anxious," EVELYN "was becoming anxious". ""

⁽" After "being anxious", EVELYNE "became even anguished". ""

⁽" Between "anxiety's states", EVELYN "became even more anxious." ""

⁽" Brief, EVELYN becomes downright mad, mad – ally; and she never, ever, never, ever, never, and ever, would stop "to talk nonsense". And in this context of "to talk nonsense", she would say to her mother, for example: ""

⁽" Evelyn, so talking to her mom Madam Simone Durand, wife MULER: "What I liked in" this here called Julio, "that before procure me what "will then be" "says my sleep repairman" that "eyes closed, so to speak", he let himself be guided by blinding me Evelyn. Ah!, when I thought for example our four mouth lips combined together [mixed if you like]! And "this gun" fled! He really escaped! Certainly there is in my memory, others lips; other lips, as I have known before! But in any case, they were not the same! Those other lips – here turned out to be far inferiors! They "drooled" too often saliva in "my valve". And besides, their tongues knew undertake no movement! But, they were there, that poor Evelyn memories for me! But then, he is, in my life "hymen" JULIO with him; there was always in moments of great feelings of inner joy and great satisfaction; moments such as those I have always known and yet always with this one, even when the moment I began to cohabit with him matrimonially, poor memories crossing [certainly periodically] my mind, as for example, neuralgia and against which precisely I did everything to forget; but unfortunately alas!, I just could not! But, it is only then that the memories! And now I find myself far from Paris especially, I find myself here in Corbeil – Essonne with my parents. True, not prevent others weirdoes I had known before, also knew [as for himself JULIO] "kicking kidneys". In short, [and do not have disgust quote this verb, mom], they knew "overlap". But what makes the difference with JULIO; that it in this matter (See what I mean Mom?), he knows how to do everything! When I think, for example, in "My valve," his tongue knew perfectly ensure the synchronism movements to and fro; his tongue knew perfectly ensure the synchronism of movements go and back and just; and those of other movements of the tongue, for example, those of articulation with my tongue to me Evelyn. In short, the language of JULIO knows perfectly synchronized movements back and forth and all other movements with my tongue to me Evelyn without such "drooling at me with saliva inside my mouth"; while supporting this synchronized action, using various small licks precisely on my tongue to me Evelyn! Humm mm! In addition, this JULIO knew "down in the cellar!" Otherwise expressed: Also, this JULIO knew "give his tongue to the cat" (You still know what I want to tell you mom? The Cunnilingus, what?!); "He knew me, give a phone call," always with various small licks, but of course at the base of the meatus; just something that they, my other conquests before Julio, did not know me procure; or perhaps "they were reluctant" to make me procure that! JULIO But for him, there was not a little reluctance in this! Even that sadistic Seducer of GIRAUD, which made me lose my Julio in question, in truth no idea (really so: not at all, at all), make me sure all these synchronic movements. Ah!, if only that day – there, at the East' Station, I had listened to the advices of Julio, when it was not yet too late! Now, damn it! That's fucked up ; because he must be left to join his Maryvonne, right now – here! """

" « I admit that for finally my Rosebud and its contours; briefly: for my anatomy, Julio him, in order "to make the commissioner's hat", he sucks me Evelyn even better and better and better at superlative; as if it was for example, a bee sucking a flower or sugar. And that ah!, it's magnificence – even. And this JULIO just decided to slip away without even so far, being asked! Evelyn and tell me that I had taken considerable risks, going to try to find him in what I believed to still be his matrimonial home with his Maryvonne! Anyway, I was undoubtedly "bitch"! But eh! When you love someone like me Evelyn I love JULIO; and that someone in question is saved, without being asked! When we love and do it well the farce, not to tell you where he went eh! Then ! " " " " ".

But only here, although Yves MULER could beseech Julio Fernandez, resume Evelyn MULER!

But how he could accept her frankly, "a **Matronly**" who was very, very generously "polluted" by "another **gas**"; and he just JULIO he knew?

It would be very, very difficult for him Julio Fernandez, to accept such a combination.

It would be very, very difficult for him Julio Fernandez, to accept such a combination; because by comparing for example, Evelyn MULER with Maryvonne KEVILER, thereof, to the knowledge of JULIO, this latter had not even agreed to have "another chap" after the run of him.

"**Mister**" Yves MULER had thus giving the false promise "his **Brunette** Evelyn MULER" to bring her, Julio Fernandez, to relieve him. But the truth in such an emotional and mental state in which this EVELYN eventually end up. It should therefore not at all, ever so slightly, playing the sorcerer's apprentice with her; it should not be at all, at all, ever so slightly to lie in that way. What for? This is for the simple reason that she now expected stubbornly like what, the pretty promise that her father had given her, was actually very, very close to realization. And as this pretty promise in question did not actually materialize; then she just continue to become "mad, mad ally", "like hell".

Laval BRICE, at Yves MULER: " It should absolutely see to her. Because, if she restarts for the second time, not to take her medication; and not to eat; it simply could be fatal!".

Of those, LOÏC and LAVAL went away, saying: "Goodbye!", at Everyone.

Anyway, Mrs. Maryvonne KEVILER, wife FERNANDEZ would be happy. And she would confess [to interfere without any degree], to his father and her mother [when they left to visit them during their summer vacation in New York]: What were it not her reunion with Julio Fernandez; she would simply stop living quietly; surely and gradually.

When Maryvonne KEVILER had his second son already, of course with Julio Fernandez; she did not at all think would work again soon; if not, she would think more, to permanently outright; in order to take care this time 'it, now that almost exclusively herself (and it is to say, contrary to what it was before, when she was still living as husband and wife with Julio Fernandez), cleaning her home (Improving its characters [And for good reason!] – required). The pair (JULIO – MARYVONNE) did not have to be worry for their monthly budgets; they had even no problems for their monthly budgets even if she had stopped working. This is because that one had found a very, very good job in an Office of Workforce Services UNO; with support; or rather, by the piston of some influential friends of "Sir" Moses KEVILER. In addition, JULIO did not have to be worry for his mother; since as expected, discreetly, that one through intermediaries; he was occupied with his fate and numerical hardware (and for good reason). Anyway, Mrs. Maryvonne KEVILER, wife FERNANDEZ would be happy. And she would confess [to interfere without any degree], to her father and her mother (when they left to visit them during their summer vacation in New York): What were it not her reunion with Julio Fernandez; she would simply stop living quietly; surely and gradually. But only here, that this confession, she had never made himself JULIO; which had anyway despite everything, was informed in turn by Maryssa Fouquet, the mother of one.

MARYVONNE: " Now, it is with the "honor" that you JULIO deal! ".

JULIO: " This is fabulous! ".

"... / ... In short, Machiavellian methods; but effective; or very effective; and see: very, very effective; which would be to put into play, for example, much of the wealth in order to mount a real shot stuffed by example! ".

Another day, Loïc MORIN and Laval BRICE were still [income] to visit Evelyn MULER. When they struck only at the door; she was all happy; and she said: " Thank you! It was brought my Julio Fernandez "Descent From Poitevese ... / ..."; because I promised! It is like what was promised, we just went, my back very, very soon! So you brought him back? ".

Yves MULER who was present in the home; calm down "his **Maidenly**" to saying to her: "Calm down! Calm down! It's not Julio Fernandez! These are only my friends LOÏC and LAVAL that you know them very well!". When Evelyn MULER had only heard such a response addressed to her attention; she had always suggested to her father: " I will not take my pills! I will take over; it is because I do not have at all, at all, the will to live, including very, very well that definitely Julio Fernandez "Descent From ... / ..." is gone! ". " And I EVELYN; it is now over; it is now **Irreversible**; and therefore, it will never return to pick me to remarry "my ex – Ugliness"! I now have very, very well before it's truly finished between us! So eh!, antidepressants, you can even take "M'Sieurs" and put them where I think! This is because no matter how, I'm not going to eat. ".

By listening to this response of EVELYN, her father Yves MULER would suggest to his friends Loïc MORIN and Laval BRICE flatly: " I sincerely confess that at times, a Machiavellian mind black idea; very black; a dark idea; very dark; very, very dark, through my head! It bothers me so much head! And consequently, this idea leads me to draw such a horrible project about "the nervous breakdown" of EVELYN! Which does not always end result to all of us, "worries"! And aye!, ih"! "Worries"! EVELYN it, it is "very, very infected" "**the nervous breakdown**"! Then, her mother Simone and I YVES we are about to us: "very, very affected" "with worries" caused by "the nervous breakdown" of EVELYN exactly! ".

Loïc MORIN, at Yves MULER: " I see what idea very, very dark is it! And I beg you not to think of a very, very dark thoughts; as that! I beg you not to think of such an evil spirit! Since "your **Girlish**" will do just fine! And I'm very sure. You must not ever think about euthanasia. In addition, you will end yourself YVES inevitably sheet! ".

Yves MULER: " Euthanasia? ".

Loïc MORIN: " Affirmative!, ih! ".

Yves MULER: " No ohm! No, no! Quite the contrary! ".

Loïc MORIN: " What then? ".

Yves MULER: " This Machiavellian idea, it enters my head! When it arrives in my mind! It tells me that If I was a "good Man" fortunate like some others who have many chances in life to be! I would not, for example. ".

Loïc MORIN: " For example what not? ".

Yves MULER: " For example not hesitate a moment to ... / ...! For example not hesitate for a little while, to use methods certainly unorthodox; certainly against the Law; Briefly, Machiavellian methods; but effective; or very effective; and see: very, very effective! Which would be to bring into play, much of the wealth in order to mount a real dirty trick! ".

Laval BRICE: " But? But against whom? ".

Yves MULER: " Against the current "beauty" of JULIO "Descent From ... / ...!". At this point, I want to tell you both of you my friends; or maybe you just repeat my friends; that the current "Eva" of him, she had previously lived together with that one question! And they even had before to separate, a son! ".

Laval BRICE: " One more reason that you may not even mounted the blow against this **Thicket**; "then this Iphigenia"! Which is certainly there for nothing, at all, just about the breakdown of household of "your Cute EVELYN"! ".

Loïc MORIN: " You YVES, do such a dirty trick? ".

Laval BRICE, at Loïc MORIN: " No, I do not believe my ears that our friend YVES cans actually do such a thing! ".

Yves MULER: " And why not! ".

Laval BRICE: " Oh!, no, should no longer think of the concepts of this kind! ".

Yves MULER: " Yet if anyway! And this way, I could have as a consequence, redeem the charm of this JULIO "Descent From ... / ....". With regard to "my **Bitch**"; with regard to "my only **Pussy**"; by offering for example, a large villa or a large pavilion (; a great home if you want) and a large sum "winkles" filed in one of the banks of Switzerland or Panama! ".

Laval BRICE: " Hmm mm! For rescue "single chirping" – oblige what! ".

Yves MULER: " Indeed! ".

Laval BRICE: " Well, and say so! ".

Yves MULER: " Unfortunately alas!, I am not wealthy! ".

Loïc MORIN: " This is perhaps the better way! ".

Yves MULER: " Well, like you said LOÏC: This is perhaps the better way! This is because quite frankly, if I was fortunate! I was not going at all, at all, hesitate a little while, to the portion (since in this case "... / ... For save" "my only **Womanish**" " –actually requires, what")! Hence the fact that I was not going at all, at all, hesitate a little bit, to the passage of evil "to another split" in this case, to that currently lives with JULIO! ".

LAVAL: " It is certainly to nothing about the termination of EVELYN household, as I have already said! ".

YVES: " No matter even if it has nothing to do about the blackouts EVELYN! What would count that time: that ... / .... ".

LAVAL: " Agreed!, ih!, ih, ih! What would count this time? ".

YVES: " What, to save "my only **Ladylike**" absolutely should "another innocent **Filly**" pay instead! That's right, this idea is dark; this idea is very dark; this is very, very dark idea; this Machiavellian idea; which at times, just touch my mind! ".

LAVAL: " Ben and say so! ".

YVES: " But unfortunately alas! ".

LOÏC: " But unfortunately alas? ".

YVES: " But alas!, unfortunately, as "the **financial**" that controls everything! And I have not it! So I can only put myself in evidence! And therefore I cannot do anything at all! ".

LAVAL: " If you owned "**monetary**" as you were doing it? Or you say just like that, to play to the gallery? ".

YVES: " I ah! Not ohm! Indeed: never under any circumstances I could do it! It's like you just said my dear friend LAVAL! It is only to amuse the gallery I speak this way. In addition. ".

LOÏC: " Also? ".

YVES: " Furthermore, I told you so you both that it was only a very, very dark idea that came to touch my mind! And I confess solemnly! But only here, this does not imply necessarily that I would act effectively that way, if I would of fortune! ".

LOÏC: " Quite frankly, I'm glad to hear you say that! This is because I started very seriously indeed, very frightened, you know! ".

YVES: " No ohm! It should not! It should not be; since, I still accept as it were, the fatality; which eventually would carry along "my only **Butterfly**" in the world of stiffs! But never, ever, never, ever, I would transfer "this **unfortunate nervous breakdown** at her", to "another innocent **filly**"! Understand LOÏC? ".

LOÏC: " Understood! ".

YVES: " Otherwise! ".

LOÏC: " Otherwise? ".

YVES: " Otherwise who knows! It is indeed risk, dress up me all the names! ".

LAVAL: " For example? ".

YVES: " For example! ".

LAVAL, " Indeed!, ih!: For example? ".

YVES: " For example, we may fine and good to me to dress up Machiavelli! And about that, I want to open the way, a great parenthesis: ("This hominid" policy, Italian writer and philosopher born in Florence in 1469 and died in that city in 1527, which "gentleman" was called: Niccolo Machiavelli, and commonly known under the name of Nicolas Machiavelli, "which bimanous" in fact, contrary to the reputation that we usually stick to the person he had in his book: "The Prince" [published! in 1513] not written recommendations to follow [fact which earned him the reputation of a gallant very cunning and unscrupulous]. Rather, he wrote things that is often practiced for well control; things which precisely formally denounced! Why It's simply because in realist theory that it was developing in his time, he wanted to promote a new order, that is to say: free order, an order secular! Which a moral order were up to snatch his natural human wickedness. But only here, this philosopher is widely regarded as the incarnation of evil himself which on the contrary; he wanted above all to report. And what makes that right now, nasty "a hominid" is treated "This ape" is "a formidable Machiavelli"! And besides myself YVES in my everyday language, I get that Machiavelli nasty! If not, then each time telling people that we address by saying "MACHIAVAL" the opposite of what he is accused! So then, we do would pull at all, at all! In doing so, we make the simplest; that is to say: we consider the theory of "the gentleman" as evil. Hence, in order to close this large between – great parenthesis, I just want to reiterate that we risk such indeed dress up for me the name of Machiavelli;) and accuse me of having practiced: "doctrine [commonly considered]" "Machiavellian"; that is to say: "a wicked doctrine"! What precisely for me YVES is never help matters! Now, we indeed risk, dubbed me, LUCIFER outright; or SATAN; or BELZEBUTH [also called Beelzebub]; in other words, "the prince of demons"! Or even one of me indeed nickname may simply: "Vampire"; or and cetera and cetera. ... In short, it indeed may treat me as "bugger" no "feeling of love" or "affection against" "the tomboy" "other"; "Devil" "with no mercy"; or "friendship towards" imps "other"; "Funny" whose heart is imbued with a fierce devotion; and therefore, it is known for example "or tenderness", "or softness"; "When dealing with other kids"! Well understood? ".

LAVAL: " Sure!, I quite understand. ".

LOÏC: " YVES? ".

YVES: " All right!, ih!, ih, ih! I listen LOÏC! ".

LOÏC: " Since the sickness of "your **filly** EVELYN" turns out to be true: "heartache"! ".

YVES: " By all means!, ih!, ih, ih! ".

LOÏC: " Does she even "your woodcock EVELYN" could hardly go find her ex – husband JULIO where he is now? Do solemnly apologized for her adultery? And finally, conducting various activities of seduction vis-à-vis the latter, in an attempt to win him back? See yawn very, very strong in the sense? ".

YVES: " Frankly my dear friend LOÏC! "My **Squaw**, EVELYN" has no chance of getting there! She has no chance of reaching the culmination of such a company! ".

LAVAL: " And how? What do you mean she has no chance of doing so? ".

YVES: " I'm sure I'd already told you! But does that I still rest both of you this question: Do you know at least this one herself who took over "her" old gentleman JULIO "Descent From ... / .... ". ".

LAVAL: " It seems to me that you had already called us and even repetition ih!, yep! ".

LOÏC: " Of course!, indeed! You we'd already told and retold the same! ".

YVES: " It is Maryvonne KEVILER! ".

LAVAL: " Absolutely!, that's quite it! Aye!, ih!, it's true you we'd already told and retold the same as what: it, this MARYVONNE and him this JULIO; they had even had a son together! But so what? ".

YVES: " It is, according to those said to me among – others; and those, repeatedly herself "my **Queen bee**, EVELYN" and of course also, according to those that among – others also; she said "her ex – **Adam**, Julio Fernandez himself"; when they were still living together as a couple: "Maryvonne KEVILER turns out to be": **"A Mixed Descent From Paris"** (by place of birth); **"And On Background Kinese Descent"** (that is to say: by the birthplace of her father Moses KEVILER [formerly called: Monze KEMVILA]). And Julio Fernandez himself, being as I do not stop to tell you and repeat: **"Descent From Poitevese"** (by place of birth); **"And Background On Spanish Descent"** (and this is to say: by the birthplaces of his parents: "Sir" Patrick FERNANDEZ and Yolanda Roussel, widow FERNANDEZ [widow PATRICK, what!]). And notice how it's very, very strange that this couple one: always and always again coincidentally both, put accents on their "offspring" "And Backgrounds Descendants"; evoking; or rather, talking about their own places of birth and those of their parents; or else: from one of their parents! In short, MARYVONNE turns out to be: **"A Mixed Rear – Kinese Descending"! ".**

LOÏC: " So what? ".

YVES: " "So what?". Tell me you LOÏC? ".

LOÏC: " Very well!, ih! So what? ".

YVES: " So "the **Blonde**" is "**a sensual canon**" that repels "my **Queen** EVELYN", "in Hundred miles an hour"! "**This Brunette**", she is "a very, very nice **product of mixing of the races**"! She does not even have an example to look ever so slightly, "to soak up the sun"! "The Youth" is quite naturally, "half – tanned ahead"! Do not you understand LOÏC? ".

LOÏC: " Certainly!, absolutely!, ih! I understand very well! But so what? ".

YVES: " But! ".

LAVAL: " Certainly!, ih! So what? ".

YVES: " "This **Princess**" is "a very, very charming **Colored**" I tell you in plain! ".

LOÏC: " So what? ".

YVES: " But you two friends! You made expressly or what? You really seem to understand nothing about anything right? I say quite explicitly that "this **Agnes**" is "a **Mulatto** very, very **elegant**"! ".

LAVAL: " Aye!, Okay! We understand we thy two friends: Maryvonne KEVILER is "a **Mulatto** very, very **elegant!**" So what? ".

YVES: " Oh! Say so! But you still understand nothing about anything! "This **little Woman**" is "**a very beautiful Hybrid; very, very beautiful**"; which has only reclaim what was once hers; that is to say, "her **Noble** JULIO"! ".

LOÏC: " Aye, aye!, OK! We understand! Maryvonne KEVILER is "a **Hybrid very, very beautiful**"! So what? ".

YVES: " "This **Gal**" is "a **Latte, canon!**". ".

LAVAL: " It's "a **Latte, canon**"! So what? ".

YVES: " And then, "this **Cute**" named "Maryvonne KEVILER" owns "all this natural opportunity, so to speak", to be "the product of two different races"; a fact "that, as a result, made her, she's very pretty! A fact that makes the shot, that face her", "my Evelyn MULER" feels herself (: and according to what she told me and keeps telling me that she feels herself) **very, very complexed; very, very less**! Do you understand this? ".

LOÏC: "Ah! It is because of this ah! Ah! This is because of "the very natural beauty that Maryvonne KEVILER" benefits, it is here? ".

YVES: " Now listen to me very, very dear friends LAVAL and LOÏC! Now open very, very well your four ears my dear friends! Make yourself very, very well in both of your heads, all of whom I am going to immediately let you hear! Listen to me very, very carefully; and you will understand me eventually! Could I go? ".

LAVAL: " Aye!, of course! ".

LOÏC: " Aye, aye!, affirmative! You can go; and we're listening! ".

LAVAL: " We are listening! Go! I'll tell you two things first: It's the "all natural beauty", it is here! But we must not display any of the "this is defeatism" ahead like that! But we must not display any of "this kind of inferiority complex on behalf of" your **"Guinea fowl"**, "about beauty" eh! Ohm!, good! I said nothing! Forget it! Forget so this double reflection! And speaks those you have to say and we are listening very, very carefully! ".

YVES: " How! Needless to say no! This is of course that "this award from **Diane**" "named": "Maryvonne KEVILER" benefits: of "the all natural beauty"! To wit: "a very, very pretty **Mixed – blood**" (nothing surprising about that the Mestizos are still generally very, very nice 's); "a very, very beautiful Mulatto"; "a very, very attractive Hybrid"; "a very, very interesting Latte"; "A very, very brilliant Lady"; "a very, very lovely person feminine"; including "a gentleman" could resist very, very rarely before her presence! And do you honestly my dear friends LOÏC and LAVAL, "my Evelyn MULER"; no benefit from all these natural qualities and each other, has every little luck so slightly, to substitute "such a dream creature for" number of "Foals"? That "Weird Science" in addition, had indeed that recovered what was once hers: **"Adam**'s Julio Fernandez"? Not ohm!, My dear friends LAVAL and LOÏC! My "Evelyn MULER" has no chance of achieving the outcome "of such business"! Of course, it's hardly that: it is a "fact of any defeatism"! Admittedly, it's not at all, at all that: it is "a kind of inferiority complex in beauty as such (beauty gained through any other chemical I want to say here)"; like you two, you probably think, undoubtedly would display or logically "my dear" **"Grasshopper**, EVELYN" in front of "the Bomb that MARYVONNE"! But anyway! ".

LOÏC: " Indeed! "But anyway"! ".

LAVAL: " And be it! ".

YVES: " That's why my dear friends LOÏC and LAVAL, I did not, for example, hesitated a little while, to tell you there are a few moments [I quote] that: " ... / If I was ... "**a lucky guy**" as some other people who have many chances in life to be! I would for example not hesitate for a moment! I would not hesitate, for example, one small moment, to use methods certainly unorthodox; certainly against the Law; briefly, Machiavellian methods; but effective; or very effective; and see: very, very effective! Which would be to put into play, for example, much of the wealth in order to mount a real dirty trick against "the current rave of JULIO" "Descent From ... / ...".! " .

... / ... But unfortunately alas!, for human justice, it ultimately remain secret and unpunished. Is this the also remain, for "**the Other Justice**"? Or to pose this question differently this: These multiple crimes remain unpunished they also in the eyes of "**Justice Supernatural**"; to not say for example "**the Providential Justice**"?

Are they finally (said Yves MULER, to his two friends Loïc MORIN and Laval BRICE), were they true? Or he would say only because it was not actually wealthy? Anyway, it was very difficult to really know. But what was sure and certain knowledge, that: "The unique **gazelle** Evelyn MULER" was only a modest part – time cashier in a big – Supermarket in the Eleventh Arrondissement of Paris; and as such: so she would continue to do her job.

Only here and unfortunately alas!, for her, it would still only **five good years** with her **nervous breakdown**. Aside from the small contribution that it would receive its remuneration of part – time cashier, her father, with low income and also help her tremendously. He obviously help as he could. He would help her finally to find very good psychiatrists. But EVELYN that clearly said she was not sick! And because of this: it was sufficient only to bring for her, such as her "**Irreplaceable** and **Irreversible**" Julio Fernandez "Descent From ... / ....". So that the latter agrees to forgive. And therefore, to remarry her simply to get to finally realize: How she would be cured! She unfortunately stop alas!, take hers therapeutic pills. And when she would fall again in syncope; then straight into a coma; a deep coma; she would pull through again this clinical condition; and **she would have died**. (Oh!, that fate is hail, oh!, that eternal sleep, in no case, so far!). Compared Maryvonne KEVILER, about "this sad **nervous breakdown**" which violently oppressed both, it just, she was returned to her after her coma; then live again. Moreover, Evelyn MULER had returned to her, for her first coma; but only here for her second coma, **she would not return to her and she would die**.

And after the death of EVELYN, LOÏC, one of the faithful friends of her father YVES, being very distressed; **he would try by all means to contact** that apparently was **the basis of this whole sad situation**; that is to say: the gallant and elegant "the Thief of love Giraud ZEFRINO", to tell him the unfortunate indirect effect of the act he had committed as well. And it would do so. There happen to come into contact with "the suitor". And as a surprise: Loïc MORIN would simply make them aware of the entire plot. This is because Giraud who hardly thinking at all, at all, that this delicate mission he had deliberately subversive accepted himself to perform, "many candelabra" reward would indirectly **cause such a tragedy**. He felt so, in a kind of moral obligation, to confess; and consequently, to brief: to "Sir" Loïc MORIN, all this machination and its real purpose. And righto!, ih! It was "**the Mystery of the Universe**" **which was already beginning to manifest itself in that way**. And "**this Mystery of the Universe**" happen by one way or another, even among "Sir" and Mrs. Moses KEVILER, passing first through the home of JULIO and MARYVONNE. But only here, "Sir" Loïc MORIN (instead of going immediately to tell the facts "Sir" Yves MULER, his friend so that we study together, in which modality, we could eventually lead [if and only if it could be feasible, and also if and only if it really was worth the cost]., action at the Court but only here, him), he had some idea; some idea [according to his calculations] not bad at all. What for?

That's because he had to take this information in order to draw considerably "of **almighty dollars**" a kind of blackmail. In short, LOÏC had a numerical idea behind his head. He just wanted to try to take advantage of this sensitive information, to blackmail the boss Moses KEVILER. He had just the idea of **trying to win a fortune on this sad story**, in an attempt to transform his life. (So what was the whole moral that him LOÏC and his friend LAVAL lavished YVES?). However, Loïc MORIN begin simply and immediately, to a kind of blackmail against the father of MARYVONNE; the Sponsor of that "Machiavellian mission".

And in so doing, to silence; and this, once and for all, Loïc MORIN; which could very possibly later, to talk to many other people, in this case; and consequently: Make that way, change the course of events (for example: by simply starting, and this time, forever, his son in Law Julio Fernandez, and by implication, **to plunge once again**, "her **Cute** MARYVONNE" in **a sacred nervous breakdown, which would be much more severe** than that which she suffered once, the new depression which, she would pull through again [And for good reason!], and all the way, making him "Sir" Moses KEVILER sink himself and herself "the **Baroness**, Maryssa Fouquet", through various trials and various convictions that would ensue). They had promised to pay to purchase his silence, a sacred fortune blackmailer. They had set him an appointment in one of the premises of an old abandoned warehouse, to Viry – Chatillon, where they were going to bring him [so – called] a small suitcase with plenty of **financials** inside. The appointment was set at Fourteen Hours, a Sunday.

Then the day "**D**." and time "**T**." MOSES and "his **Countess, MARYSSA**" were not even visited the place of appointment. What had happened? What had happened, what had MOSES paid and sent some Annick Tyssandier; a **ruthless killer**, to go "**smoke**" just Loïc MORIN, **the blackmailer**. The latter, who yet could stop providing little moral lessons to Yves MULER. He, who stopped not wonder indeed that the idea very, very dark crossing the head thereof; the idea that he himself LOÏC and his friend LAVAL fought vigorously. LOÏC him yet that did not stop at all surprising that this idea very, very dark was actually practiced, but by someone else, their YVES friend. And about the "Recycling" "the same guy"; that is to say: Julio Fernandez; instead of condemning the act, he did not even do. He had simply imagined: Getting great benefits from this. And so, he also found his account, "**being physically removed altogether**". "Mister" Moses KEVILER was still as he signed a contract with the same tacit Annick Tyssandier, so that he makes the same fate, "the **Penelope's Killer** Giraud ZEFRINO"; which according to the boss MOSES, he still could inevitably cause of this sad story in many others; if it was not already done in the meantime; something that in this case, greatly surprised, him.

In any case, the note payable by the father and mother of MARYVONNE to be able to save in-extremist "their unique youth" and heiress (without the latter herself, were thus put in aware of the plot), the terrible depression that plagued her; and which would inevitably prevail in the next world; in the afterlife; in the world after death; this note was very salty.

Incidentally, the very healthy people; that is to say: the parents of MARYVONNE, which were once very honorable citizens; which had never previously been sponsors of murders; they were now become outright; thus loading their consciences not only an indirect death (which had not even too much, too soon, to be followed: that of Evelyn MULER); but also of a double direct murder, that of Loïc MORIN and that of Giraud ZEFRINO.

... / ... But unfortunately alas!, for human justice, it ultimately remain secret and unpunished.

Is this the also remain, for "the Other Justice"?

Or to pose this question differently this: These multiple crimes remain unpunished they also in the eyes of "Justice Supernatural"?

To not say for example "the Providential Justice"?

... / ... But unfortunately alas!, we could no longer work miracles. The young rider had died as a result of multiple injuries to the skull rather than on arrival at the hospital; but actually there at the scene of the accident.

Anyway, for MARYVONNE, commitment "of many **accounts**" from hers parents (without herself, the person we had wanted to save was not aware) was the only thing that brought her back to life. MARYVONNE, "their **little** one" and give them all **three grandchildren**. All in all case: **"Money may not buy happiness! But honestly, there really helps a lot**.". As already understood, old. After spending up to six good years in the megalopolis of New York, Julio Fernandez had taken steps in order to always serve in an International Organization, but in Paris; that is to say: at home, so to speak. And for that, he had taken steps to work at the Headquarters of UNESCO in Paris, for a position in the Direction of the Staff of Agents of the latter body; and that steps had also been successful. In doing so, he returned with all his family in the French capital. At this very issue, Julio Fernandez, who had never thrown negative responses were sent to him; when it was once repeated requests failed to be able to find a job more or less directly with its many degrees; he had gone to seek and found the negative response that the UNESCO in question had sent him several years ago. That said, he suggested in his "**Eva**, MARYVONNE": " When I thought I had already begun earlier steps, to enter this International Organization; and besides, it was even you MARYVONNE who had advised me to do among – others, this approach just there! And ... / .... ".

Maryvonne KEVILER, wife FERNANDEZ: " Absolutely!, it's true, I remember ih!, righty – ho! ".

JULIO: " ... / ... And the answer was negative! Besides, I've always kept that answer; as also several other negative responses that were sent to me! I looked for; and I found her. Hence, if you want, I will immediately take it and read it again to you. ".

MARYVONNE: " Go on forever. Because my memories! Although sad that we would want to think about its memories; but go ahead anyway! ".

JULIO: " That's it! Here! "I'll read it!"."

"" For a position in the Direction of the Staff of UNESCO; staff for example, the answer was: ""

"" U N E S C O

United Nations Educational,
Scientifics and Cultural Organization.
United Nations
Education, Science and Culture.

Mr. Julio Fernandez.

The Personnel Office is pleased to accuse**i** (**_Sic_**). Reception and thank you for your letter dated: November 21, 1976, addressed to: Personnel 's Office.

Reference: XXXXXXXXXXXX.

Re: Your application for the post of Unesco.

The pieces of information that you
kindly send us caught our
attention and we had to make
assess your application against
our current opportunities for
vacancies.
However, I regret to inform you
knowledge it has not been possible
to identify a position in the field of your
specialization.

Thank you for your interest
Porter (*Sic*.) The activities of the Unesco.

Paris, March 19, 1977.

Recruitment Division
Personnel 's Office.
U N C E S O " " " ".

MARYVONNE: " And yeah!, ih! ".

JULIO: " In any case my dear wife, now is a great time for me to confess that were it not for the influence and support of your father ... / .... ".

MARYVONNE: " I will yet had always said! But you also always refused. And who is right now? Huh? ".

JULIO: " In any case it's you! It is you who are right! And there is no doubt about it. My conscience compels me to admit you solemnly: What were it not for the influence and support of your father, I would wait a long time; or very long; and see: very, very long time; so as not to say that: I never was going to be able to the end of my life, to be able to find work in a Major International Organizations, such as O. N. U. or even U. N. S. E. C. O. ".

MARYVONNE: " I always said to you had and still recalled before; when we only had been living without getting married; like what, that I was going to introduce you to people who were going to boost you; ... / .... ".

JULIO: "Finally, it was the influence of negative memories of my ... / .... ".

MARYVONNE: "Yeah!, I know, your godmother. ".

JULIO: "Got it? ".

MARYVONNE: " Understood. ".

JULIO: " Thank you. ".

MARYVONNE: " It is understandable that you had seen those had to suffer at the hands of your beloved godmother; and considering all the implications! You definitely still refused to accept the support of others who are not your immediate family and especially the support from female ones. And I need not ask you, for example: What is your stubbornness, it had brought to you then? ".

JULIO: " It's true: you was right. ".

MARYVONNE: "Forget all those. We are happy now; and that's it: the basics. ".

JULIO: " You was right. ".

MARYVONNE: " Now, it is with the "honor of the joint" that you JULIO deal! ".

JULIO: " Fantastic! ".

Several years later, the father of MARYVONNE; that is to say "Sir" Moses KEVILER; or the grandfather of Lucilian KEVILER and his siblings, in order to please his little son; that is to say: to the same; when he celebrated his twenty – fifth birthday. He launched an idea to pay him **a great gift** stock. He wanted to pay him a small new car; new, but with low power, like, two horses; or four or seven horses only; since according to him, used for example in large cylindered, it was not too good. MOSES wanted to offer to LUCILIAN a small new car low power to reward his diligence in his studies and also to reward the seriousness with which he displayed throughout his behavior. Why this initiative? It was not only to be able to express such as among – others in this way then, to found joy or pleasure regained "his keel MARYVONNE" and every home; but it was to push the LUCILIAN brother named Patrick Fernandez, to follow his studies and also to perform well. For he began to follow for a while, a band of disaffected youth. Which consumed drugs. Which consumed hash [hashish]. Who ate the cam. And therefore, his grandfather MOSES held for example, encourage him to expect him also, during his twenty – fifth birthday, a pretty new car underpowered. But that's only when MOSES had posed the question to his grand – son LUCILIAN: "What kind of small new car underpowered, you like dear little son, I offer for your twenty fifth birthday? ". He was surprised to hear an unexpected response: " ... / ... So in this case, it's not a small new car low power I wish I had; but rather: a large new bike of many powers; otherwise expressed: a great new bike of many horses! Although I've never told anyone before. But yet I take this opportunity you offer me making you know that I adore motorcycles; very big bikes; very, very big bikes! ".

MOSES, at LUCILIAN: " Very, very big bikes, like, 125 cc or 250 cc, for example? ".

LUCILIAN, at MOSES: " Genre: a very, very big bike two cylinders 250 cc each; making a total of 500 cc the bike; or even (and maybe elsewhere: a very, very big bike two cylinders 300 cc each, thus making in all a very, very big rolling machine two wheels, a total of 600 centimeters cubes) for example! ".

MOSES, at LUCILIAN: " Ah!, anyway! ".

LUCILIAN, at MOSES " Uh – huh!, ih!, because: in addition, the total amount of cylinders is large; more so, there is power in the bike! And the more, me LUCILIAN, I feel the pleasure of driving this bike in question! ".

MOSES, at LUCILIAN: " When it yourself! Yep!, indeed: you wish one of the big **guns** that can exist until the moment in terms of very, very large revolving machines with two wheels what! But it is dicey! This is dangerous! It's really that dangerous ah!, dear grand – son! This is very dangerous! It's very, very dangerous! ".

LUCILIAN, at MOSES: " But dear grandpa? Do you really want to make me happy for my twenty fifth birthday or not ohm? This is because: motorcycles, small or large displacements huh! ".

MOSES, at LUCILIAN: " It's dicey anyway, anyhow! This is OK! Okay! I understand! Or to put it better myself: I quite understand; uh – huh!, I really, really understand! ".

LUCILIAN, at MOSES: " Anyway, if we reflect very well ... / .... ".

MOSES, at LUCILIAN "Yep!, ih!, ih, ih! ".

LUCILIAN at MOSES: " As I began to express it; and you grandpa you finish my sentence! Hence, I repeat once again: If we reflect very well, even for a small motorcycle engine; or even if only for a moped; or even if only for a bicycle also huh! The danger; or rather, the "dangerousity", as it is still present there, almost at any time that you drive with these machines! And he would always and still always so! So eh! To know that, do not forget the point dear grandpa, the bikes (they may be 125, or 250, or 500, or even 600 cubic inches of displacement); machines, or machineries, are always and always again; and they still remain and yet always known: break snacks! So eh! Mention the danger for motorcycles gender 500 or 600 cc to me, huh!, Grandpa! Or else maybe you already regret quite frankly, in the depths of your heart, the colossal sum it would cost you for that! And in this case, it's a whole other thing! ".

MOSES, at LUCILIAN: " Okay, I very, very much got it. ".

It is very includes very explicit, for this story of a motorcycle with the power considerably, "Sir" Moses KEVILER as we could see; he was himself caught in a trap. In doing so, he could not have another alternative: that of offering to his little son LUCILIAN, the machine that interested him, of course. He could not even insist on trying to explain this one for example, that it was very, very dangerous gear like this. Lest it rightly interprets these words as: a whimsical or sign versatile, tactile; express or implied, of a sudden reversal; an abrupt refusal. Lest LUCILIAN interpreter e.g. insistent this explanation, like what, that his grandpa MOSES regret almost immediately, having launched yet himself deliberately, the idea of paying him a very good gift for rolling its twenty – fifth anniversary . And [; that is to say: the little – son] had informed him in these words: " If we reflect very well, even for a small motorcycle engine; or even if only for a moped; or even if only for a bicycle; the danger; or rather: the "dangerousity", as it is still present there, almost at any time that you drive with these machines! And he would always and still always so! So eh!, grandpa! ... / ...! ".

Indeed, with **these big guns** gear or not, just two wheels, many people have done; and they continue to accident every day. And they even let ¾ their lives; or rather: they **continue** to let their lives.

Is this would also be the same for the young Lucilian KEVILER?

But in fact, no one knew in advance the answer to that last question. All that we knew was that during that time, "Sir" Moses KEVILER continued to meet his little son Lucilian KEVILER: " Okay, I very, very much got it. ".

LUCILIAN, at MOSES: " There's another thing dear grandpa! ".

MOSES, at LUCILIAN: " I'm listening! Tell me everything, my dear grand – son! ".

LUCILIAN, at MOSES: " I want to point out to you right away or straight away: I do not yet have a driver's license; as for a passenger car or driving license; as for the permit bikes! I do not have; or at least not yet! ".

MOSES, at LUCILIAN: " It ah!, I know. But it's not even a problem that ah!; because, as I want to please you by offering you **this sacred machine that you are mad about so much**! I am therefore quite logically obliged to pay you all, your training "pilot" in a driving school nearest you. ".

LUCILIAN, at MOSES: " Well! I remind you that I agree, for a bike very, very powerful and not a car (in addition, a low – powered car is just around ah!, no!). ".

MOSES, at LUCILIAN: " It is understood: it is not a car; it will be a motorcycle; a motorcycle very, very powerful. Make you already enroll in a driving school of your choice. And I will pay thee all that training. ".

Once said; LUCILIAN was immediately made and consequently, left to enroll in a driving school of his choice. He had certainly not had a chance to get the code right the first time: he had started in all five times. And after the fifth time precisely he got it. And each time, it was his "wealthy" grandpa who had financed all without the slightest lament, to not discourage his little son. It should say, with the same code then, theoretically: throughout the five years that would follow to obtain this code in question at that time, he could, for example, then go get the permission B; but because of this, it would no longer board code; but only if he spent five years, aye. Aye, aye!, there: he would have to also board the code. For driving also LUCILIAN had hardly had a chance to get it right the first time: he had had at the end of the fourth attempt at recovery [definitely!]. All his motorcycle license had lasted a total of over a year of training; and it had cost quite a small fortune for MOSES. But as this initiative came from himself and not for his little son. So he felt this moral obligation to pay; and that, without complaining that if only a little. Anyway, MOSES had many "**ways and means clustering**". And therefore it does not even concern for sub he had to pay for the license and buying a big bike. But otherwise, he was concerned greatly for the safety of his grand – son; because the bike; still "a very, very big bike anyway"; since he bought him "**a Kawasaki 500 cubic centimeters**" spread "**double tank**" "**250 cm3**", "for each of the two."

Unfortunately alas!, when LUCILIAN received his license and motorcycle when his grandfather MOSES had paid him "his Kawasaki 500"; the very first day it was only with the running; and it was a Sunday afternoon. He went on "**National Road 7**" that is to say: in Corbeil – Essonne. "**The National Road 7**"; a road he knew in part, very, very good; since often went by car with his friends, even in the latter town. Going there was no problem: it had arrived where he wanted to happen. But that's only on the way back and more specifically, at the height of Juvisy – On – Orge; he had not made a gaffe truck "Van Five Tons"; which was before him, hardly rolling at all. And that is in high speed, LUCILIAN had gone back inside, behind that truck. The shock was very, very violent (; namely collision between a motorcycle launched at high speed, a Five tones against parked). And therefore, it is not even worth describing: What was henceforth his physical condition: Was he still around? **Yes** or **No**? There is not even the issue. Five tones in the truck off, there was not even the driver inside at that time. And since it was a Sunday afternoon, the first people who flocked to the accident; and that they had actually noticed it was after two to five minutes later. These early people, they were motorists who followed behind. One had called for Firefighters – Emergency Personnel. And we had brought the young LUCILIAN to the "La Pitié – Salpêtrière"[1] But unfortunately alas!, **we could no longer work miracles. The young rider had died as a result of multiple injuries to the skull rather than on arrival at the hospital; but actually there on the site of the accident itself.**

---

[1] In the Thirteenth Arrondissement of Paris, near the Station of Austerlitz.

(And agreed!, ih! It was still, anyhow: "Mystery of the Universe" that would continue thus to manifest itself in that way.

And do not we have said above, that "the mystery of the universe in question just" happen in one way or another, even among "Sir" and Mrs. Moses KEVILER?

By first passing through the focus of JULIO and MARYVONNE?

And so therefore: a son of that couple was no longer here).

... / ... But they could not at all, at all, do something; to fool "Justice Supernatural or Providential Justice" [; because she is fine and well: the proof! But only here, it occurs often unexpectedly; and very rarely immediately.].

It was really sad for this calamity that overcame "this Background Progeny Kinese". But there could not do anything at all, at all. It was fate. "Unfortunately alas!", "The misfortunes (Has it used to say [that] do not come alone!"). We're not there, just beginning, for this wealthy family. The little brother of LUCILIAN which was already in the meantime, to follow his friends "bandidos" and drug addicts. The little brother of LUCILIAN which was already beginning to follow his friends who used "hash"; would enter this time in himself a first time, in this cycle of consumption "of the drug unrefined laboratory". Then beyond that, he would pass outright worldwide consumption of harder drugs, like, cocaine altogether. The family would all it, could do to save this boy [Patrick FERNANDEZ]. It had sent him to Kinshasa for example a little bit, in members of the family of his maternal grandfather MOSES. And so according to calculations by his parents [JULIO and MARYVONNE], being a little bit away from them in this way; he would inexorably be corrected once and for all. And when he would back in the Paris 's region, according to the calculations of this family, it would avoid to behaving badly; lest they again revisit in Kinshasa. But only here, in that capital here and as a result of race: Patrick Fernandez refused to eat for several days. And he would be hospitalized urgently in Kitambo 's Hospital; where he would be in intensive care. He only fails to very, very little, dying. Then with very, very good care he received there and with many chances as he would pull through. On his release from the hospital, his parents resolve only to repatriate him, to Suresnes. The family would still be a second attempt removal of the "poor" boy. He had been here this time, sent to the Island of Martinique. And holding it for the second time, away from his parents and especially all the thugs he followed in the Paris 's Region. There also wanted him to learn in this French overseas territory, away from

Suresnes, a manual trade; which he would choose himself, once he got there; and once visited a few schools training manual trades instead of just.

MARYVONNE: " Now it is a "joint of honor" that you JULIO deal! ".

JULIO: " Great! ".

For both distances then, it was mainly in order to keep him safe from various bad many temptations. But only here, again as a result of race: In very, very short time only, PATRICK fall into "a terrible nervous breakdown"; that "depressive illness" was even drawn into the world of "the afterlife". These parents had no other alternative than to make him back in this French overseas territory, as soon as possible in order to save his life in extremis. The family did everything to save the "poor" boy. But alas!, unfortunately!; it would succeed at all, at all, to stem the tide and the impact of the cam. "Sir" and Ms. Fernandez had finally decided not to give at all PATRICK "sorrel pocket"; since it simply he used to get his daily dose. When they stop offer him "the pesetas – pocket" precisely; he would only rob all. He had simply become a thief. He began by pilfer even in their own home. And given the fact that he followed a gang of young junkies who actually made among – others, multiple rackets along the way. Then, too, he would just like them.

In doing so, one evening, PATRICK and his group would stroll around in Montigny – Bauchant where they would observe by chance, "a girl" who had to pay for gasoline at a gas station. In wanting to start her car and leave, by surprise, "the lady" had just been attacked by a gang of young robbers consumers of drugs; which wanted to extort her purse; which included among – others, all his identity papers; other paper and "some chrematistics". This cohort of scoundrels was therefore precisely one where coincidentally, PATRICK belonged. "The Contessa" resisted all alone for quite a while, before another motorist 54 years at that time; which had by then also pay his fuel, do some thinking to this band of young ruffians: " "And you there"! "Let this" "behind – the penury" "of chick" [yet harmless] not quiet! ". By listening to this severe rebuke, the band had indeed left the lady outright. But only here, it was always raging against "the honest man" of 54. It had just snatch him from his vehicle; and this: force; it did extirpate him, from his "cabin"; it's because so far, this motorist was only speak from "his car". And as his engine had stopped, "behind – the misery" "this type" of

54 years; he would not even have had time to turn and run away quickly. In doing so, he was immediately taken out of his vehicle. And we immediately began after: not only verbal abuse; but also physically. Then suddenly, as if this double assault already little enough, to hurt, to an innocent motorist who, if he was not do so; he would inevitably eventually accused for example, by "the Countess" or others: we are attacked, but "the non – assistance to a person in danger" was therefore required!; and the young Patrick Fernandez took out a sharp knife he kept in his socks; and he was mercilessly stabbed "the honest man" of 54 years. He pressed his knife in the belly of "the poor" motorist outright; and this, as you might say: "It was just him hara–kiri". The other gang members did not want it anyway happens to such an extreme. It is therefore begun to reproach PATRICK; even the same type by the other young punks of his pack. But as "that wretched" motorist instantly collapsed to the ground; and he was already starting to lose a lot of blood, all the attackers were consequently eclipsed even without one was able to put their hands on, or immediately – there; nor even later. The station attendant who apparently pretended not to see all those that took place in the institution where he worked yet; because he was extremely scared for himself also [And for good reason]. "He ended up being alerted by the turn of events. "In other words": He had finally seen. And therefore he was well alerted by phone, the Police Officers and the Firefighters. On the other side, "the duchess" they were going to bite the handbag; and which had by then, the fear; scare of her life; she was all just escaped. The motorist of 54 years had been brought at the hospital[1]. On arriving there, the doctors had done everything to try to cure this Gentleman; Unfortunately, alas!, we could no longer work miracles.

A year later, after the death of LUCILIAN by motorcycle 's accident, his little brother PATRICK (; which had never wanted to tell his guilt to his parents, let alone the police, and that therefore the Society does unfortunately not able to punish him,

---

[1] In fact, we had quickly moved the man, 54, at the Clinique Of Plessis – Bouchard, on Street Gabriel PERI.

by default; it could be reached nab if only one member among these young perpetrators); it should be struck in turn by "The Supernatural" or "The Providential Justice". However, he will succumb himself, as a result of an overdose.

(And yeah!, ih! It was still, anyhow: "The Mystery of the Universe" that would continue thus to manifest itself in that way.

And do not we have said above, that "the mystery of the universe in question just" happen in one way or another, even among "Sir" and Mrs. Moses KEVILER?

By first passing through the focus of JULIO and MARYVONNE?

And there: Two children Three of this couple here, were no longer).

Their sister Yolanda FERNANDEZ lives at the age of sixteen, a big disappointment in love. And she swallows one stroke, twelve tablets of barbiturates; taking care to write in advance a brief letter to explain the reason for her desperate act and the number of pills she was about to swallow one stroke. And consequently, she would not wake up again.

(And okay!, ih! It was still, anyhow: "The Mystery of the Universe" that would continue thus to manifest itself in that way.

And do not we have said above, that "The mystery of the universe in question just" happen in one way or another, even among "Sir" and Mrs. Moses KEVILER?

By first passing through the focus of JULIO and MARYVONNE?

And there: All children of this couple here were no longer).

Mrs. Maryvonne KEVILER, wife FERNANDEZ, the mom of the three children would fall; as might be feared, of course, in "a terrible nervous breakdown"; as a result of the loss of all hers children "even stronger than she had known years earlier depression". Fate was dogging this family. Of "The Depression", she would pull the point. And she died.

(And OK!, ih!, It was still, anyhow: "The Mystery of the Universe" that would continue thus to manifest itself in that way.

And do not we have said above, that "The mystery of the Universe in question just" happen in one way or another, even among "Sir" and Mrs. Moses KEVILER?

By first passing through the focus of JULIO and MARYVONNE?

And there: A parent of two was no more).

It was, if we reflect very well, "the very untimely passing of his very, very bad characters, many years ago"; "That very, very bad characters" had finally made sure that hers parents could commit "three deadly crimes"; including a course, it was only indirect; crimes of which they were not even steins, by the Society. In order to better myself: they managed to escape justice rights. But alas!, unfortunately for them: " The Justice with a big "J" " or "The Justice Providential" or rather: "The Supernatural 's Justice" was hardly forgotten. It waited for the moment to start hitting [And how to hit! It ah!]. However they die, all their property would go naturally for the most part, to the state; since they had no direct heirs; and for a small part to share among distant family members of MARYSSA and MOSES.

Julio Fernandez was left alone in his big house that he was offered several years ago by MOSES, sly. But only here, he had wanted to hear more dating "beauties". For him: "For me Julio" "Descent From Poitevese And Background On Spanish Descent" "Attending" lobster "would only bring me nightmares". "Proof ... / ...!". In doing so, he started for the first time in his personal life, by attending the sly, downright men, to try to forget all his troubles with "beautiful sex". And worse in this story, he did not care to wear protection. It looks like himself on this subject: " What I'm doing now, I know very well that it is against nature! And consequently, it is really not ethical. But while I think, I almost always hitherto respected ethics question. And what it was it really brought me? Nothing! Nothing, if they are only nightmares; worries; and even "acute depression; which is watching me now me also, as a bonus!". ".

Julio Fernandez had therefore continued to attend "the guys" on the sly. But that's only for lack of pot; he prematurely ended his life as a result of AIDS (Acquired Immune Deficiency Syndrome).

(And nd yep ih! It was still, anyhow: "The Mystery of the Universe" that would continue thus to manifest itself in that way.

And do not we have said above, that "The Mystery of the Universe in question just" happen in one way or another, even among "Sir" and Mrs. Moses KEVILER?

By first passing through the focus of JULIO and MARYVONNE?

And then: All the parents here were no longer).

If we reflect very, very well indeed, for him Julio Fernandez, it was also "The Supernatural Justice" or "The Justice Providential" who had chastised him. What for? This is because several years ago, before they get back together again with Maryvonne KEVILER; he had not only drawn intentionally, a macabre plan against a nice lady (Mrs. Evelyn MULER);

which was nothing else, that "his legitimate filly"; which had not committed in this time, as a real sin; him JULIO: as using a subterfuge in order to get pregnant herself "without the agreement of her own foal Julio" though; it's because she only asked for, to have offspring; but even worse, he was also passed to the realization or the realization of this macabre plan. Fortunately this very nice lady was not dead. It took a little bit just so that she passes away. And despite this heinous crime, he JULIO just was not even worried. He had killed two people and indirectly [the twins] who would be born. But he was not even worried. On the contrary, he was very, very glad indeed. That's because at first: it was these twins then that he did not at all, at all, to have; while his "Judith" though.

JULIO had indirectly erase two people who would be born. But there was no concern for the simple reason; he was nabbed by anyone. JULIO had cheated by the human justice. But he had ignored; what he could not in any case fool "The Justice Supernatural" or "The Providential Justice"; which saw everything. Or to be able to express more precisely: which always sees everything. And that was only waiting for the right moment, to respond. The obstinacy of Julio Fernandez helped in part [indirectly] to "nervous breakdown"; and therefore the death of EVELYN.

For their part, "Sir" Moses KEVILER and "his Eva, Maryssa Fouquet", having become old and full aging. They would be left (in order to express ourselves in this way), with individual as: [heir; direct heir, of course], all their property they owned. While they had just done everything; and even they had used the most heinous methods, so as not to get to where they had come.

Moreover, "Sir" and Mrs. KEVILER (and not forgot to mention the worker Thierry Glorian) would anyway eventually subsequently charged against their will, in justice [human justice course]; and in addition, they would be brought, in any manner the court; where they were presented as being "behind the murders". And so they would know canker sores of justice. "Mister" Moses KEVILER and his worker Thierry Glorian would be imprisoned in Fleury – Merogis. And aye!, ih! MOSES says for example, had among – others, done everything, to hardly get one! But they were still anyway [husband & wife and not forgetting his faithful worker and friend THIERRY] got one! "There"; that is to say: "in jail"! " " " " ""

"" When MOSES thought ... / ... ""

"" Oh!, the prison! ... / ...! ""

"" And he would even hear [and even write] to the attention of some of those friends: ""

"" When MOSES thought ... / ...: ""

"" Ah!, the prison! ... / ...! ""

" When I think even the shower, it's only twice a week we could take it by Fleury – Merogis! Even simple as walking, it's a trickle. Because they can only take place by division! What is a penal division already? In fact, it is neither more nor less than a section of a given group. It is ranked arriving in prison; and that, after spending a first night in a neighborhood newcomers. And we will stay three to a cell. And it is based on crimes that have been committed. And also, it is based: that one has already been in "jail" (that is to say: that one is "repeat offender"); or that one is "primary"; that is to say: that we had never previously been in "sheet". Divisions were divided, within different branches of the prison. And overall, a division can be found in the same lane; and this, with shares and others, of the various cells. And each lane has a consequence, some cells with three prisoners and a shower room. And remnants of cells appear to be in principle, individual. "

" When I think two days of showers in the week, we find ourselves in an ultimate obligation to get up much earlier; much sooner; since it would be essential that not only the entire division can shower; but it should, even before breakfast! However, that should not be lost on the time; otherwise, we do not even have: time to dress; time to his bed; and the time to take his coffee! However, it would really make such a bed huh! For the simple reason that, in principle, supervisors ensure among – others, to this! And only after breakfast, so that theory is expected to be picked "you" to sign for the walk! "

"" When I think that, as long as it is not yet considered, it is so to speak, what monotony of prison! Monotony happily cut sometimes (but not very often also true), for appearances before judges in the courthouse, and of course, with rare visits by lawyers! ""

"" When I think of the outputs of the prison grounds, heavily dependent frequency instructions! ""

"" When I think the frequency of instructions themselves, depending on the length of pretrial detention! And when I think that more preventive detention lasts much longer; more as the frequency slows facto instructions! And that consequently, "you" out a lot less! ""

"" When I think overall, we usually see less of lawyers! Which lawyers are more concerned as it were, for big business! Which relate big! And they generally hate plead, lost in advance causes; causes such as ours! ""

"" When I think generally, prisoners see little more than twice their lawyers before the fateful date of judgment! Finally, "little more than twice their lawyers" (so to speak: Because, and here again! If and only if their lawyers decide, however, to give the penalty and that is what is difficult for causes clueless in advance!). ""

"" When I think that even to go to the instructions, you are advised that at the last moment! And this morning, a few minutes ago, before the morning alarm clock! ""

"" When I think that one "you" makes several in the paddy wagon! ""

"" When I think fatigue "you" are going to suffer for days instructions: since "you" out in the morning; and you do not come back in the evening! ""

"" When I think of all the humiliating rituals of excavations that "you" are going to have for the occasion! ""

"" When I think "the shabby little bundle picnic" that they give you for lunch such a day! ""

"" When I think the whole day is spent waiting in cells! In small cells! Cramped in the basement of the courthouse! And that with a sealed bench! Sealed to the wall! Hmm mm! With a water course, but with a screen door; and we observed all "his" doings! Hmm mm! You wait two or three in one of these tiny cells! It is expected that heavily armed guards are "you" look, for "you" bring to the Office of the judge! And one "you" leads through underground labyrinths Courthouse! What penury! If we knew we would be making the point nonsense; and that, for "a single gentlewoman hysterical"! The item cannot be committing mischief; and consequently, it cannot go much into "jail"!

And – there the questions are and they will still to be:

"Is it really worth the trouble to come out ways against – nature "one **hysterical filly**" from her severe schizophrenia; which would systematically transported her, to the death, even if she was our daughter?

And no matter how "the Other Justice precisely who she is invisible" get busy and is indeed "hysterical this filly in question" is when – even well, well, well dead, right?

And me MOSES and my Cleopatra, Maryssa and not forgetting my faithful worker and friend THIERRY, what we won after all these sordid, despicable and abominable machinations sponsored by us?

Nothing, nothing, nothing, nothing, nothing, nothing and nothing, at all, at all.

Morality: we the humans, so we should absolutely be afraid of this "Other Justice", by – above all. And thus, our behavior will be blameless. ». » « » « »"

"« » « » « "MARYSSA for her side", she would be imprisoned at Versailles. And when she thought ... / ... » « » « » « " ... / ...! " . ""

"« » " "When MARYSSA thought ... / ...". » « »"

"« "Oh!, the prison! ... / ...!". ""

"" And she also, she would even hear [and even write] to the attention of some of the friends that: ""

"" When [MARYSSA] thought ... / ... ""

"" Oh!, the prison! ... / ...! ""

"« And when I MARYSSA, I think "in prison", we are considered to be minors! ""

"" When I think "that jail", everything is done so that the inmates are accustomed to letting e.g. guided by supervisors, without even so much that one wonders: The Why? ""

"" And when I think we even hammered for example, the language we should use! ""

"" When I think that we only discuss item orders Supervisors! Otherwise, it's disobedience; and it is severely punished! ""

"" When I think you said for example: "You go through that!"; and we, we have only run! ""

"" When I think you said for example: "You close it! "; and we, we have but to comply! ""

"" When I think you said for example: "You get on your bed!"; and that, even if we have little sleep; and we, we have only run! Hmm mm! It's really sad, "the jail"! The inmates are truly considered real kids! And because of this, they have no other alternative, than to accept (: and this without issuing fewer requirements, and this without the slightest issue claims). In short, and this without the slightest issue revolts), the abusive and coercive authority of supervisors, wants! Hmm mm! The prisoners are really considered eh babies! And any guardian, ostensibly to search us, she undresses us as she wants! ""

"" And when I think that with respect to age, as for many of the guards who dig myself MARYSSA I am so to speak as their mom! The search is us; and it could not absolutely say: "No!"! Under the pretext of search us, we scrutinize the supervisor for example, healthy! And we, we could simply not say: "No!"! Under the pretext of search us, we drop the supervisor for example, the pants! And we, we could not simply say: "No!"! ""

"" And besides, it is easily searched, especially as "clothes that are accepted" for us, we can wear them (this is because: let us not forget that prisoners do cannot even dress with any clothing); "these clothes" lend themselves very, very well to these multiple humiliating strip searches! ""

"" Hmm mm! "The jail", it's something! "The sheet" is really something, eh? It's really something! Because we suffer! The one suffers "affectionately speaking" so to speak, for example! ""

" " And when you suffer so "affectionately speaking for example"; one feels that: you find yourself absolutely in need! The ultimate need to have such a loving touch "normal to express ourselves in this way!" "Normal"; that is to say: "with [your] parishioner" what! " "

" " But it is, alas!, unfortunately, alas!, that it also happens to be incarcerated! " "

" " But what to do in this case here? " "

" " But frankly what? " "

" " Quite frankly how, since it is cut "contact with her male"? Which regards myself MARYSSA: it is also found just like me, "sheet" in Fleury – Merogis? The same charge as me, of course: to save; and that, for all means (and by "our little one" the most abominable means, and therefore our heiress Maryvonne KEVILER)? And today, it and all members of the household are no longer! Yeah!, ih!, MARYVONNE that we wanted to save at all costs, is no longer of this world! All hers children too! The father of these, too! They are no longer! (And we should see: How the three of them and their parents there are already more will, it really was worth it to save and "our hussy MARYVONNE" Even if it was for us!, "the single baroness!" But anyway! Anyway, God exists! And it is God's the proof: He inadvertently us and especially ruthlessly punished all!). " "

" " "The jail", it's something! "The sheet" is really something! There are not really found in need! The ultimate need to have a "real and above normal" loving touch! "Normal"; that is to say: "with [its own] Hector self"! " "

" " Or just him "the Marc Anthony" [self as] he is: he is also found "on the tin"! Also accused thus: of ordering "the same crimes", as for yourself! "Crimes" "quite inhuman"; with hindsight, we understand like what, it was not worth above all; then really: not at all, at all the trouble to commit, indeed! Proof: What we all won in this family, which is ours! Nothing, nothing, nothing, nothing, nothing and nothing; if these are not just "family Massacre"; "Imprisonment"; "Humiliation"; "Deprivation"; "Abuse"; "Wilderness"; "Nervous breakdowns very, very acute"; "Sadness"; "Wasteland"; "Despair"; "Eternal despair"; "Purgatory"; "Purgatory forever"; "Abyss or Hell"; "Abyss or Eternal Hell"; and "Tears"; "Eternal Tears"! " "

"« And so, when you are for example, "flame", we do not know: What do exactly? »"

"« One does not know: What to do, especially since we pay for long; for very long; for a very long time! »"

"« Let it be astonished, that with such rigor prison, some women (even if they were hardly formerly lesbians); finally they have thereafter; and it sometimes unconsciously, of lesbians inclinations! »"

"« Even if the regulations of the prison environment severely punished in principle, reverse or certainly homosexuality; by isolating such as those inmates who are caught in the act of this immoral practice, in a special section called "Group S"! Although the regulations of the prison environment severely punished in principle the lesbianism certainly; but only this, it is easily tempted! »"

"« Otherwise expressed: it is a principle! Since, it just prevents hardly provided that lesbianism persists in "jail"!

"« And Maryssa from her side also, very, very exactly, it would be the same tune, like for her husband Moses: »"

"« And – there the questions are and they will still to be: »"

"Is it really worth the trouble to come out ways against – nature "one **hysterical filly**" from her severe schizophrenia; which would systematically transported her, to the death, even if she was our daughter?

And no matter how "the Other Justice precisely who she is invisible" get busy and is indeed "hysterical this filly in question" is when – even well, well, well dead, right?

And me MOSES and my Cleopatra, Maryssa and not forgetting my faithful worker and friend THIERRY, what we won after all these sordid, despicable and abominable machinations sponsored by us?

Nothing, nothing, nothing, nothing, nothing, nothing and nothing, at all, at all.

Morality: we the humans, so we should absolutely be afraid of this "Other Justice", by – above all. And thus, our behavior will be blameless. ».

» « » « » « »
.

That said, "Sir" and Mrs. KEVILER became "very, very concerned" and "very, very depressed nervously speaking, they also in turn". They would catch "acute depression". In doing so, in turn, almost at the same time (first MOSES; succumb immediately to "acute depression precisely this").

(And uh – huh!, ih! It was still, anyhow: "The Mystery of the Universe" that would continue thus to manifest itself in that way.

And do not we have said above, that "The mystery of the universe in question just" happen in one way or another, even among "Sir" and Mrs. Moses KEVILER?

By first passing through the focus of JULIO and MARYVONNE?

And there: A grandparent of two was no more).

Then, only after some time, "the same acute depression in question" would lead almost immediately "his widow MARYSSA also" to death.

(And yeah!, ih! It was still, anyhow: "The Mystery of the Universe" that would continue thus to manifest itself in that way.

And do not we have said above, that "The Mystery of the Universe in question just" happen in one way or another, even among "Sir" and Mrs. Moses KEVILER?

By first passing through the focus of JULIO and MARYVONNE?

And there: All grandparents were no longer).

In short, in their sides: "Sir" and Mrs. KEVILER did everything, using even the most heinous methods in order not to happen one day, where they had just arrived. But that's only the spouses KEVILER had thought only fooled human justice (something they had been very successful doing [And how!]). But they could not at all, at all, do something; to fool "The

Justice Supernatural" or "The Providential Justice" (for It is fine and well: But only the evidence here, It occurs often unexpectedly, and very rarely immediately!).

After "the journey" of "Episode Five", it seems very, very explicitly, that "the event" of "the Other Justice" (To wit: " A Justice with a big "J" Shift ") does not even market.

IsMaSa
-make "tenorize" (make sing in the tenor register) the pen;
-make sol–fa the writing.

The End

For almost "all this writing lying below high" "with the black anchor on a white background or a white paper"; namely: that there are among others; or to be able to say more correctly: they were then among others: "imaginary stories"; which is much more similar to "real stories" rather than anything else; i.e.: they are then among others; or in order to better express it: they were then among others: "true stories"; which is much more similar to "imaginary stories" rather than anything else.

"Irene LUCINDAÇIO,
The Girl From Jupiter
And APHRODITE".

All those who wish to continue their reading in the "Samba Style", are asked not to "miss" the next small volume to be released and which will be titled:

"IRENE LUCINDAÇIO, DAUGHTER
OF JUPITER AND APHRODITE".

"IRENE LUCINDAÇIO, DAUGHTER OF JUPITER AND APHRODITE"

"IRENE LUCINDAÇIO OF "DESCENT PORTUGUESE AND REAR – OFFSPRING CONGOLAISE" A VERY, VERY PRETTY GIRL CALLED: "DAUGHTER OF JUPITER AND APHRODITE"? ".

PREAMBLE

Ａnd in this part of the distance precisely
"The parishioner" would meet
with a "parishioner";
wherein also as,
by chance, by his lack of candor,
it would have continued,
irrational by some bad luck.

Ｂefore the years 1960 [s], a group of emigrants originally from the Belgian Congo; which would become after independence: The Democratic Republic of Congo; this group of emigrants that their ancestors are from Angola; So for this group came from the Congo (; where [he said] he did not feel better during that period very, very precisely, and therefore, it would be decided in addition, to seek a better life, elsewhere); for this group bound in principle to Portugal (where he would say that he would feel better [and through Angola, where he was about to embark on commercial vessels leaving for Europe]) ; this group would separate into several factions:

Which one would stop on the island of Sao Tome e Principe and he would not go further.

Another would stop in Portuguese Guinea (Guinea Bissau); and it also does not go further.

Yet another, would stop in Cape Verde and it would not go away too.

And the last small group would stop on the island of Madeira and it would not go away, either.

All these factions would feel decidedly better where they should theoretically stop that time for some stops. And since practically, they would feel better in these territories then precisely; then, they would say:

"Why bother to pick our "paradise" to Portugal colonized Angola, the land of our ancestors?

Huh?

Why bother to go further? ".

"'Do not tell – that is not": "Ubi bene Ibi patria?". ("Where there is good, there is the Fatherland?").

So eh!

Ohm!, good! ".

As might notice: None of these factions would reach Portugal proper. They all would establish where they would feel better.

And later some of their offspring, then yeah!, they would emigrate to Portugal; or: even a little further.

And there were even complete or even downright tiny groups: whole groups (regardless of their will, and this: several generations, and this too: through the slave trade, they ¾) would settle even among – others, to Brazil.

And we will fly over consequently, some progeny of all these groups in question, listed below senior: " Which would be "driven cross" together. And we will follow especially: those who would be in one way or another, "their paths crossed".

"And we find that: it's really" "wow"; or "pathetic" as "program". ".

In the 1960s, the Isle of Madeira[1], lived some very, very nice lady called Irene LUCINDAÇIO and known by many people: "The daughter of Zeus and Aphrodite". Given its striking beauty, "many hominids" single throw their sights on it to take the outright marriage. That one fact, aware of what she "provoked" with "the Masters" she refuses consequently, the various stresses that she would receive. In her heart, she had not yet met "soul mate". Given the fact that she knew very well as this, she was very, very nice; and that "apes" and yet still always ran behind her. So IRENE would say internally: " I can wait a little longer until I have for example, found a true "soul mate" to me. But meanwhile, for "the interest of my own carnal pleasure", I can accept myself anyway despite some various promptings boys in my neighborhood! Why not indeed? The main thing is to be very, very careful, so as not especially limited at all, get pregnant! ... / .... ". This situation was greatly worried hers parents. Subsequently, "a gentleman" single named Almeida LOURENÇO[2] would use unorthodox means to attract "this Damsel" said: "The daughter of Zeus and Aphrodite", to him. And that would be in order, to downright marrying her. Marriage precisely, would take place.

---

[1] Madeira and Madeira, and part of Portugal; especially in Camara De Lobos, the "Rua Serpa Pinto, No. 997".

[2] And capita [still] in Camara De Lobos [Madeira Island] on the "Rua Nicolau Rui Fernandes No. 234".

But only here, as the "Sir" had used a subterfuge dishonest enough to succeed his absolutely blow. It would therefore and without knowing in advance some "calamities"; which would ensure that his wife rightly make him suffer the stigma of his life, because of the confidence he would do it. And when we discover "the pink pole", called "the mouse": "The daughter of Zeus and Aphrodite" would go far; far; far, far away; that is to say: she would go where she's like, less "of shrews" and possible "Gentleman", knowing her, could continue to know her; and meet her. And in this part of the distance precisely, "this parishioner girl" would meet with a "parishioner guy"; which as also, by chance, by his lack of candor, he would have continued, with "some irrational dry spell". But only here, "her Yeoman" would never know beforehand. He would never know beforehand, like what, he was pursued that way by some "Cataclysm", given the dishonesty of himself personally. What would happen next?

In short, there, we will discover one Irene, nicknamed: "Irene LUCINDAÇIO, the daughter of Zeus and Aphrodite". An Irene that eventually would live in London certainly; one Irene but above all: from the Congo (of Congo – Kinshasa), by hers parents (; and an Irene speaking among – others languages: Portuguese, English, Lingala and Kikongo); one Irene not only as a bubbly, as appealing; but also: one Irene as volcanic that as sulfurous, that everything; and what is more, an Irene seeking and knowing how carnal games, above all: as physicals and jam – exhausting, as complicated and spiced.

This really is a program! And readers will feast at superlative.

Wanting ... / ...

" **W**ant to walk his mind;
the escape into a world;
in a world of imagination;
imagination in retrospect;
retrospection that clings infallibly in the present;
a present that will grab turn tirelessly in the future;
in the future and around the world;
this is ultimately our best inclination. ".

In short, Isaac MAMPUYA Samba is : << The Difference Blondywoodian or Hollywoodian or even downright planetary the most original in simplicity and humility of Scripture therefore which one can so exist. Otherwise expressed : That's the distinction, what ! >>.

Signed: Isaac Mampuya Samba.

NOVELS OF THE SAME AUTHOR

1 - "A True untimely Awareness."

2 - "Nervous Depression or Grief Love."

3 - "Torment of "JULIO, Descent From Poitvese" ".

4 - "An Ultimate Therapy To Save Their Children".

5 - "Impacts of the "Other Justice" ".

Also From Isaac MAMPUYA Samba :

1: Survival And Punishment Of The Slave Trade From Gabon till Congo in 1840-1880 (**VOLUME ONE**).
2: Survival and Repression Of The Slave Trade From Gabon till Congo in 1840-1880 (**VOLUME TWO**).

Series or Sub-Series:
"... / ... Their
Membership Negritude in
Africa and the World ... / ... ".

AuthorHouse ™ UK
Design & Print: Editions IsMaSa, London – Paris – Los Angeles
(ims.ismasaparis@yahoo.com) with printing

AuthorHouse ™ UK
1663 Liberty Drive
Bloomington, IN 47403 USA
www.authorhouse.co.uk
Phone: 0800. 197. 4150

The fourth cover

A series of people were in this novel **N° 5**, of **Isaac Mampuya Samba** (IsMaSa), entitled: "**Impacts of the "Other Justice"** " (; which is the logical continuation of the Flight N° 4 entitled: "**An Ultimate Therapy To Save Their Children**". {appeared to: "**Editions IsMaSa, London – Paris – Los Angeles**" [With " *AuthorHouse ™ UK*]}; and which thus marks the end of "this Sub – Series of altogether Five Episodes"), used "methods" abominable "to realize a sordid mission in favor of a couple (the couple : [MOSES-MARYSSA])". The guru of the mission in question was: a "sir" Thierry Glorian. This would write the script [And what script! Abject, of course!]. And he would grant the lead role in a "Don Juan", named "Giraud ZEFRINO". He Susceptible him more "**the Potent Analgesics**"; or rather "**the Powerful Amphetamines**"; or rather, "**the Powerful Methamphetamines**", so he does not feel pain point, about "his role" it would play devilishly; or rather noisily, to harm inevitably, to a certain Evelyn MULER, m. FERNANDEZ, defiling it copiously, so that Julio Fernandez her husband divorce her.

What a story! It was just a story, to ruthlessly clear one, the home of JULIO order to recover Maryvonne KEVILER the hands of it. In truth, it was a well-hung scenario; Thierry Glorian. And it was "that way quite clever and quite particularly Machiavellian" that the household EVELYN was wasted. And it was also "that way quite diplomatic", that it had agreed to go back to her parents. In short, it was this way that the household of "this naive **Archduchess**" had been wasted. It was as a result of false promises from a certain Giraud ZEFRINO [and for good reason]. It just would not even feel EVELYN so slightly.

And in the new household of Maryvonne, "Movies" "Blondywoodians" with all their "Inventivities"; with all their Finesses; with all their Ingenuity; short: with all their Greatness and all their Heights, will finally have, all their Explanations and Acquiescence's; and this time – here, with the Incomparable and Unsurpassable Conjugal 's Agreement; and even: with all the Complicity of her Husband, Julio. It would therefore be the Excellent Serenity or rather: the Serene Friendliness between them – two, what! And what else to say!

The consequences of such a plot would be: more stiffs. But the instigators would remain for quite a while, "unpunished". But would they, for example, through the "Providential Justice" or "the Other Justice"; "Justice with a large J" "punished" anyway despite them? And that, one way or another? This is why we chose to name this fifth monograph by Isaac Mampuya Samba: " Impacts of the "Other Justice" ". In any case, by reading it, you will find among others: the answers "These high above questions asked".

So it was then wholesale: the story of "MARYVONNE, A Filly Descent From Paris And In Background Kinese Progeny" and "JULIO, A Foal Descent From Poitvese And Background On Spanish Descendants"; whose destiny was inextricably linked.